The Mystical Thread

Books by Cheryl Lafferty Eckl

Personal Growth & Transformation

A Beautiful Death:
Keeping the Promise of Love

A Beautiful Grief:
Reflections on Letting Go

The LIGHT Process:
Living on the Razor's Edge of Change

Wise Inner Counselor Books
Reflections on Being Your True Self in Any Situation
Reflections on Doing Your Great Work in Any Occupation
Reflections on Ineffable Love: from loss through grief to joy

Poetry for Inspiration & Beauty

Poetics of Soul & Fire

Bridge to the Otherworld

Idylls from the Garden of Spiritual Delights & Healing

Sparks of Celtic Mystery:
soul poems from Éire

A Beautiful Joy: Reunion with the Beloved
Through Transfiguring Love

Twin Flames Romance Series

The Weaving:
A Novel of Twin Flames Through Time

Twin Flames of Éire Trilogy
The Ancients and The Call
The Water and The Flame
The Mystics and The Mystery

The Mystical Thread:
a legacy of love - past, present & future

The Mystical Thread

a legacy of love
past, present & future

a twin flames novel by
Cheryl Lafferty Eckl

FLYING CRANE PRESS

THE MYSTICAL THREAD: A LEGACY OF LOVE - PAST, PRESENT & FUTURE
© 2023 by Cheryl J. Eckl, LLC

Published by Flying Crane Press, Livingston, Montana 59047
Cheryl@CherylEckl.com | www.CherylEckl.com

This is a work of fiction. Names, characters, places and incidents either are the product of the author's imagination or are used fictitiously. Any resemblance to actual persons, living or dead, business establishments, events or locales is entirely coincidental.

Cover image: Skellig Michael and Little Skellig, viewed from the Kerry Cliffs, County Kerry, Ireland. Licensed from 123rf.com.

Library of Congress Control Number: 2022914024
ISBN: 979-8-9866788-0-1 (paperback)
ISBN: 978-1-7367123-9-9 (e-book)

Printed in the United States of America

For you, dear Friends of Ancient Wisdom
past, present & future

Contents

Part Two ~ Following the Thread

Part Three ~ Poignant Recollections

Part Four ~ Inescapable Records of the Past

Part Five ~ The Invisible Weaving Continues

Part One

Weaving
the Unseen &
the Seen

The Tapestry

Sarah MacCauley had not meant to write a vision of the future. But that is what happened when she invited her muse to inscribe in her journal those thoughts and feelings that otherwise might go unrecognized or unexpressed.

Immediately she had felt a stirring—a percolating sensation that bubbled along her spine and into her heart, urging her to put pen to paper. Inhaling deeply, Sarah had listened closely and began to write the words that were streaming into her receptive mind.

Thousands of years before Éire's druids warmed themselves in cloaks of purest wool, and centuries before Egypt's pharaohs donned kilts of finest linen, master weavers in mythic times worked at their looms as if before an altar, so sacred was their labor.

For they were creating exquisite tapestries to grace temples of light and halls of justice in an Atlantean civilization long-buried beneath the ocean waves.

Treasured were these masterpieces for their delicate artistry and the touch of magic they contained. Intertwined in warp and weft, threads of white, gold and silver, blues and greens and ruby hues illumined mysteries of ancient wisdom, forgotten now in the mists of time.

And yet.

In recent years, unseen hands in ethereal realms have been weaving a different tapestry. Visible only to those with quickened senses, this work of art is proof to certain souls of light of their earthly sojourns that began in starry realms in eons past, before history or memory convinced them they were two, not one.

Through countless trials of heart and soul, these stalwart friends have learned—and must learn again—that the fabric of community is only as strong as its weakest threads. Discernment is a requisite to ensure love's victory. For things of this world are not as they seem, and the invisible weaving does continue.

As Sarah pondered the meaning of the sudden outpouring, she remembered that this was not the first time her muse had sent her portents of future events, though she had not experienced a rush of prophetic inspiration for quite some time. *At least this piece doesn't name a specific person,* she reassured herself. As her friend Glenna might remind her, she had reason to be wary of intruding upon the private life of another.

Still, the mysterious words had quickened in Sarah's being a vibrant sense of inner knowing—though of what exactly, she could not say. Only time would tell. This she knew to be true. Myriad experiences in past lives had taught her that the future is, indeed, veiled.

Sarah had not written much since publishing her novel last Thanksgiving. Today she had been reflecting on how she might begin to fill the empty pages in her journal now that her active toddler twins, Gareth and Naimh, had finally worn themselves out for the afternoon. They were napping soundly, giving Sarah some time to herself.

Her husband, Kevin, had taken his wolfhound, Hero, for a long romp at the beach. So the only sound in the house was the gentle breathing of two little ones and the contented purring of Sprite, the mini-panther cat who had squeezed in next to her mistress in the nursery's overstuffed chair where Sarah loved to watch her children sleep.

I suppose I shouldn't be surprised by the tapestry image, she thought.

After all, she'd been gazing at the weaving she had purchased during her first trip to Ireland. At the time, she had been more enthralled with the colors and artistry of the piece than with the actual design that depicted a group of people sharing a celebration.

Nowadays, those figures reminded Sarah of the Friends of Ancient Wisdom—the community of modern-day mystics that had formed around Fibonacci's Esoteric Bookstore and Coffee Shop. As she gazed at the tapestry—which she had hung in the nursery where the twins could see it—she imagined the forms and faces of cherished friends and family looking back at her.

There at the center of the gathering were Fibonacci's owners, Lucky O'Connor with his wife and soulmate, Róisín. Although these two kept a low profile, they were, in fact, adepts of remarkable spiritual attainment. For several years they had been mentoring a growing number of seekers who were finding their way to Fibonacci's.

A young woman named Charlotte was one of these eager seekers. Her willingness to help out anywhere and everywhere, along with her stunning raven-black hair and cobalt-blue eyes, had already brought her to the attention of many in the community.

Sarah easily identified herself and Kevin in the tapestry. They were standing and smiling in rapt conversation with their dearest friends of many ages—gifted seers Debbie and Jeremy Madden and multi-talented Glenna and Rory O'Donnell. The three couples called themselves the Twin Flames of Éire to honor the deep ties they had shared in first-century Ireland and because each one's spouse was the twin of their own soul.

All six had become mainstays at Fibonacci's.

Debbie was doing a heroic job as manager of the coffee shop that had been renamed "Róisín's." Jeremy was head of finance for the computer company that Sarah's brother, Brian, owned.

Former Broadway actress and happily pregnant Glenna was creating a drama program for children. She was blossoming as new life grew within her, while her husband, Rory—a former Irish monk and popular history teacher—was assisting Kevin as bookstore manager.

All of the businesses were now located in a single city block where the coffee shop and bookstore had moved after a devastating fire.

As Sarah slipped into a deeper state of contemplation, she felt her heart swell with love for these friends of her soul. *We six have certainly overcome some desperate challenges throughout the ages,* she mused.

Only a few short months ago, they had won a costly victory over the sorceress Una and her consort, Arán Bán—individuals who had persistently tormented their twin flames in both recent and ancient times.

Now the entire Friends of Ancient Wisdom community was grieving the death of Róisín—who had made the ultimate sacrifice to defeat Una. When Sarah thought of their dear friend's selfless act, her heart ached for all of them—especially for Lucky. It was hard to imagine him cheerfully serving customers at Fibonacci's coffee bar without the support of his wife's nurturing presence and visionary gifts.

Still, I know we are healing, even as things change, Sarah reassured herself. And changes there were, aplenty.

Debbie's older sister, Cyndi, and her husband, Phelan MacGrath, had bought Lucky's house with money from the sale of her health food business that was part of the Fibonacci's block. The new owners were renting that space, and the MacGraths had come on board as employees at the coffee shop and bookstore.

Lucky was residing with his longtime friends, Tim and Maggie O'Toole—a pair of ageless adepts who acted as mentors and godparents to adults and children alike.

And in the midst of all these transitions, Sarah had agreed to help Lucky compile his memoirs into a book.

Fortunately, when she needed quiet time to write, family would be available to watch her little ones. Her parents, Eileen and Patrick Callahan, were eager babysitters. Brian and his wife, Ivy, and their seven-year-old twins, Kerry and Kaitlyn, lived just down the street. Having them close was a comfort—almost like living in their own Irish village of old.

A tiny cry from Gareth interrupted his mother's reverie. She watched and listened, anticipating the end of her quiet time. But the little boy soon settled and returned to dreamland.

Gazing once more at the weaving that had sparked her imaginings, Sarah viewed it with fresh eyes. *We really are like a tapestry,* she thought. *All of us woven together in strands of love—past, present and into a future that remains unknown until experienced.*

Love's Promise

JULY 31, LATE AT NIGHT - AT THE HOME OF TIM & MAGGIE O'TOOLE

Lucky knew he was lucid dreaming. He was too alert to be lost in the mists of deep slumber. With remarkable clarity, he was experiencing past, present and future simultaneously.

He'd been dreaming about his soulmate, Róisín. Oh, how profoundly he missed her wise counsel and the many ways she had helped him find joy in this life. Now his soul was reaching farther back into a more distant past, trying to bring much older recollections into the present. Despite the pain such openness might cause, he knew it was time.

For the feminine spirit he sensed with him in this moment was as real as himself. Here was his twin flame, his soul's other half, the singular companion of his heart whose presence brought back memories of difficult lessons and vivid insights that Lucky rarely allowed himself to entertain.

"Flavia." He spoke the word tenderly. The sound of her name, the way it nestled in his heart, warmed him from within. And it frightened him. For if he allowed her love to live in his being, the pain of losing her must live there, too. And that he feared he could not bear.

When a tear escaped his deep blue eyes, he shook his head. It would not do to be sentimental. Not when courage and the storytelling skill of a *seanchaí* were required. He must impart to his present-day heirs his legacy of hard-won wisdom before his days on planet Earth expired.

The details of his life experiences were personal to him. Yet the stories of events that had transpired during embodiments which many of them had shared were meant to lead his inheritors into an enlightened future. He could not leave them with such an important task undone.

Fully alert now, Lucky was not surprised that Flavia's radiant image began to materialize before his wakened sight. The lithe figure. The flaxen hair. The soft blue eyes only a shade lighter than his own. When they had been together those long centuries ago, she used to gaze into his eyes and tell him she could see herself reflected there.

Had she always seen herself in him? She said she did. Even though they were so different in that lifetime. He, such a sober young man. She, so carefree. At least she was free of cares in those few stolen moments when she could slip away from her father's disapproving presence.

Tonight, in this midnight hour, there was no obstacle to their oneness. No external obstacle, that is. The problem had always been within him. Lucky took a deep breath and prayed to *An Síoraí*, the Eternal One, that he might hear the voice he had shut out far too many times in the past.

"You must tell them." Flavia spoke to him now with such tenderness, he wept. "You must tell them, Lúcháir," she repeated, calling him by the name he had rejected as a child in this life. Not the name as she'd known him. He was called Quin in those days. Yet his soul was Lúcháir. She hoped by using his inner name she might call him out of the misery he still carried.

"I cannot, Flavia," he protested. "I cannot bear rehearsing the terrible way you died. After so many earlier tragedies, losing you killed me. I fear it will again."

"Take yourself down from that cross, Lúcháir. I have been free for nearly two thousand years. You are the one still suffering. I long for you to join me, *mo chroí*—here in this beautiful realm where there is no pain, no separation. Where the joy you have learned to live in this life will be permanent and we will be together, at last."

"Tell me how, Flavia. I know you've said it before. I promise I will take your words to heart this time."

"Very well, *a ghrá*. The joy that our dear Róisín helped you learn to express will be great beyond imagining when you finish the work that only you can complete. To achieve the reunion you and I long for, you must go back through the pain of separation. To reach the end, you must return to the beginning, which was also an ending. And in that return is the rebirth that will live on in us forever.

"For the sake of your legacy's heirs, for the sake of your soul and mine, the story must be told. Tell them, *a ghrá*, no matter how troubling the task of remembering. Share with them our story—the whole of it. There are lessons locked in the past that can only be released as you speak them."

She waited for his response, but he was silent. She tried again.

"Do you not remember why wise master druids like yourself taught that their ancient knowledge be passed on orally?"

He hesitated, but agreed at last. "I do, and I would hear you remind me. Listening to the reason from you embeds it in my heart and gives me courage."

"I fear I may be spoiling you, *a ghrá.*" She used to tease him like this when they sat together in the green and pleasant land of Albion that was their home. Ah, such peace had been his then. He with his head in her lap as she stroked his forehead with her delicate hand.

"Pay attention, Lúcháir," Flavia admonished him for letting his mind wander. "Follow my voice and I will remind you."

"I am awake, *mo chroí.* I will not fall asleep."

"Like mystics and storytellers of all ages, the original druids knew the power of spoken words to anchor deep comprehension in the very cells of the speaker and to elevate the understanding of listeners. Illumination is carried on the breath, in the tone of the voice, the resonance in the heart, the posture of the body and the consciousness that uses words to convey the truth of wisdom's presence.

"When you speak the memories that will emerge if you allow, you will learn of yourself and of me and of the 'us' that we knew long ago. Tell them, Lúcháir, and find me in the spaces where Spirit infuses all of life. My darling—soul of my soul, heart of my heart—faint not. I am here and I will be with you as you speak. Never doubt that I love thee."

The Adepts

Lucky, darlin', are you ready?" Maggie called through the door to the suite of rooms her friend had been occupying for several months.

"Sarah just called to ask if you still want her and Ivy to bring their twins. I told her you were counting on it. They'll be here in a couple of hours. Tim and I thought you might like a bit of a chat before they arrive."

Being one in heart and mind with Lucky, Maggie had not hesitated to reassure Sarah that her toddlers and their precocious cousins were as welcome in her home as they were at Fibonacci's. Those family ties must be reinforced at every opportunity.

Lucky opened the door and smiled into the reassuring countenance of the remarkable woman who had been his colleague and sister on the spiritual path for ages.

"You've the right of it, *a chara*. This gathering wouldn't be complete without the little ones. They're as much a part of my legacy as the stories I'm bound to tell their parents. Give me a minute and I'll be right with you."

Lucky closed the door to his room and rubbed his hands over his face. He pulled his once-ginger-red mane into the ponytail he wore down his back and slipped a pinky ring with five rows of clear diamonds onto his right hand. Taking a deep breath, he opened the bedroom door, crossed the threshold and joined his gracious hosts for the serious endeavor of recording his legacy which they were about to begin.

"Ah, Maggie, 'tis grand!" Lucky exclaimed when he saw the abundant buffet she had set out for their guests. "*Go raibh míle maith agat, a chara*. You warm my heart."

"'Tis an important day," she smiled. "Tim and I want to be sure our friends are comfortable. As well as yourself. Come sit with us, lad." She motioned to the sofas adjacent to the turf fire that was burning cheerfully in the living room fireplace.

As soon as they were seated, Maggie focused her crystalline blue eyes on Lucky's darker ones. "I have a question for you."

"And I have an answer. I know you're concerned."

"I am, so I must ask: Are you truly ready? This telling of your lifetimes is likely to be a mighty challenge. Can you bear it?"

"I must, *a chara*. I've promised Flavia. There's no turning back. No avoiding the heartbreak. And I *can* bear it because I've got you two here in the physical and her in Spirit. Things were different two millennia ago."

"Aye, they were that," agreed Tim with a smile that said he wasn't worried. "So they're all coming, then? Your Twin Flames of Éire and the others?" His own crystalline blue eyes that matched his wife's danced and he clapped his hands together like a schoolboy anxious for a treat.

Lucky nodded, and Maggie gazed into the fire, pondering.

"I think today's group needs a special name," she said thoughtfully. "There are more of them now and 'tis is a new day. The Twin Flames of Éire will always be strong. Those three couples have been through so many adventures together. But you're creating a larger gathering."

"I've thought about that," said Lucky. "What about 'The Weavers'?"

"Why 'The Weavers'?" Tim wanted to know.

"I got the idea from Sarah when I asked her to help me turn my memoirs into a book," said Lucky. "We were talking about how the children and adults coming today are woven together like a tapestry. Each one is weaving the threads of their unique self into the whole."

"'Tis true," Maggie agreed. "And that makes you the foundation on the loom, Lucky. You know, the plain warp that gets wound onto the frame before the colorful threads of the weft are intertwined to make the design."

"'Tis a lovely metaphor," Lucky said, reflecting. "Though..."

"...is there something more apt for this group?" Tim finished his friend's thought.

"I suspected you were reading my mind," Lucky laughed. He and Tim nearly always knew what the other was thinking.

"I'm wondering if this group is more like a *claddagh*." Maggie was still musing. "You know—the ring with the hands, a crown and a heart. The meaning fits. Hands for friendship, crown for loyalty and heart for love."

"Still too metaphorical," said Tim. "What's a word that carries the same meaning? Something everyone can relate to?"

"Aye. Like a ring, but not a ring," said Lucky.

The three friends paused, pondering, searching inner guidance.

"Companions!" Maggie declared. "The Circle of Close Companions."

Lucky nodded. "Sure, and haven't we been the closest companions for many a lifetime. The words carry an intimacy that speaks to the loyalty of these friends of my heart. I know I can count on them."

"And they can count on you," Tim agreed. "I like the name."

"So would Róisín," Lucky added wistfully.

"She would." Maggie took up the thought. "Our lass would say, 'A circle keeps every companion mindful of the others.'"

Lucky nodded again. "Kevin's still my main heir, as he's always been. But when he looks 'round the circle, he'll be assured of the support he needs."

"You know who else will love the circle arrangement?" Maggie chuckled and answered her own question. "The twins Kaitlyn and Kerry. Those two seven-year-olds are already wanting to be included in everything to do with the Friends of Ancient Wisdom."

"And rightly so," said Lucky. "They're the future for all of us. Even for you two, should you ever take off to *Tír na n'Óg*, Land of the Ever-Living."

Tim and Maggie smiled at each other but made no comment. When they turned back to their own companion of ages past and present, a cloud had settled on his brow.

"Don't worry, lad," said Tim, his eyes soft with understanding. "And you can be sure I *am* reading your mind. Maggie and I will be here as long as you need us. Our Master has made it clear he's not sending us on any missions if we're meant to hold the light for you and your Circle of Close Companions."

Lucky's eyes misted. "*Go raibh míle maith agat, a chairde,*" he said again. "You've never let me down."

"We're not about to start now," Maggie assured him. "Now, what else is on your mind?" Tim started to answer for his friend, but stopped when his wife laid a hand on his arm.

"Let him speak for himself," she smiled. "Go on, lad."

"I want to say 'thanks' to you both for giving me a place to meditate and grieve and to collect my stories as my legacy for future generations."

"You had to come here," Tim said with conviction. "You've got a grand portal to higher planes there at Fibonacci's, and we've got a different one here. You're obliged to keep the businesses open for your inquiring public. We have no such requirement. We've spent many a year focusing massive amounts of light energy on this property to create a forcefield worthy of the Masters."

"So you have," agreed Lucky. "And you're right about this being the only place my legacy could be spoken into the physical. The records of the past that my Circle of Close Companions and I are going to uncover could not be activated or survived anywhere else. That I know as a personal fact."

All three fell silent as images of difficult experiences they had shared in more than one embodiment came to mind. They were highly sensitive to the dangers of the endeavor upon which they were embarking. One in heart and mind, they rose from their seats and repeated a solemn vow which they had affirmed in their souls more times than they cared to count: "There is no turning back!"

As they remained standing in silence, Tim decided a change of mood was in order before the others arrived.

"Do you think your Circle of Close Companions will catch on to how long we've been working on creating *Teach an tSolais*—our House of Light?" he grinned.

"Why, Tim, how could they?" Lucky clapped his fellow adept on the shoulder. "You don't look a day over a thousand."

Gathering

"Do you ever wonder what's next?" Kevin asked Sarah as she rushed—he thought unnecessarily—to finish feeding Naimh. Their auburn-haired daughter and her identical twin brother, Gareth, were not making the chore easy, even with their father's help.

Infants no more at nearly one year old, their talent for making a mess was exceeded only by their glee in doing so. Violet eyes sparkled, little rosebud mouths grinned and tiny voices giggled as Hero and Sprite joined in the fun by gobbling up tidbits the toddlers dropped.

Their mother was not amused.

Sarah pushed a loose strand of long auburn hair, a shade darker than her daughter's, out of her hazel-green eyes and gave her husband a look that said she meant business.

"At the moment, what's next is for you to help me get these two washed, dressed and buckled into their car seats in an hour."

"You know that's not what I meant," said Kevin. Determined to make her laugh, he caught her by the waist and planted a kiss on her cheek. His tactic worked and Sarah paused, a cloth for wiping baby faces in her hand.

"I know," she admitted. "I only wish we had more time to understand how to outpicture our inner wisdom. Retrieving our past spiritual attainment as the druids Ah-Lahn and Alana is one thing. Living in that refined state of consciousness as modern-day mystics is another entirely."

Sarah lifted Naimh from her high chair, and Kevin followed them up the stairs to the bathroom with Gareth wriggling in his father's arms.

"Maybe helping Lucky write his memoirs will reveal our next great encounter with ancient mysteries." Kevin started running bathwater and pulled a tiny shirt, damp from breakfast spills, over his son's head.

"I could do without a dangerous one," said Sarah as she tested the water's temperature and eased her daughter into the tub. "I'm enjoying a taste of normalcy. I suppose it's naïve to think these days will last."

"Have they ever?" said Kevin.

"Not that I recall. Hand me the baby shampoo, will you, Hon? We've got to hurry."

The five couples who were gathering for Lucky to begin sharing the stories that would become his legacy had decided to meet at Fibonacci's and then follow Kevin, as he was the one with directions to the O'Tooles' home.

No one thought it strange that they had never been there before today. The circumstance was not for lack of hospitality. Far from it. Tim and Maggie were the most hospitable of people. However, they were often away on special missions for the Masters of Wisdom who sponsored the community at Fibonacci's, so they rarely entertained.

Of course, everyone was aware that Lucky had required the unique solitude which the O'Toole home provided for him to grieve the passing of Róisín—*a chara dhílis*, the dearest friend of her soul, as she'd called him with her final breath. And he'd needed time to collect his thoughts for the memoir that Sarah had promised to help him write.

Lucky's announcement that he was ready to begin sharing stories from his present and past lives and the O'Tooles' invitation to gather at their home made today's event a special one—especially as it coincided with *Lughnasa*, the traditional Celtic feast day of First Harvest.

Sunday, August 1 had seen more than the usual number of tourists filling the tables and stools at the coffee shop. Cyndi and Debbie had stayed busy until closing time at 2:00 p.m. Kevin and Rory had worked the midday rush at the bookstore, but agreed that their employees could handle any afternoon business.

For a usually talkative group, the atmosphere in each vehicle was surprisingly subdued. Two sets of twins had instantly fallen asleep in their parents' cars as the adults contemplated their individual relationships with Lucky. There was the past, of which they knew only a portion. The present was really only this moment. And the future could make them anxious if they let it. No one wanted to admit that Lucky's purpose in gathering them together was to complete his legacy so he could leave them.

They had mixed feelings about listening to his stories, lest the hearing of them should hasten his departure. Nevertheless, they had accepted the O'Tooles' invitation. Whatever would be would be.

Teach an tSolais was situated at the end of a secluded lane in an older neighborhood that gave the appearance of being more of a forest than a place for homes that emanated the weathered comfort of former days.

In fact, you could not see the O'Toole house behind a dry stone wall that stood as high as two men—one atop the other's shoulders. Towering over the wall were massive ash, oak and beech trees that in a couple of months would be ablaze with the rich golds, oranges, crimsons and occasional deep purples of autumn on Long Island.

The wall's fortress-like appearance was relieved by a wrought iron gate created from interweaving filigree designs like those found in ancient Celtic artwork. In anticipation of the visitors' arrival, the gate was open. As the last vehicle passed through, it closed without a sound.

The company parked along the curved gravel driveway that arced in front of an expansive, well-trimmed lawn where the one-story house stretched—almost languidly. A walkway made of smooth limestone slabs led from the driveway to the front door.

Compared to the dramatic entrance to the property, a visitor might be excused for considering the house rather plain.

That is until one studied the fine stonework that surrounded the thick oak front door. Until one noticed that the adjacent window panes were leaded glass. Until one's eye caught sight of the *fleur-de-lys* and spiral patterns that had been intricately carved into the long wooden planks that acted as siding. And until one noticed the conical roof of a fifty-foot-tall round tower standing majestically behind the main house.

Then one would know for certain that this was no ordinary dwelling. Which is what stopped Glenna as if she'd seen a spectre from the past.

"Oh my God, Rory, look!" she exclaimed, grabbing her husband's arm and pointing to the tower. "It looks just like..."

"Clonmacnoise," was all he could say with a shudder of recollection. He had not dared to think about round towers since he and Glenna had been taken prisoner near one by Arán Bán.

In a past-life scene that had played out on the astral plane, that man would have killed their souls, had it not been for swift intervention by Kevin and Sarah who—as directed by their Master Saint Germain—had appeared in their identity as druids Ah-Lahn and Alana. That event was months in the past, but seeing the conical form again shook Glenna and Rory to their core.

Eagerly anticipating his guests' arrival, Tim had opened the front door, intending to issue a hearty *céad míle fáilte!*—a hundred thousand welcomes. Instead of smiles, he saw only faces arranged as in a tableau reflecting expressions of concern.

Instinctively, the Twin Flames of Éire had moved together in mutual support that had become their way of being in the world. Nothing could threaten any of that tightly bonded mandala without the others rushing to their aid.

"*A chairde,* my friends!" called Tim as he hurried toward them with apology in his voice. "I should have warned you about the tower. We built it as a place for special prayers, just like the old monks did. You remember, Rory?" He addressed the young man who was standing with both arms around his wife, beads of cold sweat glistening on his forehead.

"I do, yes," Rory nodded and slightly eased his hold on Glenna.

"But it looks so much like that old tower," she said warily.

"Don't worry yourself, lass," Tim said. "There's no malignant forces lurking in these precincts. Too many angels surround this place for any-thing other than benevolent beings to get in. You're safe here."

Smiling broadly, he continued. "Come in now, and welcome. Maggie's got a grand feast laid out for us, and I know Lucky's wanting to greet you."

Rory breathed a sigh of relief and released Glenna from his embrace. Tim gently offered her his arm and led the company of friends from past, present and future into his home. Enfolded in the man's gracious aura, they crossed the threshold and stepped into a fairyland.

Crystalline Wonders

Or had they passed into an etheric temple of light? Sarah and Kevin, who had visited those luminous retreats, were certain they had entered such a place—so radiant was the atrium where sunlight streamed through a skylight, reflecting onto white marble tiles.

They were greeted by a rose quartz fountain that splashed gaily before them. Along walls that shimmered with inlaid crystal, elegantly placed benches upholstered in dark burgundy velvet provided seating for guests who might wish to meditate in the peaceful cool of the atrium.

Norfolk pines graced the corners and reached nearly to the ceiling while two enormous amethyst geodes stood like twin pillars on either side of an archway that opened into the main living area.

"Uncle Lucky!" cried twins Kerry and Kaitlyn as they broke away from their parents. They had spied the man they adored beaming at them from the next room and rushed into his embrace. The adults were right behind them, gathering around for their turn at hugs.

"*Beannachtaí Lughnasa!*" Maggie called out her festival blessings from the long marble kitchen counter where she had set out trays of *hors d'oeuvres* and cold drinks. "Make yourselves at home. We've lots to eat. Sit where you like here or on the terrace. Lucky will let us know when he's ready to start."

She reached down to scoop little Naimh into her arms and Tim did the same with Gareth before the lad could toddle away from his father.

"Don't worry, my girls." Maggie smiled at the concerned faces of Ivy and Sarah. "It may not look it, but this house is quite child-proof. They're welcome to explore—as are you."

"Your home is gorgeous!" exclaimed Glenna. "And I don't have to be asked twice to enjoy this lovely buffet."

After Tim's reassurance, her voice was stronger, though Rory's hand remained on her shoulder to steady her and himself. He exhaled the breath he'd been holding and stroked his wife's cheek.

"You'd think I don't let the lass eat," he joked and began filling his own plate from the abundant refreshments. "I'm a bit peckish myself. Seeing your tower has given me an appetite."

"I'll join you," said Phelan. Being a newlywed, he was vividly aware of how a man's concern for his spouse could instantly swamp him and leave him shaken, even when the wave passed.

Cyndi followed close behind her husband. Being surrounded in so much beauty and reflected light was making her woozy. This experience was all very new to her.

The others let the two couples fill their plates while they wandered around, admiring the furnishings. Many of the tables were made from cleverly carved crystals, fossils and geodes. Multiple *objects d'art* invited closer inspection. Some of the pieces appeared to be very old.

Ahead and to the right of the kitchen, a living room offered casual ease. Sofas covered in soft tapestry fabric were arranged in conversation areas in front of a green stone fireplace where a cheery turf fire danced.

Interesting, thought Kevin as he relaxed in the welcoming space. The outside temperature was well over ninety degrees, yet here in this tranquil home, a cozy fire felt just right.

The living room extended further into a large dining area, where a large oval walnut table with seating for at least twelve sat in front of floor-to-ceiling windows. French doors opened onto a terrace that overlooked a large body of water at the end of another expansive lawn and glorious gardens that were bursting with color in the bright summer sun.

Phelan was pleased that Cyndi was eating with Glenna and Rory in a quiet corner where Debbie and Jeremy soon joined them. He was too restless to sit. He noticed that Ivy and Brian had freed Lucky from their twins so, plate in hand, he walked over to his fellow Irishman who was gazing into the fire.

He noticed that Lucky's ponytail had more grey in it these days. The big man's back was still straight and strong, but he seemed thinner than the last time they'd spoken. That had been at the real estate closing when he and Cyndi had finalized their purchase of Lucky's house, where they were still settling in.

"Is that the bay we see across the terrace?" Phelan spoke softly so as not to disturb the man's reverie. "I didn't know it curved around here. Truth be told, I'm not sure where we are."

Catching a gleam in Lucky's eyes, he grinned. "That's intentional, isn't it? And if I'm not mistaken, that's Connemara marble." He pointed to the fireplace surround that was fashioned of stone in an unmistakable green.

Lucky turned to face the young man.

"You're a bright lad, Phelan. I'm glad to see it. I know you're still finding your way at Fibonacci's, but have faith. You have much to offer the community. Let the path unfold for you. I know it will."

"'Tis grand of you to remind me, Lucky," said Phelan with a grateful smile. "Things have been moving really fast since I landed in New York on Saint Patrick's Day. I do have some questions I'd like to ask you—separate, like, apart from your own stories. Could we have a chat sometime soon?"

"'Twill be my pleasure. Now, help yourself to more food and join your sweetheart. We'll be starting momentarily."

While Maggie was answering questions and making certain that her guests were getting what they wanted to eat, Tim was showing Jeremy and Brian around the main living areas. He enjoyed telling stories about the artwork and crystals that were placed throughout his home—especially to anyone as interested in building, architecture and design as these two young men were showing themselves to be.

Pointing to several highly polished clear crystals, he explained, "These are Lemurian Star Seeds. The tabletop they're resting on is rose quartz. Those blue clusters in the corner are very rare aquamarine. We've got many more crystals in the bedroom suites down the corridors to the left and right. Those rooms are private for now, but I can assure you they're as luminous as crystal caves. Let me show you the spa."

Leading the men through the French doors, across the terrace and into a separate wing of the house that contained a hot tub and swimming pool, Tim stopped before a three-foot tall blue pillar that rested on a low pedestal fashioned from the same stone.

"I've a particular fondness for these pieces. You'll recognize the stone as lapis lazuli."

"Amazing," said Jeremy. "How old are they, if I may ask?"

"Very old, lad," Tim nodded. "Very old indeed." Deftly changing the subject, he turned to a softly lit alcove on his left.

"Now here's something you won't see every day." He gestured toward a full-sized bath tub made from a giant amethyst geode whose interior had been smoothed to a silken sheen.

"Soaking here is a grand way to rejuvenate," Tim chuckled at his wide-eyed guests. "Someday I'll show you the quartz crystal chair that we use only on very special occasions."

"A person could live forever in a place like this," Brian remarked as he and Jeremy followed their host back through the French doors and into the dining room where the others were assembling.

"That's the idea," said Tim with a wink as he encouraged the men to fill their plates at the kitchen counter. "We'd best gather now. Lucky is ready to start. Be sure to sit with your wives for this first session. They're wanting you with them."

While the men took their seats around the dining table, Brian couldn't help thinking to himself how much this large property with its wealth of artwork and crystals must be worth. Without a doubt, more than his computer company and the entire Fibonacci's real estate block combined.

Beginning

Come, *a chairde,* and gather 'round," said Lucky, taking his place at the head of the dining table. He smiled as he gazed into the faces of loyal companions from ages past who were seated around the oval.

"We'll be like King Arthur with his knights and ladies seated in council at the Round Table. I don't recall them gathering to eat, but you're welcome to bring your plates if you're still enjoying Maggie's buffet. We'll have daylight for hours yet, but I'm mindful of the little ones' schedule. So, let's begin our session. Sarah, darlin', are you recording?"

"I am now, so you can start any time," she answered, switching on the little audio recorder that would catch every word of the stories she was certain would be flowing swift and sure from Lucky. The man was a gifted *seanchaí* who needed little prompting to share a tale or two. Sarah knew better than most the importance and urgency of today's gathering.

"*Go raibh maith agat, mo chara.*" Lucky was tempted to address her as daughter, which is how he often thought of her. If she remembered, she hadn't told him. Still, how appropriate it was that she was helping to bring his legacy project into the physical. Still musing, he took one more minute to appreciate the expressions of curiosity and anticipation that shone on the faces of his stalwart friends.

"I was going to commence by asking what you're most interested in hearing about from my past or present, but I think I'll start by answering the question I see furrowing Brian's brow. 'Why exactly are we here?' the man wants to know. Am I right?"

"Am I that obvious?" Brian said, trying to keep his voice light.

"Not always," replied Lucky with a hint of seriousness. "Though at the moment, yes. So I will answer your question, which is the right one. I want us to be of one mind and heart for this assignment that I must fulfill before I can depart this world."

As a single voice, Sarah, Debbie and Glenna uttered an involuntary sigh. They were already united in their reluctance to let him go.

Lucky nodded in recognition. "I know, lasses, but it can't be helped. Each of our souls has its destiny, its obligations to life. As much as I might want to stay with you for decades, 'tis not to be. My race is nearly run. Truth be told, I'm longing to join my sweet twin flame in our land of the ever-living, where she has waited for me many hundreds of years."

Husbands and wives took each other's hands and moved a little closer to their partner. They could well remember their own longing before they found each other in this life.

"Go on, Lucky," said Debbie in a tone of conscious resignation. "We're here for you as you've always been for us. Give us the story. We're ready."

"Then, so am I," Lucky began. "This is less a story than a statement, but 'tis the beginning. Some of you were there when our Róisín made her ascension and joined her twin flame, who came out of the Great Silence where he'd been abiding for a very long time."

Many eyes, including Lucky's, misted as the company remembered that incredible scene.

"Oh, how I longed to cross over, too. Even though Róisín was not my twin flame, she and I have been together as devoted soulmates for more lifetimes than I care to count. Staying behind when she left was a trial to my soul, I can tell you. The details of selling my house to Cyndi and Phelan and getting me settled here with my compatriots Tim and Maggie has kept me anchored in the physical plane. But for weeks I wondered how I could go on without my faithful helpmate.

"Then one day, the great Master Saint Germain appeared to me in spirit and gave me my next assignment. I can tell by the expressions on your faces that many of you have had the experience of receiving instructions like this, whether you're waking or dreaming.

"So, this grand Brother of Light says to me, 'Lúcháir (he calls me by my birth name), you have a legacy to impart to the inner circle of our Friends of Ancient Wisdom. Do this for them, for yourself and for your twin flame, and you will complete the mission that has long been yours to fulfill.' Since then I've felt his presence, though I've rarely seen him.

"Of course, I wondered how to accomplish this mighty task. I've been kicking around this old world for countless centuries, so there is many a story to tell and a fair number of insights to share. I've been feeling the need to collect this memoir into a book. But, I'm a *seanchaí*, a storyteller in the oral tradition, not a writer.

"Fortunately, our Sarah is a writer and she has agreed to be my scribe. She'll put all these tales into a form that I hope will last long after we're all on our way to higher realms."

"I'm honored to help," added Sarah.

Lucky gave her a grateful nod and continued.

"As you know, every *seanchaí* needs an audience. A story's no good unless it's shared heart to heart, soul to soul. In fact, I don't believe a story can truly come to life unless there are hearts open to receive it, in person or later in a book or recording. That's where you come in—if you will 'lend me your ears,' as Marc Antony famously requested."

"We will," the group answered as one voice.

Lucky's heart swelled at their response. He knew they had little idea of what they were agreeing to, but that was part of this initiation—the spiritual test his Master had only hinted that he and his Circle of Close Companions must pass through together.

"Well then," he lightly clapped his hands together to change the mood. "That's all there is to that story for now. So let me ask: What tales do you most want to hear about my past? I can sense some curiosity about the future, but I'll remind us all that future events unfold in their own time. We shall see what we shall see when it comes to that. Who wants to start?"

"I will," offered Glenna. "I'd like to know about your childhood and why you go by Lucky and not Lúcháir, although I may have some idea." A knowing chuckle rippled around the table.

"What can you tell us about the history of our group that's gathered here?" ventured Rory. "Many of us are aware of a tight bond that goes back eons. Are there lifetimes we haven't discovered yet?"

"There are, indeed," said Lucky. "There's more than one story involved in that telling. We'll just see how much I'm allowed to reveal."

"Even now, you're not permitted to tell us everything you know, " commented Jeremy. He was not asking a question.

"That's right, lad," agreed Lucky. "My leaving a legacy doesn't mean I can reveal details of your past lives that you're not ready to deal with."

"I understand," Jeremy said quietly. Then he added, "Personally, I'd like to know how you became an adept."

Lucky chuckled. "Another mighty tale and one I may not know the answer to. Have I actually become an adept? I suppose time will tell."

"Where do our children fit into your legacy?" Ivy asked. Her expression had been thoughtful since she and her family arrived.

"We fit, don't we Uncle Lucky?" Kaitlyn chimed in followed by Kerry who asked, "Do you know the Rose Lady? I know you do. Where did you meet her? Does she visit you like she does us?"

A grimace flickered across the faces of Ivy and Brian, while the others laughed appreciatively. The twins never failed to make their presence known—as did Naimh and Gareth, who babbled and giggled and waved their hands excitedly when their cousins spoke.

"I believe the children may have answered your question," Maggie commented. She walked around the table and gave Ivy a quick kiss on the cheek as she eased the youngsters out of their booster seats. They were getting restless as were Sarah's twins. Gareth and Naimh were showing signs of needing their afternoon nap, which they could take in their stroller.

"Come with Aunt Maggie, *mo pháistí*," she said to Kaitlyn and Kerry. "Let's walk around the garden. I'll show you where the fairies hide."

"We know where they are," the twins whispered to each other as they eagerly followed her through the French doors.

"Who's next?" Lucky felt time slipping away. He needed to bring the adults back to the matter at hand.

"I'll go," said Debbie. "Before Róisín left, she shared many insights about the spiritual path, but she never told us about your lives together as soulmates. I'd be grateful for what you could share with us."

"I'd love to hear about your twin flame," added Cyndi. "I don't recall hearing much about her." She took Phelan's hand. He kissed her on the cheek and asked the next question.

"I'm fascinated by the esoteric collection in the bookstore. I've heard the story about old Joshua giving you the books, but what else can you tell us about how the bookstore started?"

"I'd like to know more about how you and Róisín became close friends with Maggie and Tim and how you founded Fibonacci's," said Sarah. "I guess that's two questions."

The group fell silent. All of their questions appeared to have been asked. Lucky looked over at Kevin, who was lost in thought.

"Kevin, lad, do you have a question you'd like me to answer?"

"What? Oh, sorry. I was just thinking back to what I know from my memories of being Ah-Lahn. I'm sure there are stories I've never heard about your embodiment as Old Quin, the *ceann-druí* or chief druid that Ah-Lahn replaced in first-century Ireland.

"I remember him as a fair, but tough disciplinarian—although, when I was finishing my studies to be a master druid, I thought he was especially stern with me. He seemed to carry a deep sorrow that he was unwilling or unable to voice to any of his students or his peers—as if he'd closed the door on a pain too terrible to utter. Are you able to open that door now?"

Lucky closed his eyes for so long that some at the table thought he might be joining the MacCauley twins in a nap. When he opened his eyes, he seemed to be gazing into a distant realm.

"Kevin, you have some idea of what you're asking, but not all. I'm sure that story is one of the difficult ones Saint Germain insists on my telling. Thanks for the nudge, but we won't start there.

"One thing I can tell you is this: Our Master has reminded me that the foundation of every tapestry must be solidly threaded on the loom before the intricacies of design are added. So, before we delve into the most challenging recollections of my legacy, I believe we are wise to begin with gentler memories."

Lucky smiled at the wave of relief that rippled through the group.

"Thank you, my dears, for this grand beginning. You've given me lots to ponder. Meanwhile I feel a beautiful *Lughnasa* evening beckoning. Let's adjourn and enjoy the rest of our holiday. Now, I know you're all very busy with raising children and running your businesses. But could you see your way clear to meeting every Sunday after the coffee shop closes?"

"Yes!" declared the group, with hearts and voices in perfect synchrony.

"*Go raibh míle maith agat, a chairde.* Until Maggie and Tim send me packing, I'd like us to gather here in this forcefield. Some of what I am bound to tell you is best relayed when surrounded in light and blessing."

Lucky gently pushed his chair back from the table and stood. He was about to send them home when Tim stopped him.

"Aren't you forgetting something, lad?"

Lucky looked at him quizzically.

"The name," Tim prompted.

"Right you are, lad. I did forget."

Lucky turned to the group. "What Tim means is that he and Maggie and I have been thinking that we need a unique term to differentiate this group from the wider Friends of Ancient Wisdom community. In your positions of responsibility and by your past connections with me and with each other, your original mandala of three couples—the Twin Flames of Éire—has expanded."

"Sounds reasonable," said Brian, thinking to himself. *I hope it's not something weird.*

Lucky stifled a grin and glanced at Tim with a wink that warned him not to respond to Brian's very loud thoughts.

"We kicked around some ideas and finally came up with the Circle of Close Companions. What do you think?"

"I like it," said Kevin. "Even though a single individual must wear the mantle of leader, being able to share the burden in a circle of oneness is a powerful blessing."

"I agree," said Glenna. "Whatever the future may bring, there's safety in a circle, a mutuality of care and respect. I feel like we've been creating this expanded mandala for a long time. Now we can be more conscious of our bonding and the love that holds us together."

"Being aware of our mutual commitment is vital," added Debbie. "Our past experiences with the Twin Flames of Éire proved that. Now that I'm doing my best to fill Róisín's shoes, I am sensing a future of greater subtleties and hidden challenges that require all of our efforts. I have a feeling some of those details may come to light in your stories, Lucky. Am I right?"

"You are, darlin'. We shall see what we shall see—all of us. Off you go now. Come, give me a hug and I'll see you in a week."

An Agreement

The sun was dipping low by the time Sarah and Kevin finished tucking Gareth and Naimh into their cribs for the night. The little ones had been especially frisky after their naps and had insisted on playing when their parents would have preferred a light supper and an early night.

Now awake himself, Kevin decided that Hero needed a walk before he and Sarah relaxed with their evening cup of tea and conversation. While they were out, Sarah considered checking the recording of this afternoon's session with Lucky, but she soon abandoned that idea.

Instead, she opted for a quick bath while Sprite kept her company. She had the tea brewed and ready when the front door opened, signaling the return of man and dog. The happy wolfhound bounded in, greeting Sarah as if he hadn't seen her in weeks. Kevin was pensive.

He sat and sipped his tea, not saying a word. Without deciding if he was actually hungry, he picked up a scone that Sarah had laid out on a plate she'd bought in Ireland, then changed his mind. He looked his wife in the eye and spoke soberly.

"Are you sure you can handle being Lucky's scribe—considering how busy the twins are keeping you these days? I know you promised him, but I got a sense today that this legacy assignment is going to be a big one. I don't want you getting too tired."

Sarah felt her solar plexus tighten. After all the emotional ups and downs she and Kevin had been through together and how persistently they had worked to master their lesser selves, she still had a tendency to get defensive when she felt him question what she was doing. She took a breath and answered him directly.

"Are you really saying you don't want me shutting you out when I get embroiled in writing?"

"That's part of it."

"I know I've done that. It's something I have a hard time with. But as close are you are to Lucky and considering that you'll be taking over for him like Ah-Lahn did for Old Quin, I know you are deeply part of this story."

"I definitely felt that today," Kevin agreed.

Sarah reached over and took her husband's hands in hers. "I *want* to include you. What I don't want is for us to lose the depth of our connection. We've worked too hard to get to where we are. I promise not to put that communion in jeopardy."

Kevin raised her hands to his lips and kissed them, but he didn't say anything. Instead he looked down and closed his eyes.

Sarah felt his attention slip away.

"May I ask you for the same promise?" No response. "Kevin?"

"Huh? Oh, sorry. I'm here." He released his wife's hands and rubbed his forehead.

"Where did you go?"

"I'm not sure. Just thinking."

"I know what you're like when you're thinking," said Sarah. "This is different. You were disappearing all afternoon and now, again, you're miles away."

"Sorry. You were asking me something."

"I was asking for your promise not to jeopardize our connection. If I start shutting you out while I'm working on Lucky's stories, I want you to call me on it. And if you start drifting away, I want your agreement that you'll come back to me when I call you. Will you do that for me? For us?"

"I will. I promise."

"Good. Now will you tell me what has so intensely captivated your attention all afternoon and evening?"

"I would if I could. If I knew what I was sensing. At the moment, it's just a disturbance. Like an old memory that wants to surface and that part of me doesn't want to remember. Does that make sense?"

"Of course, it does. Wasn't I in that same state when you rushed to Ireland after our big blow-up two summers ago?"

Kevin nodded and sipped his tea. The scone looked more appealing now and he took a big bite.

Sarah continued. "You wouldn't let me push you away. I'm more than willing to do the same for you."

She felt her solar plexus tighten again—for a different reason. She sucked in a breath. "Hon, we may have to really watch out for each other. I'm sensing this is a record that neither of us wants to deal with."

"I think you're right." Kevin studied the expression on his wife's face. "I know you are." He pushed back from the table and stood behind his chair.

Hero and Sprite perked up from where they had been snoozing on one of the oversized dog beds they shared. They always sensed when something was bothering their humans. The dog walked over and flipped Kevin's hand onto his own big head for a scratch. Sprite curled around the man's legs.

The atmosphere in the room lightened.

Sarah freshened their cups of tea and ventured, "Do you want to ask Lucky privately?"

"No, I'm not sure what I would ask him. Let's just see what unfolds. I know his stories will be very enlightening. We may both gain some insight into the natural order of things."

"I'm fine with that." Sarah rose and joined her husband. They switched off the kitchen lights, double-checked the nursery room monitor and climbed the stairs to the peaceful sanctuary of their bedroom.

Concerns

Conversation was the need of the hour for the other couples, as well. Even after the relatively casual afternoon they had spent with Lucky and their closest friends, they were beginning to perceive their roles as being more than that of receptive audience for some lively recollections.

"Do you trust Maggie and Tim? I mean completely?" Glenna posed the question that had been on her mind since she and Rory confronted the spectre of a round tower at the O'Tooles'.

"I do," answered Rory, "though I'm thinking maybe you don't."

"I want to. I know they're ancient friends of Lucky's and I love him dearly. But I don't want to get drawn into some kind of scenario where we have to go to war again."

"I doubt that's what Lucky has in mind," said Rory.

"And you're not sure, are you? Our experience with the whole Arán Bán and Una drama was more than enough for this lifetime. He tried to kill us at Clonmacnoise and she did kill Róisín. We didn't think that was possible, but it happened."

"I know, *mo mhuirnín.*" Rory reached over to take Glenna's hand, but she pulled away and started to cry.

"I'm sorry to be so weepy. It's these silly hormones." She dug into her pocket for a tissue. "I don't want to be in danger, Rory. I want you and me and our baby to be safe. To just live our lives and be happy. To be a family. To do ordinary things."

"Glenna..."

"No, please hear me. I don't want to be a hero and I don't want you to be one either. I've lost you in too many battles. Promise me you'll stay safe this time. Don't leave me, Rory. I couldn't bear it!"

She was still sobbing when he pulled their car into the parking space they had rented in their apartment building's garage. Rory didn't want his pregnant wife navigating stairs and slippery sidewalks in bad weather.

"Glenna, look at me. I'll talk to Lucky. If you don't want to be part of his story sessions, you don't have to. And I won't if you don't want me to. Okay?"

"Okay. But I don't want to let the others down or make Lucky feel like we're abandoning him. I'll be alright. I'm tired and that tower frightened me. Maybe Tim could give us a demonstration of how those structures are supposed to work. That might help."

"There's the brave lass I married." Rory leaned over and kissed her.

"Um, that's nice," sighed Glenna. Then she shifted abruptly. "Ooh! I hate to spoil the moment, but could we hurry inside? I have to pee and I'm not sure how long I can wait."

Rory whipped off his seat belt and rushed around the car to help Glenna out. He offered to carry her to the elevator, which she laughingly declined.

"You're a darlin' man, Rory O'Donnell," she said in her best imitation Irish accent and breezed through the doors he opened for her.

Phelan did carry Cyndi into their house, which still showed the signs of their moving in. His wife had fallen asleep on the way home and was so groggy that he simply picked her up and brought her inside.

"How romantic," she crooned when he eased her onto their bed. She tried to sit up, then fell back on the pillows. "I'm sorry to be such a noodle. Something about being in that atmosphere with all those crystals made me really sleepy. I don't understand."

"It happens sometimes," Phelan said gently as he untied her shoes and removed her nightgown from its hook in her closet. "Do you need help with this?"

"I wouldn't mind, since you're so accommodating," said Cyndi coyly.

"Always happy to serve, darlin'. Let's get you comfy and then there's a subject I want to discuss with you."

"Do we have to talk at this very minute?"

"We do, yes, though I think we'll make it quick." Phelan grinned as he helped her into her nightgown."

"Okay. I'm all yours. I mean I'm all ears." Cyndi laughed and snuggled under the covers. "What is so serious that it can't wait?"

"I've been thinking about how tired you've been the last couple of weeks. And, yes, I know there's more than one reason for that, *mo chroí.*"

Cyndi fluttered her eyelashes as if she had no idea of his meaning.

With some difficulty, Phelan swallowed and went on.

"The other reason is that you're working too many hours at the coffee shop. Debbie seems to be thriving as the new Róisín, but I'm wondering if the new Cyndi isn't doing as well."

Tears suddenly welled up in his wife's eyes. She looked down as if to hide her true feelings from the husband she was still getting to know.

"I didn't want to tell you," she admitted. "I was afraid you'd think I was lazy. In a way, we hardly know each other. Everybody is working so hard to make Fibonacci's a success. I want that, too. But I feel like I'm in over my head."

"Tell me." Phelan kicked off his shoes and sat beside his wife. She was right. They were still getting to know each other.

"Our old health food store was mine and I could operate it the way I wanted. This is different. The pace is faster. The customers expect things to be the way they were when Lucky and Róisín ran the business. I don't have their touch or even Debbie's. All these changes are overwhelming. I feel like I don't fit." Cyndi practically wailed the last sentence.

"Ah, darlin', come here." Phelan drew her close. "Why didn't you tell me? I could have helped. I'm here to help you now. And I've come up with a plan that's going to be better for me, too."

"What's that?" Cyndi sniffled.

Phelan turned her around to look at him.

"I'm going to ask Lucky if he'll share his Caffeine Alchemist blends with me. I'm sure Kevin and Debbie will let me take over some of your responsibilities at the coffee shop. You and I need to spend more time together. We could create new herbal teas and tinctures from plants in our garden room and maybe make up some products that Stacey and Stan might like for the health food store—now that they own it."

"Oh, that is so wonderful. Thank you, my darling husband." Cyndi dried her tears and looked into his eyes. "Are you finished talking now?"

"I am."

"Good. I'm not tired any more."

"What did you see today?" Debbie asked Jeremy as he maneuvered their SUV through the Sunday evening traffic of people driving home from the beach. She noticed his pleasure in the way this new vehicle handled.

"While Tim was showing Brian and me his crystal collection, I saw a few orbs that looked like glistening, transparent spheres. Most of them contained scenes of people in different time periods and activities. Some were only filled with light of various colors."

"Was Róisín in any of them?"

"Not that I detected," Jeremy said as he parked the car.

"I was hoping I might see her," said Debbie. "You know, I thought maybe she would be around to help Lucky with his legacy. The fact that she wasn't tells me he's got this."

"I agree." Jeremy unlocked their apartment located on the third floor of Fibonacci's tower and followed Debbie into the kitchen. Placing his hands on her shoulders, he gently turned her toward him.

"I love coming home with you. I don't think I can say that enough. Making a home with you means the world to me."

Debbie put her arms around his neck and nestled her face against his chest. They stood that way for several minutes, neither of them willing to pull away.

At last, Jeremy smoothed her white blonde hair. "Do you want something cold to drink?"

"There's iced tea in the fridge."

"Perfect." He poured two glasses and handed her one. "Will you come sit with me in the living room? I have a question for you."

"You're being rather mysterious. What's on your mind?"

Jeremy sat where he could look at Debbie.

"Though it hasn't been long since you and Cyndi took over running the coffee shop, I've seen you accelerating in consciousness. When I watch you talking to customers or your employees, I can see a golden light all around you."

"That is so sweet. But not really a question."

"I'm getting to that. What I want to know is: Do you see me accelerating, too? I don't ever want to hold you back from your mission of using the torch of illumination Róisín gave you. I wouldn't want to crowd you or dampen your light."

"Oh, Jeremy, you wonderful man. There's no chance of that. Shall I tell you what I see?"

"Will I like it?"

"I believe so. I see a man who grows more comfortable in his own skin every day. A man who is a thoughtful and calming presence, a support to me and also to Kevin. I think the weight of responsibility lies heavy on him these days. Your presence eases that burden. He knows he can depend on your quick mind, your integrity and your willingness to tell him the truth."

"I feel the same about him. He's an excellent leader. What else?"

"I feel your strength growing in me. And because of that, I'm more comfortable in my own skin. I didn't know I wasn't. But with you in my life, I feel clearer. Better aligned with my inner sight. More able to function from my heart."

"I do feel that in you. Is there more?"

"There is. I see us moving together on a luminous cosmic highway. I know I wouldn't have that sense unless we were both making progress as two halves of a precious whole. Does that answer your question?"

Debbie's light green eyes misted as she felt herself melt into the deep pools of Jeremy's gaze.

"*A ghrá,*" he whispered. "You humble me. Thank God we found each other."

Ivy's Request

Sarah had finally found time in her morning to review the recording from yesterday's meeting with Lucky and to begin creating the initial transcript. It felt good to be at her desk again. If the twins would stay asleep for a nice long nap, she could get some work done.

She would not be doing any editing until she had a hard copy manuscript for her and Lucky to work with. She knew from transcribing her own journals that apparently insignificant comments could be key to insights she would have missed otherwise. She wouldn't make that mistake. Not with material as important as Lucky's legacy.

She was setting up the necessary computer files when her cell phone rang. It was her sister-in-law, Ivy. Her voice was strained.

"Sarah, I'm sorry to bother you. I'm sure you have a million things to do. My morning was crazy getting the twins off to their summer program at school. Do you mind if I stop by? I really need to talk to you."

"Of course, Ivy. Is everything alright? You sound stressed. Are the twin okay?"

"Oh, they're fine. They were still jabbering this morning about Uncle Lucky and Aunt Maggie and Uncle Tim and their house and all the fairies and gnomes they could see. They can't wait to go back."

"How delightful," said Sarah. She made a note to include observations like that in Lucky's book. "I was sitting where I could watch them pointing and explaining to Maggie what they were seeing as they walked around her garden. But there's a problem?"

"There is. That's what I need to talk to you about."

"Then come right over. I'll put on the kettle."

Five minutes later Ivy rang the doorbell at the MacCauleys' town house that was only two doors away from the similar one which she and Brian had bought earlier in the year. In a way, she missed living in the Boston area, but being close to family was a boon.

"I brought muffins," she declared when Sarah opened her front door. Ivy felt guilty about dumping her problems on Brian's sister, but Sarah was the only person who might understand.

"You didn't have to, but I'm glad you did. I forgot to pick up baked goods from Fibonacci's yesterday, so my cupboard is bare. After Maggie's feast, I didn't think I'd eat for days. But you know how that goes."

Sarah was making small talk to get a sense of Ivy's emotional state. She had never seen the young woman quite so frazzled. Her long, copper-colored hair was tightly pulled back and she wore no make-up. Unlike her usual tidy appearance, she was wearing a baggy t-shirt, faded denim shorts and flip flops that looked like they'd just wandered in from the beach.

Sarah ushered her sister-in-law into the kitchen and pulled out a chair at the table.

"Ivy, sit down and take a deep breath. Whatever is bothering you will be better if you don't stop breathing. Have some tea and a muffin and tell me what's going on. Are you and Brian having problems?"

"No, it's not like that. Well, I guess it is—sort of. Oh, I don't know. It's really not about us. It's about the twins and this whole storytelling thing with Lucky. I'm confused and Brian is upset. I guess neither of us realized what we'd agreed to participate in. It's all this stuff about past lives that you and Kevin and the others are so comfortable with. And the twins are seeing fairies and gnomes and talking about their Rose Lady. It's too much, Sarah."

"Okay. Deep breath in, let it out. Again."

Sarah couldn't help remembering childbirth classes. Ivy's condition had that kind of urgency. After a few deep breaths, she calmed down.

"There you go. In one way I'm not surprised to hear this, except I thought Brian was opening up about the Rose Lady and the fact that Kerry and Kaitlyn can see into other realms."

"So did I," said Ivy, her emotions a combination of frustration and disappointment. "I mean, he's the one who planned our trip to Ireland last month. But once we got there, he was more interested in the pubs and nightlife and talking to business people than in exploring his family's roots and learning about the culture."

Ivy took another deep breath and gathered her thoughts.

"Brian liked Dublin and Galway, and he loved going out on boats. The sea definitely captured his attention. But otherwise, he seemed anxious to come home."

"I'm sorry to hear that," said Sarah. "I was hoping that Ireland's thin places would open Brian to the ancestry he's been rejecting—much to our mother's consternation."

"I'd hoped so, too," said Ivy dejectedly. "Anyway, he and I discussed Lucky's legacy project last night and we'd like to be excused. Gosh, that sounds like we're skipping school. What I mean to say is that Brian doesn't feel like he fits with the whole past lives idea. He's still happy being part of Fibonacci's as a business. Just not as a spiritual thing."

"What about you, Ivy? Do you feel like you belong to the Circle of Close Companions? You've had your own experience with the Rose Lady."

"I know and I'd like to hear Lucky's stories. If I don't participate, even a little, I know Kerry and Kaitlyn will be disappointed. But I'm stuck in the middle. When Brian gets upset, he can be harsh with the children. I don't want that to happen. I don't know what to do."

Sarah reached across the table and took Ivy's hand.

"Okay, let's think about this. First of all, nobody's forcing you to attend the sessions with Lucky. He's got such a big heart. I know he was just trying to include everybody with whom he feels a deep connection. And he's determined to finish every detail of his assignment."

"That's really very sweet," admitted Ivy.

"I'm sure Lucky would tell you and Brian to consider his story sessions as an opportunity, not an obligation. But what are you going to do about Kerry and Kaitlyn? Their inner sight is a big part of who they are."

"I know and I don't want them to feel ashamed or unloved because they have special abilities." Ivy teared up at this thought.

"I have an idea," said Sarah. "Maybe, if Brian knows he doesn't have to attend the story sessions, he'll be relieved and then he won't mind if you join us. Would you still want to come? Kevin and I can bring you and the children, if you like."

"I'm not sure," Ivy hesitated. "I guess I could show up at least one more time with the twins." She paused and ate most of a muffin. "I just had a thought. Do you think I could talk to Maggie?"

"That's a great idea," agreed Sarah. "If anybody can help you figure out how to make life work for you and your family, it will be Maggie O'Toole."

Maggie answered the phone herself and immediately agreed to meet with Ivy. "Be sure to bring Brian," she insisted. "Let's have no secrets or divisions between you. I'll be happy to see you both this Wednesday morning while Kerry and Kaitlyn are in school."

She hung up before Ivy could protest that Brian might not want to join them. She would just have to tell him they had an appointment with Maggie O'Toole and that was that.

Two days later, Tim opened the door before they could ring the bell. "Maggie's in the living room," he said and ushered them in. "I'll leave you three to your conversation. Lucky and I are going sailing this morning."

"Come in and welcome," said Maggie cheerfully. She invited them to sit by the fireplace and poured the tea she'd prepared into sturdy mugs. Then she went straight to the point of her proposal.

"Brian, I'm grateful you accepted my invitation to join Ivy. I want you to know that I'm here to help you, not to tell you what to do—though I am old enough to be your mother and I do know a thing or two about children with special gifts. I once was one myself."

She offered them a confident smile and continued.

"I would like to work with your children to help them learn to use their gifts of inner sight and hearing without being a burden to others or to themselves. Kerry and Kaitlyn are old enough to learn the lessons every person with these abilities must learn."

Brian's expression was neutral. Maggie could see why he was such an effective negotiator. She went on before he decided to interrupt.

"What I will not do is make those gifts go away. In fact, I hope to help them develop—in a safe and practical manner. Debbie and Jeremy can tell you that knowing how to work with second sight makes life flow along more smoothly. All I ask is that you love your children for the blessing they are and for the gifts they possess. They can be a help to the world if you'll let them be themselves."

She paused, expecting an answer. "Can you do that? Ivy? Brian?"

Ivy nodded in agreement, but Brian looked apprehensive.

"I don't want them to be silly or weird. I just want normal children."

"Oh, Brian," laughed Maggie, "there's no such thing."

"What do you mean?" *Who is this woman who acts as if all the world's wisdom is at her fingertips?* he wondered.

Maggie smiled to herself as she caught the image Brian was vividly projecting. He would not appreciate knowing how easily she could read his thoughts. Her intuition was showing her a lot about this accomplished man. *He has so much fear,* she realized. *We'll have to help him with that.*

Warming to her subject, she went on. "Would you get rid of your own intelligence and business acumen? Or your ability to design new products and services to offer through your computer company?"

"No, but that's not the same as seeing fairies or rose ladies."

"To some people, your talents are exactly that magical. You have a highly refined sense of how things work. You understand the mystery of electronics and how to be financially successful as well as innovative."

"I suppose so."

"Even for folks who have similar talents, they don't possess your unique combination of natural abilities. Whether you realize it or not, Brian, you're tapping into hidden realms of your own inner genius. You've had to learn how to use that genius effectively, have you not?"

"Yes, I have."

"And he's done a fantastic job," Ivy interjected. She was genuinely proud of her husband's accomplishments.

"Well then, do you see that appreciating another person's talents is all a matter of perspective? You've good hearts, both of you. Pay attention to those hearts and you and your children will thrive."

Brian blew out a breath. "Okay. We'll give it a try. How do you suggest we proceed?"

"I appreciate your willingness, Brian," said Maggie earnestly. "And you, too, Ivy." She paused briefly to let them feel her sincerity.

"I suggest that we set up an afternoon program for Kerry and Kaitlyn. With your approval, I'll pick them up from school once or twice a week. I'll bring them here to my house, feed them a light snack, give them a lesson and then bring them home. Our first lessons will focus on teaching them how to protect their awareness so they stay safe from any malicious forces that might try to piggy-back onto their openness."

Brian and Ivy looked worried again. Maggie hurried to reassure them.

"Don't worry, my dears. Since they were conceived, your children have been under a powerful spiritual protection. Now they will learn to take some responsibility for their own safety, which is as it should be."

"You do understand, don't you?" said Ivy.

"I do, yes—as do Sarah and Kevin. We'll be doing the same sort of training with Gareth and Naimh when they get older." *And by then their older cousins will be explaining everything,* Maggie chuckled to herself.

"Let me say again, you need not be concerned. We are committed to keeping your precious children as safe on the inner as you do on the outer. All will be well, I promise."

Memory or Prophecy?

Kevin woke up gasping. For air. For reality. He opened his eyes—saw nothing but darkness. Where was he? He turned his head, his mind clutching at the bright green numbers on the digital clock. 3:00 a.m.

Thank God he was in his own room with his wife sleeping peacefully beside him and his big dog making snuffling noises beside the bed.

Reality. At least he hoped so. He might still be dreaming. No, that wasn't a dream. That was a nightmare. And not like any he'd had before. Not in this lifetime.

The emotion had been overwhelming. Still was. Like a wetsuit clinging to his skin and darkening his heart to all that was good and true and beautiful about his soul.

He needed coffee. And a walk through his house where he could touch the familiar furnishings that made up his home environment.

Could he slip out of bed without waking Sarah? Yes, if he was careful. But Hero would wake up. The dog didn't miss anything. Maybe he wouldn't bark if Kevin eased him out of his doggy slumber.

Okay. Quiet. Quiet. Quiet. Sarah stirred, but didn't wake.

"Hero, buddy, wake up," Kevin whispered, gently ruffling the hair on the wolfhound's head. Brown canine eyes popped open, but no bark.

"Good boy, come with me. Shhhh. Good boy."

Man and dog tiptoed down the carpeted stairs and into the kitchen. Kevin switched off the house alarm and walked out the back door to let Hero do his business. "Quiet," he whispered. "No barking."

Mercifully, there was a breeze blowing off the Long Island Sound. Like a man who'd nearly drowned, Kevin filled his lungs over and over with air that carried the scents of sea and summer flowers.

Yes, he was coming back now. *Terra firma* under his bare feet. He walked gingerly across the patio's slate tiles and ventured onto cool green grass that sent the feeling of vibrant life tingling up his legs. He stretched his arms. Did some deep knee bends. Drank in more fresh air.

Hero walked back to his human. How did the dog know not to run or bound as was his habit?

"Good boy," Kevin said again. He and his perceptive canine padded inside and gently closed the back door.

He gave Hero a treat and started making coffee.

Pouring water, measuring the grounds, switching on the appliance. Actions he had done a million times all took on the meaning of ritual as he thanked *An Síoraí*, the Eternal One, for his life, his family, his home.

While Kevin waited for the coffee to brew, his thinking mind came back to life. Should he reconsider his decision not to speak to Lucky? The inner sense that he had identified as only a disturbance had broken through into a full-on nightmare.

Today was Friday—before the sun had thought to rise. Could he wait until the weekend to speak to Lucky? Maybe the man's first story would shed some light on this night's excursion into the astral plane.

Of course, that's where I was, Kevin told himself as he poured his first cup of coffee. In the meantime, he was obliged to tell Sarah what he'd seen. Or actually what he hadn't seen. The sensory blackness had been enough.

Kevin had promised her truth and openness. Here was a test of that promise. He finished his coffee and set his cup on the counter. He turned to walk upstairs and wake her, but there was no need. His wife was already in the kitchen, wrapped in her fluffy yellow robe, her eyes not quite open.

"Oh, good, you made coffee." She crossed to where Kevin was standing. She poured herself a cup and took the first welcome sip. Only then did she look at her husband's face.

"Hon, what's wrong? You're pale and sweaty. Did you have a nightmare? You should have wakened me."

Sarah spoke softly as she always did when the children were asleep. Instinctively, she put her hand on Kevin's forehead and stroked it as he had seen her do many times with their twins.

"I didn't want to wake you until I pulled myself together," he whispered and poured himself another cup of coffee. "I'm glad you're here now. Will you sit with me? Maybe I can make sense of where I was and what was happening."

He took his seat at the head of their kitchen table, then looked up hopefully before Sarah sat down. "Do we have anything to eat? Please tell me your mother baked scones yesterday."

"Yes, my mother baked scones yesterday and we've got lots." Sarah opened a tin filled to the brim with Eileen Callahan's pastries. Kevin let out a sigh of relief and closed his eyes as he ate an entire scone before speaking again.

"I'm not sure where to start," he admitted. "Maybe you could ask me some questions. The details are already starting to fade away. It's that same sense that part of me doesn't want to remember. What I won't forget is the vicious feeling of the nightmare."

"Okay," Sarah agreed. "Let's start with you. Did you recognize yourself as Kevin or Ah-Lahn?"

"I was me—my soul, I mean. Modern Kevin and then later an older version of Ah-Lahn. Not an older person, but an earlier embodiment. Like I was having two dreams at the same time."

"Did you have a sense of location?"

"The main scene felt modern. Like a conference room with harsh lights and uncomfortable metal chairs. Very utilitarian."

"Go on," said Sarah. "You're getting it."

"So I'm in this room and there a few other people there, but I don't see any faces. I can't tell if they are men or women. What I do know is that they are in charge, and I'm being held in this place against my will."

"Was it like a prison or maybe someplace where you might have been interrogated?"

"Hmm." Kevin closed his eyes, trying to remember the scene.

"It's possible that an inquiry was being held. I was beginning to get a sense of what was going on when the scene changed. That's when I had the feeling of being that earlier version of Ah-Lahn."

He stood and began pacing around the kitchen.

"There were different faceless people now, and this scene felt raw and personal between me and them, whoever they were. The thing is, I couldn't identify them in the dream, but I did know who they were. In fact, I think I knew them really well."

"Do they remind you of anybody you know now? Somebody from our community?" Sarah checked herself. "I hope not."

"I can't tell you. And I guess that's about all I can tell you, except for the energy. You know, I said the scene felt raw. The emotion was like that and more. I would call it primal."

"That's so weird."

"Definitely weird. Anyway, whatever these people had done, they had done it to me personally. But they were berating me as if their deeds were my fault. Anyway, I was so angry that I wanted to kill them. Honestly, I wanted to rip their hearts out. I think that's why I woke up."

Sarah shuddered. "Now I'm glad you didn't wake me."

Kevin paused and sat down again.

"You know, one thing about this event is that it didn't give off that element of protection like we've experienced in life reviews. Even when the scenes have been intense, they've felt sponsored. We knew our Masters were in charge. We still had to go through some awful scenarios, but our souls were never in danger from the recollection."

"You're right," Sarah agreed. "I've never thought of it that way, but everything we've been through has been for a spiritual purpose. The other thing is that, even when we've been in battles with evil forces, we haven't been angry."

"That's right," Kevin went on. "Remember how when Arán Bán's treachery ended the life of Ah-Lahn's son and the two men were locked in the final event of Arán Bán's life. The emotion Ah-Lahn was feeling for his mortal enemy was compassion."

Sarah picked up Kevin's thread. "Through all of these events with us and the Twin Flames of Éire, we have worked hard at never descending to a consciousness of anger or vengeance. Don't you think that's one reason we've been able to achieve the union of mind and heart we have now?"

"Absolutely," Kevin nodded. "And this was different. It was almost as if a malignant force was trying to trick me into committing murder that would have trapped my soul on the astral plane."

"Hon, that is really terrible."

"Tell me about it." He raked his fingers through his dark brown hair and finished his coffee.

"I have one more question—that I don't really want to ask," said Sarah.

"Go ahead." Kevin took her hand.

"Was I there? Was I in that room with you? If I had been, I hope I would have tried to stop you from committing murder. I'm sure our being together would have prevented you from doing anything deadly."

"I agree, but you weren't there. The violent emotions I was experiencing were very personal. Something had been done to me. I can almost remember pounding on my chest at the injustice of whatever it was. Of the horror and hatred I was feeling toward these people. And they were mocking me. That was a real blow to my pride, I can tell you."

"That is so unlike you. I can't imagine you or Ah-Lahn or whoever you were in that embodiment thinking such thoughts."

"Well, we haven't been exactly perfect, you know. That's one reason we're both still here. Anyway, it's possible that your soul could have been involved peripherally. But that wasn't what was on my mind right before I woke up."

"Thank God you did."

"No kidding."

"Do you think you should tell Lucky about this? Or Tim and Maggie?"

"Before you came downstairs, I was considering just waiting for the weekend to see if Lucky's first story might shed some light on this nightmare. But now that you've helped me remember more details, I don't think I should delay." He checked the clock on the kitchen wall.

"It's almost 5:00 o'clock. I'll call Lucky in a couple of hours and ask if I can drop by later this morning for a chat with all three of them."

"Do you want me to go with you?" Sarah started loading their cups into the dishwasher and putting away the scones. Just then, a couple of little voices could be heard over the nursery monitor.

Kevin shook his head. Five o'clock was earlier than Gareth's and Naimh's usual rising time, but this had already been an unusual morning.

"You're welcome to come with me, as long as you don't have anything else to do," he said with a grin.

Sarah felt her heart expand with a love she could not have imagined two years ago. Hearing her children call for her in the morning was such a pleasure. She returned her husband's grin.

"I do seem to have another pressing engagement. And I still have to review the notes I've typed from our first session with Lucky. You go ahead and please give them my love. I'll be eager to hear what they have to say about your nightmare."

Kevin was sitting across from Lucky, Maggie and Tim by the green marble fireplace where a turf fire burned. He was grateful for its comforting light which eased the heaviness of the images and emotions his story vividly created in his friends' minds.

Maggie had set out tea and fruit on the coffee table that anchored the conversation area where they were seated, but no one was eating.

"This is unexpected," said Lucky, not hiding his concern about Kevin's experience. "I knew my stories were likely to spark recollections from the Circle of Close Companions. If that happened we were going to explore them in sponsored life reviews. Nightmares were not part of the plan."

"What do you think it means?" asked Tim.

"It means we'd best be very careful," said Maggie firmly. "Do you think the dream could be a prophecy?"

"Could be, but I'm puzzled," said Lucky. He rose and stood by the fire, resting his arm on the mantle. "When our Master gave me details of my assignment he indicated that our timing was good—like a respite from the battles our community has been through. I got no sense from him that we were facing any imminent threat."

"Have you asked him for clarification?" Maggie asked, refreshing their tea.

"No. I've been listening, but I haven't picked up anything," said Lucky. "Meanwhile, I think we'd best plan to use the tower on Sunday. Tim, are Rory and Glenna open to that since you gave them a demonstration?"

"They are. The lad's on fire to try it out with the group and the lass is as game as he. They're quite a pair."

Maggie nodded. "'Tis a good thing she was willing to let you show her how the old towers were meant to work."

She turned to Lucky and Kevin. "Glenna was so frightened that first day, I told Tim we had to do something. The lass is pregnant and more sensitive than she lets on."

"She is that," smiled Tim. "I was proud of her. She listened while I explained how we'd built the tower and how we use it. She admitted that Rory had explained some of the science the old monks used, but being inside a functioning sound and meditation chamber made it all real to her."

"Good for her," said Kevin. "I'm looking forward to experiencing the tower myself, but I'll wait for Sunday. My question is: Do you think using its forcefield and harmonic resonance will be protection enough?"

"'Tis been our secret weapon for a long time," Maggie assured him. "When we raise your group consciousness to a higher level than whatever negative forces may be anticipating, I'm sure Lucky can go ahead with his grand stories."

"And we'll keep a weather-eye on happenings around Fibonacci's," said Tim.

"Agreed." Maggie, Kevin and Lucky spoke as one voice.

"One thing this tells me," Tim continued, "is that the Masters of Wisdom are pouring buckets of light energy into our community right now. Otherwise, why would malignant forces decide to attack Kevin and make him violate his own principles in his sleep?"

Lucky agreed. "The nightmare may be a record of your own karma, lad, but pushing it to the surface is not the purview of the dark ones. As far as our Master is concerned, we've plenty of moves remaining in this old chess game."

Glendalough

Lucky's entire being was alive with a sense of anticipation as his listeners gathered on sofas and comfortable chairs in the living room of Tim and Maggie's home. He had taken the *seanchaí's* traditional seat in front of the ever-present turf fire that created an atmosphere of comfort and safety.

"The story I'm about to tell you isn't the one I thought I'd be sharing today," he explained. "As we know, priorities on this spiritual path we're walking have a way of changing, so we're following the lead of *An Síoraí*, the Eternal One. 'Tis grateful I am that you've all pushed through any old obstacles to your being here today."

Until that morning, none of couples had been entirely certain that they *would* push through the obstacles to their providing Lucky with the audience his stories required. Fortunately, everyone had rallied.

Even Brian had decided he wanted to hear more from Lucky—for the sake of Ivy and their children, if not actually for himself. His conversation with Maggie had given him a fresh perspective.

While Brian was pensive, Lucky's bright blue eyes were twinkling. "Tim and I have a surprise for you. We decided a story would make it more meaningful.

"This answers your question, Sarah, about how the lad and I became such close friends. Kevin, you may enjoy hearing about your namesake. And for one or two of you, don't be surprised if you recognize yourselves in this tale. I expect that may happen often before this legacy of mine is complete." Lucky winked at Rory and began.

There are eras in history when individuals and groups attune to cosmic forces and respond to those energies by changing how they behave or how they think. At that point, transition from one state of consciousness or stage of development takes place in their lives.

One day, a person unknown to them appears on the scene—someone with an idea straight from the heart of *An Síoraí*, the Eternal One. Like the storytellers of old, this stranger has a way of communicating that sparks inner recognition and enthusiasm on the part of the listeners who are ripe for change.

Seeking their own taste of the Divine, these folks pick up on the brilliance and experience a conversion. They hasten to become followers, devotees, students and builders on behalf of those like good Saint Patrick, Saint Ciarán of Clonmacnoise, Saint Columcille of Iona, or even the famous lady bishop, Saint Brigid of Kildare—people who were called by a mystical vision or an encounter with angels or other heavenly visitors.

These saints are remembered for the trails they blazed throughout Éire and beyond, founding monasteries and turning druids into abbots. Which wasn't all that hard.

You see, belief in the soul's immortality and the threefold nature of the Divine had been held long before Saint Patrick preached about the Trinity. Some say he destroyed druidism, but his fight was with the serpents who had corrupted the old faith. A fascinating tale that is, but 'tis a story for another time.

Anyway, there were other saintly figures in Éire whose minds and hearts, though educated by man, were elevated by Nature herself. Saint Kevin was such a person.

He was born during one of these transitional eras. A lover of learning with an aptitude for asceticism, he became part of what was called the Green Martyrdom. Because the druids had so easily converted to Christianity, there were no Irish martyrs in Patrick's day or for hundreds of years after.

So the Irish monks, never at a loss for creative solutions, fashioned themselves after the Desert Fathers of the East. They sought out the most inhospitable locations they could find, like the rocky outcropping of Skellig Michael, where they could live and pray in seclusion. Of course, that didn't really work.

For one thing, when left to herself, the land of Éire flowers abundantly with food from land and sea. And, being innately social folk, the Irish couldn't seem to stop themselves from gathering around the hermits. Monasteries were the natural result.

That's what happened to Saint Kevin. After being ordained as a monk, he took himself off to a lush, secluded valley nestled between two lakes in the Wicklow mountains. There on a hillside overlooking one of the lakes, he discovered an ancient cave that became his habitation for over seven years.

Of course, not even a hermit can hide his light under a rock forever. Eventually, folks found out about this holy man who would teach and guide them if they asked. As more pilgrims made their way to what became known as Glendalough, Saint Kevin finally relented and allowed some of the monks to build him a little beehive hut made of stone.

They created mud and wattle huts for themselves, which is how the Glendalough monastery came to be founded around AD 544 and where Saint Kevin served as abbot, more or less continually, until AD 618 when he died at the age of 102.

Now, where do Tim and Lucky come in? you'd like to know. Well, I'll tell you.

Imagine yourselves living in the middle of the sixth century. That's where we encounter two lads with a particular longing. Like many Irish of the time, they raised cattle with their families and farmed some crops to feed their people.

They'd absorbed the Celtic Christianity that permeated the countryside and were content with their lives, with a single vital exception. You see, the lads shared a gift that was common in the people of the land, though perhaps not as strongly felt by some as by them. They loved stone. And they'd come to love Saint Kevin, who they'd met after some of his itinerant monks encouraged the lads to visit him.

'When he looks at you,' the monks reported, 'the man's eyes can hold you tethered to his very soul. Or like he's lending you a piece of his heart because he knows you need it.

'He's quiet, interior, self-contained—like his life is a sort of perpetual meditation on realms unseen. But when he speaks, you feel the clouds part, whether they're in the sky or your head.'

Well, that's all the urging the lads required. At the time they were both unmarried, so they bade their families farewell and hurried off to the glen between two lakes in time to help build the stone beehive hut that Saint Kevin had decided was maybe better than living in a cave after all.

Although the man spent most of his time in prayer, he would come out regularly to sit in the sun and greet folks who needed his attention or who'd recently arrived at the monastery to visit or stay.

As good fortune would have it, the lads arrived on just such a sunny day. At first they didn't know where to go. But when they saw a crowd of people, they knew that must be where they would find the abbot. Sure enough, there was Saint Kevin, standing by his hut, ministering to his flock.

He was of medium height and presented a strong figure. He tended to the thin side from all his fasting, but he was not weak. His hair was dark and his eyes were shades of blue and grey that changed like the color of the sea when the light brightens or dims from clouds passing overhead.

The man was warm as a sunbeam. As the lads got to know him, they thought he was like the stone he loved so much. That sounds contradictory, but 'tis not. It was like Saint Kevin could attract light from the ethers and store it up in his cells for those moments when woman, man, child, bird or beast would come to him for help or healing.

Oh, how the lads wanted to be like him!

Once in a while, when they knew he'd be secluded in his stone hut, they would row a borrowed currach boat over to the opposite side of the lake and scramble up to the cave that came to be known as Kevin's Bed.

It was so narrow and short, they had to crawl in. Then they'd pray and chant and meditate. You know, sometimes there'd be a vibration, like the cave was alive. Or the air would shimmer with spiritual vibrations. One time they stayed up there over night and they heard the mountain speak.

Those experiences changed the lads so they poured their hearts even more fervently into their work—as has been the way of stone masons who've built the grand temples and cathedrals that humans still raise up to the Eternal One, no matter what century they're born into.

Now, back to Glendalough. What they don't tell you in the histories is that those seven years spent tucked into the rocky bosom of the earth had taught Kevin a thing or two about the life force in certain stones.

You see, just like the Egyptians and probably the Atlanteans before them, the saint began to realize that some stone emits life-sustaining energy that it has absorbed from the sun. When he meditated and chanted his prayers in his cave, the stone shared that light with him.

'Tis no wonder he ate so little and lived so long. He was full of energy from the cave. He made sure his monks built his hut of the same stone, so his life didn't change all that much. Except for the fact that he was surrounded by the people he had tried to avoid in favor of the animals who also loved him.

However, being a real saint, Kevin was generous of heart and keen of mind. He decided to share his secret with the community that was growing around him. It takes a fair amount of labor to build with stone and there was plenty of timber in those days, so there was no point in his suggesting that mud and wattle wasn't going to create the architecture of the future.

Instead, he described what he'd heard passed down from the druids about Egyptian engineering techniques and how they'd built their pyramids as energy collectors, not tombs. They created their structures to detect and store cosmic rays. One purpose was to direct those rays into the earth to help their crops grow.

The ancients were also aware of the healing power of sound. The interiors of their pyramids were constructed like sound chambers that amplified the vibrations of their chants to enhance meditation and healing.

So Saint Kevin declared to his community, 'We'll build our own energy collector tower that's shaped like the interior of the Great Pyramid. We'll meditate and chant in there and the stone will give off cosmic energies to help our crops grow and to raise the consciousness of our people while they thrive physically.'

That's what the lads and many others set to doing. At the time, nobody knew to call what they were building an antenna, but that's basically how the Glendalough tower and the others going up around Ireland functioned.

Of course, it took years to build a hundred-foot-tall tower. But the lads were there from beginning to end, even though some of the books will tell you it wasn't finished for centuries.

You see, they learned from Saint Kevin to sleep near the stones that were meant for the tower. And handling them day after day gave the lads stamina like they'd never experienced.

They just kept building and living. As the tower grew taller and taller, they knew it was going to work. Already the crops planted close by were flourishing. So was the community. The seventh century that followed was a time of massive expansion of the monastic movement in both learning and building. 'Twas a grand time to be alive!

Now, there's all manner of tales about Saint Kevin and blackbirds and other animals. He was definitely a miraculous man and you can read those stories. The point is that the lads and at least one of you became like brothers as they worked with stone and raised their voices and their souls in the mighty tower as it rose higher and higher, casting its powerful gaze out over the glen between two lakes where it would survive storms and fierce attacks for over 1400 years.

Lucky's bright blue eyes glistened as he recalled those days of a life well lived. He looked across the room at Tim who nodded with approval at this first of the many tales that would unfold at *Teach an tSolais*.

None of Lucky's listeners spoke right away. Their eyes were misted with a faraway expression that showed they had traveled in their imaginations to the scenes they'd felt as well as seen.

Rory was especially rapt with his own memories. He turned to Lucky and smiled, folding his hands in front of his heart in a gesture of thanks and recognition.

"Now then, *a chairde*." Lucky spoke gently as his friends returned from their musings of the past to the present. "Are you ready for the surprise Tim and I have arranged for you?"

"I know I am," answered Glenna cheerfully. She had felt the quickening of Rory's entire being as he saw himself working alongside Tim and Lucky in those long-ago days of tower building. She'd had no sense of herself being with them in that labor, but she was delighted that her husband now understood more about his own fascination with stone towers.

"Grand!" said Tim, as he rose from his seat. "If you'll follow me..."

"Tim, darlin'," Maggie playfully stopped him. "Let's give our friends a bit of a break. I'll put the kettle on and we can sample the lovely snacks Debbie and Cyndi brought us from the coffee shop."

"Ah, sure, darlin'." Tim grinned back at his wife of countless years. "Help yourselves, everybody. Lucky and I will collect you in about fifteen minutes, if that will suffice."

"Make it twenty, and we're all yours," laughed Ivy as she hurried to follow Kerry and Kaitlyn into the kitchen. "Brian and I have a couple of hungry children to feed."

"Right you are, lass," chuckled Tim. "Right you are."

Vibrations & Visions

"Maggie, now I see why your gardens are so lush," Debbie exclaimed as she and the other Companions strolled across the back lawn toward the structure affectionately known as Tim's Tower.

"And why they're planted in circular patterns," added Sarah.

Cyndi chimed in. "I always thought it was odd that the plants in Lucky and Róisín's garden room were arranged in circles with a granite obelisk in the center. Now I understand. No wonder that room is like a paradise."

"Oh, 'tis the man's scheme, though I do appreciate the results," said Maggie with a grin as she inhaled the fragrance of roses and lavender and dozens of seasonal blooms that were a treat to the senses.

"On overcast days like today, I can even imagine myself back at Glendalough. Oh, yes, I was there—tending Saint Kevin's crops while the lads were fitting their stones into place. We started growing food in rings around the outside perimeter almost as soon as they established the base and built up to where the door would be placed."

Sarah had been watching Kevin and Brian walking ahead, each of them holding an excited twin by the hand. She was grateful that Gareth and Naimh were spending the day with her parents so she could fully participate in the afternoon's activities.

She turned to Maggie and said with a knowing smile, "I get the feeling that Saint Kevin wasn't the only one who lived to a very old age."

"We Celts were a hardy folk. We did have to contend with the odd attack from some Irish gang, but we had long been a people very knowledgeable about Mother Nature and her healing ways. When our good Saint Kevin revived the ancient knowledge of stones, we kept on living for many a year."

Maggie perked up suddenly. "Come along now. The man's fairly bursting to tell you about his big experiment here on the shores of Long Island."

They gathered around the enormous tower and craned their necks to look all the way up to the conical roof that was also made of stone. Light appeared to reach inside from eight small rectangular windows that were located far up the tower. The four highest were placed directly below the roof at right angles to each other.

"Those top windows are set on the four cardinal directions," explained Rory. "I've studied the Irish towers and they're all the same."

Lucky clapped him good-naturedly on the shoulder and smiled.

"Oooo!" exclaimed Kaitlyn. "Lift me up, Daddy, so I can see."

"Me, too, Uncle Kevin," declared her brother. "I want to go inside."

"So you shall, lad," agreed Tim. He was standing next to some portable stairs that led up to the entrance, which was nearly nine feet above ground level.

"If we were a group of monks coming to chant and meditate, we'd be climbing up a rough ladder," he began. "But since our merry band includes you lasses and little ones, we've put up these stairs to make getting in and out safer. Follow Lucky and I'll bring up the rear."

In no time, they were all inside, standing like a little tour group, ready for the next explanation from their local guide. The atmosphere inside the tower was slightly cool and dimly illumined, even with light from the entrance behind them.

"What is this material on the floor?" asked Ivy. "I guess I thought it would be stone, but it looks more like soil, though not like soil."

"'Tis crystal that's been finely crushed almost to sand," explained Tim. "That's part of the secret to how these towers work. Adjusting the level of fill at the bottom of the tower is how we tune the frequencies to attract the electromagnetic waves we want to focus inside."

He looked around the group to make sure all were assembled.

"If you're willing, we do have a sturdy ladder to climb to the next level. Kaitlyn and Kerry, you let your daddy and your uncle boost you up. Glenna, lass, are you alright?"

"I'm fine, Tim. Don't worry. I've months to go before I waddle."

Very carefully they all made their way up the ladder where they were seated on a wooden platform that stretched around the circumference of the tower. Tim and Lucky pulled up an insert to cover the opening. Now, they could see how light flowed in through the high windows. When Tim spoke, they heard how the tower was as resonant as a Gothic cathedral.

"Normally, there would be several more wooden floors set at precise levels in the tower," he explained. "But we like to use just this one level so we get not only the exact vibration that supports meditation, but also the amplification of our chants that bounce off the stone around and above us.

"That's the effect the ancient Egyptians produced in the Great Giza Pyramid because those floors were all stone. We're still experimenting with our tower to figure out how to get the best effect."

"This is amazing," said Brian. "I'm impressed. And you said this tower at fifty feet tall is only half the size of the one at Glendalough?"

Tim nodded. "Truth be told, I had no easy time convincing the planning board of our village that I wasn't building an eyesore that was going to blow over in a hurricane. Many of our trees are over fifty feet tall, so we're well hidden. And these walls are double-layered with rock and dirt fill between them. They'll stand."

Lucky knew his friend could talk for hours about tower construction, but he wanted everyone to experience why they were sitting on a wooden floor perched more than seventeen feet above ground level.

He spoke up to move things along.

"One reason the old monks prayed before sunrise and then again at sunset is because the cosmic rays that are most conducive to meditation are strongest at dawn and dusk. We're either early or late for those services, but I'm sure our tower will do its part."

An enthusiastic Tim nodded in agreement as Lucky continued.

"To give you an idea of how sound can be amplified in a structure like this, let's sound the OM together. Then, if that goes well, we'll meditate for a few minutes. Tim has tuned the floor to the meditation frequency, so you may notice a difference in your ability to relax and let go."

"We've never had this many people in the tower at one time," Tim added eagerly. "This should be interesting."

"We'll not make this a lengthy experiment," Lucky assured the group.

"We're only meant to have a taste of what Saint Kevin's monks experienced centuries ago. At the end of our meditation, I'll softly sound the OM to bring us back to the present. Everybody okay?"

He looked over at Ivy's husband who appeared to be having an internal conversation. "Brian?"

"Yeah, I'm okay. Big stretch for a computer guy, but I'm game."

"And you were Irish before you were a geek," teased Sarah. "Still are, as far as I can tell." She reached over and ruffled her brother's very red hair. "Come on, little brother, you can be both."

"Watch it, big sister, or I'll bonk you with my shillelagh," Brian grinned back at her.

Lucky chuckled at the siblings "Right. Let's get started."

He closed his eyes and centered his awareness in his heart. When he was set, he sounded the OM and immediately felt it rising within him with unusual strength. The others joined in, matching and harmonizing with his tone.

Instantly, the tower was filled with the sound as if a hundred voices had joined in. Tones far deeper and higher in pitch than normal human throats could produce were resonating. The very stones seemed to sing.

The Circle of Close Companions were accustomed to chanting the OM continuously for several minutes. This they did, then in one accord, their voices faded and they slipped into deep meditation. If asked by an observer to describe the sensation, they would have said it was like being cradled in a downy comforter of pure, radiant light.

Had the adults opened their eyes—which not even Brian was tempted to do—they would have perceived the interior glowing with light energy now emanating from the stones.

Of course, that is exactly what young Kerry and Kaitlyn saw when their bright blue eyes popped open the minute the meditation started. Fortunately, they were sitting on either side of Maggie, who was holding each of them by the hand. The twins loved being in her aura. As soon as Tim and Lucky closed the opening in the wooden floor, they had scrambled over to sit with her.

'Tis a good thing, Maggie thought to herself. Holding their hands, she could feel so much energy vibrating through their small bodies that

she half expected them to start levitating. Taking a deep breath, she consciously grounded herself, which caused the twins to look up at her like two ecstatic angels.

Maggie knew what they were seeing because her own clairvoyance was highly developed. She squeezed their hands and mouthed "watch." Without letting go of their hands, she wiggled her index fingers up and around the tower and smiled encouragingly. Here is what they saw:

At first they perceived a soft golden glow emanating from the stones. The adults were also taking on that glow. The energy began to move in distinct waves that undulated around everyone's bodies, including their own.

During the chanting of the OM the children had been so energized they'd wanted to run around. But now they felt calm, even tranquil, while their senses were becoming extremely clear.

As they watched, the wavy lines of energy began to spiral up to the peak of the tower. They knew their bodies were sitting still on the floor, and yet they became aware of their souls lifting out of those bodies into another dimension that was congruent with the tower.

Kerry and Kaitlyn had experienced similar sensations in the company of the Rose Lady, who often visited them and sometimes took them flying to her home in *Tír na n'Óg*. This was similar yet different. The atmosphere was very bright, as if they were surrounded with sunbeams—in the light and of the light.

Aunt Maggie was with them. She looked young and beautiful. She had never appeared old to the twins, yet now her hair shone like sunlight on snow and her body was almost transparent.

She looked like one of the tall white angels (the twins knew they were called seraphim) whose forms were barely visible, except for a thin line of shimmering gold that traced the outline of their bodies and enormous wings. Countless numbers of them were arrayed in rings upon rings that encircled a luminous building that glistened in the distance.

One very stately seraphim wafted over to Maggie and the twins and said in a voice that rippled through them like a harp glissando, "Welcome."

That "welcome" conveyed more than a vibration. It was a state of being, a level of consciousness that absorbed them into itself. Like an actual presence, that "welcome" enfolded them in an exquisite embrace, as if a radiant Divine Mother desired nothing more than to infuse them with a love so profound it could light up a million Milky Ways.

Oh, how the twins wanted to stay with her! But Aunt Maggie was squeezing their hands again, and Uncle Lucky was chanting the OM. Very softly and far away at first, then growing louder as they felt their souls ease back into their bodies and they opened their eyes.

Kerry didn't remember closing his eyes, but then that did happen sometimes when the Rose Lady came to visit. He and his sister looked around and saw that the tower was no longer glowing. Aunt Maggie had released their hands and they were sitting in the same position as they had been a few minutes earlier.

The only difference was a certain brightness in the eyes of the adults who gazed back at them. There was a look of amazement on those faces as they smiled at each other. Spouses were holding hands, making sure they were actually physical. But no one spoke.

Instead, they stood while Lucky and Tim carefully removed the floor insert and pulled the ladder into place. As the other adults began climbing down the ladder, Kevin and Brian walked over to the twins. Each man hoisted a child up on one arm.

With the little ones firmly hugging their necks, they carried them one-handed down the ladder, then out the door and down the stairway to ground level. There they set the twins on their feet as if they bundled seven-year-olds out of round towers every day of the week.

Lucky was the first to speak. "I suggest you take some time in the gardens and feel the earth under your feet."

"I think we could all use a bit of grounding," quipped Rory.

Maggie held out her hands to the twins. "I'll take these two back to the house. We'll put the kettle on for one of Róisín's special teas that will do just that. We want you well settled before you venture into traffic."

"You're right there," said Phelan. "I feel like my molecules have been rearranged."

"No kidding," agreed Brian. "I'm ready for whatever magic that tea can produce. Ivy and I will go with you, Maggie."

Lucky and Tim decided to follow them, which left the four remaining couples strolling peacefully around the rose garden.

The sky had cleared to a robin's-egg blue. Late afternoon sun was making diamonds on the still waters of the bay. Seagulls called and wheeled overhead. Still holding hands, Sarah and Kevin and the others stopped to admire roses of countless variety—stunning in color and fragrance that had never smelled so sweet.

"I'm not sure my molecules have been rearranged, but my senses have certainly been heightened," said Kevin as he breathed in the redolent air.

"Mine too," agreed Sarah. "And look!" She pointed back toward the tower. "Do you see what I see?"

They all did. Superimposed over the tower and standing nearly as tall, was the figure of man. He was clothed in the robe and sandals of a sixth-century Irish monk.

As the couples gazed in amazement, he blessed them with the sign of the cross. Then, pressing his hands together over his heart, he bowed deeply and vanished from their sight.

Surprises

It was a bright ray of summer sunshine, not her alarm, that woke Ivy the following morning. Groggily, she rolled over and squinted at the face of her cell phone that was always close at hand.

Seven-thirty! Her mind started racing. How could that be? She should have been up an hour ago. Had she forgotten to set her alarm last night? Or had Brian switched if off before it could wake her?

How could he let her sleep in today of all days? Didn't he remember this was the twins' first session of a special summer program at their Montessori school? Of course, they already knew their teachers and classmates, but that was beside the point. Nobody is late to school on the first day!

Ivy threw on a pair of jeans and the dark green silk blouse she had laid out the night before. At least that would give her the appearance of an organized mother, she thought as she twisted her hair into a quick knot atop her head.

She was marginally presentable, but how was she going to get her children fed and dressed, in the car and walked into their classroom in less than an hour? She rushed to the hallway outside their rooms. "Kids, come on! We've got to hurry!"

No response. Where were they? Was she losing her mind? Then she heard them. Two cheerful little voices chattering away to their father in the kitchen.

Brian? In the kitchen for breakfast? Maybe she *was* losing her mind. Her husband was usually driving to his office at Fibonacci's by this time on a Monday morning.

But there he was. In the flesh. Sitting at the kitchen table with the twins who were finishing their breakfast and dressed in school clothes.

Not the ones Ivy had planned on them wearing, but close enough.

Kerry spied her standing in the doorway and called to her excitedly, "Mommy, look! Daddy made us cimmamon toast and scrambly eggs and PBJ sammies for our lunch!"

"We dressed ourselves," said Kaitlyn proudly.

"Yes, I see," was all the comment Ivy could manage.

"Good morning," said Brian. He got up from his chair, poured his wife a cup of coffee and walked over to where she was still standing in the doorway. "Here you go, Vee. Come, sit down and drink your coffee."

"Mommy, you look sleepy," observed Kaitlyn. "Daddy told us not to wake you..."

"...so we've been extra quiet," Kerry finished her sentence.

"I hope you're not mad," Brian said a bit sheepishly and resumed his seat to finish his own breakfast. "You were so peaceful this morning, I decided to let you sleep in. I think I've done everything right. Except for brushing their hair. Kaitlyn drew the line at personal grooming. Are you okay driving the kids to school? I have a meeting at 9:00 that I need to prep for."

Ivy nodded her head. "Sure, sure, that's fine. Good job, you guys. I'm amazed. But come on. We need to wash hands and faces and do your hair." With practiced efficiency, she rose from her chair and plucked them from their booster seats in a single motion.

"Tell Daddy 'thank you for everything'."

"Thank you for everything, Daddy!" cried the twins together and scampered off to the bathroom. "See you later!"

Ivy paused by Brian's chair and grinned at him.

"Just one question: What happened to you in that tower? Or are you a changeling the fairies have substituted for the real Brian Callahan?"

"Oh, ha-ha." He mocked a laugh and looked up into his wife's deep green eyes that twinkled at him. "No more sleepy mornings for you if you're going to be sarcastic." He grinned and thumped his arms and chest. "Nope, as far as I can tell, no changeling here. Just your hubby."

Then he grew serious. "About what happened yesterday in the tower, I haven't decided yet. Actually, I was going to ask the twins about their experience to help me figure out mine, but morning chores took longer than I thought. I wasn't exactly sure how to ask them when they were busy describing—in great detail—what they're going to learn at school today."

"Probably for the best," said Ivy, wondering. *What would I have asked the twins to help me figure out my experience?*

Brian checked his watch. "Gotta run. See you tonight."

"Hurry up, Mommy!" Kaitlyn called from the bathroom. "We can't be late for school."

"Coming!" Ivy dashed off to brush two little heads of bright red hair.

Even after Brian was settled at his desk, he was only half-focused on the spreadsheets he was supposed to be reviewing for his second and third meetings of the day. Instead, his mind wandered back to Tim's Tower.

Was the statuesque female figure he'd seen during his meditation the Rose Lady his children claimed to see regularly? Probably not. The twins always said she wore a pink gown and a gold circlet with a gemstone on her forehead. Plus her hair was a deep gold and she often smelled of roses.

No, the woman he'd glimpsed for only a minute—or was she a goddess and was there a difference? Anyway, she had worn a brilliant white robe. She'd been surrounded with what Brian thought must be angels. The vibration she was gently emanating was one of profound love for his soul and a concern she either could not reveal or that he could not perceive.

I should have asked, Brian chided himself. But then the woman had faded so quickly from view that he couldn't have asked, even if he'd been able to form a question in that meditative state.

He was still musing when his secretary knocked at his open door.

"Brian, your nine o'clock is here. Stan Conway, owner of the health food store. Your renter, remember?"

"Oh, right. Thanks, Sandy. Send him in."

An unusual guy to be operating a health food store, thought Brian as Stan Conway strode in like a man on a mission. He was tall, about six-one, tanned and lean. A strong man in his prime, probably around forty. His black hair was well-trimmed and his dark brown eyes seemed not to miss a thing. He had about him a certain polish, almost a sheen, that he likely used to draw people to him. In the back of Brian's mind there was something familiar about the man, but it was fuzzy. Like his experience in the tower.

Forcing his mind to focus on the present, he walked from behind his desk and extended his hand, which the other man shook with a firm grip.

"Good morning, Stan. Have a seat. Would you like some coffee?"

"No thanks, I've had my allotment for the day." Smiling congenially, Stan took the indicated chair across from Brian with the air of someone accustomed to being listened to. He immediately launched into the speech he had prepared for this encounter.

"I appreciate your seeing me on a Monday morning when I didn't offer a reason for the meeting. Truth is, I didn't want to tell your secretary that I was coming to brag."

"Oh? Then you've brought good news?"

"I have. The store's doing great since we bought it from that young woman. My wife, Stacey, and I are an excellent team. She has a real flair for retail and design. I keep the books, deal with vendors, manage the cash flow—that sort of thing—so she can innovate to her heart's content."

"Sounds like a perfect match."

"It is. Stacey's already added some new gift items and is creating her own line of products for the holiday season. She's expanding the selection of oils and herbals that returning customers still ask for."

"Congratulations," said Brian. "As your landlord, I'm glad to hear that your business is thriving."

"That it is," agreed Stan with obvious pride.

The man was certainly honest about coming in to brag, thought Brian.

Stan continued. "Which brings me to the real reason I'm here. I'd like to engage your technical expertise for a computer system upgrade and a new website. We need to expand our infrastructure to keep pace with business growth. Nothing worse than not meeting demand."

"I agree," said Brian. He enjoyed talking businessman to businessman and here was a double bonus. His tenant was also proposing to become a customer. "How would you like to proceed?"

"Stacey and I agreed that, since our business is part of the Fibonacci's block, we should get to know you better. We'd like you and your wife to join us for dinner at our house tonight. Say around six o'clock? I know it's short notice, but when Stacey gets an idea like she did this morning, we try to act on it right away. We can have a friendly chat and also start the ball rolling on what I think we're going to need in the technical department. What do you say?"

"It *is* short notice, but hang on. Let me call Ivy." Brian hit speed dial on his office phone. "Hello, Vee? It's Bri. Listen, I've got Stan Conway in my office...Uh-huh, the one who bought Cyndi's store. He and his wife are inviting us to dinner tonight....I know. He apologized. Will six o'clock work for you and the twins?...Yeah, good idea to call my mom. She and Dad have been lobbying for more time with their grandkids....Hold on, I'll ask him."

He turned to Stan. "Ivy wants to know if she should bring anything."

"No, no. Just bring yourselves. Stacey's already got things covered."

"Vee, he says not to bother. I'll be home by 5:30. Bye."

"Nice people," commented Ivy as Brian drove them home later that evening. "For some reason, I didn't expect to like them, but I did. I could tell you and Stan were talking the same language—computers and websites, inventory and cash flow."

Brian looked over at his wife appreciatively. "It *is* the world I know. The world you and I have built together. I'm hoping you'll be part of this project. It promises to be a big one. I can really use your expertise."

"Oh, Brian, you're such a romantic," Ivy teased him. "That's interesting. Stacey said the same thing to me while you and Stan were talking—about needing my expertise, that is."

"Really?"

"Uh-huh. She asked if I'd like to help out in the store a few hours a week. It's funny how it came up. She does these intuitive card readings for people. Angel cards, that sort of thing. So, she's looking at the cards she had me draw from a colorful deck and she says, 'I see wonderful success and much happiness for you and your family. And projects for you and

Brian to do together'."

"That *is* interesting." Brian was intrigued.

"I know. Especially now that you're saying you'd like me to be involved in the project for them. Stacey didn't say anything about Stan hiring our company and I didn't bring it up. She just asked if I might like to spend a few hours in the store with people—adults, you know—in addition to being a mother and a programmer working from home."

"Would you want to work in a store?"

"I think I might. And if I'm working there, I'm sure to have some ideas that could be helpful for website design."

"Excellent. Let's keep it in the family."

"That's what I thought. The MacCauleys, the Maddens, O'Donnells and the MacGraths all have their niches at Fibonacci's. This can be ours. I know we've always had the computer business, which is how we were able to buy the new building. But this feels special somehow."

"They're perfect, aren't they?" Stacey was speaking to Stan while they cleaned up the dining room and kitchen after tonight's dinner with the Callahans.

"They are. Exactly who we need. I knew I could count on you to find us the right opportunity. And look where we landed. Talk about fate."

"All a matter of timing and patience, my love," cooed Stacey as they walked upstairs to their master suite. "And paying attention to the signs that are given. Of course, your charm makes all the difference."

"Shall I show you how charming I can be?" Stan slipped his arm around his wife's waist and drew her to him.

Stacey giggled and tossed her head. The lights switched off by themselves.

Perception or Mirage?

Friday afternoon, August 13 - at Fibonacci's

Kevin and Jeremy were seated at one of the larger tables at the back of the coffee shop. It was the middle of the month when they reviewed cash flow reports for Fibonacci's coffee shop and bookstore.

It was Friday and they were both weary of being in their respective offices. So they had agreed to meet amidst the welcome flow of humanity that was the reason for their businesses and Brian's operating in the same building which filled most of a city block.

The students and adults who made up their growing study group called the Pythagoreans would be assembling in an hour. That left the men as much time as either one cared to devote to spreadsheets on a warm August afternoon.

Jeremy also enjoyed sitting where he could watch his wife in the role she had inherited from the coffee shop's namesake, Róisín.

Graceful as a nature spirit, Debbie moved easily between customers and employees—offering a kind word to a first-time patron, a gentle admonition to a young barista, a bit of advice to one of the many souls who homed to her these days. Wisdom seemed to grow in her the more she shared it.

Kevin was pleased to notice that Phelan was also finding his place as the new Caffeine Alchemist—Lucky's old moniker. He and Cyndi were becoming a very efficient team behind the bar and in the kitchen.

The obvious love they shared permeated the shop's atmosphere whenever they worked together. Customers could feel it and brought their friends in to enjoy the coffees, teas, baked goods and lunch items that tasted better at Róisín's than at any other coffee shop in town.

In less than an hour, the two men had completed their spreadsheet review and were enjoying coffee and a muffin along with a few moments of contemplation before the study group arrived. Jeremy broke the silence.

"Have you ever met a shark?"

Kevin raised his eyebrows and smiled at the man he was glad to rely on. "Are you forgetting that I worked at Nordemann Financial several years before you came on board?" He sampled a blueberry muffin that Debbie had brought to their table.

"So you did," admitted Jeremy, smiling appreciatively at his wife as she returned to helping customers. "Guess it's hard for me to equate the man you are now with Karl and Greta Nordemann's single-minded manager."

"And you're equally as different today from the whiz-kid investor I met before you moved from the Manhattan office to Long Island City," acknowledged Kevin. "Yet here we are—still doing financials."

"Under much more pleasant circumstances," added Jeremy.

"So, what's this about sharks?" asked Kevin. "We've both dealt with plenty of them in our time."

"When you met one, how did you deal with him or her?" Jeremy was probing as his detailed mind was wont to do.

Kevin thought a minute. "I'd personally handle their account, watch them carefully and pay very close attention to what they were saying or not saying. Usually the key was in what they weren't saying."

Jeremy nodded. "That's what I did. Just wondered if we were on the same page."

"We usually are," said Kevin. "Are you thinking of diving back into dangerous waters? Doing some risky investment on the side?"

"No way. But I do think we may have a shark in our midst."

"I can't imagine who." Kevin was genuinely puzzled.

"Have you been in the health food store recently?"

"No. I've never been prompted to go in. I take it you have. And you saw something."

"I have and I did," confirmed Jeremy. "Earlier this week Debbie asked me to pick up a remedy she'd run out of, so on a break I popped over to Conway's."

"Was something wrong?" Kevin was immediately concerned.

"No. In fact, everything appeared to be running really well. The store was clean and organized. Stacey was helping customers, who seemed to be happy with the selection of products. Stan was working the cash register, cheerfully ringing up sales and chatting in a steady stream of conversation as if he'd been in the health food business all his life.

"They were both very solicitous of me. Glad to assist me with my purchase. Always good to see me. Say 'hello' to Debbie and Cyndi. All the right pleasantries."

"Then what? You've described the surface. What was underneath? What wasn't being said?" Kevin's inner senses were tingling.

"That I couldn't tell you. In fact, I couldn't seem to penetrate the outer circumstance of a well-run business that was doing a brisk trade to very satisfied customers."

"And? There was something else, wasn't there?"

Jeremy nodded. "It was just a flash before what I would call a 'veil of perfection' came down. When I walked into the store and caught sight of Stan pulling in the cash, I heard the word SHARK. I swear to you, for just an instant, I thought he was smiling a big toothy grin like *Jaws* rising out of the water."

"If anybody other than you was telling me this, I'd think they were imagining things," said Kevin. "But I trust you, Jeremy, and your ability as a seer. You're not given to flights of fancy. However, I don't know that there's anything we can or should do."

"I agree. Cyndi sold the business to the Conways, free and clear. Other than Debbie, none of us ever had an interest in her shop and now, neither does she. My only concern is if something 'off' is going on at the store that's part of Fibonacci's building complex."

Kevin drained his coffee cup and set it on the table.

"Here's something interesting. The other day Sarah told me that Ivy is going to work with Stacey a few hours a week while the twins are in school. And Stan has hired Brian's company to create a new website and upgrade their computer system."

"Yeah, Brian told me there would be developments on the financial side. Do you think that's a problem? Should we say something?"

"No." Kevin drew out the word as he thought. "My brother-in-law is well-accustomed to swimming with sharks. That's how he and his smart lawyers out-maneuvered A. B. Ryan when that old crook tried to ruin Lucky financially."

"Brian's definitely sharp," agreed Jeremy.

At the sound of cheerful voices coming through the door, Kevin looked up. The first few Pythagoreans were gathering at the coffee bar, ordering their refreshments before the study group session.

"I don't think we have to worry. If anybody can stay one step ahead of a shark, it's Brian Callahan. But, Jeremy..."

"Agreed. I hear what you're not saying. I'll keep my eyes and ears open, just in case."

"Good man," said Kevin as he folded up the spreadsheet printouts and tucked them into his briefcase. "Let's go talk Pythagorean philosophy. I'm ready for a different approach to numbers."

Childhood, Part 1

Two weeks had passed since the Circle of Close Companions had met at Tim and Maggie's home. Gareth and Naimh had caught colds and Sarah had been under the weather until a couple of days ago.

The delay could not be helped. However, the more perceptive of the group had been concerned that an obstacle might arise if they allowed too much time to pass between sessions.

And so it did.

It wasn't that Ivy and Brian didn't want to join the others for Lucky's stories. Their experiences at Tim's Tower had left them very interested. Their priorities had changed, that's all. Business was business and they had a new client to tend to. A client who promised to pay very well.

"No Ivy or Brian today?" Lucky looked around the room, then let his eyes rest on Sarah. He already knew that her brother and sister-in-law would be absent. Maggie had told him. But he wanted to observe the look on Sarah's face when she repeated the news.

"I am sorry, Lucky. We tried to convince them to come, but they're working on a big project for the health food store owners. They said it's very timely and they need to bow out for now."

"What about the twins? Couldn't Kerry and Kaitlyn have come with you and Kevin? I miss the children, Sarah."

"We know you'd like to see them, darlin'," Maggie intervened. Lucky had become uncharacteristically emotional these past few days. Usually a pillar of tranquility, something was bothering their old friend.

Maggie couldn't put her finger on the cause and she wasn't sure Lucky could either. He'd been spending more time in Tim's Tower since their group meditation two Sundays ago. Except for today. The weather had turned rainy with enough wind to make tower-sitting uncomfortable.

Kevin stepped in. "Kerry and Kaitlyn are at our house with Gareth and Naimh and Sarah's parents. They're playing games with Grampa while Gramma bakes and then they're watching a movie. Hero and Sprite are keeping everybody company."

Lucky sighed, his face a picture of resignation. He'd known all along that these couples would be the ones he could count on. Sarah and Kevin, to be sure. Debbie and Jeremy. Glenna and Rory. Cyndi and Phelan. As long as they stuck with him and the O'Tooles, he'd be fine.

"Are you feeling melancholy, darlin'?" Debbie perched on the arm of Lucky's chair by the fire.

"I suppose I am," he confessed. "Going back over my childhood memories, which is what I was after today, made me miss dear ones that are gone, passed over to the Other Side. Truth be told, I'm lonesome for them and I'm lonesome for my own trip through the veil."

Debbie put her hand on his shoulder and kissed the top of his head. She tried to stop the tears that filled her eyes, but one trickled down her cheek onto his.

Lucky reached up and patted her hand.

"There now, lass, don't worry. I'm not going anywhere yet. I have to wait for the Wise Ones to send a car for me. So far, nobody's offered me a ride."

"Alright," said Debbie. She stood up and gave him a friendly nudge on the shoulder. "Then you'd best get on with the storytelling, lad, so your fare is paid in full."

That made Lucky laugh. He wiped his eyes and cleared his throat. "So I shall. Go sit with your sweetheart, darlin'. I'm fine now."

"What story do you have for us today?" Glenna asked encouragingly. "You said that our tower adventure was out of sequence. Are you going back to the beginning of this life or the beginning of time?"

"I've considered that very question," said Lucky, warming to the subject of his many lives. "We may not always go in sequence, but today we'll start with this current life because it leads into what is surely one of the most important episodes of my sojourn through the trials and triumphs of life on this blue bauble we call Earth." He paused to check with his scribe.

"Sarah, darlin', are you set?"

"Already recording, Lucky. Go ahead."

Lucky gazed off into the distance to where the best stories go for safe-keeping until a *seanchaí* breathes them back to life, and then he began.

Once upon a time, there was a lad called Lúcháir. 'Twas a name he disliked with a fury only the young know when faced with what seems to them a massive injustice.

Unfortunately, his mother adored the name. She'd yelled the word meaning *welcoming joy* the minute she realized that she'd given birth to a healthy boy after bearing four girls. The lad was certain his mother called him by name more than she did any of his sisters, just so she could hear herself say the word.

What he should be called in daily conversation was a block of stumbling between him and his mother that worsened as he grew older and the taunting at school grew more mean-spirited. Why adults allowed children to bully their classmates was something the lad never understood.

'Stand up to them,' his father had urged, and so he did. The lad had inherited the height and heft of his father's people, and he sprouted tall and tough at an early age.

It mattered little to him that the schoolmaster expelled him for fighting. He didn't plan to be a scholar. He didn't know what he was going to be, but he figured he would find out soon enough.

In the meantime, he declared his name to be 'Lucky' and dared anyone anywhere to say otherwise. The funny thing was that in his secret heart he liked the name Lúcháir. He just wished he'd given it to himself.

He often imagined that he'd been out on a grand adventure, risking life and limb. Then he'd come home to a glad welcome that bubbled up through his body like a mountain spring, joyful in its witness of his safe return because he'd accomplished something noble and the world within and around him knew it was so.

At age fourteen, when he left home to make his fortune, that grand adventure hadn't happened yet, but he knew it would. Or strangely, maybe it already had. But not in this life.

That was the other odd thing about Lucky. When he was very young, he used to sit and dream about the lives he'd lived and the grand things he'd done in centuries past. He didn't tell his family, and he certainly didn't tell his acquaintances who were sure to make his life a worse misery than it already was.

Instead, he read and he dreamed. Though he had no plans to be a scholar, he devoured any books he could get his hands on. There weren't all that many in his tiny Connemara village, so he read the few he had until he knew them by heart.

His favorite was about King Arthur and his knights and their daring deeds in search of the Holy Grail—the cup used at the Last Supper. The cup was said to have been carried to England and buried on the Isle of Avalon, called Ynys Witrin in olden times.

There was magic in that tale that was personal to Lucky. More due to the location than the story itself. Which was odd, because he loved a good story. But memories—yes, he was sure they were memories, not imaginings—of Ynys Witrin and the prominent hill where Michael's Tor now stood haunted his dreams until he decided he must travel to England and see for himself.

Lucky paused and drank from the mug of tea Maggie had placed on the table next to him when he began his story.

"Did he go to England?" Cyndi asked eagerly.

"Not for many years and not in the way that most people travel there. But that's getting ahead of our story. Here's the way it was in the lad's youth."

There was a lake, you see. One of many. Connemara is a land of lakes and mountains and cliffs where waves crash relentlessly against the ancient stone. Where vast bogs still provide fuel for the turf fires that warm the Irish—body and soul.

Even today, the lad's birthplace is a timeless landscape where the heart is free to expand. In his youth, he relished those grand expanses, testing their edges in the quest for answers to questions he'd yet to form in his mind.

He could feel the questions, sitting like solemn guests, waiting at the threshold of consciousness, trusting that the time would come when he would offer them the hospitality of recognition.

For then the journey, the quest, would begin in earnest. The path he had walked in lifetime after lifetime, each one bringing him closer to a destination, would become clear.

One question had slipped into the lad's full awareness. It had been born with him—wrapping him in his cradle more surely than the blankets his mother had swaddled him in as a newborn.

He couldn't remember ever being without this question, though he couldn't penetrate its meaning. He was aware only of its presence that greeted him in waking and sent him off each night to slumber's dreamtime.

'Is this the life?' The query would come to the lad gently, kindly. Almost like a promise or a comfort that enfolded him in possibility.

Then he would hear it again, rising up from deep within his soul or spoken as if by an external source, almost like a challenge. Yet, in his childhood mind, he knew not the meaning of: 'Is this the life?'

So he pondered by the lake. Listening and watching for a sign. As the lad sat musing by the lake, he began to have visions of the past. Of ancient times and places far removed from the wind-swept dampness of lakes and bogs.

He saw images of events that took place in a desert land. Events that broke his heart and made him wonder at the tears that would not cease until he had risen from his pondering place and tramped back home across the rugged hills. Or until he had ventured far out on a spit of land to stand upon a cliff where the crash of wave and howl of wind buffeted him, demanding that he hold strong.

At other times, he saw himself in England or on the eastern shores of Ireland. 'Tis not so far in these days of easy travel, yet a universe away for a lad with no money and fewer prospects. That was a situation that must be remedied.

And every waking moment, he was aware of the question abiding in the recesses of his soul: 'Is this the life?' He knew that one day he must give answer, but for many years he did not know how to try.

Childhood, Part 2

Sunset would not come for several hours. Yet in the living room of Tim and Maggie O'Toole's home, the imagined atmosphere of Connemara brought a closeness of grey skies and cool temperatures more real than the rain that was currently drenching Long Island.

Had Lucky's listeners been asked, many would have admitted to feeling stiff winds from the Atlantic blowing through their hair. A few reached up, convinced they would touch the wet of salty spray on their heads.

Rory's eyes shone as he eagerly spoke the room's consensus. "What happens next? Will you leave us so unsatisfied? Or is that the *seanchaí's* ploy for guaranteeing a return audience?"

Lucky chuckled. "Aye, lad, you've found me out. Now I'll have to try another trick to keep you coming back. But given the elements currently pitting themselves against us, you may have to stay for another story, if you're willing."

"Don't you dare send us home," declared Debbie with a grin.

"Maggie, darlin', what's the forecast?" asked Lucky.

"Heavy rain, letting up in an hour or so."

"Very well, then. A quick break and we'll follow the Connemara lad as he goes forth to discover the deep things of his soul."

The lad preferred speaking his native tongue in the *Gaeltacht*, but his English was very good, as it must be for an Irishman to make his way in the world beyond his rural home.

'Twas the way of the druids whose lineage he shared. Being

a culture whose tradition was an oral one, they cherished the language of many lands. We know that during Roman times they were a highly educated people who knew Greek and Latin and could make themselves understood in Hebrew, a language not unlike their own.

Conversing among themselves they preferred the vernacular, but they never let someone speaking a foreign tongue prevent them from being understood. If others refused to comprehend their insights into the workings of the world on inner and outer planes, 'twas not the fault of speech.

The lad was sure he could make himself understood anywhere he went. But where should he go? Without a plan, he tarried another several days by the lake, hoping for inspiration to rise from the water like the mysterious hand that had seized the dying Arthur's sword. He was certain that messages could surface in just such a miraculous manner.

Ironically, one did. Though not as he expected.

On the morning of the fourth day, the lad walked once more to the lake. When he'd awakened that day, he'd made a decision. Absent any clear sign, he would walk to the village of Letterfrack and hitch a ride on the first vehicle going in any direction.

Probably not surprising to anyone who has sat by still bodies of water waiting for concrete signs of anything other than the odd fish rising to feed, the lad saw nothing and received no definitive inspiration.

Resigned at last, he left the lake, possibly for the final time, and strode off purposefully towards the village. Strangely for someone intending to travel, he'd packed no clothing. Nor had he asked his mother for some money to tide him over. He knew she would think him foolish, as perhaps he did himself.

After two hours, he arrived at the village without a coin in his pocket and nothing but dreams in his head. There were no vehicles in sight. The village was deserted.

Then he remembered—'twas Sunday afternoon. Instead of going to mass, he had daydreamed the morning away. And now he was in the village at a time when everyone would be at home. There would be no commerce today, no lorries traveling to or from larger towns. No shopkeepers or tradesmen looking for a willing lad to take on any work they might offer.

Depressed, he sat on the curb, his head in his hands. He was surveying the sorry state of his life, when a voice spoke.

'Can I help you, lad?'

Looking up, he saw the local priest, Father Kenneally. The man had been out for a stroll around the village, as was his habit on Sunday afternoons.

After visiting the home of a parishioner who'd fed him his midday meal, he liked to wander around the empty shops and peaceful cottages, quietly blessing them in his soft voice, wishing them Godspeed in all their endeavors and praying for peace and good will among all the Irish, no matter their religion.

For this good priest was a man of tolerance amid these times of trouble in Ireland. Divisions were strong and, sadly, people were ignorant of the larger principles that could govern their lives if only they would allow.

'Are you in trouble, my son?' the priest asked more earnestly.

'No, Father, I'm not in trouble. I'm not in anything,' the lad admitted and showed the respect he'd been taught by standing to address the priest and removing his cap.

'I've been looking for a sign and none has appeared. I was going to hitch a ride to anywhere, but there doesn't seem to be one. I'm stuck.'

'What sort of sign, my son?' The priest was big on signs and had often prayed for them himself.

'A clear direction for my future. I've watched for days and seen nothing.'

'You know how they say that watched kettles never boil?' the priest asked with a gleam in his eye. The lad nodded.

''Tis the same with signs. Like souls or fairies, they're shy and won't reveal themselves when faced with a steady gaze like you've been putting upon that lake. You have to come at them from the oblique. Like you're not staking the whole of your life on their appearance. Otherwise, you seem a threat. 'Tis the intensity of your attention, you see. You can scare off even a very determined sign if you're too forceful.'

'Is that what I've been doing, then?' asked the lad, amazed at the priest's uncanny wisdom.

'More than likely.'

'What shall I do instead?'

'Does your family know where you are?'

The lad shook his head and looked down at his shoes.

'I thought not,' said the priest in a kindly tone. 'Here's what you do. Walk on back home. You've still plenty of daylight. Tell your family you've been given an opportunity by me, Father Kenneally, and you're to start first thing tomorrow morning.

'Let your mother know she's not to worry about you. She'll help you pack your belongings. She may even give you a few coins. And she'll kiss and bless you on your way. Do you believe me, my son?'

'I do, Father. I don't know why, but I do. Thank you. I'll see you tomorrow.'

'I'll be expecting you.'

So, that's how the sign the lad had been praying for revealed itself once he stopped watching the lake's still waters like a hawk tracking its prey.

Father Kenneally was right, of course.

The lad went straight home as instructed, and the scene was exactly as the priest said it would be. Right down to the lad's mother helping him pack and giving him a handful of coins. She didn't call him Lúcháir, but only 'my boy' as she kissed him and blessed him on his way. His father said, 'I'm proud of you, son. I always knew you'd be lucky.'

And so he was.

Rural audiences of other decades often did not greet the end of a well-told story with applause. Such displays are a more modern custom. It was the purview of the host to reward the *seanchaí* while the praise of others was bestowed in the form of private compliments or small gifts discretely tucked into the storyteller's hand or pocket.

Lucky's audience suffered from no such reticence. They clapped and exclaimed and thanked him for giving them the next part of his story.

"That was wonderful," declared Glenna. "You would have been a fine actor, Lucky. I know a few Broadway professionals who could learn a lot from you."

"Thanks, darlin'. You warm my heart. All of you. I'd love to keep you longer, but you'd best be heading home while the rain's stopped and the wind's calm."

"I'm glad we'll be all here next Sunday," said Cyndi as she, Phelan and the others said their good-byes. Everyone agreed.

"I hope she's right—that they'll all be here," Maggie whispered to Tim when the Companions had gone to their cars. Lucky was standing by the front door, seeing them off.

"I know, lass," said Tim. "We'll do what we can, but you know they must make their own choices."

"I do. That's what concerns me."

What If?

August in Maggie O'Toole's garden bloomed its welcome to this morning's visitors with a blaze of fragrance and color. Last Sunday's vigorous rainstorm had only heightened the yellows, oranges and reds of day lilies. Asters, echinacea, clematis and dahlias added rich purples, blues and pinks, while the sunny faces of rudbeckia, daisies and tall sunflowers made every view a cheerful one.

Moisture-loving hostas were spreading their broad leaves in lush, shady beds that nestled under lofty ash and birch trees that sheltered the property. Bees and birds were everywhere. Hummingbirds zipped in and out of their favorite nectar plants—all to the delight of Naimh and Gareth who in only a week's time would be one year old.

Today, Maggie and Tim were supervising the children as they toddled along curving garden paths while Lucky and Sarah worked at the dining table. He was reading transcripts from the first three sessions she had brought over this morning for his review.

Assembling his stories and comments into book form would happen later. For now, Sarah wanted to be sure her friend was pleased with how his storytelling was proceeding. She also wanted to talk to him about an issue weighing on her mind. But that could wait until he'd read through the typed pages she had placed in a binder so none would be lost.

She understood the mix of emotions that accompany the experience of seeing your stories on a printed page, even if they're only in draft form. Somehow handling those pages makes the stories permanent in a way that telling them does not.

The *seanchaí* has faith in the nature of stories to remain alive as long as they are told and retold, heart to heart. But what if the tradition wanes?

Eventually, stories can die and with them an entire culture may cease to exist, like that of the original druids. Only fragments of their wisdom remain as myths or legends that most people regard as fiction.

Lucky and Sarah hoped that publishing his recollections would keep them alive long past the twenty-first century which they and the Friends of Ancient Wisdom community were currently inhabiting.

She watched his face as he focused on the words he'd spoken to his closest friends. He made a few notes in the margins, adding or subtracting a word here and there. For the most part, he seemed content that he was proceeding as he'd meant to do.

Sarah could tell when Lucky reached the end of the stories he'd told on Sunday because he looked up from the page with misty eyes. She had included in the transcript all of the comments from his listeners.

As a writer, she was very aware of how doubt can ride in at the most inopportune times to make you question the worth of your work. Should that happen to Lucky, she wanted him to have these pages so he could read for himself the expressions of love and appreciation that spoke the value his friends placed on his presence in their lives—not to mention how much they enjoyed his stories.

Lucky closed the binder and held it to his heart before handing it back to Sarah. *"Go raibh míle maith agat, a chara."*

"Tá fáilte romhat," she answered him in Irish. "You're welcome, Lucky. I'll take the transcript home to incorporate your changes and this will be our working copy. In the meantime, here are the comments from all of us who love you. So you don't forget."

She handed him a separate, smaller binder.

"I'll print out your listeners' comments separately each week and we'll tuck them in here. It's not quite the same as saving love letters tied with a red ribbon, but the sentiment is the same."

That image made Lucky laugh. Then he turned to her, his expression serious. "I know there's something worrying you, *a chara.* I can see it in those hazel-green eyes of yours. There's a cloud dimming the light I usually see shining out from you."

"I sometimes forget how much you do see, Lucky," Sarah smiled. "What I wanted to say is this: I'm sorry that Ivy and Brian didn't join us last Sunday. I know they're suddenly very busy with their new project for the Conways, but I really was hoping they would make time to be with our group."

She stopped a minute, puzzling. "Do you suppose the fact that they're not twin flames—and the rest of us are—makes them feel like a fifth wheel?"

"Could be," said Lucky. "There's probably more to it. But we've no point in speculating into why any of us makes the choices we do. They have a business to run, as does everyone at Fibonacci's. We can't blame them for wanting to make a success of their endeavor."

Sarah nodded. "I see that. It's just that I've always been concerned with how materialistic Brian can be. How he puts business before any-thing else."

"Isn't that the way of life when you're young and wanting to make your mark in the world?" Lucky was watching Sarah closely. She had no idea in her outer awareness of the deeper reason for her concern, but her soul knew.

"There's nothing wrong with well-earned monetary gain," Lucky con-tinued. "'Tis often the sign of considerable mastery."

"What about ill-gotten gain?" Sarah was shocked to hear herself ask such a question.

"Well now, that's a different sort of ability, isn't it? You don't suspect your brother, do you?"

Sarah answered quickly. "No, I don't. But I am aware of how anything that glitters has always attracted him. When he was little, the shinier the toy, the better. As he grew up, the more powerful the electronic gadget, the sooner he was in line for the newest model. Same thing with cars."

Lucky raised an eyebrow and chuckled. "Sounds like many a lad I've known in my life."

"Yes, I know." Sarah returned his smile. "But here's what does have me concerned: I caught sight of Brian's face while Tim was showing him and Jeremy around the house at our first meeting. While he was expounding on the crystals, I didn't see appreciation in my brother's eyes. I saw envy."

Sarah stood and walked over to the French doors that led out to the terrace. She could see her children toddling around on the lovely green lawn with Tim and Maggie shepherding them along. She turned back to the dining table where she and Lucky had been working.

"I don't want that for my brother. Brian has always found a way to pay for what he desires. He's earned his rewards. But what if he desires something he can't or shouldn't have? What if somebody dangles a shiny bauble in front of him that jeopardizes his family?"

"Sarah, darlin', you of all people should know that asking 'what-if' gets us nowhere. The future will find us soon enough. There's no point in worrying about events that may never come to pass."

"You're right, of course. Kevin said the same thing this morning at breakfast." Sarah gazed once more at the bright summer day that bathed the back garden of *Teach an tSolais* in sunlight.

"I look at our babies and I can't help wondering about Kaitlyn and Kerry. I know that Ivy is doing her best to understand them and accept their special gifts. Maybe Brian will, too. I can only hope."

Lucky rose from his seat and stood beside her. "Don't worry, darlin'. Maggie's got those twins under her wing."

"I'm glad to hear it. I just hope her span's broad enough."

"Broader than you can imagine, *a chara*."

Taking Sarah by the hand, he opened the French doors and led her outside to the terrace. "Come along, lass. Let's bring your babies inside. They're probably ready for lunch and Uncle Lucky needs a hug."

A Dilemma

Ivy was torn. Actually, she felt like a piece of salt water taffy being pulled six ways by people who all wanted a bite of her. Not that anyone was aggressively demanding that she go their way. They didn't need to. The implicit expectations were sufficient.

She knew that Sarah and Kevin, Lucky and the other couples were disappointed that she and Brian had missed last Sunday's gathering. The twins were making it plain that they wanted to hear more of Uncle Lucky's stories and why couldn't they go with Uncle Kevin and Aunt Sarah if Mommy and Daddy were busy?

Stacey had already phoned to set up a schedule for Ivy to start working a few hours a week in the health food store. And Brian wanted her to come to his office this afternoon to start mapping out the basic structure for Stan's inventory control program and how it would interface with the updated website.

The biggest pull of all was the one inside herself. Ivy had never mentioned to anybody what she'd seen during their group meditation in Tim's Tower. Obviously, each person's experience was private—uniquely meaningful to them. As was hers. But she needed to tell somebody. She couldn't help feeling there was an answer to her dilemma in what, or who, she had seen. She'd had only one previous experience with otherworldly visions. This one was far more dramatic.

Maybe she could talk to Sarah. They were close now. Helping each other with childcare had brought them together as only mothers of young children can bond. The mutual concern and understanding of the sheer magnitude of daily chores and responsibility was a shared burden that eased the weight for both of them.

But this was different. Sarah was deeply involved in recording and transcribing Lucky's legacy stories to fulfill his obligations to the Masters of Wisdom. That was more than enough to add to her already full plate. Nevertheless—and later Ivy wouldn't have been able to say exactly why—she dialed the MacCauleys' home number.

The phone rang several times. Ivy expected the call to go to voice mail, but Kevin answered.

"Hello?"

"Kevin, it's Ivy."

"Hi there. We missed you last Sunday."

"I know." The fact that she said nothing else caught Kevin's attention. He proceeded casually.

"Sarah's not here right now. She and the twins are still at Tim and Maggie's after meeting with Lucky. Shall I have her call you when she gets home later? She just sent me a message that she and Maggie are relaxing on the terrace while the twins are taking a nap."

Ivy hadn't expected this turn of events, but she took it anyway.

"Kevin, I need to talk to somebody." She hesitated. "No, never mind. It's nothing. You probably have to get back to work and I'm supposed to meet Brian at his office in a couple of hours."

A person didn't need to be a reembodied druid to detect the despair in Ivy's voice. This was one of those moments when the future of lives could tip one way or the other. Kevin knew a lot about those moments and determined not to let this one pass.

"Ivy, whatever is bothering you isn't nothing. Do you want to come over and we'll have a chat? I don't have to be back at the office for a while."

"If you're sure you don't mind."

"If I minded, I wouldn't have offered. You know me that well." He made his point gently.

"Yes, I do."

"Then I'll see you in the two minutes it takes to walk from your house to mine."

"Okay, thanks. I'll be right there."

Ivy knew if she delayed she would lose her nerve. She dashed up the street to the MacCauleys' house and rang the doorbell.

"One minute, that's a record," chuckled Kevin as he opened the door to his sister-in-law. "Come in. Would you like some tea or coffee?"

"No, thanks. But could we sit at your kitchen table? I need something substantial to lean on."

"No problem. Go on in."

Kevin had seen Ivy injured from the car accident she and Brian and their twins had suffered two winters ago. He had seen her frustrated with being a mother of two highly gifted children. He had seen her glowing with love for her husband and pride in his accomplishments. But Kevin had never seen her this distraught.

He poured them each a glass of water and sat in his usual chair—head of the table. The chief druid's seat. He was glad for the wisdom and insight that always accompanied the united consciousness of his past and present attainment. He sensed he was going to need it.

Ivy laughed nervously. "I feel like I'm going to confession, except I've never been to confession."

"That's okay," said Kevin congenially. "We don't have a closet with a sliding screen, so the kitchen table will have to do. You can speak to me in confidence, if that's a concern."

"I appreciate your saying so. I don't mind if you tell Sarah about our conversation. If she'd been home, I was going to ask for her advice. But I would like to keep this between the three of us. Can I tell you a story? It's not a short one."

"Of course. I always have time for a story from people I care about."

How interesting, thought Kevin. He remembered having a similar conversation with Lucky the first time they'd met at Fibonacci's. Then he'd poured out his burdens about his future and his relationship with Sarah.

As the two men became better acquainted, Kevin realized the depth of Lucky's ability to see into the hearts of others. Now he was offering his sister-in-law the same support.

Ivy hesitated again. "I'm not very good at this—storytelling, I mean. Certainly nothing like Lucky or Sarah."

"Just slip into the scene and let the story carry you," urged Kevin.

"That's what the Rose Lady told me."

"You saw the Rose Lady?"

"I did. That's what I want to tell you about."

Ivy sipped some water and took a couple of deep breaths. "I guess this isn't really a story as such. More of a recollection for now.

"That's fine, Ivy. No pressure. So you've seen the Rose Lady?"

"Yes, last Sunday and once before. After the car accident when my arm was broken. Sarah had told me a story about a goddess and then when I took a nap with my twins, the three of us had this vision together.

"Kerry and Kaitlyn knew all about the Rose Lady and her temple that looked like a rose made of crystal. It was so beautiful and peaceful. I felt such love from her. She really did look like a goddess.

"I always wanted to see her again, but I never did. Not until we were all meditating in Tim's Tower. Maybe I can only see her when I'm with people who don't doubt her existence."

"Could be," said Kevin when Ivy looked at him for confirmation. "Go ahead. I'm following you."

"Okay, thanks, Kevin. I'm glad I can talk to you."

"So am I, Ivy. Now, tell me about last Sunday."

Visibly relaxing, she took another sip of water and continued.

"I could tell from the way all of you chanted the OM that you are accustomed to the experience. I'd never been to any of your services, so when the sound started reverberating through the tower like there were hundreds of voices chanting, there was so much energy vibrating in and around my body, I wasn't sure I could hang on.

"I didn't dare open my eyes, and when everyone started meditating, I did the same. Like I had done that before. Almost immediately, I felt myself lifting off, but it wasn't my body. It was my soul. I could feel my soul rising up to the ceiling and as soon as I reached the peak, *whoosh!* I was in another dimension.

"And I knew where I was. I was in the Rose Lady's temple. Even though I was alone this time, I was so excited that I ran past the rose quartz fountain and the hanging baskets of flowers and the reflecting pools. My entire being was consumed with the knowledge that I had to get to her.

"That desire must have propelled me to her, or maybe it called her to me. I'm not sure. Except that suddenly I was standing with her in a beautiful room with walls covered in light pink silk and lush, dark green carpet on the floor. The room was sparsely furnished with only a long bench upholstered in dark burgundy velvet with spirals and other symbols like the ones on the O'Tooles' gate embroidered in gold thread.

"The Rose Lady motioned for me to sit on the bench. As soon as I did, a goblet of the most refreshing beverage appeared in my hand. Of course, I drank it and the goblet instantly disappeared.

"Only then did I notice that on the wall in front of me was a large screen, like in a movie theatre. The Rose Lady spoke to me very gently, in her angelic voice.

"She said, 'Watch the screen, my dear. As soon as you notice scenes appearing, step in and let the story carry you. You will not see me, but I will be with you every minute. Have no fear, this experience is for the tutoring of your soul.'"

Ivy stopped speaking and looked imploringly at Kevin. "Is this making sense? I hope so, because I think what came next is what I've heard you and Sarah refer to as a life review."

"You are making perfect sense. And I have a suggestion. Sometimes, when you're explaining to another person what you saw on the screen, it helps to slip back into the scene exactly as it happened and tell the story in the third person. Can you do that?"

"I'll try," Ivy said so softly that Kevin knew she was already there.

"And don't worry," he said. "I'll be right here to help you come back."

Ivy closed her eyes. With the vivid recall worthy of a *seanchaí*, she began to narrate what she had seen.

Ivy's Life Review

At the Rose Lady's Temple

On the screen a thick mist appeared and then quickly dissolved to show a young man—tall, robust, dark-haired and dark-eyed. He was a warrior and, by all accounts, a skilled one. A man admired by the people of his village called a *túath* for his ability to fight off the frequent cattle raids that were part and parcel of those times.

He was particularly admired by the beautiful young woman at his side. She was his wife. She wore her dark red hair in a long braid. Her deep green eyes gazed at her man and no one else.

She was nearly as tall as he—intelligent, a woman of many skills which she had inherited from generations of those who understood the ways of Nature and animal husbandry. They were a powerful presence in their *túath,* and others deferred to them.

Not her older brother, of course. He had become a master druid of considerable spiritual attainment. His position and knowledge elevated him to the highest rank of society. Nevertheless, they were close kin who enjoyed each other's company whenever their labors allowed a visit.

The warrior and the young woman had been in love ever since they were old enough to pay more than passing attention to the opposite sex. As was the norm of their culture, they married in their teens and had several children by the age of twenty.

Despite ongoing skirmishes with other tribes, theirs was a fairly peaceful life. That is, until the woman's husband brought a fellow warrior into their home.

He was a stranger who'd been caught stealing cattle, though he swore he'd only been on his way to the sea and was in the wrong place at the wrong time. In the mêlée that often accompanied cattle raids, the man's shoulder had been grazed by the horn of an angry bull. The wound was not deep, but it was painful and he had begged for mercy.

The young woman's husband believed the man and brought him home for a meal and some rest. The stranger appeared to be in need of friendship, which the couple gave him without considering the possibility of unforeseen consequences.

In a couple of days, the stranger, who was fair-haired and brown-eyed, was healthy enough to resume his travels. However, deciding that he liked the *túath* where he had landed, he asked if he might make himself useful. As cattle-raising was labor-intensive and required sustained physicality, the couple agreed that his obvious strength and willingness to tackle any task were more than welcome.

The stranger was also possessed of a winning personality. He had a way with children that the young woman's husband did not. Soon the little ones were following him around while he tended their family's herd.

Naturally, this did not sit well with the warrior. He began to find fault with the man, who was a stranger no longer. In fact, he was becoming more like family—not only to the children, but also to the warrior's wife.

She and the stranger were often seen together, feeding and milking the cows. Breeding time added a certain dynamic to their conversation that others in the *túath* began to remark upon, though not directly to the warrior.

And then one day, as circumstances are wont to do, things changed.

The stranger and the warrior's wife had walked far from the *túath* in search of a cow and calf that had strayed away from the herd. Neither of them had thought anything of the situation until a sudden rainstorm caught them in the open and they sought shelter in a secluded, rocky outcropping.

They had not planned to find themselves in one another's arms, but the harsh wind and pelting rain forced them close. She nestled against his warm chest, and he stroked her long hair. In that moment he declared his love for her. She was the reason he had asked to remain in the *túath*. She was the love he had sought his entire life. Could she honestly say that she did not return his affection?

Of course, she could not deny her own feelings. And weeping with the mixture of emotions she knew she would regret on the morrow, she gave herself to him.

Although the warrior's wife had tried not to admit her growing affection for the stranger, her husband had already detected a change in her response to himself. When his wife and her lover returned to the *túath* much later that day, violence erupted.

The two men fought. The warrior, being more skilled in combat than the stranger, severely wounded the man so that he lay dying in the wife's arms. She felt his soul leave his body and wondered how she would ever live without him.

Ivy sat quietly with her eyes closed. Kevin did not disturb her. After a few minutes, she opened her eyes and spoke.

"The screen turned misty again and that's all I remember. I wanted to ask the Rose Lady what it all meant, but then I heard Lucky quietly chanting the OM and I whooshed back into my body—like suddenly coming awake from a dream."

She sighed deeply and looked across the table at Kevin. His blue-green eyes were intently focused on her. He was very familiar with the after-effects of a life review. He watched this woman, who had clearly been his younger sister in another lifetime, to ensure that she emerged from her vivid recollection emotionally intact.

"Drink some water, Ivy," he said offering her the glass she had only sipped from. "How are you feeling?"

"A bit vague, I guess. Can you explain what I saw?"

"I could, but I believe the details are yours to discover. Why don't you just sit while I make tea and find something for you to eat, to ground you."

Ivy didn't object and closed her eyes while Kevin put on the kettle and made them both a sandwich.

"Are any details clearer to you now?" Kevin asked a few minutes later as he poured cups of strong black tea and served their food.

"Not many and I'm not sure what it all means."

"Why don't you tell me what is clear and maybe the meaning will reveal itself."

"Okay. I know we were in Ireland in a village called a *túath*. I know you were my older brother. I also know that Brian was the warrior and I was his wife. What I don't know is who the stranger was. I could see him clearly, but I got the feeling that the Rose Lady wasn't allowed to reveal his identity to me. That's one of the things I was going to ask her before the screen went misty and our group meditation ended."

"Anything else?"

"I'm puzzled about the intense attraction I felt for this other man. I love Brian and I've never been tempted to stray. I know we're not twin flames like the rest of you are, but we have a good marriage."

"Can you detect the lesson here? The Rose Lady said this scene was for the tutoring of your soul. Any idea what she meant? Try digging deeper."

"Okay. These life reviews are meant to show us our past karma, aren't they? And where we may be vulnerable in the future?"

"They are, yes. Does that fact answer the question that brought you here—about what you should do moving forward?"

Ivy closed her eyes and thought a minute. The message became clear.

"Regardless of what may be going on in our lives right now, I need to stick with Brian. I have an obligation to be true to him. If he needs me to work with him on the Conway's project, I'll do that. I'll just have to figure out a way to keep our twins connected with all of you."

"Good lass, as Lucky would say," said Kevin. "We'll do our best to help you. All you have to do is ask."

After Ivy left to meet Brian, Kevin did not return to his office. Instead, he remained sitting at the kitchen table, musing on his own future.

He knew he was born to lead. He'd been more than aware of that fact when he was an Atlantean priest. He'd known it as the trusted adviser to Pharaoh and his Queen in 18th-Dynasty Egypt. He'd been an able, though short-lived, chief druid in first-century Ireland when he was Ceann-Druí Ah-Lahn.

Even as a lad in this life, he'd known that others looked to him for leadership. At a high school reunion, which he'd been reluctant to attend, one of his former football teammates told Sarah how her husband inspired the other players. "If MacCauley was on the field, we believed we'd win. And we usually did."

Kevin wasn't arrogant. Far from it. Sure, he was confident of his strength of mind and body, but he saw no reason to lord it over others. In fact, the bardic aspects of his nature sometimes beckoned him to a poetic life. But more often, circumstances prevailed that brought his leadership qualities to the fore.

For his willingness to take on a leader's responsibilities and for his sense of humor that appeared at surprising moments, people—including his mother—would ask Kevin's opinion when faced with problems they were challenged to resolve.

He rarely gave them a quick answer. What they received instead was the product of his thoughtful consideration (often based on wisdom gained in past lives)—a creative solution that had not been immediately evident, but that untangled knotty issues with good will and good humor.

Now, at the age of forty, Kevin felt himself a man well-primed to once again take on the mantle of *ceann-druí,* whenever his friend and mentor departed this world. Only Sarah was likely to call her husband by his title, and only Lucky understood the truth of their ancient relationship.

The passing of the leadership torch had not happened yet. That day would arrive soon enough. Meanwhile, a certain awareness came to Kevin that he was gaining in mastery. His conversation with Ivy had shown a light on his inner nature that was becoming like an outer garment.

He felt the growing power of his attainment. And in that sense he also realized that the tests of his mastery would not be easy. He was preparing for the future, but he wasn't there yet. He and his Close Companions were on a path with destiny. They would look to him to lead them through the dark nights that might threaten when Lucky took his leave.

Those challenges may come soon. A sudden warning from Kevin's voice of inner wisdom reverberated through his being—body, mind and soul. 'Twas a sobering thought.

His reverie ended when he heard Sarah's car pull into the garage. He brought his awareness back to the task at hand and quickly went out to help her bring the twins inside. They had napped again on the way home from *Teach an tSolais* and were ready for playtime.

"Was that Ivy's car I passed on the way in? She was driving like a woman on a mission."

Kevin checked his watch. "I think she was late for her meeting with Brian. She was here longer than expected telling me about the life review the Rose Lady gave her during our meditation in the tower on Sunday."

"Wow. I didn't get anything like that in the tower, did you?"

"No. Nothing but lots of light and a feeling of peace, for which I was very grateful."

"Me, too. What did Ivy tell you? Are you allowed to share?"

"Normally I wouldn't, except she had actually wanted to speak with you. We're to keep this between the three of us, but she wants you to know what she saw. She relies on you, Sarah, and I'm glad.

"So am I. Let's take the twins outside so they can play in the fresh air with Hero and Sprite, and you can tell me about Ivy and the Rose Lady."

Defending What's Dear

Sarah was wide awake and so was Sprite. The sleek feline with green eyes had been her full-sized panther spirit guide in many past lives. No less vigilant now, she was embodied in the smaller, mini-panther version.

Seeing her mistress's brow furrowed with sleeplessness, Sprite leapt onto the bed, landing quietly with barely a ripple. She curved her body against the woman's chest and began to purr.

Sarah pulled her perceptive cat closer and relished the soft motorboat sound and vibration that often brought on the slumber she sought. Tonight that was not to be. When she failed to drift off, she sat up carefully so as not to wake Kevin, who was sleeping soundly.

Gathering Sprite in her arms, she tiptoed into the twins' room and curled up in the soft overstuffed chair where she had nursed her babies. She loved sitting alone in this room late at night or very early of a morning when she would watch her children sleep.

The fact of their existence was a miracle that still astounded her. After two miscarriages, she had despaired of ever having a family. Now here they were—Gareth and Naimh, friends from ages past, souls who had begged to be born to her and Kevin. They nestled in their cribs, enfolded in an atmosphere that swaddled the nursery in a blanket of peace and serenity.

Sprite was purring again, though now the vibration was more urgent, or perhaps inquisitive. Sarah's spirit guide was inviting her to look deeper into her own mind and heart. To listen to the voice of her inner wisdom that had a message for her.

Her thoughts turned to Kevin. Although over the centuries they had been apart more often than together, she was his wife by design. They were twin flames—two souls created in the beginning from the same cosmic blueprint as one bright ovoid of light.

She shared his passion for poetry, philosophy, music and history—in different modes and measure, to be sure. But at their core they were one in soul and spirit. Warrior, bard and druid lived in them both. Balancing those aspects was a dance they each sought to master as inner guidance told them when to act or when to stand down. When to speak or when to be silent. Following that rhythm was the challenge of their individuality and their mutuality.

Tonight the warrior was on Sarah's mind. She had witnessed Kevin in combat and knew she could be as fierce as he. She'd proven that in the battle she and her sister Twin Flames of Éire had fought and won to rid the Universe of the sorceress Una. In those dreadful moments, Sarah had felt a powerful presence of the Divine Feminine coursing through her as she wielded sword and shield.

Thankfully, that terrible confrontation is now months in the past, Sarah thought as she made her way back to bed. She was suddenly tired enough to sleep. Yet, as she drifted off, she felt in her bones that she would fight again, to the death if necessary, anyone who threatened those she loved— her community, her husband, the children she had carried in her womb, nursed at her breast and sheltered in her arms when they were fretful, colicky or teething.

A mother bear had nothing on Sarah MacCauley when it came to defending what she held dear. Beginning with her own life.

"Sarah! Wake up! You're having a nightmare!" Kevin was shouting and struggling with his wife who was flailing her arms, kicking him in the shins and screaming into the pillow that had become wedged between her face and her husband's head.

He tossed the pillow to the floor and grabbed Sarah's hands to stop her from hitting him. He pinned her arms to her sides and held her as close as he could. She was gasping for air. When she wildly opened her eyes, he could tell she wasn't seeing him.

"Sarah, *mo chroí,*" he said gently. Focusing his eyes on hers, he began crooning to her in Irish and English. *Bí fós, a ghrá.* Be still, my love. *Le de thoil, teacht ar ais.* Please, come back. *Táim anseo agus tá tú slán.* I'm here and you're safe."

After what seemed like an age, Sarah blinked once then closed her eyes with an enormous sigh. Kevin eased his grip as he felt her relax.

Finally, she looked at him, "*Táim anseo.* I'm here." She sighed heavily again and welcomed the pillow that Kevin tucked behind her head.

"What happened?" she said at last.

"You tell me," said a confused Kevin. "All I know is that I was sound asleep and then shocked awake because you were kicking and screaming and flailing around like you were fighting for your life."

"I think I was," said Sarah weakly.

"What do you remember? Do you want me to get you some tea first?"

"No, I'm fine for a minute. I don't want to forget any details. The image is already disappearing. Like it's trying to hide from my calling it to mind. All I remember is that I was a very young child. Maybe three or four. I was fighting off somebody larger—two teenagers, I think. They were smothering me with a pillow."

"Were they trying to kill you?" Kevin was really alarmed.

"I don't think so. Maybe just trying to scare me. Which they certainly did. I couldn't breathe enough to scream. I was kicking and trying to hit them. I think I landed a few blows. But, oh Hon, I guess they landed on you, didn't they?"

"Good thing, too, so you didn't accidentally suffocate yourself with that pillow. You were really far gone. Even when your eyes opened, you were somewhere else."

"And now I'm freezing." Sarah began to shake uncontrollably. Hero and Sprite jumped up on the bed and wrapped themselves around her while Kevin covered her in the thin blanket they used during the summer.

"Stay here with the fur kids and I'll bring you another blanket and some hot tea as fast as I can." He started to dash from the bedroom, then turned when Sarah said his name.

"Kevin?"

"Yes?"

"Check on the babies, will you?"

"Absolutely. Don't try to go anywhere."

Hero licked Sarah's very wan face and that made her chuckle weakly. "Don't worry. I'll be right here."

When Kevin returned minutes later, he was glad to see Sarah sitting up. He hurried to her with a mug of hot tea, which she gratefully accepted, and a warm blanket, which he tucked around her shoulders—the only part of her body that Hero and Sprite were not covering.

"Oh, that's much better," sighed Sarah, sipping her tea.

She paused for moment and gazed up at the ceiling. Then looking at Kevin with a serious expression, she furrowed her brow and said, "I was wondering where you were."

"What do you mean? I was brewing tea, checking on the twins and finding another blanket."

"No, no." Sarah shook her head. "Not here—in my dream. While you were rushing around like my warrior, I was trying to remember more of the scene. But all I got was a frantic thought running through my mind. As I tried to fight off my tormentors, I was crying to myself, 'Where is he?' I know that sounds strange. It's probably nothing. You know how things get mixed up in nightmares."

"No kidding," said Kevin, probing his mind for an answer. "I'm sorry, Hon. I don't know what to say. Except that if I was supposed to be there, I'm sorry I wasn't. No child should be treated like that."

She finished her tea and set her empty cup on the bedside table.

"Do you think you can sleep now?" asked Kevin.

"I can if you'll hold me. I need you to hold me like you'll stay with me forever."

"You know I will, Sarah. And I *will* be glad to hold you, if the fur kids will give you back to me."

They both laughed at how thoroughly ensconced she was by her two very determined protectors.

"Good job, you guys," said Kevin, as he eased Hero and Sprite off the bed. "I'll take her from here."

Musings & A Request

Debbie leaned comfortably against the doorway that led to the kitchen at Róisín's Coffee Shop. As she often did these days, her light green eyes scanned the room while she offered silent prayers for customers and staff alike.

Until recently, she had not realized that this simple act of blessing was one that Róisín herself had performed daily for all the years that she and Lucky operated Fibonacci's. Now that Debbie had assumed Róisín's role and bore her torch of illumination, she vowed to carry on the tradition.

Much had been destroyed in the horrific fire that burned the original Fibonacci's Coffee & Tea Merchants and Esoteric Bookstore to the ground. Fortunately, all of the books, priceless artwork, antique tables and chairs and most of the coffee shop's essential equipment had been removed prior to that terrible event. Unfortunately, the wonderful old mahogany bar and masterfully crafted shelving that held teas and coffees from around the world had been a total loss.

Debbie sighed and put a hand to her heart. There was still grief, but not nearly as much as might be expected from similar circumstances. Thanks to the financial wizardry and astute legal resources of Sarah's brother and the determination of the entire Friends of Ancient Wisdom community, Fibonacci's had a spacious new home.

Brian had hired master craftsmen in all the trades, and they had achieved the miraculous. Anyone who did not know better would have thought they had packed up and moved the old building intact to its new location, so accurately had the reconstruction been accomplished.

The larger, rebuilt Fibonacci's was housed in a building of nearly the same age. The distinctive interior red-brick walls and rounded exterior front entrance that joined two side streets were nearly identical.

As Debbie continued gazing around the coffee shop, she smiled at the vibrant energy she felt permeating the room. Late August was high tourist season and business was strong. Word of mouth was positive. Many locals had claimed Róisín's as their favorite meeting place. They enthusiastically recommended the beverages and baked goods to visitors.

There are many reasons for the good reviews, thought Debbie. One of them was her sister Cyndi's husband, Phelan.

Debbie could understand why their founder Master Saint Germain, in his guise as alchemist F. M. Bellamarre, had employed Phelan as his assistant in Ireland. The young man seemed to be everywhere at once—brewing special coffees from the blends Lucky had shared with him. Bussing tables if necessary. Restocking food items in the display case.

He had a knack for noticing what needed to be done and seeing to it—always with a twinkle in his blue eyes that lifted everyone's spirits and kept the staff from taking themselves too seriously.

He was especially good with the tourists, charming them with his Irish brogue and stories of Celtic lore. The man was a born storyteller, very much like his fellow Irishman, Rory.

We should ask them to organize some sessions of stories and Irish music, Debbie said to herself. She made a note to talk to Kevin about how they might arrange such a new enterprise. She was certain that Glenna would jump at a chance to bring in some of her musician friends. That would really put Fibonacci's on the map.

Debbie's attention was drawn once more to how Phelan was helping his wife integrate with the Fibonacci's community of modern-day mystics. Until the dramatic events surrounding her own wedding, when she and Jeremy had been under psychic attack, Cyndi had never shared her sister's connection with the group. Róisín, Glenna and others had helped her understand more about their beliefs. And now the Close Companions were being very kind to Cyndi as she increasingly saw herself as one of them.

Phelan's profound love for his wife was making all the difference. The sale of her health food store had been a big change for her. Now with Phelan at her side to answer questions about spiritual matters, reassure her and encourage her continued experimentation with herbs and essential oils, she was blossoming like the exotic plants that grew in their home's garden room, which Róisín had planted many years earlier.

Debbie was also grateful that Phelan's managerial skills were freeing her for the growing number of one-on-one conversations that individuals and couples were requesting of her.

I'm beginning to feel like a personal coach, she smiled to herself. *Should I make it official?* Another interesting thought.

Still, she had to admit that something was bothering her. Nothing to do with the coffee shop. She was convinced that all was well there. However, every so often in the past couple of weeks a ripple of concern would pass through her body.

The sensation would appear as only a momentary flutter in her solar plexus, but it always caught her attention. There was no definition to it, only a vibration that felt like a subtle warning. And, Debbie noted, these ripples had actually become more frequent in the past week since she and others had experienced the amazing vibrations in Tim O'Toole's tower.

With all of these thoughts going through her mind, somehow Debbie was not surprised when Kevin entered the coffee shop from the rear door by the kitchen. He looked around, spotted her and walked over—clearly a man with a purpose.

"Debbie, do you have a minute?"

"I always do for you, *a chara.* Especially when concern is written all over your face. Let's sit in the back booth."

The back booth was traditionally where serious conversations were held. It contained an unusual energy that encouraged deep connection. No one knew exactly why. The back booth at the former Fibonacci's had produced the same effect in its occupants.

Kevin slid into the seat across from Debbie. They had been close friends for many embodiments and still shared an ease and a frankness that both trusted implicitly.

"This won't take long," he began. "Are all of the main Companions here today?"

"They are, yes. Everyone except Sarah, of course. You see Cyndi and Phelan behind the coffee bar. Jeremy is in his office. Rory and Glenna came in earlier. He wanted a coffee before he opened the bookstore, and Glenna filled her thermos with our special pregnancy tea blend. She's in the ballroom working on her drama program for children."

"Good," said Kevin. "Would you be willing to collect them all in the ballroom in about thirty minutes?"

Debbie looked puzzled.

"I know it's a strange request. I can't really explain right now except to say that Sarah and I have something we need to discuss with all of you and we don't want to interfere with Lucky's session on Sunday."

"That sounds serious," said Debbie. "Of course everyone will come. Do you want to join Jeremy and me in our apartment? It's more intimate than the ballroom."

Kevin looked away, thinking. "Normally, I would accept the invitation. But in this case, I actually want to open the curtain that protects the altar and the sun disc. I don't want anybody to be burdened by what we have to share. I think being in that forcefield will help."

"Alright, then," agreed Debbie. "You go home and get Sarah. I'll gather the troops."

She and Kevin moved from the booth and stood facing each other. She put her hand on his shoulder.

"Don't worry, Kevin. Whatever weight you and Sarah are carrying, you know we'll bear it with you. We always have and we always will."

His eyes misted as he reached up and briefly placed his hand on hers. Nodding, he turned and departed by the back door to the lot where he had parked his car.

Forewarned Is Forearmed

Thanks, everybody, for coming on such short notice," Kevin began when they were all assembled. He and Jeremy had arranged chairs in a semi-circle in front of the altar. The golden sun disc shown brightly in the rays of late morning light that streamed through the ballroom's floor-to-ceiling windows.

"You know we'll always come running when the *ceann-druí* calls," quipped Rory with his ready smile. "Seriously, Kevin, you only need to ask when you or Sarah need our support."

The others chimed in, "Absolutely. Definitely. How can we help?"

"Well, technically, Lucky is still *ceann-druí*," said Kevin, answering Rory's offer. "Though I suppose this is good practice for us all." He did not need to reference their mentor's eventual departure from this world.

"If you'll stand, I'll light the candles and offer an invocation. When Sarah and I share what we feel compelled to tell you, I'm sure you will understand the importance of being in this forcefield."

With the grace of one who has conducted rituals for many a lifetime, Kevin solemnly lit the dozen candles on the spiral candelabra that stood man-high on either side of the altar. Facing the sun disc, he repeated the invocation that the druids of ancient Éire and Lucky himself had used for centuries.

O Spirits of East and West, South and North, give ear, we pray, to our supplications. Angels of our world and the next, bless this assembly with your protection and inspiration.

Beloved An Síoraí, O Eternal One, may the words of our mouths and the deeds of our hands bring health and abundance to all our people and safety to our homes, our leaders and those we love both near and far, here with us and in gracious Tír na n'Óg, Land of the Ever-Living.

Kevin turned and addressed the group. "Let's tighten the circle now and then be seated." Everyone moved their chairs to form an unbroken ring, a symbol of the mystical tie of their soul group.

Sarah spoke first. "For the past few days, Kevin and I have been debating if we should share with you the nightmares we've experienced. And, if so, what we should say about them. His was a couple of weeks ago. In fact, his describing the event to Lucky and the O'Tooles is what prompted our session in Tim's Tower."

"I hope you'll forgive us for not telling you then," said Kevin. "But, honestly, we didn't know what to make of the event except for Maggie's insistence that we need more protection."

"I, for one, understand not wanting to share one weird nightmare when that might be all it is," offered Jeremy. "If I went around talking about my dreams, you might wish I'd be silent."

Everyone laughed appreciatively.

"That was our conclusion," Sarah continued. "That is, until last night when I had my own nightmare. It wasn't the same scene. In fact, it was very different. But there was something similar in each event that made us realize that whatever was coming after us might also attack you."

"Both nightmares did feel like an attack," added Kevin. "Definitely not the way the Higher Self communicates with the soul through dreams or in meditation."

"Then I think you'd better start at the beginning," said Debbie.

"I need to add one thing," said Rory, taking Glenna's hand. "I don't want anything to happen to Glenna's baby."

"Nor do we," said Sarah. "That's why we're here at the altar and why we're not taking any chances. Forewarned is forearmed. We mean to stay that way."

Glenna squeezed Rory's hand to let him know she was okay.

"We do understand, Sarah. You and Kevin came to our rescue when we were in grave danger. We will not abandon you." She looked around the circle at the faces of her dearest friends. "Or anyone of our mandala, no matter what. Please tell us what you want us to know."

Wow!" Phelan spoke for the entire group when Kevin and Sarah finished relating the details of their experiences. Eyes were wide as each one pondered how these nightmares might relate to themselves and their spouses. For a minute, no one said anything else.

Jeremy was musing. "Now I appreciate why you wanted us to gather here at the altar," he said quietly.

"Thank you." Sarah nodded to him. She was sitting across from the Maddens. "We are grateful for your support. And I sense something more than appreciation flickering in the awareness of you two seers."

Debbie did not hesitate. "Your experiences remind me of something. Not the particulars, but the vibration of menace, even violence." She turned to her husband. "Do you know what I mean?"

"I do, as far as the vibration," Jeremy agreed. "I can't tell you anything specifically. Except I think it may have to do with the attack on our community of Tearmann when we were all together in first-century Ireland."

He turned to Rory and Glenna who had been embodied as the druid Riordan and chief bard Ollamh Gormlaith. "That event was devastating for you two."

Rory put his arm around his wife's shoulder and pulled her close. She rested her head on his chest. "I'm sure this time it won't come to that, *mo mhuirnín*," he said gently. He looked intently at Kevin, silently asking for confirmation of his assurance to his beloved.

Kevin nodded and said solemnly, "That is why we are here. I agree with Sarah that forewarned is forearmed. Fortunately, we are better able to withstand treachery than in first-century Ireland."

Looking around the circle at the faces focused on his and hoping to alleviate some of the concern he observed there, he explained, "Our mandala is stronger than we've ever been. We have greater protection as a result of the victories we've won, the prayers we know to give and because of the spiritual attainment each of us is garnering. We have greater access to the Wisdom Masters than in ages past. And we know a lot more about the wiles of dark forces."

"Besides, Arán Bán and Una are gone forever," said Glenna. She was determined to be brave and wanted her friends to feel her resolve.

"That is true," Debbie agreed. She wanted Glenna to feel seen.

She continued, "And that knowledge does make a difference. Still, we know that evil never sleeps, even when one of the worst of our ancient adversaries has been removed. I agree with Kevin and I am not afraid. I take these nightmares as warnings, perhaps even a grace, despite their ominous nature. Should they actually be prophetic, I take heart that prophecies are meant to be broken. I know we can do that if we stick together."

"Yes!" declared the group as a single voice.

"Thank you all," said Kevin with deep affection. "Does anyone want to add anything before we go back to our other work?"

Other than his initial surprise, Phelan had been silent throughout the discussion. Now he spoke thoughtfully, "I'll add only that F. M. Bellamarre always said, 'The future must be lived to be known.' My guess is that we're meant to go on living—with an increased sense of vigilance—and we'll see what *An Síoraí*, the Eternal One, has up his divine sleeve. I'm sure the force behind these nightmares is not the only one involved."

"Right you are, Phelan," said Kevin.

His face was bright with a radiance that was apparent to those in the circle. United in consciousness, they thought to themselves, *Yes, whenever the time comes for Kevin to take over from Lucky, he will be the ceann-druí we need to lead us forward.*

Kevin did not let on that he sensed their thoughts. Though he was deeply touched, first things must come first.

"If you'll all stand," he said, "I'll extinguish the candles and seal this session. God willing that no other obstacles arise, we'll gather again on Sunday at *Teach an tSolais.*"

Part Two

Following the Thread

Lúcháir

A touch of autumn brought a noticeable tang to the air and slightly cooler temperatures to the lush gardens and enormous trees that surrounded Tim O'Toole's round tower. Myriad hues of crimson, gold and orange were soon to follow.

Change was in the air. Which meant the couples were not surprised that each had asked if they might arrive early in order to meditate in the tower for a few minutes before Lucky's story session. They laughed, shook hands and hugged as they alighted from their cars at the same time and walked to the front door as a united body. None of them doubted that they were in this together—whatever "this" might turn out to be.

Before they could knock, Tim opened the front door. His guests felt him open his heart even wider. "Come in and welcome. Lucky's waiting for you by the tower. Maggie and I will bring up the rear."

More comfortable now with the physical requirements of entering the tower, the couples quickly made their way up the stairs and ladder to the wooden platform and sat quietly. As was their custom, they joined Lucky in sounding the OM and slipped gently into a peaceful meditation.

After twenty minutes, a very serene group made their way back to the house and took their seats before the cheery turf fire that set the atmosphere for Lucky's stories

As they were all getting settled, Kevin spoke. "Before we begin, I want you all to know that I've had a conversation with Ivy. Based on what she told me and Sarah in confidence, I am firm in my belief that she needs to support Brian in his business project. If they feel that they can participate with us in the future, I'm sure they will."

"What about Kerry and Kaitlyn?" asked Debbie. "I know they loved being part of their Uncle Lucky's storytelling."

"They're content for now," Maggie explained. "With approval from Ivy and Brian, I'm giving them their own little program on how to use their special gifts and protect themselves from malevolent forces. This way, they get to visit with Lucky on their own. At the moment, they are happy with the arrangement."

"Where are your twins, Sarah?" Glenna wanted to know. "I love seeing how they change week to week." She rested a hand on her belly. She could feel her own baby changing as it grew week to week in her womb.

"They're with my parents," said Sarah with a sigh. "I'm almost over feeling guilty about not bringing them. I know their souls want to be here, but their toddler bodies are so active that they require constant supervision. Letting their grandparents babysit is the best solution."

Then she added, "Besides, if they start talking about seeing fairies and gnomes, nobody will try to stop them."

Kevin gave his wife a look that spoke volumes.

"I'm sorry," she blushed. "That was a really snarky thing to say about my brother when he's not here to throw it back at me."

Sarah was seated next to Lucky. He looked at her and said quietly, "We'll let it go this time, lass." However, something in his tone told her she had best not repeat the comment.

He quickly changed the subject. "Now, who's ready to hear what happened to the lad, Lúcháir, as he made his way through adolescence and beyond?"

Like a class of elementary school children eager for storytime, the adults all raised their hands. Though it had been only a week, it seemed an age since they had gathered around the man who was weaving them into his legacy like the best *seanchaís* of ages past.

The next morning, as the lad walked to the village, ready to begin his new life, he thought of himself as Lúcháir. He said the word aloud and claimed it. *Lúcháir!*

Here was not so much his name as his action. He was welcoming joy into his life. To his mind, the sun shone brighter than ever. The world around him gleamed with possibility.

The Unknown beckoned with promise. 'Twas a thing of brilliance that glimmered out from the mountain tops and sparkled on the lakes and ponds he passed.

At first he strode past the lake that had been his pondering spot for the whole of his life so far. Then he turned and walked back. This was farewell, like he was leaving an old friend. He doffed his hat and folded his hands together at his heart as a sign of gratitude.

He stood like that for a full minute. The lake's surface was a perfect mirror, reflecting a smattering of thin clouds that sailed silently across a sky of uncommon blue. The lad was turning to go when the surface rippled. Before his eyes it seemed to part as a shape rose up from the water.

Others might have said 'twas a fish rising to feed in the early morning light, but the lad knew better. Fish don't glide up out of the water, hang in midair, then slide back down in exactly the same spot like a hand extended in salutation, then withdrawn.

Here was a sign. His destiny was sealed. At last, his life had been acknowledged. He felt like one of Arthur's knights. One of those chosen for an elite quest. In that moment, Lúcháir vowed not to fail his liege lord or himself.

From that day forward, Lúcháir was the lad's private, secret name. Father Kenneally knew it, but he didn't use it. Instead, he called the lad by his family name: O'Connor—the same as university men were addressed. The lad was 'Lucky' to his friends and he soon had many, for the kindly priest insisted that he return to school in the village.

'You're bright, O'Connor,' said Father Kenneally. 'As long as you are under my supervision, you'll not neglect your studies.'

Committed to this life of work and study, Lúcháir grew into a young man. He graduated from the local secondary school where the nuns were fair, though strict teachers. Being immersed in the parochial atmosphere, and with Father Kenneally's encouragement, he decided he might have a vocation as a priest.

So, off he went to seminary in Limerick.

You'll not be surprised to learn that his roommate was a fellow named Tim O'Toole. The young man was full of chatter and stories that brought Lúcháir out of himself. Soon Tim and Lucky (always that name to his friends) were rollicking good mates who stretched more than a few boundaries of seminary decorum.

However, by the end of the first term, Lucky had developed doubts about his ever being a priest. He persevered through freshman year, though more for his roommate's camaraderie than affection for the curriculum.

'What'll you do?' Tim asked as he and Lucky packed up for the summer break.

'I have a job with a bookshop in Limerick. When the fall term starts, I'm going to take some business courses.'

'That's quite a turn from the priesthood.' Tim shook his head.

'Not so much,' replied Lucky. 'I've thought it out. Serving God or customers is not so different. Seems to me that all creatures have needs that a shop or business can fill. 'Tis only a matter of hospitality. You'll be doing the same in your parish.'

'Then I wish you well,' said Tim. 'Still, I think I'll stay on and be a priest for a while. That's my assignment, anyway. Then I'll reconnect with the lass I was married to before and we'll pick up our mission for the Masters where we left off.'

Lucky had always suspected his roommate of being a very unusual sort of person. Now he knew it for a fact. Was Tim talking about this lifetime or another one? Regardless, in the conversation that followed, records of their past associations as mystics and seekers after truth opened up for him.

Tim assured him that, though their lives might take different turns, this reignited friendship would carry them through many a challenge and mighty missions on the spiritual path they were walking with the Wisdom Masters.

'Stay in touch,' he said the next morning. 'I want to know how your business studies go. And I'll be glad to meet the lass you're going to marry. She's a fine one, Lucky. Treat her well. She deserves better than what she's got at the moment. You can make her happy.'

Time passed as time is wont to do. And so it was that, after a couple of years, our lad decided one day to eat his simple lunch of ham on brown bread in the park around the corner from the bookshop where he was pleased to be employed.

As he approached his favorite spot, a bench that sat under an oak tree, he saw her. A lovely young woman about his age was resting on the bench with a little boy who was four or five years old.

Lucky felt his heart soar in instant recognition. The lass was beautiful. Her eyes were emerald green. Her long hair was flaxen gold in color and looked as soft. He knew he'd known her in ages past. Surely, here was the woman his friend Tim had predicted he would marry.

But then his heart sank. The child by her side had the same coloring and features, only in miniature. How could that be? He watched closely. Sure enough, a wedding ring flashed in the sun.

He was transfixed by the sight, at once elated and grieved. Despite her belonging to another, Lucky was drawn to speak to her. Then a tall man with a pinched face and straight black hair strode over to the bench and stood menacingly before the pair.

The little boy shied. The woman reached to console him, but the man grabbed her arm and wrenched her to standing. Just as abruptly he let go of her and growled something Lucky couldn't hear. Immediately the woman picked up the child and, head down, followed the man without a word.

Lucky barely stopped himself from rushing over and pulling the woman and her little boy away from the man. But then what would he have done? Fight the man to the death?

A tempting idea. Lucky had grown tall and strong. He figured he could probably take his opponent. Though, on second thought, he wasn't so sure. The man was thin but wiry, with an air of meanness that said he wouldn't go down easy.

Lucky watched them leave—the man now pushing the woman ahead of him, she clutching her child. He decided to follow them at a safe distance. When he saw them enter a shabby building, he knew he'd found their dwelling.

Checking his watch, he realized he was late in returning to work. He couldn't afford his pay to be docked for missing even a few minutes. Still, he knew he'd be back.

He would watch and pray like a guardian angel. The lass with the flaxen hair was his destiny. That was sure. And equally certain it was that *An Síoraí*, the Eternal One, had a plan. Lucky must bide his time, be it long or short.

As it turned out, the wait was not long.

"To be continued," said the *seanchaí*, his eyes twinkling at the crestfallen faces before him.

"Lucky, if you didn't have us hooked before, we surely are now," said Glenna. The others agreed.

"As it should be, darlin'," he replied, clearly pleased at the success of his storytelling. "Don't think I'm not tempted to keep you here for several hours more. But you have lives to live and responsibilities to keep. We've time enough for all the tales I've yet to share. Besides, we have a surprise for you. Are they here, Maggie?"

"They are, and you've never seen such eager faces."

She opened the front door and in burst Kerry and Kaitlyn, followed by Ivy and Brian along with Eileen and Patrick Callahan, who each had a toddler in tow.

"What a wonderful surprise!" Sarah exclaimed, clapping her hands.

"I know their birthday isn't until Tuesday," grinned her father, "but we couldn't pass up this opportunity to celebrate with their cousins and very special friends. Do you have the cake, Maggie?"

"I do, with all the trimmings."

From a large box that had been sitting in plain sight in her kitchen, she produced an enormous three-layer cake decorated with white icing and tiny angels and fairies and gnome figurines that appeared to be playing in a forest of green icing trees. The effect was magical.

"Ivy and Sarah, come give me a hand," said Maggie. "We'll lay out these treats on the counter so everyone can be served."

For another hour, children and adults feasted on the cake and ice cream that Eileen had delivered to Maggie the day before in anticipation of this surprise. She had known that Sarah did not have time to plan a big party, so she had applied her own considerable organizational skills to do the job.

With Gareth and Naimh playing on the floor with their cousins, who were showing them how to use the new toys that had also appeared along with dessert, Sarah kissed her mother on the cheek.

"Thank you, Ma. I hope you know how grateful I am to have such a thoughtful and accomplished mother."

"I do know," said Eileen with a lump in her throat, "and your gratitude is a precious gift to me."

As everyone prepared to leave, Lucky turned to Eileen and Patrick. "Are you willing to take Gareth and Naimh home? I need a word with Kevin and Sarah before they go."

"Of course," said Patrick. "As far as I'm concerned, the more time with these two kiddos the better."

Kevin and Sarah walked to the front door with Lucky as he bade the other couples good-bye. "*Slán abhaile, a chairde.* May you go safely home, my friends. I'll see you soon."

Then he turned to these two who carried more of his hopes for the future than they could possibly imagine.

"Let's go sit on the terrace while you describe what you shared with the others about Kevin's nightmare, which you've told me about—and about Sarah's, which you've not told me. The Companions were very keen to support you today."

"You don't miss a thing, do you, Lucky?" said Kevin smiling.

"Not yet," answered the man.

Learning the Business

The following week was a busy one for the Circle of Close Companions. In fact, anyone watching might have thought they were keeping themselves busier than usual. Perhaps so time didn't drag until they gathered again with Lucky. Or perhaps so their minds were too occupied to dwell on the troubling images the nightmares of Kevin and Sarah had conjured in their imaginations.

Ivy was also busy. She had spent the past several days working with Brian to sketch out the structure for Stan Conway's computer and website upgrades. She had always enjoyed this part of the design process and now had a double reason to support her husband's business.

Today was her inaugural foray into working a few hours in the physical store under Stacey's supervision. She was as nervous as a child on her first day at school. For the life of her, she couldn't remember why this had seemed like a good idea.

Stacey had said to dress casually. But in her anxiety, Ivy had chosen a silk tunic a shade lighter than her copper-red hair, dark navy-blue leggings and short navy boots with chunky heels. She was especially thin these days and appeared more like a model than a clerk. To Ivy, a well-styled outfit was the same as armor. She was determined to wear it well.

When she walked through the store's front door, Stacey took one look at her new employee and felt green envy boil up like a poison. Her black hair was as long as Ivy's, but she'd never been able to pull off the sweep-over-one-shoulder style. She'd always been too full-figured to wear such a slimming outfit.

However, determined to keep to her original plan, she cooled the bile of inner bitterness with outer sweetness.

"Ivy, my dear," she gushed, "look at you! What a beautiful outfit. My customers will forget what they came in for when they catch sight of you."

The swift change of expression on Ivy's face told Stacey that her ill-disguised barb had stung after all. She hastened to apologize.

"Oh, dear, I meant that as a compliment. What I meant to say is that you'll add some class to the store. That's a good thing."

"Okay, I guess." Ivy wasn't accustomed to being the center of attention and wasn't sure she liked it. To cover her discomfort, she changed the subject to the reason she was there. "What can you tell me about the store?"

"Stan and I thought we'd start you on the cash register so you get a feel for what customers are buying. You don't have to remember the names of the products right away. Everything is barcoded, so all you have to do is scan and ring up the sale. I'll be right here to answer questions.

"Most people pay with credit cards, which they run themselves. A few still pay with cash. I assume you're good with numbers, so you can make change. Anyway, the cash register tells you the amount. Once you've completed the sale, put the items in a bag and hand the customer their receipt."

"Should be easy enough," said Ivy. "I'm sure it will make sense as we go along."

Ivy was glad she had promised to work her first shift only from 8:30 a.m. to noon. By the time she returned home, her entire body ached. She was definitely going to wear flat shoes next time. Her feet were registering a serious complaint about standing in heels.

Otherwise, the morning had moved along quickly. She hadn't made any major mistakes, and the customers were very understanding. Stacey had stayed with her, except for one rather odd event when three men wearing suits and carrying briefcases came in asking for Stan.

Stacey was instantly flustered and hurried to the back room to call her husband. While the three men waited, one of them kept his back to the others, his eyes fixed on the front door. The second seemed to be scanning the store, his eyes darting from section to section. To Ivy's enormous discomfort, the third man openly ogled her. None of them said a word, but their presence was unnerving.

The fact that they were silent allowed her to hear Stacey speaking to

Stan in a low and angry voice. "I thought you said they weren't coming till this afternoon."

"Well, they're early, aren't they?" he growled. "Deal with it."

Stan immediately strode out to greet the three men. Without shaking hands with them, he ushered them into the office situated in the far corner of the back room and shut the door.

Stacey hurriedly returned to where Ivy was standing at the cash register. The younger woman's eyes were open wider than usual. Otherwise, she gave no inclination that she had heard the Conways' brief altercation.

"Now then," said Stacey, a bit too cheerily, "what questions do you have?"

"Maybe you could show me around the store while we don't have any customers," Ivy suggested. "I would like to learn where various products are located."

"Oh, yes," said Stacey, suddenly remembering that she had not given Ivy a complete tour of the store.

About fifteen minutes later, Stan emerged alone from the back room. "Those were product salesmen," he explained to the two women as if they were both new employees. "They apologized for interrupting business and left by the delivery door."

He cleared his throat and puffed out his chest. His full attention went to Ivy. "So, how do you like our little enterprise?"

"It seems very efficient, although I can't say more than that the cash register works," Ivy admitted.

"And you did very well for your first morning," said Stacey, then she added eagerly, "It's nearly noon and I'm sure you tired, so why don't you run along." She was practically herding Ivy out of the store. "Don't forget your purse. We'll see you on Friday, same time."

"Yes, that will be fine." Ivy retrieved her bag from under the counter. She started for the front door, then turned back to ask a question—which died on her lips.

Stacey had spun around to face Stan and was poking him in the chest. Was the woman saying, "You've got to be more careful." Ivy didn't really want to know.

Ivy's morning shift on Friday went smoothly and she began to get an idea of where the various items were located. She laughed at herself when she noticed that the shelves were all clearly labeled with little signs that said:

VITAMINS, MINERALS, HOMEOPATHY, PROTEINS, TEAS, ESSENTIAL OILS

There were also sections for cards, books and what Stacey seemed to take special pleasure in identifying as "Ritual Products" such as candles, incense, smudge sticks, crystals and a variety of oracle cards.

"I'm going to be adding clothing, jewelry and my own tea and oil blends in the next month or so," she said proudly. "That's one reason we're updating the website and computerized inventory control."

Ivy nodded. "Brian and I are mapping out a scope of work so we're in sync with your timetables for rolling out the new product lines."

"That's wonderful," enthused Stacey. "I can see Stan was right to hire your husband's company. You're both so clever. And I understand that your children are as well."

Ivy raised her eyebrows and nodded. "Clever is one way to put it."

"You mean they have special gifts?"

"Yes, although we don't emphasize that. They're really just normal, happy, creative children."

"Of course, naturally." Stacey was all ears. "When I did your card reading the night you came for dinner, I could tell that you're doing an excellent job of raising them. If you ever want to bring them by the store to see where their mother is working, I would love to meet them."

"That's kind of you," said Ivy. "They're spending quite a bit of time with their grandparents, who also babysit for their little cousins. And they're being tutored by Maggie O'Toole, so their lives are very full. But I'll ask if they'd like to stop by. They do make their own decisions."

"How interesting," Stacey commented aloud to Ivy—then silently to herself, *Yes, very interesting, indeed.*

Longing for Éire

"Have you seen the lad?" Tim asked Maggie, referring to Lucky. Despite their respective ages, throughout the many years of their acquaintance, they had remained "lad" and "lass" to each other. "His listeners will be here in a couple of hours. He seemed a bit off this morning. I want to make sure he's fit."

Maggie looked up from the book she was reading. "He said he was going to have a ponder by the bay. He did have a look of melancholy about him."

They walked to the French doors that opened onto the terrace. Their old friend was sitting by himself on the bench facing the bay's still water. Tim put his arm around Maggie's shoulder. She put her arm around his waist.

"I'll surely miss him when he finally heads off to *Tír na nÓg*," said Tim wistfully. "Do you ever think about us going?"

"Not really," said Maggie. "We can do so much more here. At least I still feel that way. Do you?"

"When I see the children's bright faces, yes. I'm still of a mind to stay and do our best for them."

Maggie gave her husband an affectionate pat on the back. "Then go see what you can do for the lad. He's got miles left on this journey. Buoy him up. We don't want any of the others worrying about him."

A soft breeze was blowing off the bay when Tim sauntered across the lawn toward the water. He approached the bench where Lucky sat.

"Mind if I join you?" he said softly, not wanting to startle his friend.

Lucky raised his head and shaded his eyes. He looked surprised to see

Tim, then laughed. He'd been miles away.

"Have a seat, lad." He slid over to make room. For several minutes they sat quietly, watching the seagulls wheel and cry. A sailboat drifted across the water in the distance. It was altogether a peaceful scene.

"Reminds me of my pondering spot in Connemara," said Lucky at last. "I used to sit there for hours, imagining myself as one of Arthur's knights."

"Do you still?"

Lucky chuckled. "Not much these days. Today I was letting my mind rest on the water, like one of those glass spheres that used to hold fishing nets. 'Tis odd—how little snippets of memory come drifting back into recollection. An event here, an event there, for no apparent reason other than to say, 'This also happened.'

"They create no specific narrative—these memories—only a glimpse into a larger story too vague to be told. And likely no purpose in the telling. Snapshots in a photo album with too many blank pages to create a coherent timeline."

Both men continued gazing out across the bay. Not turning to his friend, Tim asked, "Are you doubting the telling of your life's stories?"

"Not that. Any tale that is complete in my mind, I'm happy to share. 'Tis part of my agreement with our Master. No, I was just watching these bits of memory float by like pieces of driftwood."

"Can you name any of the pieces?"

"People my family used to visit. I felt like an odd observer who didn't belong. They were my parents' people, not mine. I didn't talk much around them. They all seemed strange. Perhaps I did to them. I know I was mighty relieved when we'd go home."

The delicate "plash-plash" of the bay easing back and forth along the shore settled like a comfort around the two men.

"I wonder if I'll ever go back—to Connemara, I mean," said Lucky.

"Do you want to? Things will have changed in thirty years. You've changed."

Lucky chuckled. "They'll probably think I'm a Yank."

"That they will, if they listen to you," agreed Tim. "But if they take a good look, they'll see a man who is Celt to his bones. That's what's calling you, isn't it?"

Lucky nodded, his gaze casting far beyond what his eyes registered.

"'Tis like the Éire over there is pulling the Éire that still lives in here." He put his hand to his heart. "Sometimes the longing overwhelms me and I feel like I'll die from the ache."

"Then we must book you a visit," said Tim with his gift of insatiable enthusiasm. He stood and started walking around, his mind immediately full of plans—as if the decision had been made. "Who do you want to take with you?"

"I don't suppose I could take all eight adults from the Circle of Close Companions."

"Not unless you want to shutter Fibonacci's for a fortnight."

"Probably not a good idea," Lucky admitted. "I'll think on it."

"Ask our Master, why don't you," suggested Tim.

Lucky paused, formulating the question in his mind. He felt an answer land without his speaking it.

"Here's a thought: What if I took Sarah, Kevin, Debbie and Jeremy? Rory already runs the bookstore and he wouldn't leave Glenna with her being pregnant. Cyndi and Phelan could easily manage the coffee shop."

Tim was right there with him. "Maggie and I could be available to help where needed and to hold the spiritual balance while you five visit your old haunts."

"You make me sound like a ghost."

Tim rested his hand on Lucky's shoulder. "No, lad, but you are tipping towards the Spirit side of things. We'd best get you to Éire and back before *An Síoraí,* the Eternal One, decides to complete the process."

That made Lucky laugh. He stood and joined his friend as they walked back to the house. They could feel Maggie wondering if they were going to eat before the couples arrived.

"Don't say anything to them," said Lucky. "The hardest stories are yet to come and must be told first. We can work on logistics, planning and the like. Then none of the couples will argue that they can't all be gone at the same time. Of course, they might have a point. Is it wise to take our four key people overseas all together?"

Tim thought a minute. "It might be the only way to finish—to flush out the circumstances behind Kevin's and Sarah's nightmares. Some rats only show themselves when the big cats are away."

"'Twill be a mighty initiation for whoever goes," said Lucky. "We'll have to see how the future unfolds before any of us can decide."

"What have you two been plotting?" Maggie asked the minute they came into the house. "You've the look of schoolboys planning an escape from your lessons."

"Ah, darlin'," said Tim, putting his arm around her waist and pulling her into a dance. "I haven't surprised you in a hundred years, have I?"

"No, and you'd best not be about starting now. Sit down for your lunch, both of you, and tell me what has you beaming like Ivy's twins."

Maggie listened as they told her of Lucky's longing for Connemara, their idea of who would go with him and who would stay to manage operations at Fibonacci's. She sat quietly for a minute, gazing over the cup of tea in her hand as she often did when she was listening for inner guidance.

"Well, what do you think?" Tim asked eagerly. Planning travel was one of his favorite pastimes.

"I think if Kevin and Jeremy dispute your reasoning, they'll have the right of it," said Maggie firmly. "Think about it, lads. And I know you don't want to, but consider. As much as I'm sure Sarah would want to go, she has two toddlers who need their mother. Debbie is still finding her sea legs when it comes to operating the coffee shop. Jeremy is the finance manager for Brian's business. He could cover for Kevin, but nobody is trained to take over for both of them."

Tim and Lucky reluctantly nodded. They finished their sandwiches and Maggie cleared the table. She always thought best when her hands were busy.

"Here's another thing to consider: Aside from visiting your homeland, Lucky, what is your purpose in going to Connemara? Is it possible you're being prompted to go because there's some task that can only be accomplished there? Not only for you, but for someone else?"

"Who are you thinking of?" asked Lucky.

"Kevin seems the logical choice," said Maggie. "He's the one who'll be taking over for you at Fibonacci's, just like Ah-Lahn did for Old Quin as *ceann-druí*. The situation is too similar to be coincidence. Sarah will want to go, and part of me feels that she should. But there may be ways to include her without her leaving these shores."

"You're a wise woman, Maggie," said Lucky. "'Tis already September. We don't want to wait so long that we're braving the gales of a Connemara winter. I'll talk to Kevin and Sarah and we'll consult our Master as well. As we're considering all this, I can feel that more is going on than my being homesick for the land I left over thirty years ago."

"Come in and find your places, *a chairde*." A smiling Tim greeted the couples as they arrived and then escorted them through the atrium that was glowing with sunlight streaming down from the skylight and reflecting upon the rose quartz fountain.

Still no Ivy and Brian, he noted. *Probably just as well.*

"Lucky's bursting with tales for you today," he said. "You've asked, some of you, about how he met Róisín. Today you'll hear all, so I hope you've come ready to stay for a while. Maggie's set out tea and scones. Help yourselves and prepare to be enlightened."

No further coaxing was necessary. Lucky was already in the *seanchaí's* seat by the fire. Sarah took her place to his right with her recorder. Kevin and the other eager listeners gathered attentively. This was a story they had waited a long time to hear.

Lucky gave himself the pleasure of fastening a loving gaze on each smiling face. Surely this was family as it was always meant to be. A bond unbreakable of hearts melded together over centuries of common cause.

The longing in the older man's soul took on a new cast—one of hope that he would be leaving them with a legacy that would aid their own search for the sweetness and power of a mission fulfilled.

Meeting Róisín

Lucky finished his tea. Carefully placing Maggie's antique cup in its saucer, he leaned back in his chair. His gaze drifted out to days gone by. His voice became clear, as one of the dearest times of his journey through these realms of time and space came vividly into recollection.

As we saw, Lucky waited and watched, though not as often as he wanted. He was busy at work and could rarely get away to the park where he'd first seen the young woman and her child. Even when he did find time, they didn't appear.

'Twas only on weekends that he was able to make his way to the tenement he'd seen the unfortunate party enter. One day, he took a circuitous route, lest anyone think his interest unsavory or his presence unwelcome. The sight that greeted his eyes brought him up short.

In front of the building stood a lorry marked REMOVALS. Two heavy-set men were loading a few sticks of poor furniture into the van as a clutch of neighbors watched, their faces drawn and shawls pulled close.

Lucky approached a women with the least unfriendly expression in a crowd likely to be suspicious of his inquiry. 'What goes on?' he asked in as casual a manner as he could manage. 'I had meant to visit the family that lived here.'

'Then you're no more than passing acquaintance,' the woman replied gruffly. 'There's been tragedy in this house.'

Lucky felt his heart sink. 'What sort of tragedy?'

'Criminal. Death. Grievous injury.' The woman was short on details. She peered into Lucky's face. Seeing genuine concern, she went on.

'I'll tell ye, then. That man was the worst husband a lass could ever find herself saddled with. Taken to heavy drink for lack of work, he was. He beat her bad once or twice, on account of her protecting her son from the man's violence. Then he robbed a shop and harmed the owner, so the *garda* were after him.

'He was hiding at home. A foolish act. His whereabouts was well-known. When the authorities pounded on the front door, he ran for the back. Just then, the little boy stepped into his father's path and was knocked down the stone steps leading to the poor excuse for a garden.

'The man bounded over a wall, but the *garda* were waiting for him when he turned into a side street. A chase was on and he might have escaped except for the lorry that was loaded too heavy to avoid hitting him square. The man died on the spot. No great loss there.'

Lucky no longer tried to hide his anxiety. 'And the wife? The little boy? What of them?'

'Gone to hospital. The child hit his head bad on the stone steps where he fell. We don't know if he'll live.' She gestured to the neighborhood gaggle who'd been nodding and voicing confirmation as she'd told the tale.

'Which hospital? St. John's?' Lucky's voice rose in pitch as he tried to extract details from the women.

'Likely so,' answered a different neighbor. 'The lass has family close by. Why she didn't go to them sooner, no sane person could tell. Maybe they're with her. She'll not be comin' back here, that's sure.'

Lucky took off like a rocket, then stopped mid-flight and turned back. 'What's her name?' he shouted.

'Róisín,' called the first woman.

'Róisín what? Did she take her husband's name?'

The women looked at each other, searching their memories while Lucky stood impatiently in the middle of the pavement.

'Cullen,' said one at last. ''Tis Cullen. He was a Clare man. That's all we know. Don't be askin' us any more questions.' They turned and bustled away, obviously discussing him.

As if his own life depended on it, Lucky ran the few blocks to St. John's Hospital. By sheer good fortune, he managed to avoid careening into other pedestrians or turning an ankle on the rough pavement. He dashed up the steps to the entrance and breathlessly told his purpose to the nun on duty.

'I'm looking for a young woman and her little boy. She's Róisín Cullen. I don't know the lad's name. She may have family with her.'

The nun looked him up and down. Perspiration was beading furiously on his brow and his clothes were in disarray from his cross-town sprint.

Nervous under her scrutiny, Lucky stammered. 'I've been to seminary. I'd like to help them. I'm a friend of the family.'

The sister knew he was telling only a partial truth. Nuns can detect a falsehood at fifty paces. Yet he was so obviously concerned for the child's well-being, if not the mother's, her eyes softened.

'Third floor, turn right at the top of the stairs.'

'Thank you, Sister.'

Lucky took the stairs two at a time, then halted at the nurse's station. What would he do if he found Róisín? He'd never said a word to her.

The supervising nun was more sympathetic to his inquiry and gave him a piece of paper on which to write a note.

'They're in the hallway, just there.' She pointed three doors down where a young woman was huddled with an older man and woman. 'The doctors are with the boy now. It doesn't look good.'

Lucky felt like an invader. How could he disturb such a scene? Yet his inner voice urged him to speak to the family—if only to say who he was.

'I'm sorry to disturb you,' he said gently.

The trio looked up at him with stricken faces, eyes red-rimmed from crying.

'My name is Lúcháir O'Connor. You don't know me, though I hope some day you will. I've been a partial witness to your misfortune. If I can be of assistance or comfort in the future, please let me know.'

He handed the father the note he had hastily written. 'I work at the bookshop at this address. I'm always there if you ever want to contact me. Meantime, I'll pray for you.'

As Lucky had hoped she would, Róisín looked directly into his eyes. They held each other's gaze for only a moment, yet long enough for him to feel a flash of profound soul recognition spark between them.

'*Go raibh maith agat,*' said her father softly. Róisín looked down again, nestling deeper into her mother's embrace.

Lucky said no more. He'd clearly been dismissed, though the father had offered a faint smile. Still, he felt his mission had been accomplished as much as was possible in this sad moment.

'*Beannachtaí daoibh,*' he said to the family and took his leave.

After that brief encounter, a full year and a half passed with no sight of Róisín nor word from her family. Lucky did pray for the child and his mother, though he eventually surrendered the thought of seeing them again to *An Síoraí,* the Eternal One.

He was well aware that instances of past-life recognition did not necessarily bear fruit. Sometimes a single glimpse was all that was required in a given life. The important thing was to walk the path one faced until, or unless, circumstances proclaimed a change of direction.

So Lucky completed his business courses and continued working at the bookshop. As when he was a lad, he found himself enthralled with mythologies and works on Celtic culture and mystic lore. The more he read of the hero's perennial spiritual journey, the more keenly he felt his own awareness of ethereal realms increasing.

What developed in him during the nights alone in his tiny flat above the bookshop was not exactly second sight, but it was certainly a growing sensitivity to the other side of life.

When the shop's elderly owner retired, Lucky took over daily operations. He found he had a knack with customers and, despite general economic difficulties in Limerick, he built a steady business. He was able to pay the landlord his due as well as keep a roof over his own head and food on his table.

As weekends were busy times for shoppers, he closed the shop on Mondays and gave himself the gift of exploring the rough-and-tumbled history of Limerick and the storied Shannon River.

He particularly loved sitting in the ancient quiet of St. Mary's Cathedral. Founded in the twelfth century, the simplicity of its stone walls and wooden monk's stalls that had been carved with mythical creatures hearkened him back to medieval times.

Many days he sat across from the statue of an angel whose serene face always comforted him. Sometimes he thought she looked at him and smiled as if to assure him that all would be well, as long as he didn't lose hope.

In the past two weeks, he'd been obligated to leave the bookshop in the care of a trusted employee named Peter while he attended his mother's funeral. Again, he'd felt like he didn't belong with the extended family that gathered.

He was grateful when his sisters told him they would care for their father. They would sell the farm and move their parent in with the eldest sister. Lucky needn't worry.

As he rode the bus back to Limerick, he felt a door close on his childhood with firm finality. And, as they say often happens, another door opened.

'There's a letter for you,' said Peter when Lucky entered the shop the next day, an hour past opening time.

''Twas delivered by a handsome lass with flaxen hair and the greenest eyes I've ever seen. When I said you'd gone to bury your ma, she left for an hour and then came back with this letter.'

He handed Lucky a sealed envelope addressed to Lúcháir O'Connor. The handwriting was neat with a certain elegance that conveyed refinement without being pretentious.

'I'll read this in the back, if you don't mind, Peter.'

Not waiting for a reply, Lucky hurried to the room that served as office and storage. His hands trembled as he sat in the antique wooden desk chair and unsealed the envelope. Inside was a hand-written letter whose message flew straight to his heart.

Dear Mr. O'Connor,

Please accept my condolences for the loss of your mother. As you know, I am well-acquainted with grief, which is why I have not been to see you sooner to express my gratitude for your kindness on that terrible day at St. John's.

To answer the question I can imagine you asking, my little boy, Tómas, did not live. He lingered for a day, but his injuries were too severe. Well-meaning people said it was a blessing. He would have been in a vegetative state for the rest of his life. But he was the only child I will ever bear. Losing him was a knife in my heart.

I can also hear you wondering where I have been. That is a happier answer. My grandparents on my mother's side still live in the Golden Vale. Their farm was always my refuge and has been more so these past eighteen months. They have understood, perhaps better than I myself, what a wound was opened in my soul. So they let me heal as Nature was able to bring me back to a semblance of myself.

I feel this sorrow may be with me for a long time, but I am now ready to forge a new path in life. Which is what I came to see you about.

I need a friend. Our brief encounter told me that you and I have been soul friends in many ages. I hope you do not find that an odd thing to say. I trust you know exactly what I mean.

Your employee said you would return on Tuesday, the day

you will be reading this letter. As the friend I pray you are already, will you meet me for a late lunch today at the pub around the corner from your shop? I will be there at half-one and we can talk.

If you do not wish to meet, naturally, I will understand and I'll not trouble you again. However, should you feel prompted to explore how we might support each other further in this life, I will consider the opportunity a great blessing.

Is mise le meas, Róisín

P. S. When I first stopped by your shop, your employee called you Lucky. I found that amusing, as I do consider our meeting a lucky interval in the midst of misery. I imagine that you prefer the nickname, as Lúcháir may have earned you a fair share of taunting from schoolmates.

However, you will always be Lúcháir to me. In my soul I feel that our meeting was a gift of welcoming joy from the heart of *An Síoraí,* the Eternal One.

The group sat quietly as Maggie poured a fresh cup of tea for Lucky, then served the others. The *seanchaí's* eyes were moist and he took a couple of deep breaths before continuing.

"So, that's how my darlin' Róisín and I reconnected in this life. I did join her for lunch that Tuesday. We talked through the afternoon into dinnertime and on into the night. Afterwards we rarely left each other's company. When my employee, Peter, announced that the book trade was not the future he'd envisioned, Róisín came to work with me in the shop.

"We knew we were meant to be together, so I contacted my old friend Tim O'Toole, who was still a priest. (Though not for long. He was soon to be married.) He performed the ceremony, and we were off on our new life.

"As you know, Róisín and I were not twin flames. You were there when her soul's twin joined her as she made her ascension from a glorious etheric temple. The tale of my own twin flame is for another day. And I do promise you'll hear it."

"There's more to the story of you and Róisín, isn't there, Lucky?" Sarah still had her recorder going, so as not to miss any details.

"To be sure, lass," said Lucky with a wink. "And you'll like the next part of that story, as it pertains to how we met our Master Saint Germain when he first began physically interacting with us as F. M. Bellamarre."

A sudden rain shower darkened the afternoon brightness. Lucky's mood changed abruptly.

"Be mindful, *a chairde*," he said and they all caught the warning. "The more I tell you, the more stealthily malignant forces may try to interfere. Watch and pray. There are interesting times ahead, though I don't know what just yet. You can be sure I'll tell you when I do."

Possibilities

The next morning, Lucky was up before dawn. 'Twas an easier task these days, as sunrise came later in September. He sat on the side of his bed and listened through his room's open window.

Birds were singing, beckoning the sun to rise. Lucky loved the fact that all manner of feathered creatures sang while it was still dark. 'Twas one of Nature's reminders that life embraces each new day as it if were the first of Creation.

He moved to the easy chair across from his bed and listened closely. He had gone to sleep last night with the beginning of a plan for returning to Ireland in October. He'd drawn up a rough itinerary with the sights he wanted to share with his traveling companions—whoever they might turn out to be.

His mind had wandered once more across Connemara's rugged hills and soft valleys, along her massive cliffs and pounding waves, beside her still lakes and over her vast bogs until he felt himself there once more. Aye, 'twas a grand plan that had rested in his heart as he drifted off to sleep.

Yet with a new day appearing in the faint glow of pre-dawn twilight, he wasn't so sure. Was it longing for his boyhood home that beckoned him with an ache so strong he clutched his heart? Or was it the Éire of a much earlier time where unfinished business called for his attention?

Lucky felt Maggie and Tim stirring in the kitchen. He was very sensitive to vibrations these days. He found comfort in the movement of his hosts as they went about their daily routines. They never intruded, yet he was assured of their presence and their watchful awareness of how he was faring during this crucial time of his soul's waning journey on Earth.

If he didn't emerge from his comfortable suite of rooms to join them for morning tea, Maggie always set a tray with a pot of her special blend and a plate of scones on the table outside his door. Lucky waited briefly, then retrieved this welcome gift of hospitality. He would visit with the O'Tooles later—after he'd considered the fresh perspective his inner guidance was offering.

Today is Labor Day, Lucky remembered as he poured his first cup of tea and resumed his seat by the window. A good day to reflect on all that had been accomplished at Fibonacci's over the past several years—in their old location that he and Róisín had owned and now in the larger building that Brian Callahan's investment had made possible.

The coffee shop and bookstore would be busy today with locals and tourists celebrating the balmy weather that marked the end of summer. A new moon brought a promise of fresh beginnings. And yet, Lucky was all too aware that his task had more to do with endings.

He finished his tea and stood by the window, gazing over the bay's placid waters. Morning was breaking easy now in soft blues and luminous golds. The serenity of this place was a balm to Lucky's soul. He wondered that he should feel such a need for calm.

Was a storm brewing? He'd felt a disturbance yesterday after telling the story of how he and his beloved soulmate, Róisín, had met. He missed her terribly these days. More tangibly present with him than his own twin flame, Flavia, who had departed this Earth two millennia in the past, Róisín had been a stabilizing presence when old sorrows had temporarily burdened him. Now he must find that grounding in his own being.

So, what was this about Connemara—or not Connemara after all?

Yesterday's story had included mention of his mother's funeral. The felt sense of a door closing suggested that the unfinished business which had settled into his awareness was not waiting in the land of his birth in his current life. Could it be that his life as Ceann-Druí Quin was yet to be completed?

Lucky thought about how the Master had sent Sarah and Kevin to Ireland, to the site of the ancient *túath* of Cois Abhann. There they had discovered and reactivated the ruined wisdom grove of Ard-Mháistir Óengus. In so doing, they had retrieved fractured pieces of their souls from their lifetime as Ah-Lahn and Alana.

Living several day's journey to the east in the *tuath* of Tearmann, Ceann-Druí Quin had possessed his own grove. Upon his passing, Arán Bán had claimed it when he temporarily filled Quin's position. And then, much to the younger druid's angry disappointment, the grove had become Ah-Lahn's seat of authority. But the grove of Ard-Mháistir Óengus in Cois Abhann had always held the most power. Apparently, it did yet, if Sarah's and Kevin's recent experience was any criterion.

Lucky suddenly felt a sense of his own fragmentation—a sensation that his vibrant nature had masked for as long as he could recall. Perhaps that awareness of incompletion was one reason for his waffling between his birth name and nickname. Despite his significant powers of spiritual adeptship, there was an empty place in his soul that he had never been able to fill.

And what about others in the Circle of Close Companions? Did they also experience unsatisfied longings that only Spirit could complete?

The time is drawing nigh, he heard his inner voice declare. A different way forward appeared as a possibility.

Would Éire's Ancient East be his destination, and would Kevin be his sole companion? The two of them together had resolution to achieve. Not so much with each other, but with forces of darkness that had plagued them both since time immemorial.

Sarah would be torn between going with them and remaining at home to be with her children—and to complete her appointed task of assembling Lucky's stories into a proper memoir. The three of them would have to devise a solution.

A word flashed into Lucky's mind: "technology." Of course, bilocation was as easy as a video conference call. Besides, the couple continued to practice their telepathic skills. Maintaining Sarah's participation would not be a problem.

Pleased with these ideas, Lucky dressed for the day and joined his hosts in the garden where they were admiring the profusion of blooms that heralded a glorious autumn.

Had Sarah known of Lucky's thoughts, she would have been glad of his conclusion that she should remain home to tend her children and work on his memoir book. That project was becoming more challenging than she had expected. Especially today because her mother was not able to babysit while she transcribed all of yesterday's story session.

Fortunately, Charlotte had enthusiastically agreed to come over on short notice. Sarah wasn't entirely sure of having someone new care for her twins. But they would be at home, so she could supervise, if necessary.

Charlotte was immediately taken with Gareth and Naimh. "Oh, they are beautiful!" she exclaimed as two toddlers looked at her from their high-chairs where they were finishing their morning snack. "Have their eyes always been violet? I don't think I've ever seen such bright little faces."

"Yes, they were born with violet eyes," said Sarah as she lovingly wiped those little faces. "I'm grateful they've stayed the same color. Why don't you help me get them cleaned up for playtime. You can hold Gareth while I change Naimh. He always waits for his sister."

When Sarah led Charlotte into the nursery, Hero and Sprite trotted along beside them.

"You'll get used to the fur kids watching your every move," she laughed. "They view themselves as the twins' primary caregivers. The rest of us are merely their assistants."

"I see," said Charlotte good-naturedly. "I'm glad to know my place. Speaking of place, this is a charming room. So peaceful. I..."

Eyes wide, she halted mid-sentence. Her attention was riveted on the tapestry that hung on an adjacent wall. Sarah saw her astonishment. If she hadn't already started changing Naimh's diaper, she would have instantly taken Gareth from the young woman's arms.

"Charlotte, are you okay?"

"Oh, yes. Sorry. I'm just surprised to see such an exquisite work of art in a nursery. I've done a fair amount of weaving myself, so I appreciate the quality of artistry involved in creating such a piece. What a treat for the little ones to meditate on as they get older."

"My thought exactly," said Sarah. "I'm glad you understand. It's our community, you see. Look closely. You may find yourself in there."

Complications

Meanwhile—just as Lucky was doing—Ivy was also thinking about what was going on in her life.

The partnership between Callahan & Logan Computer Systems and the Conways was humming along. Brian and Stan were making significant progress on identifying user needs for tracking new inventory and increased sales. And her own several hours a week working in the store were providing her with important insight for the website designer.

She was personally more comfortable as well. No more strange men with briefcases came to the front of the store. They may have met with Stan in the office, but Ivy didn't have much reason to venture into the back room. In fact, Stacey had made it clear that her role was out front, which she preferred anyway.

The only snag had occurred last Saturday when she decided to bring Kerry and Kaitlyn in for a visit on a day when they weren't in school. The twins were excited to see where Mommy was working. They had visited the health food store when Cyndi owned it. On that occasion, they were fascinated by all the little bottles and boxes and interesting smells that tickled their noses when they got to test some of the essential oils.

This visit was different. As soon as they walked through the front door, they stopped and refused to go any further into the store. Kerry grabbed his sister's hand and Kaitlyn buried her face against Ivy's trousers.

"Oh, what beautiful children!" exclaimed Stacey as she walked briskly toward them. She knelt down to their eye level. "And what gorgeous red hair." When she reached up to stroke their heads, both children visibly recoiled. Stacey felt the rebuff, but forced herself to go on smiling at them.

Ivy was surprised that the woman would be so forward, although she realized that Stacey was probably unfamiliar with how sensitive young children could be. She herself was becoming accustomed to the woman's effusive personality and usually dismissed any discomfort she might have felt in their interactions. Now she had to say something.

"I'm sorry, Stacey, sometimes they're shy when meeting people for the first time." Actually, the twins were never shy, but Ivy didn't want to say so. Flustered, she continued. "Kerry, Kaitlyn, this is Mrs. Conway. Won't you say 'hello'?"

They hesitated.

"Children," she repeated in her instinctive "mommy" voice.

"Hello," said Kerry quietly, but he didn't look at Stacey. In fact, he didn't look around the store as one might expect his usual curiosity to prompt him. Kaitlyn leaned harder again her mother's leg and said, "Mommy, my tummy hurts."

"Oh, dear," apologized Ivy. "I guess this wasn't a good idea after all. Kaitlyn did eat her breakfast too fast this morning. Maybe we'll try again another day."

"That's fine," said Stacey. Anyone observing the expression on her face would have thought she meant exactly the opposite. But Ivy was too busy ushering her children out the door to notice.

"What is the matter with you two?" she demanded as soon as they reached the family passenger van and she'd buckled them into their car seats. "I've never seen you be so rude. That lady is paying your daddy for a big project. I expect you to be more polite next time."

"We don't want to go back, Mommy," said Kerry firmly. He reached over to his sister and patted her hand. Her big blue eyes filled with tears.

"It's scary," whimpered Kaitlyn.

"Did you see something?" Ivy was concerned now. As much as she disliked the fact that her twins had second sight, she couldn't discount their obvious negative reaction to merely entering the health food store.

"Uh-huh," answered Kerry.

"Do you want to tell Mommy what it was?'

"No," answered Kaitlyn. "We don't want to talk about it."

"And promise you won't make us tell Daddy," said Kerry.

"Okay, I promise." Ivy pulled away from the curb and shook her head as she drove them home. If this was their determination as seven-year-olds, she couldn't imagine what they would be like as teenagers.

On the following Wednesday during their after-school program with Maggie, the twins showed no such reticence in relating their experience. However, as proof of the self-control they were learning, they waited until they were sitting at her kitchen counter, finishing one of the healthy snacks she always fed them.

Kerry looked over at Kaitlyn and she nodded. They had practiced what they were going to say and who was going to tell what part of the story.

"Aunt Maggie, can we tell you something?" Kerry asked.

"It's important," added Kaitlyn.

"Of course. Do you want to sit by the fire?"

Both children hopped off the stools where they had been perched and hurried to one of the sofas. They scrambled up together and sat side by side, facing the woman they knew they could trust with their visions.

Kerry began. "Mommy took us to the healthy store on Saturday so we could see where she works sometimes."

"Did you enjoy that?" Maggie already knew the answer.

"No-o-o-o," said Kaitlyn, drawing out the word. "The lady was scary and there were cobwebs and black things hanging on the shelves."

"Do you mean the store needed to be cleaned?"

"No" said both twins together.

"Did your mommy notice anything?"

"No, but we did," Kerry explained. "And we told Mommy we don't want to go back. We made her promise that we don't have to tell Daddy what we saw."

"She was unhappy with us," said Kaitlyn. Her little mouth drooped sadly. "We don't like making Mommy unhappy."

"I know you don't," said Maggie thoughtfully. "What did you do when you got home?"

"We went to Katy's room and talked to Archangel Michael like you taught us," explained Kerry.

"Did the bad images go away and did you stop being scared?"

"Yes," the pair answered. They were proud of that accomplishment.

"Very good," said Maggie. "You know, your mommy or your daddy may ask you to visit the store again."

"We don't want to," objected Kerry.

"I understand," said Maggie, "though sometimes we have to go places and see people we'd prefer not to. But that doesn't mean you have to be scared or that dark things will hurt you. Shall I teach you a way to create a bubble of light around you in case there is a next time?"

"Yes!" Two little faces brightened at the thought.

"Good. I'm not saying that you have to shut off your ability to see things. That would be denying your gifts. What we're going to learn is how to see yourselves in a sphere of sparkling energy that nothing bad can penetrate. You can even practice seeing this light around your mommy and daddy when they're at the store. Or at other times when you might want to keep them safe."

"Yay!" exclaimed Kerry. "Can we have another snack first?"

"Of course you can, darlin'. Right this way."

Sleuthing

That same morning, Ivy had gone to work as soon as she'd dropped off the twins at school. She wanted to speak with Stacey before the day's activities made conversation more difficult.

And she was curious. What had her twins seen that had changed them into shy, withdrawn children who wouldn't speak to a new person? They were usually outgoing, eager to make new friends. What was so different about walking into the Conways' store?

They weren't only changed. They were frightened. Especially little Kaitlyn. Kerry had tried to comfort her. Brave boy.

When they were back home and Kaitlyn was drinking fizzy water to settle her tummy, Ivy had asked them again if they wanted to tell her what had frightened them. Again they declined and spent much of Saturday afternoon together in Kaitlyn's room. She could hear them talking, but couldn't make out what they were saying.

By dinner time they were back to their bright, expressive selves and had remained so throughout the weekend. On Sunday Ivy had considered taking them to *Teach an tSolais* for Lucky's storytelling session. But Brian had suggested a trip to the wildlife park where the twins could ride ponies, feed goats and giraffes, and circle the park on the brightly painted train called "Old Timer."

What might I detect if I were entering the store for the first time? Ivy wondered as she parked her car and approached the store. She opened the front door carefully and sniffed. Was there a distinctive odor? Nothing other than the strong scent of incense that Stacey burned. "To freshen the energy," she had explained.

Was the place dirty? Ivy was sure it wasn't. She dusted the shelves and swept the floor herself when she wasn't needed at the cash register.

Why had the twins taken an instant dislike to Stacey? Ivy liked her. She liked Stan. Then a question flickered across her mind. Did she really like the Conways? She wanted to like them. That was almost the same thing. Besides, they were Brian's important clients, and she had already promised to support her husband's business.

As Ivy walked toward the front of the store, she wound her way around some of the aisles. She felt nothing unusual until she passed by the ritual items. Then, ever so briefly, she felt a shiver run up her spine. The sensation was hardly more than a ripple, although she instinctively wrapped her arms around her body.

For protection? Of course not. How foolish, she chided herself. *That was just some cool air. Probably the air conditioner.*

Ivy moved to her usual station at the cash register and tucked her purse under the front counter. When Stacey emerged from the back room, she hastened to start the conversation she'd felt was necessary.

"Good morning, Ivy," said Stacey. "You're here early."

"I wanted to apologize for my children's behavior on Saturday," she began. "They're not usually like that. Kaitlyn did have a tummy ache."

"Oh, my dear, don't think a thing about it," said Stacey, waving a well-manicured hand. "I know children have their little ways. And I can be rather forceful. I'm not in the least offended. How could I be when they are so adorable? Those blue eyes and red hair. I'm sure they turn heads when they're out in public."

"Yes, they do," agreed Ivy. She decided to explain her own behavior. "I was just checking out some of the new products that came in yesterday. Did we get in more crystals?"

"Oh, yes, and they're quite powerful," smiled Stacey. Then she changed the subject back to the twins.

"Ivy, dear, I do have one question about your children. Kaitlyn and Kerry, is it?"

"Yes."

"Well, dear, you mentioned that they were spending some afternoons with Maggie O'Toole. I was only wondering if you were comfortable with the amount of time your precious ones are in her company."

"Shouldn't I be? Do you know something I don't?"

"Oh, nothing like that. I was just thinking that sometimes women who don't have their own children may try to monopolize the little ones of other women. Exert undue influence, you know. I certainly wouldn't want Maggie—who I'm sure is a lovely person—I wouldn't want her to drive a wedge between you and your children. Of course, it's always an unconscious thing. Nothing overt. But you must be careful, my dear."

Ivy's brow furrowed.

"Oh, now, I've made you worry," cooed Stacey. "That was certainly not my intention. I'm sure you and Brian know what you're doing with your children. Pay me no mind." She touched Ivy's shoulder affectionately.

"You're both such lovely people with a beautiful family. We haven't known you long, but Stan and I are already very fond of you. And of course we have a vested interest in your well-being since you're doing so much for our business," she added with a noticeable lack of humor.

The front door opened and Stacey's manner changed. "Speaking of business, customers are coming."

Stacey had said that Ivy shouldn't worry about the amount of time Kerry and Kaitlyn were spending with Maggie, but of course Ivy did worry. The next Sunday she convinced Brian that all four of them should join the Circle of Close Companions for at least part of the afternoon. If he didn't want to listen to Lucky's story, he could go for a walk around the property.

She didn't tell him that she wanted to observe their children while they interacted with the adults. She wasn't raising any red flags yet. She knew that any doubt from her would immediately cause her husband too much concern. She would just keep her eyes and ears open for any behavior that seemed untoward. She genuinely liked Maggie and hoped she could continue to do so.

Besides, she hadn't had a chance to talk to Sarah or Kevin since she'd told Kevin about her life review with the Rose Lady. They were family and she missed them. Why did life have to be so confusing?

Family Time

"Gramma! Grampa!" shouted Kerry and Kaitlyn. As frequent visitors to the O'Tooles' home, the minute Brian parked the family van and freed them from their car seats, they had shot through the open front door, past Tim and across the atrium, expecting to see their Aunt Sarah and Uncle Kevin and other good friends from Fibonacci's.

Indeed, all those people greeted them with warm smiles and happy "hello's." What thrilled the twins was the sight of their grandparents who were each holding one of their little cousins, whom they adored.

Gareth and Naimh squirmed to be let down for hugs from their older cousins and soon the foursome was heading for the French doors.

As usual, Sarah's mother was quick off the mark.

"Sarah, Ivy, come with me," said Eileen. "It's going to take all three of us to manage this crew. Lucky, Tim, Maggie," she called to their hosts, "do you mind if we walk around the garden and visit before story time? Then we can put Sarah's little ones down for their nap."

"Take all the time you need," Lucky answered cheerfully. "Looks to me like the Callahan family needs a bit of a reunion."

"Grand," Eileen said and motioned to the two young mothers. "Come along, girls, let's enjoy the flowers while Brian talks to his father."

Patrick walked over to where Brian was standing and extended his hand, which the younger man welcomed.

"Son, it's good to see you where we can talk."

"You, too, Dad. Sorry, I've been really busy the past few weeks with the big project for Stan and Stacey Conway's health food store. New computer system, website upgrade, the works."

"That's terrific. Other projects going well?"

"They are. In fact I'm thinking of asking Hank to come down from the Boston office for a few days to see if he might add some mental muscle. He's hired a talented manager, so he can get away for a few days. Plus, I think he's itching to see what we're up to in New York."

"Can't blame him for that."

Father and son strolled across the lawn and down to the water's edge where the bay lapped peacefully on the sandy shore of the small beach that formed along the curve of the O'Toole property.

They turned and gazed back at Tim's Tower.

"Quite a structure," commented Patrick.

"Did Tim give you the tour?" Brian asked with a knowing smile.

"He did, along with all the statistics a numbers man like me could possibly want. You, too, I imagine."

Brian nodded. "Did he take you inside?"

"He did. We even sat on the wooden platform for a few minutes. I could definitely feel something. Tim promised me more on my next visit."

"I'm surprised to see you and Mom out here today," said Brian.

"After the impromptu birthday party, your mother and I have been angling for another invitation so we could get a better idea of what all the excitement's about. Kevin has explained the basics, but being here in the tower—well, it's remarkable. Have you spent any time inside?"

"I have," said Brian. "Several weekends ago, Ivy and I were here with the whole group. It was, as you say, remarkable."

In the way of father and son approaching a difficult subject, they stood once more in silence, looking at the tower. Finally, Brian spoke.

"Dad, have you ever had—visions?" He hesitated to use the word, but out it came.

"You mean like otherworldly kinds of images or feelings?"

"Yeah."

"Well, the first one was the day I met your mother. But I guess that's not really what you're talking about, is it?"

"Not really. Besides, I've heard that story more than once."

Both men chuckled. Brian screwed up his courage and continued.

"I mean like feeling yourself lift out of your body, then seeing bright white light all around you and being greeted by a female figure who looks like a goddess and then she gives you a warning but doesn't stick around long enough to explain it."

Patrick stifled a laugh. His son sounded like young Kerry when the lad got excited about a complicated story he wanted to tell before somebody interrupted him.

"That's quite a mouthful."

Brian turned to face his father. "Do you think I'm crazy?"

Patrick put a hand on his son's shoulder. "No, and you don't think you're crazy either, do you? You believe what you saw."

Brian blew out a breath. He turned away, then back again.

"I do. I just wish I knew what it meant. What was that goddess trying to tell me? The scene was really beautiful, but I had a lot of questions. Then the whole thing ended and I was back in my body."

"Have you spoken to anybody else about your experience?"

"I haven't had the nerve."

"These are good people, Brian. The O'Toole's, Lucky, Kevin, your sister." Brian rolled his eyes.

"Okay, I know Sarah gives you a hard time. That's what older sisters are for. Believe me, your Aunt Millie taught me all about that. Anyway, these folks are obviously well-acquainted with matters not of this world. If you ever do feel like talking to them, I know you'll find a listening ear or several."

"Thanks, Dad. I'll think about it."

Both men looked up in time to see Eileen waving them in.

"Looks like the general is calling in her troops," said Patrick with a good-natured chuckle. His wife had a way of taking charge, no matter the circumstance. "I'd like to listen to Lucky's story. Are you up for that?"

"Yeah, I think I am," said Brian. He rested a hand on his father's shoulder and the two walked back to the house to join the others.

The peace of *Teach an tSolais* settled around Kevin like a cool breeze. He hadn't realized how the expectation of trying to fill Lucky's shoes weighed on him of late. That and the uncertain meaning of the nightmares he and Sarah had experienced.

Grateful to have no obligations this afternoon, he strolled around the property, observing the individuals he cherished and for whom he felt responsible. These were his friends, his family, his wife and children. The beloveds of his heart. He was reminded of how Ah-Lahn had loved the community of Tearmann. Here they were again.

What will the future hold in this age? he wondered as he watched them.

Phelan and Cyndi were collecting seeds and taking cuttings from plants which Maggie said they should add to their garden room.

Kevin was glad to see the Callahan men having the conversation he was sure they both needed.

Jeremy and Rory had joined Tim by the tower for another discourse on the harmonics of round towers based on paramagnetic qualities of the stone used to construct them.

Gareth and Naimh were already tired from their wobbly walk in the garden. When Sarah brought them inside for their nap, Kevin followed.

It warmed his heart to hear Eileen and Maggie chatting about topics as wide-ranging as food, faith and fairies. He chuckled to observe how much his mother-in-law resembled the ageless Mrs. O'Toole in mannerisms. They were both Irish to the core.

Kaitlyn and Kerry were sitting by the turf fire, deep in conversation with Lucky. The affection between the three was palpable. Their body language suggested they spoke as equals and understood each other perfectly. Once Kaitlyn reached up and patted Lucky on the cheek, as if to relieve him of some burden.

The only vignette that gave Kevin pause was the image of Debbie and Glenna. They were seated in a corner away from the others. Their heads were close together with brows furrowed and they were speaking in purposefully low tones. *Some concern there,* Kevin noted.

He started to walk over to the women, but then Eileen began calling everyone inside while Maggie ushered Kerry and Kaitlyn to a back room to watch a movie about *The Little Prince.*

Kevin promised himself that he would speak to Debbie tomorrow to find out what was amiss.

Meeting the Master

"Make yourselves comfortable, *a chairde*," said Lucky as everyone was finding their seats. He smiled broadly at the full house of friends who had gathered on this bright Sunday afternoon.

"Are my little redheads settled with their movie?" he asked Maggie.

"They are. And Sarah's twins were tired enough to stay asleep for a good, long nap," she replied.

"So you'll have to do with us old folks," quipped Patrick.

Lucky nodded. "And it's glad I am that you're all here. 'Tis a treat to have everyone with me for today's story, which is an important one. I owe you more about Róisín and me to bring us up to the present. Next week we'll be heading into the distant past that many of you were part of."

Lucky leaned back in his chair and picked up the thread from last week's story.

As I was telling you, Róisín and I met in Limerick after the death of her abusive husband and her little son, Tómas. And though in a bold move to introduce myself I'd offered to help her and her parents, I hadn't seen or heard from her for eighteen months.

When I did, the reconnection was still there. We married as soon as we were able and she moved into my small flat above the bookstore.

Now that was a cozy arrangement. As we owned no more than a few clothes and even fewer material possessions, we did just fine. You see, we were saving our money to go to America.

We were ambitious to make something of our lives. We longed to serve people in a bigger way than Limerick seemed to offer.

We often prayed to *An Síoraí*, the Eternal One, for guidance. We were both big on signs. But, as I had learned from Father Kenneally, they had a way of not showing up if you looked too hard. So, our work became our prayer.

We stocked a wide range of books—some new, mostly used—and we made a point of knowing what every book was about. When someone came in to browse, we'd ask them, 'What is the most important thing to you in your life? What do you value the most?'

You see, we didn't ask what kind of book they were looking for. Half the time, they didn't know themselves. They'd come in hoping the book would find them.

When we learned what they valued above all other things, we'd hand them a book that spoke to their heart in a way they most likely wouldn't have found unless it jumped off the shelf. I've seen that happen in special cases. Our job was to aid in the jumping so folks felt a bit of magic in the connection.

Afore too long, we gained a reputation for being real helpful in all manner of life's most trying circumstances and even in its celebrations.

Róisín got the idea that we should serve tea for an hour or two in the mornings. Pretty soon we had a store full of people. They were talking about books and buying books. They were talking about life and helping each other with their problems. A regular community of intelligent, thoughtful, compassionate people was forming all around us.

In a very short time we needed a bigger store. As good fortune would have it, our little shop was only half of what had been a larger enterprise. I'd never known it, but there was an old door between two halves of that building. It had been blocked by a heavy bookshelf that hadn't been moved since I'd worked there.

One day, Róisín said to me, 'We need to move that shelf. The answer to our problem is behind it.'

I got a couple of lads to help. We moved books and the huge shelf and, sure enough, there was a door and what looked like a false wall. The business next door had folded some time in the past. Upon inquiry, the landlord said we could rent it for a song.

That doubled our space and gave Róisín room to set up a proper tea and coffee service along one wall. It took some days to clean and repair and move stock around. And, you know, our customers all pitched in like it was their store as much as ours.

Many of them said they felt that Róisín's Bookstore and Tea Shop—for that is what we renamed the business—they said they felt that Róisín's was their home away from home.

Ah, 'twas grand, I tell you. We had such fun in those days. We almost forgot about our dream of emigrating to the USA. We were fulfilling the other part of our desire to help people by giving them a place to help each other through simple human kindness. Then something happened to once more set our sights on the West.

Lucky paused to drink some tea.

An especially bright sunbeam flowed in through the French doors, illuminating the living room where the Companions were enthralled with his description of how their own community had begun in Ireland. Their eager expressions urged him to continue.

Late one Sunday afternoon, on a day much like today, we were closing up shop when a gentleman walked in. He was dressed in the fine woolen trousers, waistcoat and tweed sports jacket that distinguished him as a man of some means.

His leather shoes were those of a well-prepared traveler who'd been strolling around town. He carried a walking stick and, immediately upon entering, took off his dark green felt hat.

He appeared to be in his prime, probably in his mid-forties. He wore his light brown hair longish. His beard and mustache of the same hue were well-trimmed. Such features were notable, but there were two more that arrested our attention.

His eyes, which might have been mistaken for a light blue, were actually violet. On his right hand he wore a gold ring with a large amethyst stone set with diamonds and rubies.

I was more than a bit discomposed by the unusual nature of his appearance, so I was not as hospitable as I might have been.

'I am sorry, sir,' I said. 'We're about to close, but could we help you find something in the next few minutes?' I was very tired and really did want my tea and an early night.

Then Róisín touched my arm. 'Ask him,' she said—meaning I should ask the man our standard question.

'Forgive my manners, sir,' I corrected myself. 'Please have a seat and a cup of tea.' I was surprised to see that Róisín had made a fresh pot. She said later she'd been prompted. So she poured us each a cup and we three sat together like old friends.

Feeling myself relax, I began again.

'If you will permit me, sir, we have a question we like to ask all our first-time guests.' I could hardly call him a customer. The man radiated an air of such refined gentility that one was inspired to treat him with great respect.

'I will be happy to answer,' he said in a voice that rang of music and magic.

'What is the most important thing to you in this world?' I asked. 'What do you value most in your life?'

Never in all the months that Róisín and I had been asking that question did we receive such an answer. The man closed his eyes for a moment then opened them with a faraway gaze. Here is what he said:

'Ah, my friends, you have touched the heart of the matter that all people of good will should ask themselves if they are to live productive and generous lives: *What do I value most?*

'Many will speak of their families, their friends, their faith. If they are rural folk—especially here in Ireland where ownership of land has been at the center of strife for centuries—they will wax poetic about their few acres or their tiny garden plot in the city.

'Those with affection for Nature's many creatures will speak fondly of their sheep and pigs. You can still identify the Celts by their love of cattle, which for many remains the measure of their wealth.

''Tis perhaps surprising how few list their abundance of possessions or financial wealth as being most dear. Although we may surmise that those who do so would not be sitting with us in your charming establishment.'

The man's violet eyes twinkled as he said this.

'As you may note, I have thought deeply about the subject of value, because to answer the question is to venture to the core of one's being. I have long pondered what motivates me above all other qualities or essences that flow through my veins and what I cherish most deeply in those friends I meet in my travels.

'Therefore, my answer is a single word that illumines a complexity of manifestations. That word is *Freedom*.

'Above all other qualities of life and being, I value freedom. And where I find true freedom most profoundly expressed is in the soul of a person who is at liberty to do the work he or she was born for.

'The soul that is free is the soul who is allowed to give its gifts to the world. For in that offering, creativeness is sparked and a sense of co-creativity with *An Síoraí*, the Eternal One, is born.

'A soul who is deeply immersed in its reason for being is free from all sense of limitation. Time collapses into the present moment and space expands as a universe of opportunity that lives in the individual's heart of hearts.

'The rarely told truth of freedom is that it cannot be denied to a soul who understands its immortality. Though death and forces of evil minds may breathe their foul breath on such a soul, in the final hour that one will rise on wings of angels, alive forevermore, eternally free.'

At some point in his discourse, the man had risen to his feet and was now standing behind his chair. His violet eyes sparkled in the waning afternoon sunshine. Later Róisín and I agreed that his aura had been ablaze with waves of violet, purple and golden light.

For several minutes we simply sat and gazed at him. We felt ourselves enveloped in a radiance that lifted our own souls into a profound experience of the freedom he had spoken about so passionately.

At last he smiled and resumed his seat.

'Thank you, friends, for the opportunity to speak from my heart. In a moment I will have a question for you. But first, I have been remiss in not introducing myself. F. M. Bellamarre, at your service.'

He handed us each a calling card printed on fine ivory stock. Embossed in dark purple ink was his name, followed by the letters A. M. C.

'I do not recognize your credentials, sir,' I said.

'Please call me F. M. All my friends do, and I assure you that we have been and will be again the dearest of friends. To answer your inquiry, I am Alchemist, Master of Community. You will not be surprised to know that the vibrant gatherings you have created here have drawn me to you. Together, you both have passed an important initiation, which allows me to pose my own question.'

We both nodded eagerly.

'How soon can you leave for America?' he said as naturally as if he were asking for another cup of tea.

If you've ever wondered at the expression, 'knock me over with a feather,' that was Róisín and me.

F. M. continued. 'To come to the point, I have need of you in New York. If you are prepared to sell your business, I have a buyer with cash in hand—one of your community, as it happens.

'A good friend of mine, who lives in a charming area of Long Island, owns an esoteric bookshop. He is nearing retirement and wishes to bequeath his stock of unusual books to someone who will appreciate the unique quality of his collection. He will be pleased to sponsor your emigration from your homeland.

'I will provide you with other details. The question is: Are you ready for the adventure of many lifetimes? If so, my friends, I can accommodate you.'

Well, I don't have to tell you that Róisín and I were ready in two very compact weeks. Cash in hand. Bags packed. I think we had only one bag each. We already had passports, so we were on our way. We took the bus to Shannon Airport. Next stop: JFK in the USA.

Friends of F. M.'s met us at the airport in New York and got us set up in a comfortable apartment on Long Island. Before we knew it, we were working for the old fellow we only ever knew as Joshua at his shop called Fibonacci's.

And that's how we all came to be sitting here today. The rest of the story belongs to you, *a chairde.*

As a single body, the Circle of Close Companions leapt to their feet. They were clapping joyfully. Their eyes glistened and were more than a little moist as they encircled Lucky in a group hug that no one felt silly about—not even Brian.

Suspicions

The minute Kevin entered the coffee shop at Fibonacci's on Monday morning, Debbie hurried over and hooked her arm through his.

"Won't you step into my office?" she grinned, repeating the joke they shared about the magical qualities of the back booth. Then she added more seriously, "If you hadn't stopped by, I was going to track you down."

Kevin knew she was trying to keep her tone light, but her worried expression said otherwise. "What's going on, Debbie? I saw that same furrowed brow on your face and Glenna's on Sunday. Is she okay? Her pregnancy's still going smoothly?"

"Yes and no."

Kevin looked puzzled.

"Yes, Glenna is doing great. In fact, I can just hear Róisín saying, 'That lass was born to have babies.'" Debbie smiled. "She's doing fine now."

"But she wasn't?" Kevin prompted her to elaborate.

"No, and that's what I need to talk to you about. On Sunday Glenna pulled me aside and started speaking in a low voice. Here's what she said:"

Debbie, I don't want to be an alarmist, but I think there's something going on at Conway's Health Food Store that you should know about.

A couple of days ago I went in to pick up some more of the special herbal pregnancy blend you and Cyndi recommended. I didn't see it on the shelf, so I asked Stacey about it.

'Oh, we're not carrying that any longer,' she said. 'I'm creating my own line of remedies now. You should take this one.'

She handed me a packet of her mixture. I don't remember

what she called it, except *Pregnancy Support*. I noticed that I started feeling kind of queasy, but that still happens if I've been overdoing. I had run more than a few errands that morning.

Stacey was very pleasant. Wished me well with the baby. Said she was making lots of improvements to her product lines. Encouraged me to let her know if I needed anything. That sort of thing.

When I got home, I was unusually tired and decided to lie down for a while. After a few minutes I felt better and remembered that I hadn't taken the remedy. I poured a glass of juice and pulled the packet out of the bag it was still in. I opened it to stir in some of the powder, like I've always done.

The minute I did, such a wave of nausea hit me, I had to grab the counter to steady myself. I picked up the packet again and—I'm not kidding, Debbie—I heard a loud voice shout, 'No!'

I don't know if it was my inner guidance or the soul of my baby. Anyway, the warning was so loud, I immediately threw the packet into the garbage and went back to bed.

That's where Rory found me when he came home for lunch. When I told him what happened, he was ready to storm over to the store and give Stacey an earful of strong Irish displeasure. I asked him not to until I'd had a chance to speak to you or Cyndi. Once he'd fed me some broth and made sure I really was okay, he agreed—though I've never seen him so upset.

"This isn't good," said Kevin.

"No, it isn't," said Debbie, "but I'm not sure what steps to take. I can't blame Glenna for throwing the packet away, though I wish she hadn't. Cyndi and I could have sent it to our lab for analysis. We've always worked with a compounding pharmacy to make sure our blends are safe."

She continued. "Kevin, I don't want to wait on something like this—until one of Cyndi's former customers or a new customer actually gets sick. Realistically, though, there's nothing much we can do, is there?"

"Not at the moment. Not unless Glenna wants to complain directly to Stacey. As the affected customer, she's the only one who could say anything right now."

"I wouldn't ask her to do that," said Debbie. "You and I know that our Glenna is more sensitive than many."

"Agreed. Rory would have our hides if we put her in that position." Kevin paused and looked away, thinking.

"It is troubling that this has come up. Only last week, Jeremy and I were talking about the strange atmosphere he sensed in the health food store, though nothing was obviously amiss. We agreed that the situation is tricky because Conways are the business owners. They rent space from Brian. We have no say in how they operate their store."

Debbie nodded. "I know Cyndi had to sell so she and Phelan could buy Lucky's house and come to work here. Still, I wish circumstances had been different."

"I agree," said Kevin. "But unless Stan and Stacey are breaking the law or not abiding by their contract, we'll just have to watch and wait to see if anyone else from our community reports being adversely affected."

"You're right," said Debbie. "It does deeply concern me to think that Stacey's inexperience—and for now I'm willing to call it inexperience—could actually harm somebody, especially a pregnant woman. In the meantime, I've asked Cyndi to make up some of her remedy for Glenna. I hesitated to tell her why. Still, she needs to be aware of the situation."

"Yes, she does," said Kevin. "I'll have a word with Brian. He and Ivy are working closely with the Conways on their big computer project. I won't ask him to intervene, but he also needs to be aware that there are ripples in the Fibonacci forcefield. Again, it's mostly watch and wait."

As it happened, they did not have long to wait. Later that morning, one of the more outspoken members of the community—a woman named Lynn—marched into the coffee shop with her obviously pregnant daughter, Haley, in tow. She stomped over to the coffee bar where Debbie and Cyndi were chatting amiably between customers.

"I want a word with you two," said Lynn in a voice that carried across the room. She flung a partially opened packet of herbal powder labeled *Pregnancy Support* on the counter and declared, "What do you have to say about this?"

Debbie and Cyndi stared at the label and blanched. It looked exactly like the packaging they had developed for their store, "Conroy's to Your Health." Now it read "Conway's."

"Lynn, I am terribly sorry you had a bad experience," said Debbie, not reacting to the woman's accusatory tone. "Actually, there is an explanation. As you see, the label says Conway's not Conroy's. However, I can tell we have a bigger issue here."

"We do, indeed," said Lynn, refusing to be placated. "This stuff made my daughter sick."

Haley was standing behind her mother where she could mouth the words, "I'm sorry," to the two women at the counter.

Debbie took the cue. "Lynn and Haley, will you have a seat and some tea? Cyndi and I would like to hear exactly what happened."

"I told you what happened," Lynn insisted. "These herbs made her sick to her stomach and she hasn't had that problem for several weeks."

"Mom, come on," Haley pleaded. "This isn't their fault."

"Well, maybe not," grumbled Lynn, "but I still want to know what they're going to do about it."

Debbie signaled to the baristas on duty to take over serving at the counter. She ushered the two women to a table away from other customers while her sister brought over mugs, a pot of tea and a plate of muffins.

"Can you tell us about your experience?" Cyndi asked as she sat and poured the tea. When Lynn started to speak again, Haley deftly stopped her with a firm hand on her mother's shoulder.

"I'll tell them, Mom. Although it was Sunday afternoon, I knew the health food store would be open. My husband's out of town and I was bored, so I drove over to buy one of the neonatal remedies Glenna had told me about. She swears by Cyndi's herbal blends. The store was really busy, so I just searched around the shelves marked PREGNANCY, found the blend I was looking for, paid and left."

"Tell them how you felt driving home," Lynn insisted.

Haley looked up at the ceiling and sighed.

"Okay, Mom. On the way back to the apartment where I live with my husband, I had stopped for a red light and this wave of...I don't know..." She waved a hand in front of her face.

"A wave of negative energy," Lynn supplied.

"Yes, a wave of what I guess you could call negative energy came over me. It was really fast. I mean, it had stopped by the time the light turned green. But I did decide to rest when I got home. I think I actually took a nap. Once I felt better, I poured a glass of juice, like Glenna said she always does, and stirred in a teaspoon of the powder."

"Tell them how you felt then, Haley."

Debbie noticed that the calming tea Cyndi had served didn't seem to be having the desired affect on Lynn.

"Mother!" said an exasperated Haley. "I'm getting to that. Okay, so I didn't notice anything at first. Then after about two minutes, my stomach started cramping. I ran to the bathroom because I felt like I was going to throw up."

"Did you?" asked Cyndi, truly concerned.

"I did. And it really frightened me. I didn't have my cell phone handy, so I sat gripping the toilet until the nausea passed."

Lynn took over the conversation again. "She did finally call me. By the time I got to her she was as weak as the baby she's carrying, but otherwise she seemed fine. I wanted to drive right over here and demand why you two were peddling dangerous herbs, but Haley said to wait until today. So here we are."

"And we're very glad you are," said Debbie sincerely. "What would you like us to do for you?"

"I want you to tell that woman to stop selling that product." Lynn slapped the table in front of her.

Debbie reached over and touched her hand calmly. "You see, Lynn, since we don't own the store, we can't actually do that. But you and Haley can register a complaint, which I feel certain Stacey will graciously accept."

"She was always a loyal employee when she worked for me," added Cyndi. "I'm sure this was just a mistake on her part." Debbie caught her sister's eye and nodded to the packet that was sitting in the center of the table, encouraging her to continue.

"Are you going to return the product for a refund?"

"You can bet we are," said Lynn with emphasis.

"As you are more than entitled to do," Debbie agreed. "Would you mind if we kept a small sample? We'd like our lab to test the blend to see if we can determine what caused Haley's body to react so violently. We don't need more than a half teaspoon."

"Keep as much as you like," said Haley. "I don't even want to touch the bag we brought it in. Mom, we should go now." She turned to Debbie and Cyndi. "Thanks for listening to us."

"We're always here for our community," said Debbie as mother and daughter prepared to leave. "Please let us know if you have any more concerns. And good luck with your baby. I forgot to ask, when are you due?"

"February 14," Haley said with the glow of pending motherhood. "I'm going to have a little Valentine."

"Same as Glenna," commented Cyndi. "Good for you."

"Come on, Haley," said Lynn. "I'm still going to tell that woman what I think of her merchandise."

As soon as the two women had left the coffee shop, Debbie carefully tipped the sample of herbal powder into a plastic baggy. "I'm taking this to the lab right now," she said, "and then I'm going to talk to Kevin and Jeremy. We may not have results for a couple of days, but when we do, I think we may have to take action."

"You'd better be careful." Stan pulled Stacey into the back room and was only moderately successful at lowering his voice. He closed the door, but Ivy could still hear them arguing from her station at the cash register.

"Don't you go after me, too, Stan Conway," Stacey snarled back at him. "There's nothing wrong with my herbs. I've read all about them and I watched Cyndi for enough months to know what I'm doing. That woman just wanted her money back, even though they'd used more than half of the powder. Her daughter looked fine to me."

"Just the same, I don't want any trouble here," growled Stan. "The last thing we need is those Fibonacci's people snooping around or asking questions. It's bad enough that Ivy works here."

Stacey glowered at her husband. She liked Ivy, even if the woman did manage to look stunning just showing up for work.

"While we're on the subject," Stan barreled on, "I think it's time you got rid of her. Hasn't she learned enough about your new products for whatever the web designer needs?"

Stacey threw up her hands. "If you say so. You're the boss."

"Don't you forget it. I've got bigger deals coming to a head and I don't need Brian's little wife seeing things she shouldn't. I'm getting ready to make the big pitch to him and I don't want any interference."

Stan always knew he'd gone too far when Stacey's aura started throwing off sparks of red and orange. She could be dangerous and he needed her on his side. He reached over and pulled her to him. She resisted at first, then snuggled into his embrace.

"I'm sorry, Sugar," he crooned. "You know I didn't mean to blame you. You're doing a great job and I really mean that. Will you forgive your mean old husband for being cranky?"

"Of course, Sugar," she cooed back at him. "Now go to your meeting and make a million dollars. Your mean old wife wants a new car."

They both laughed, forgetting that Ivy was standing on the other side of a very thin door.

The Pitch

At half past noon, Stan Conway strode into Brian Callahan's office like the man he was—self-assured, keen of mind, sharp of wit and without an honest bone in his body.

Brian didn't know that, of course. Perhaps, far back in his mind the recollection of his vision of the goddess's warning from that day in Tim's Tower might have made him wonder if she had referred to Stan. But that fragment of a signal never reached Brian's outer awareness. All he saw when Stan Conway swaggered over to his desk and sat down was a man he genuinely liked.

They could talk business like colleagues. There was an easy, unspoken understanding between them that Brian had never been able to share with his brother-in-law, Kevin, or with Jeremy, who handled the finances for the New York branch of Callahan & Logan Computer Systems.

He supposed the difference was the fact that he wasn't really part of their Circle of Close Companions. He liked all of them. But when it came right down to it, he and Ivy were outsiders. Their children fit in with these people, but he and his wife didn't.

On the other hand, Stan seemed to grasp the complexities of what he was asking Brian's company to achieve for him, and that was pleasing. Most clients were oblivious to the hundreds of hours required to implement an integrated inventory and cash-flow system that interfaced seamlessly with a company's website.

"If you approve the fine points of our scope of work, we can move directly into the first phase of implementation," Brian explained to Stan as the two stood side by side at the long worktable in the Callahan office. "We have secured all of the components. We need only your final okay."

"You have it," said Stan. "Everything looks very professional. If your team can produce what you've got here on paper, I'll know for sure they're worth the money I'm paying you."

"That's why you hire the best." Brian stood to his full his six-foot-three height and rolled up the plans.

"Yes, indeed." Stan looked at his watch. "Hey, it's later than I thought. Have you had lunch?"

"No. My morning was back to back."

"Then let me treat you to a fine meal. To celebrate what promises to be a very productive working relationship."

Stan was glowing with enthusiasm. Brian caught his mood. He readily agreed and buzzed his secretary.

"Sandy, I'll be out for a couple of hours. Please take messages till I get back....Okay, thanks."

The afternoon shone like one of those clear September days that made New Yorkers forget there could ever be oppressively humid heat, blasts of cold northeasterly winds or the occasional hurricane. Today was a day for miracles. Brian could feel it in his bones.

Stan appeared to be of the same mind. Simply enjoying the weather, the two men walked four blocks to the local five-star hotel whose gourmet restaurant was famous across Long Island. The doorman ushered them into a lobby that glinted with money and power.

"Not the kind of place where I usually pop in for lunch," Brian remarked. He had rubbed elbows with plenty of high-powered attorneys in his day, but they had never taken him to lunch like this.

"What good is life if you can't splurge once in a while?" Stan smiled broadly as he stuffed a bill into the *mâitre d's* hand in acknowledgement of the excellent table where the man seated them.

"What'll you have to drink?" he asked when the waiter appeared. "Make mine Scotch on the rocks with a twist. Brian? I know you don't usually drink. Maybe just this once?"

Brian did hesitate, but not for long.

"Well, since we're celebrating—glass of Pinot Grigio."

"Good man."

When the waiter returned with their drinks, Stan ordered lunch for them both. "We'll have two of the chef's specials. Okay with you, Brian?"

"Sure." He couldn't remember ever being treated so grandly. It wasn't only the wine that was going to his head.

Throughout the meal of excellent veal parmigiana, Stan told stories of some of his other successful business ventures. The man loved making money, that was obvious. He appeared to have considerable skill in doing so—which caught Brian off-guard when Stan mentioned over gourmet coffee and cheesecake that he was running a little short. He hoped that Callahan & Logan Computer Services could extend the payment schedule they had previously agreed upon.

"Sorry to burden you with what I assure you is merely a temporary set-back in my cash flow," Stan said in his most apologetic tone.

"Well, this is a surprise," said Brian, "especially considering the very expensive lunch we've just enjoyed."

"Oh, that's nothing," said Stan, brightening. "The hotel owner and I go way back. I've brought him a lot of business over the years so he welcomes me as his guest. I don't take advantage, of course. Only for very special occasions."

"That's good to hear." Brian paused, mentally tallying the status of his own cash flow. "The problem is, Stan, my business is running very close to the bone right now. Buying the Fibonacci's building was a major outlay, not to mention all the remodeling and new construction costs. Besides those expenses, I've hired a couple of extra programmers to handle the main requirements of your job.

"Truth be told, our Boston branch is carrying the financial load right now. As long as both of our businesses continue to do well, we expect to pay down some of our debt fairly soon. I'm sure you realize that we were counting on your contract to speed that process along."

Stan folded his hands under his chin and looked down at the table, which the waiter had now cleared, except for refilling the men's coffee cups. Anyone observing the businessman might have been forgiven for believing he prayed.

After a full minute, he raised his head and focused his dark brown eyes on Brian's blue ones. "I was afraid that might be the case. Let me assure you again that I will do everything in my power to see that you are not negatively impacted by my temporary difficulties. In fact, I believe I have a solution."

"I'll be glad to hear it," said Brian, slipping into the calm negotiating mode that had served him well in the past.

"I was hoping you would say that." Stan leaned across the table. "Here's the situation: I have been doing business with some close associates who, for the time being, shall remain anonymous. I know I don't have to explain the need for confidentiality in delicate financial transactions."

"Naturally," Brian agreed, wondering, *Where was Stan going with this?*

"Excellent. Part of the delicacy is that my associates do have money to invest. Unfortunately, because of my current difficulties, they are not willing to back my health food store enterprise. It's really a matter of them not understanding that market. Their position is firm, although I explained that once we get the new computer system and website operational, we'll be able to do mail order as well as in-store retail, which will more than double our sales."

"That's impressive," said Brian. "But how does that help either of us in the short term?"

"See, that's why I like working with you," Stan nodded appreciatively. "You go right to the heart of the matter. Here's the solution: My associates are willing to pay you directly on my behalf, as a way of buying into my business. A sort of insurance policy, they said."

"How would that work?"

"They will open a checking account at their local bank in the name of Callahan & Logan Computer Systems with you as the account owner. You will invoice me regularly, preferably at the end of each week. I will pass on the invoice to them and they will deposit that amount in the account for you to draw out to pay your expenses."

"That seems like a lot of extra paperwork." Brian didn't see the logic. "Why don't they just pay you so you can pay me?"

"Well, you see, that's the unfortunate thing about our relationship. Some years back we had a silly disagreement. At the time, they declared they would never do business with me again. Since then, bygones have become bygones, but the trust we once enjoyed has not been completely reestablished. This is a way for us to do exactly that. And you can help in healing an otherwise very solid relationship."

Brian paused briefly, then explained, "I'll have to check with Kevin and Jeremy and my business partner, Hank, before I can agree. Kevin and I have taken over from Lucky O'Connor as co-owners of the Fibonacci's building. Hank and I are co-owners of Callahan & Logan Computer Systems. Jeremy handles my company finances. So you see, I'm not the only decision-maker. I'm sure you understand."

"Oh, I do," Stan said, opening his arms in an expansive gesture. "That is the tricky thing about being in business with family and close friends. I had an uncle once—great guy—but he always seemed to get in the way of my financial decisions. I finally had to let him go."

He looked searching at Brian.

"You see, the current problem is that my associates don't know any of you. I've never dealt with your other partners, so I can only vouch for you. My associates have made it clear that the only way they'll consider this arrangement is if the money goes directly to you."

"I see," said Brian. This was one of the toughest negotiations he had ever dealt with. He took in a deep breath and blew it out. "You've put me in a considerable bind here, Stan. I've already invested time and money in salaries, new hardware and software. If I don't get paid, I'm likely to default on my loans."

"We certainly don't want that to happen," said Stan. His tone was very sympathetic. "Why don't you sleep on it—confidentially, of course—and let me know in the next couple of days what you decide."

He waited a beat then continued.

"And while we're discussing financial matters, I expect you already have a couple of invoices for me."

"As a matter of fact, I do." Brian pulled an envelope from his jacket pocket and held it out like an offering. "I was hoping you could take care of these today."

Stan eagerly took the envelope and put it in his own breast pocket.

"Excellent. I'll forward these to my associates. They can literally have money in the bank in three days."

Stan checked his watch and stood up from the table.

"Sorry to rush off now, Brian. I need to get to my next appointment. Let me know what you decide. I realize this may be a lot to consider. But you won't regret it, I assure you."

Brian also stood and extended his hand. Stan took it in both of his and looked his new partner in the eye, nodding knowingly.

"Okay, then," said Brian, doing his best to sound more confident than he felt. "Thanks for the fine meal. I'll be in touch."

"How did it go over lunch?" Stacey asked Stan when he returned to the health food store.

"You've heard the old cliché: 'Like shooting fish in a barrel'?"

"That easy?"

"That easy. Do you have the cash I promised them? They'll be here at three o'clock."

"In your locked desk drawer. Same as always."

"Good girl."

Stan Conway gave his wife a massive hug and strode back to his office to count his money.

Family Secrets

Henry Wadsworth Logan (aka Hank) had decided to drive to Long Island. He would need his own car to get around and he hoped to see some of the Manhattan sights he hadn't visited since he was a boy.

He'd spent Friday night in Cambridge with his parents—the folks who loved all things poetical, especially Longfellow. Hence his own name. The couple always wondered what gene pool had spawned their technically inclined son. But the three of them got along well because they'd made a point of learning from each other. A rare quality.

Truth be told, he rather liked his birth name—as long as people called him Hank. He appreciated the connection with the famous poet that Cambridge claimed as its favorite son. Sure, he was more a technician than a poet. Still, he did have his soft side. He just kept it tucked away most of the time so his peers would take him seriously.

Hank could have reached Brian and Ivy Callahan's home in less than five hours. Instead, he decided to extend his journey and prolong the welcome solitude and quiet by taking back roads, avoiding the interstate highways as much as possible.

September was his favorite time of year for a road trip and he needed the break. Today was Saturday, so he would miss the urban commuter rush. That added ease to his plan.

As he headed west toward Marlborough, he was reminded that he'd always considered the lush forests and farmlands of Western Massachusetts, Connecticut and New York as some of America's most beautiful countryside. He was a city boy at heart and knew he would go stir-crazy if forced into a rural lifestyle. For today, though, taking his time through the

Berkshires, along landscapes beginning to turn the golds and crimsons of autumn, he felt the balm his soul had longed for.

Now that Hank was alone, he could admit to another longing. He missed Bri and Vee—their nicknames from the old days. He missed hanging out with them at their home in New Bedford, same as when they were in college. They'd been solid friends in those days when he and Brian—two young, ambitious computer wizards—had started a small company in their dorm room. Hiring Ivy had been a stroke of genius.

Thinking back in time as he bypassed Worcester, Hank remembered how his life had seemed complete when he realized he was in love with Ivy. And how that life had suddenly crashed when Brian moved into her apartment.

For a few days he'd questioned if he should walk away from the whole situation. But Bri, and especially Vee, had been good to him, including him in their lives. They seemed unaware that they had broken his heart.

He'd finally stitched up that heart, told himself not to be foolish and got down to business. With the three of them working together, the company they created had taken off like wildfire and none of them ever looked back.

Until recently, Hank realized. Of course, he held out no expectation of anything changing. Bri and Vee were parents now—to the twins he was eager to see again. No, this trip was only for an extended visit and to check out the Long Island branch of Callahan & Logan Computer Systems.

After all, he was a partner, though he'd never had the time or the help to leave Boston for more than a day. Now that he'd hired a terrific manager named Dev, he was free to breathe some new air.

Bri and Vee had insisted that he stay in their spare bedroom so the three of them could talk shop into the wee hours if they wanted. And Brian's parents had suggested that Hank might want to spend a few nights with them if the constant activity of a household with two vigorous seven-year-olds started to crowd him—since he'd always been single.

That circumstance was a puzzle, especially to Brian's mother. Why a tall, strong, well-built, thirty-something man with a thatch of dark blond hair and a poet's deep brown eyes had escaped matrimony was a mystery that Eileen Callahan intended to solve.

She had already decided that Hank should join the Callahan family of Massachusetts transplants on Long Island. Finding him a suitable mate would be the perfect incentive to keep him among them. To fill that need, there were a number of attractive young women among the growing Friends of Ancient Wisdom community that gathered at Fibonacci's.

Of course, Hank was not to know of her plans. For now, that would be her secret.

The object of Eileen's plotting decided on another detour that took him into the Mount Washington State Forest. He would be later than planned for lunch in Rhinebeck Village. But the peace of walking even a portion of a well-groomed trail along a rushing mountain stream through a red oak forest would be worth it.

Yes, he mused, as he ambled along, not minding how far he walked, he would definitely spend time with Eileen and Patrick Callahan. They had always opened their home to him, like a second set of parents. And he looked forward to seeing Brian's sister, Sarah.

When Brian had gone to live with Ivy, Hank had imagined that he and Sarah might become an item. Then she'd moved to New York, met Kevin and that was that. So be it. He missed all of them. And realized more than he'd admitted to himself that he needed to be with them.

As he got back on the road, Hank wondered what Brian would think of his idea. If they sold the Boston branch, they could concentrate all of their efforts in New York. There must be plenty of work in the Big Apple. And they could pay down some of the debt they had agreed Brian could incur to finance purchasing and remodeling the Fibonacci's block.

The secret he'd barely told himself, and that he had carefully kept from Brian, was that he was weary of Boston. Hank was ready to expand his own horizons.

A plan began to form in his mind that he hadn't dared to entertain before. Now it seemed so logical, so all-around practical, that he couldn't imagine why he'd never had the courage to tell Brian the truth. But then, success in life and business was all about timing, wasn't it? What could be more perfect than to take bold action right now?

He couldn't wait to tell Bri and Vee his idea.

As soon as he reached Rhinebeck, he texted both of their cell phones to say he would be there around six o'clock. He hoped that wasn't too late. Ivy answered that his timing was perfect. She would hold dinner until he arrived.

Brian's was the next secret that soon would come to light. He'd made up his mind that same Saturday morning. *Nothing ventured, nothing gained,* he'd told himself. Despite figuring and re-figuring for the whole of the past week, he had finally seen no other way forward. He'd always done business by the book. This deal with Stan's associates was just a slightly different book. That's all.

He'd thought about talking to Hank, but he knew his partner really liked running the original location of their business. Though still the best of friends, they liked the autonomy the distance between Boston and New York gave them.

The truth was that Brian was afraid. And sometimes fear makes you do things you shouldn't—like leaping before you've asked for the help that is right in front of you.

He went for a walk so Ivy wouldn't hear him making the call that would change everything. Stopping by the bay where it was quiet, he rang Stan's cell and found him at home. The man expressed no surprise that Brian was going ahead with the deal.

"You'll have the checkbook in hand and money in the bank by next Tuesday," Stan promised. Then gushing over the luck that was arranging everything the way he'd planned, he enthused, "Great doing business with you, my friend. See you next week."

Brian wished he could feel the same. Still, he was relieved to have these details settled before Hank arrived. He'd been on edge all week. Now he could relax and enjoy his partner's company.

Hank was another person who understood how business operates. Stan would like him. Brian briefly considered introducing the two, but then thought better of it. Too much going on to muddy the waters.

"Uncle Hank!" Kerry and Kaitlyn practically bowled him over the minute he came through the door. Their mother had promised them a surprise that would arrive around dinner time and, wheedle her as they might, she would not divulge a single clue. Now they knew why.

"How did you guys get so big?" Hank asked, bending down to where he could talk to them. They loved that about him. When they were really little they would crawl up on his lap. Now he looked around for a chair where he could meet them eye to eye.

"We took our vitamins," Kerry explained.

"And we get lots of fresh air and exercise," Kaitlyn announced with the authority she'd learned from a nutritionist's podcast her mother had been listening to.

Before Hank could find a place to sit, they took him by the hand and insisted on giving him a tour of their rooms where they could show him their treasures and share some secrets. They also wanted to know if he could see the spirit beings that were their friends—though they had to be discrete about asking. That's why they were taking him to their rooms.

"Hi, Vee! Hi Bri!" he called back over his shoulder as the twins led him away like a cherished captive. "We'll be back soon—I hope."

The parents stood with arms around each other's waist and smiled at the departing trio. Such was life with Kerry and Kaitlyn.

Dinner could wait a little longer.

Hank's Proposal

The three friends did talk through dinner and late into the evening—long after the twins had been reluctantly tucked into bed with promises of more Uncle Hank time tomorrow.

Hank thought Brian and Ivy looked tired, even a bit distracted, though the stories and memories they shared cheered them all. He figured he probably looked tired as well. Everybody needed a break.

Ivy said 'Good night' at ten o'clock. The twins were early risers, no matter the day. The two men finally retired at twelve.

The next morning—Sunday—they went to Fibonacci's after a lazy breakfast so Hank could be given the grand tour and meet the people who were making their businesses a success.

Brian had invited everybody to meet at Róisín's Coffee Shop for introductions. Kevin and Sarah came with Gareth and Naimh. The O'Donnells, the Maddens and the MacGraths all arrived in fine form and took Hank to their hearts as one of the family.

They had such a fine time showing Hank around and telling stories that they all stayed for a light lunch. Debbie and Cyndi managed to pull together a reasonable meal from the various wraps and the day's soup which they had begun offering now that the weather was turning cooler.

Soon it was time for the group to be leaving for the O'Tooles'.

"Ivy, why don't you come with us?" Sarah urged her sister-in-law.

"Thanks, but the twins and I are going to the beach."

"Can Uncle Hank come with us?" asked Kaitlyn.

"No, sweetheart," Brian explained. "Daddy and Uncle Hank have business to discuss. We need you to keep Mommy company."

The timing was Brian's idea. He and Hank were due to review the financials for Boston. He knew that was Ivy's least favorite part of the enterprise and said so.

"Are you trying to get rid of me?" she asked with a flirtatious grin.

"Never." Brian leaned over and kissed her on the cheek.

Hank barely stopped himself from blurting out, "If he ever does, I'll take care of you." He didn't say it, but he thought it.

"Nice digs," Hank commented as Brian opened the door to his office on the second floor of the Fibonacci's building where Callahan & Logan Computer Systems was located.

"I spend a lot of time here," said Brian. "I wanted it to be comfortable and well-furnished so that high-powered executives like my business partner would be impressed." He grinned.

"Mission accomplished." Hank nodded appreciatively and sat in one of two side chairs in a conversation area. He gathered up his courage as Brian retrieved bottles of mineral water from a small refrigerator and took the other seat.

"This is great, Bri. I hope you'll think what I'm about to propose is equally great. So I don't lose my nerve, I'll get right to the point. Please let me finish before you say anything."

"Okay. The floor is yours."

Hank took a deep breath and leaned toward his partner and friend.

"We've had a solid run in Boston and I've really enjoyed operating that part of the business since you moved here. But, frankly, I'm feeling stale. What would you think about our selling the Boston branch and my moving here to Long Island so we could concentrate all our efforts in New York?"

Brian couldn't have spoken if he'd wanted to, so Hank continued.

"I need a change, Bri, and I miss you guys. The friendship has always been as important as making money. Besides, with the cash influx from selling Boston, we could easily pay down some of the Fibonacci's debt I know you've been concerned about. What do you think?"

Hank expected his old friend to be surprised, but he didn't expect him to look like he'd been punched between the eyes. Brian bolted up from his chair and started pacing around the office.

"Good God, man," exclaimed Hank. "What's wrong? I've never seen you react to anything like this. What's happened to calm, collected master businessman Brian Callahan?"

The man turned and faced Hank. His eyes were stricken in a sort of wild combination of fear and grief. "I think he got lost in the weeds and forgot to talk to his real partners," he said wearily.

Hank didn't know what to say. He started with the obvious.

"Well, I'm here now. Do we need to retrieve Ivy from the beach?"

"No, I want to leave her out of this."

"Then sit down and tell your best friend what's going on."

"You're not going to like it."

"Tough."

Twenty minutes later, both men were stone silent. Brian was shocked to hear himself tell his friend what he'd decided to do—only that morning. Hank was shocked that his business partner hadn't trusted him enough to ask his advice.

"You know what this sounds like?" he said, hoping to bridge the gulf that could swallow them if they didn't act. "Money laundering."

Brian's hand went to his mouth. He'd been standing and pacing while he related the exact sequence of events. Now he sat and ran his hand through his hair for the dozenth time.

"God, you're right. How could I be such an idiot not to see that?"

"As your best friend, I have to agree. But I can't blame you. Under the circumstances, I might have done the same thing. You never know."

"Actually, I don't think you would have," said Brian. "Between the two of us, you've always been the better man."

"Yeah, well you were more innovative. Let's postpone campfire songs for now and figure out our next steps. We should probably contact your attorneys first thing in the morning. If this is what we think it is, we need to be sure you and the businesses are safe."

"Definitely." Brian was relieved to have the situation at least out in the open, if not resolved.

Hank was still thinking. "The main question is: Can you get out of this deal? Did you sign anything in writing about the bank account?"

Brian smiled grimly. "No. I don't think money launderers write up contracts stating how many thousands of dollars they're going to shift around to make dirty money look clean. The only agreement I've made with Stan about getting the company's invoices paid was verbal."

"Good." Hank nodded. "And just to confirm, you haven't received that checkbook, which means you haven't written any checks, right?"

"Right. The last thing Stan told me was that I'd get the checkbook on Tuesday. That gives us through tomorrow to put a stop to whatever scheme his so-called 'associates' are putting place."

Both men were silent until Hank had an idea.

"Do you suppose you could get Stan to come here tomorrow, maybe late morning, for a meeting with both of us?"

"Probably. I'll tell him I'd like him to meet my partner—a man who also understands what it means to be a real businessman. He'll like that. He enjoys showing off. I'll make it sound very causal, friendly."

"Let's hope we can keep it that way."

"No kidding."

Brian checked his watch. Late afternoon was fading into early evening and dinner time. "Ivy and the kiddos will probably be home by now. We should get back."

He looked at Hank, who was drilling him with the purposeful look he remembered. "We should tell Ivy, shouldn't we?

"Yeah, but how much?"

"Let's just see how the conversation goes. I don't want to worry her. But if we're in trouble, she'll be furious if we've kept her in the dark."

They both rose to return to the Callahans' home. Brian turned back to his friend.

"Hank?"

"Yeah?"

"You really are the better man."

"Whatever you say, boss."

When they walked through the back door into the kitchen, Ivy was busy preparing dinner for the adults. Kerry and Kaitlyn were already eating their favorite mac and cheese. As soon as their father and adopted uncle sat down at the table, their faces brightened. They didn't have to be asked to give a report on their beach experience.

"We built a big sand castle and then a gynormous wave came in and carried it off," Kerry said with appropriate hand gestures to demonstrate the watery destruction.

"We found a sand dollar and pretty shells. See?" Kaitlyn held out her small hand to show the men her still slightly sandy treasures.

"We had ice cream, but not too much so we didn't spoil our appetites for dinner," added Kerry. To prove his point, he finished his sizable bowl of what he called "cheesy noodles" and took a large swallow of milk.

"That sounds like lots of fun," said Hank appreciatively. "Did you see any whales?"

"We did, but they weren't very close to the shore today," explained Kaitlyn.

Kerry almost said, "We did see undines playing in the water," but he caught himself and managed instead, "We saw lots of seagulls and little birds with tiny legs."

Brian surprised his wife by offering to help her, something he rarely did. "Vee, is it bath time for the kids? Hank and I can finish dinner if you want to get them ready for bed."

"Really? Wow." Then she turned a suspicious eye on Hank. "Where did you pick up this stranger? You left with my husband. I'm not sure I recognize this man."

"Oh, just my positive influence. Isn't it early for bath time?"

"It's way too early," Kaitlyn protested. "Besides, Mommy made us take a bath when we got home to wash off the beach."

"We could watch a movie with Uncle Hank," Kerry proposed.

"Okay, but only a short one and then it's off to bed," agreed Ivy with a laugh at her friend. "Maybe you can convince Uncle Hank to tuck you in when the movie is over. Remember teeth brushing."

"Yay!" The twins climbed out of their booster seats and hurried off to the family room.

"I don't mind, Vee," Hank assured a bewildered Ivy. "Besides, Brian needs to talk to you."

"I do? Or, right. Yeah, I do."

"That's good," said Ivy as she put the casserole she'd been assembling in the oven, "because I need to talk to you."

Hank left the room with a knowing look at Brian. He hoped this conversation would go well.

"Lady's first."

Ivy took at seat at the kitchen table adjacent to Brian and sat up straight in her chair.

"Here's the thing, Bri: I don't want to work at the health food store any longer and I don't think you should be dealing with Stan. There. I wasn't going to blurt out that last part, but that's how I feel."

"You don't? Why?"

"It's hard to explain, really. The place is starting to give me the creeps."

"Go on."

"Well, during the first shift I worked there, these three men came in wearing dark glasses and suits and carrying briefcases. Stacey and Stan had an argument about that and then they went to the back room with Stan. I didn't see them leave."

"Did they do anything they shouldn't?"

"Not really. Except that one of them leered at me and another one kept watching the front door like he didn't want to be seen in the store. And there's more. The other day a woman stormed in with her pregnant daughter demanding her money back because one of Stacey's herbal blends made the daughter sick. The Conways argued about that, too. I guess they thought I couldn't hear them, but I did."

"What did they say?"

"Something about not wanting 'those Fibonacci people' snooping around and asking questions."

"Anything else?"

"Yes, and I guess I should have told you about all of this. Soon after I started helping out, Stacey expressed an interest in meeting the twins. So one Saturday I took them to the store to see where I was working."

"That sounds okay."

"Well, it wasn't. Almost as soon as we entered, they both freaked. They drew back and looked more frightened than I've ever seen them. Kaitlyn clung to me like she was about to be eaten by a monster and neither of them would look at Stacey. Kerry murmured 'hello,' but that was it."

"I wish you'd told me. Did they describe what they saw?"

"No, and they made me promise not to tell you because they didn't want to talk about it. As soon as we got home, they went to Kaitlyn's room and started talking to each other. A little while later they came out and they seemed totally fine. I didn't think much more about it until I started feeling weird vibes from Stacey. And, frankly, from some of the new merchandise she's carrying."

Ivy reached across and took Brian's hand. "I don't want to go back there, Bri. I wish you didn't have to do any work for them. I know we need the money, but..."

"Don't worry, Vee." Brian squeezed her hand. "I think we may both be off the hook."

"Really? How?"

"Well, Hank thinks we should sell the Boston branch so he can move to Long Island and help us concentrate on building the business in New York. Then we wouldn't need Stan's contract."

"What a relief." Ivy looked at her husband. She hadn't noticed the shadows under his eyes until now. "There's something else, isn't there?"

Brian closed his eyes for a minute and took a deep breath.

"Yeah, there is. You have no idea what a relief this actually is. You see, earlier this week Stan told me that he was having financial troubles, which meant that he might not be able to pay for the work we've already done on his big project."

"That's weird. He always acts like he's rolling in cash."

"I think he is, Vee, and that's the problem. The bottom line is that he floated this idea about some unnamed associates of his who would pay our company's invoices for him. They were going to set up a bank account in my name that I would use to pay related expenses."

"Brian!" Ivy interrupted him. "That's money laundering."

"I know that now. I'm an idiot not to have spotted the con. I was desperate and I didn't know what to do. Stan knew I was in a tight financial spot and used it to trap me."

Ivy sat back in her chair. "I can't very well say, 'You should have told me,' can I?"

"No, but I should have told somebody. Hank got here just in time. No money has changed hands, so that's good."

"What are you going to do? What if Stan is running some kind of illegal operation on Fibonacci's property?"

"Hank and I have a plan. Tomorrow we're calling my attorneys for their advice and we're having lunch with Stan to see if we can ease out of the whole computer contract." Brian blew out a breath. "When are you scheduled to work at the store again?"

"Tuesday. I was taking tomorrow off while Hank was here."

"Good. Then your working there should be a moot point."

"Bri, I do have one question: Have you told Kevin or Jeremy?"

"No. This all happened fast and I convinced myself the situation was strictly a Callahan & Logan Computer Systems problem. Let's see what happens tomorrow and I promise I'll talk to them."

They were holding hands across the table when Hank returned. "Something smells good," he said, eagerly inhaling the aroma of casserole. "I'm mighty hungry after being on twins duty."

Ivy and Brian turned to him. Their expressions said what he wanted to know.

"You told her?"

"Everything."

"And I'm on board with both of you," Ivy assured them.

"Good," said Hank as he joined them at the table. "When do we eat?"

Part Three

Poignant Recollections

Prologue to the Past

Nearly the autumn equinox, Lucky remarked to himself as he prepared for the day's story session. *Another season of transitions. How many more will I experience?* he wondered.

He was pondering his next recollection. This one was going to be tough to tell. He'd nearly postponed the session, but then decided that cowardice would get him nowhere. He had awakened that morning with such a pain in his chest he thought he might be having a heart attack.

Of course, he knew he wasn't. He was fit as a flea. This was only his resistance to urging from his precious friends, all in spirit now, who had always insisted that he take the adept's solo path up the mountain of being.

All of the twin flames couples who had been at Fibonacci's that morning were chatting gaily to each other about how delighted they were to meet Hank. Not until they were seated and finally looked in the direction of their beloved *seanchaí* did the expression on Lucky's face halt their conversation mid-sentence.

"*Beannachtaí daoibh, a chairde,*" said Lucky with an expression of love and longing that nearly broke their hearts. Was he departing today?

"No, my dears," he said, reading their minds. "I'm not yet bound for *Tír na n'Óg.* We have some centuries to traverse together first, and I fear these may be the most difficult stories for you to witness. And witness is what we shall be doing this afternoon.

"Although I've pondered for many days how to bring you into these recollections, I find myself not entirely sure of the best way to begin. So I will first tell you how I myself began to recall the challenging lifetime that my outer mind had refused to remember.

"You won't be surprised when I tell you it was Róisín herself who said I must go deep into my soul to retrieve an understanding of why I am the joyful man I've been in this life. And why I had been so different in a previous one.

"Kevin, lad, you asked if I could tell you why Old Quin was such a tough disciplinarian and why you felt that he singled you out for his most exacting lessons. Today's story will answer the first of your questions, but not the second. That insight may come later. More than that I cannot tell you—except to say that we must complete this story today. There are forces at work that we cannot forestall."

Lucky breathed in to gather himself and sighed a sigh so deep that his listeners could feel it emanating from the farthest reaches of his soul. He finished the cup of tea Maggie had placed on the table beside him, settled into his chair and began.

You might call this the Prologue, as the actual past-life story comes later. But we must begin here because this is one of the miracles of my life with Róisín.

You see, in those early days of our marriage her gift of clairvoyance was already highly developed. She'd had second sight since she was a child and her grandparents on her mother's side had given her many years of training during her visits at their farm.

After her little boy died, she went to stay with them—to heal and to receive the kind of instruction that only advanced adepts receive. Not all of this was from her grandparents. Still, they provided the setting for that training to be given.

Almost from our first conversations and, to be sure, from the first days of our marriage, she began teaching me prayers and mantras and practices meant to open my inner sight in a way it hadn't been in this life. Of course, I'd had many flashes of past lives and insights into the workings of my soul, but they'd been like glimmers, dreams, occasional visions—nothing that lasted.

Right away our practices intensified and I could actually feel a resistance in my being, as if a memory was sitting back stage in a big theatre and I was preventing it from taking center stage in my awareness.

'There are things I don't want to remember, Róisín,' I said to her in protest.

'Then, *mo chroí*, those are the memories that are most vital to your soul. We'll not force them to consciousness, but neither must you block them when their time arrives.'

We let the matter rest and I faithfully did my prayers so that my outer mind was not an obstacle to my soul or to the mission that Róisín and I had together. For she'd been very clear that our being married in this life was the key for many other souls.

I believe she could see your faces, *a chairde,* even though many of you weren't yet born into this life.

One Monday morning in late September—the day of the week when our bookshop on Long Island was closed—we were finishing our coffee after breakfast when Róisín spoke my name with great tenderness.

'Lúcháir,' she said, as she focused her deep emerald eyes on me. 'Have you ever experienced a full past-life review?'

I answered that I did not think I'd had such an experience. She raised her eyebrows and smiled at me, ''Tis not one you would easily forget.' That was all she said until later that day.

As afternoon was melting into twilight, she took my hand and led me to the living room of the cozy cottage where we lived at the time. She lit a fire in the fireplace. The flames appeared un-usually lively, throwing off sparks of many colors.

We sat together on the loveseat that served as our sofa, facing the fire. Róisín turned to me and said simply, '*Mo chroí*, the time has come. Are you ready to remember?'

Without hesitation, I answered, 'I am.'

"That is the end of the Prologue, *a chairde*, though 'tis only the beginning of the story. For what happened next was the real thing—a full life review.

"The other stories I've told you have been elaborations on events that I've remembered from this life. What I'm about to share with you is the life review itself, exactly as it happened. You see, these experiences can be recreated from the Book of Life—the imperishable records of akasha—when circumstances allow and when our Master sponsors them, which he is doing for us today."

Eight pairs of eyes were wide in amazement, excitement and for some, a certain amount of trepidation. Lucky read their meaning.

"There is nothing to fear in what we are going to share. Maggie and Tim are here to invoke light energy and protection around us. When you feel your souls lifting out of your bodies, have no concern. Our trusty guardians will make sure everyone comes back to full consciousness and in one piece."

"That we will," said Tim reassuringly, and Maggie added, "We won't leave you for a minute."

Lucky continued. "First, I'll ask you to move your chairs so you're each facing our lovely turf fire. Once you're situated, we'll close our eyes and sound the OM together, as we've done many times.

"When I bring the chant to a close, open your eyes and focus on the flames. By then they will be dancing like orbs of colorful light. When one of them beckons to you, take a breath and step in. In the moments that follow, you will experience this life review exactly as I did."

Lucky paused and let his gaze rest lovingly on each one of these souls who were about to witness the most transformational events of his many past lives.

"Your questions are welcome, if you have any," he said.

Phelan reached for Cyndi's hand to reassure her. Having worked as assistant to F. M. Bellamarre, he had experienced a couple of personal life reviews. He was eager to attend one of another person.

Sarah spoke confidently to her friends. "I know many of you have gone through your own life reviews. I'm sure this will be similar. What I want to say is that, for several years, Kevin and I have used this orb technique of stepping out of our physical bodies and into our soul bodies. It definitely works and you will feel no ill effect."

"Let the story carry you," added Kevin. "Treasure awaits in the orb."

To seal their mutual resolve, each spouse looked into the eyes of their twin flame. When they felt themselves in contact with the soul essence of their beloved, they turned to Lucky with a nod that said they were ready to experience this profoundly personal life review.

"Very well, then," he said. He took several deep breaths to center his consciousness in his heart. Feeling the presence of inner courage he knew he would need for this session, he began intoning the word that would carry his Close Companions into scenes of the most pivotal embodiment of his many lives.

"OMMMMM."

The group continued the chant for several minutes until they noticed Lucky drawing it to a close. As each one was directed from within, they opened their eyes and beheld a veritable Christmas tree of dancing orbs.

Rather like cherished pets drawing close to a favorite human, each orb seemed to choose one of the company as its own. Maggie and Tim heard the couples take a deep breath together, like a choir preparing to sing, and their soul bodies disappeared into the light of their individual orbs.

The Best of Friends

Fourteen-year-old Quin raced away from the hazel grove where he had spent several hours memorizing the next stanzas of the ancient laws that the *ard mháistir* had presented. The tide was turning, which meant the ship bearing his friend and the lad's uncle should be arriving soon.

Quin knew their route to the Isles of the West by heart. They would sail the length of the Mediterranean, through the Straits of Gibraltar, across open water to avoid the treacherous Bay of Biscay, north to the southern shores of Albion, around the island's westerly tip, up the wide Bristol Channel to the River Parrett—and then up the River Brue to the marshy waterways that surrounded Ynys Witrin.

On the few occasions when Quin had sailed back from Éire after visiting his family, he would have taken a similar route once his boat crossed the *Muir Éireann*. He had always wondered what it would be like to travel around the world. His friend Racham had told him stories from when, as a small boy, he had accompanied his mother's uncle on several voyages. Now that the two lads were older, Quin hoped to hear tales of grander adventures.

Over the past five years, during the time that Quin had been studying at the renowned druid university at Ynys Witrin, the boys had met twice. ("Racham means 'friend' in my language," the lad had explained on their first meeting.) Their common interests and like-mindedness had forged a strong bond that contained no small amount of humor.

Quin was a serious student who rigorously applied himself to learning the vast sweep of mystical and practical knowledge that was communicated orally. Anyone embarking on the path to become a master druid knew that he or she could expect to complete a course of no less than twenty years to gain proficiency.

One day Racham had come upon his friend when Quin was working out a particularly difficult passage. In moments of deep concentration, the lad had a habit of furrowing his brow so intently that Racham could not help but laugh.

"You look like one of the ancients, Quin. All you need is an elder's long white beard and no one will suspect you of being a student. I think I shall call you 'Old Quin' from now on."

The nickname had stuck. Even some instructors began addressing their young and very capable student as if he were one of their age. Years later Quin would wonder if Racham had known that life's circumstances would make him old before his time.

With no such worries on his mind, Quin was buoyed by the morning that had dawned bright and warm. The sun was high in the sky, sparkling on broad patches of water, tipping the thick marsh grasses with flashes of gold and silver.

He convinced himself not to stop to watch the many species of water-fowl feeding. He did hesitate once to gaze at the giant cormorant which his rapid pace had startled into flight. He was usually quiet along the footpath in case a stately heron or snowy egret was standing still in the shallows, watching for its next meal.

Quin promised himself he would bring Racham here to talk while they watched for beaver and playful otters to surface. But not today.

Skirting the farmlands where cattle grazed placidly in the distance, he noticed how tall the crops of wheat and barley were growing. The summer weather had been fair so far, promising a good harvest.

When he came to the base of the *Cnoc Glas,* the very tall hill that dominated the landscape, he quickened his pace and made straight for the shore of a smaller hill that came to be called Wyrrall, where the river had carved a natural landing place and a wooden dock had been built.

There he sat and waited, turning his body to the right, his eyes search-ing the western horizon for the sails that would signal the arrival of the ship owned by Racham's great-uncle known by the title *Nobilis Decurio.*

As minister of mines for the Roman government and a distinguished

Roman citizen, he had acquired enormous wealth in the tin and lead trade. He often disembarked at Ynys Witrin, which was a primary transfer point for the ore that was produced by the mines he oversaw in the Mendip Hills located half a day's walk to the north.

For many years, the Decurio had been trading with Rome, Phoenicia and the Levant, where he was a leading member of an elite religious order. He was held in high esteem by all who knew him. Here at the spiritual center of Ynys Witrin, he was especially well-respected by the druids with whom he shared many beliefs and practices.

Some said that he himself had studied at their universities as a youth, as did the sons of many top Roman families. Now his nephew could do the same—even as that young man was steeped in the Mosaic scriptures and mystical teachings of his homeland.

The traditions had much in common, as Quin had discovered early in his acquaintance with Racham. That commonality strengthened the bond of friendship between them. 'Twas a connection that would have profound consequences.

In fact, the Decurio, his niece and her son had family ties with the druids through their shared ancestry that reached far back into antiquity. Like these great mystics of the Isles of the West, the Decurio understood the interrelatedness of all mystery teachings whose essence pointed to the soul's ability to make direct spiritual contact with its divine source.

Part of his success in trade was his ability to speak to the soul of anyone he met—not as a manipulation, but as his sincere dedication to the truth that lived in the heart of every person born of the Divine. It was this truth that he emphasized to his nephew in their travels—and that he would live to see that magnificent soul embody and proclaim for all time.

In light of the Decurio's character, his personal connections with the area of Ynys Witrin in particular and his vast knowledge of topics material as well as spiritual, the local warrior nobility—the renowned Silurians—always welcomed him warmly. So did the workers who gathered ore from stream beds and cliff sides to be smelted into ingots for transport in the merchant's vast fleet of ships.

Racham dearly loved his uncle. Quin came to do the same.

At last, sails billowed into view and the ship anchored in the river's deep water. The young man stood and watched as a smaller boat was launched. Yes! Being brought ashore were Racham and the Decurio.

Eager beyond words, Quin stilled his heart as he had learned in one of his earliest lessons as a neophyte student of the ancient mysteries that had been taught by the druids for over two thousand years. As soon as the boat docked, he held out a hand first to the Decurio and then to his nephew.

Although a crowd had gathered to welcome the travelers, these three stood alone for a brief moment, exchanging the double-handshake of friendship. Then the Decurio strode across the landing platform to greet the delegation of senior druids and high-ranking Silurian nobility who had come to pay their respects.

The two youths—boys no longer—stood silently in shared admiration of the impressive company of leaders assembled before them. Nobility was the word that came to mind. There was a magnificence of body, heart, mind and spirit that radiated from the auras of these men and women. Most particularly from the Decurio himself.

As the assembly made their way to the village where formal discussions about trade and what the Romans were plotting would proceed, Quin felt himself profoundly moved. Racham sensed his friend's emotion and guided him in another direction.

"Let us walk on," he suggested. "Uncle will be in conversation for many hours. He and I will find each other at our lodging in the village."

As they walked, Quin's mood lightened. Stopping a moment, he looked at his friend with mock appraisal. "You are as tall as I am, though I believe I can still out-wrestle you."

They both laughed. Indeed, the youths appeared equal in vitality, though Quin was one year older.

Racham's stature spoke to the carpenter's trade he was learning from his father and from his growing ability as a sailor. Quin's training also involved extensive physical exercise. The university curriculum at Ynys Witrin included what some might consider the Greek ideal of a strong mind in a strong body. Of course, the druids knew they had established the principle long before the Greeks thought of it.

In silence, the two friends walked some distance from the landing until they reached a broad, flat area half way between Wyrrall Hill and *Cnoc Glas*. Racham stopped and looked around, slowly turning in a circle as if analyzing the view.

"Yes," he said, "this is the location Uncle told me about. It will do."

"For what?" asked Quin.

"I want to build an altar, a small tabernacle for my mother."

"Did she come with you?"

"No, but one day Uncle will bring her to Ynys Witrin. I want a sacred place I have built with my own hands to be prepared for her. While I am here for the next few months, I will use the tabernacle myself."

"How soon do you expect your mother to arrive?"

Racham turned away from Quin and stood gazing out to the west where the river met the sea. "Not for some time yet," he said softly, as if his grey eyes saw far into the future.

The mood passed and he turned back to his companion.

"Come, Old Quin. I will tell you about my plans. You are familiar with the area and building techniques your people use. Will you help me create my mother's tabernacle?"

"Gladly. I imagine that places of worship in our watery land are very different from your home in the desert."

"Very different," Racham agreed, "although our essential spiritual teachings originate from the same ancient sources. What we know in our hearts flows from a fount of wisdom that was known in Atlantis and Egypt and that illumined glorious golden ages of the past."

"Yes. I often sense the antiquity of certain words as I repeat them in my lessons. I can feel them reaching far back in time, as if the esoteric knowledge that has been collected here at my university came from the very foundation of the world."

Racham nodded in acknowledgement.

"As we build together, perhaps you can recite for me the latest histories you have memorized. I confess that I have fallen behind in my druidic studies since Uncle and I were last here at Ynys Witrin."

"You know I will be speaking the vernacular of our oral tradition."

"Do not worry. I will understand you," Racham assured him. "I have not forgotten the language used at Ynys Witrin Besides, words convey only a fraction of the meaning of ancient wisdom. Vibration carries all."

For the next ten weeks, Quin and Racham worked together, creating the small tabernacle which they would use and that would be in place for the young man's mother, whenever she might travel to Ynys Witrin.

Quin was amazed at Racham's dexterity as he worked with wattle. The materials obeyed his hands as if he'd been weaving willow and hazel branches all his life.

"Wood contains life force, even when no longer attached to its source tree," he said, stating a truth of which Quin was already aware. Druids cherished the oak, hazel, beech, alder and hawthorn trees that formed their groves. Each species of tree and plant held esoteric meaning. Many furnished medicines and remedies that had been used for centuries.

Still, he found it fascinating to watch Racham measure and cut and assemble with a carpenter's skill. His friend built with an eye keenly attuned to beauty as well as function.

Soon Quin was not the only local youth who gathered to help build and to talk. Some entertained the others with songs and tales of ancient Celtic lore. All found themselves enthralled with the stories Racham told them about his life in the Levant and travels with his uncle.

He also shared knowledge of Rome he had learned from the Decurio, "Though I fear we may come to grief from them one day," he said so quietly that none but Quin heard.

As the warm summer air began to hint of autumn and the changing weather that could make sea travel perilous, work slowed. It was almost as if the young people resisted completing the building, lest it hasten the departure of the friend they all agreed was the most remarkable person they had ever met.

On the day the merchant ship anchored in the river's deep channel and a small boat lay peacefully tied to the landing dock, they knew the time for farewells had come.

As the stately friends of *Nobilis Decurio* assembled by the shore to bid him safe journey and speedy return, Racham pulled his friend aside and laid a well-bronzed hand on his shoulder.

"Old Quin," he began with a gentle smile, "I am going away now."

"I understand. I console myself with the knowledge that we will have rich conversations when you return. Perhaps you will bring your mother on your next visit."

"That is possible, though I will not return for many years. You see, old friend, my next course of study calls me to the Far East. There are vast deserts to cross, long rivers to navigate and majestic mountains to climb before I begin the mission that is mine to fulfill."

Quin looked into his friend's deep grey eyes. Their expression was inscrutable.

"Never fear," Racham continued. "I will return. Perhaps only once more. But, ah, what stories I shall have to tell you!"

"Then fare well and be safe." Quin suddenly found speech difficult and struggled to swallow the emotion that had lodged in his throat.

His companion in the ancient mysteries appeared to have the same problem with his throat. Finally, Racham managed a smile.

"Study hard, lad. Perhaps you will fall in love while I am away."

They shook the double handshake of friendship and said not another word as the Decurio and his nephew boarded the small boat that carried them back to their ship and a sixteen-year separation that was filled with adventures and many lessons for Quin and Racham.

Flavia

When you're young, sixteen years can seem like an eternity. Yet as Quin matured, he found time speeding up, as if the sun had risen and set before he'd accomplished all that he had planned upon waking that morning. The passing years held many important life events. The most significant being his acceptance as a master druid.

To earn that status, he had been studying and serving at Ynys Witrin in Albion for over twenty years. Once or twice he had sailed across the *Muir Éireann* to visit his family in the *túath* of Tearmann. While there this past year, he had included an excursion to Cois Abhann to meet with Óengus, head of the Brigantes druids.

Though less than a decade older than Quin, Óengus had demonstrated extraordinary skill for one of his age and had been unanimously elected *ard mháistir* by the combined druid councils of this large tribe. He was now establishing his own school following the model of Ynys Môn, the illustrious university where he had studied.

The two men had felt an instant kinship.

"I hope you will return to Éire," Óengus urged. "We need you here."

"I am beginning to understand that my life as a master druid is not my own," said Quin. "Only *An Síoraí*, the Eternal One, knows for certain where life will take me. For now, my heart lies in Albion."

"Aye, the lass with flaxen hair and soft blue eyes," chuckled the *ard mháistir* with a knowing grin. "Bring her home with you," he urged. "We always welcome royalty, you know."

"That I do," Quin nodded, "though she may not agree, even with your generous invitation. The future has yet to reveal itself."

Though he had a strong desire to remain in Albion, he also knew that much was expected of him. He had grown up with an equally strong sense of duty to his family in Éire. They had served as *ceann-druí* to the Brigantes chieftains of Tearmann for generations. Truth be told, he secretly hoped that his heritage would lend him the necessary gravitas to be nominated by the Druid Council and then selected by Ard-Mháistir Óengus to follow his family lineage when the time came.

Perhaps such distinction would convince Flavia to return with him to Éire. Still, as Quin sailed back to Albion and the sweet companionship of the young Silurian noblewoman he hoped to wed, his mind turned to the events surrounding the difficult circumstances of their relationship.

The Silurians took their status seriously, for they were the dominant tribe in the southwest of Albion. In Éire the head of a clan was called *Rí*, which meant not quite a king, yet more than a petty tribal chieftain. On the other hand, a Silurian leader was considered a king and was addressed as such.

This was the family of the beautiful lass with the flaxen hair and soft blue eyes with whom Quin had had the misfortune to fall in love. *Yes*, he reflected, *my feelings for Flavia carried all the markings of misfortune.*

Their connection had been instantaneous and just as swiftly opposed.

The girl's father—a lesser noble in the Silurian royal family—was possessive in the extreme. He had been older when the lass was born. Her siblings were all male and prodigious warriors, so the father expected that his daughter would look after him in his dotage. He was not ready to hang up his sword and shield just yet, but he knew that day would come.

His wife had died when Flavia was eight years old and the daughter had clung to her family, as was natural under the circumstances. That is, until she met Quin.

The young man was as dark-haired as Flavia was fair. His eyes were a much deeper blue. In fact, in later years, some would say of him that his eyes would grow darker than the ocean at midnight when he was in the throes of righteous indignation that could seize him when confronting the torturous brutalities that people inflicted upon each other out of greed or lust or inexplicable, unmitigated hatred.

As fate would have it, twelve-year-old Flavia had accompanied her father and other relatives to the landing at Wyrrall Hill to bid farewell to the *Nobilis Decurio* and his nephew. Her older cousins had been full of tales about these two exceptional individuals—the resplendent merchant and the lad named Racham whose kindness and wisdom had captivated people of all ages at Ynys Witrin.

Flavia had begged her father to bring her along so she might see what all the excitement was about. She was enthralled by the size of the ship and the number of sailors required to manage its sails and oars. The authoritative figure of the merchant did not disappoint. And she could well understand why her cousins had chattered on about the handsome nephew who carried himself with a dignity far beyond his thirteen years.

Accompanying the large assembly of well-wishers, Flavia had watched the dramatic scene of the ship's departure. However, she soon discovered a more riveting sight in the tall young druid who stood gazing after the ship as if part of himself were sailing out to the western horizon.

When her father became distracted by more senior members of the Silurian entourage, Flavia slipped away and approached the youth. Being of a naturally tender heart and a healer by instinct, she touched his arm.

"Are you sad because your friend has gone away?"

Quin started at her touch and turned at her gentle words. Their eyes met and souls swam into each other like twin tributaries flowing to a vast, ethereal sea. They simply could not speak. He placed his hand on hers and held it there. Time stood still. Heart locked into heart and lifetimes melted into a single moment of powerful recognition.

At last, he opened his mouth to form an answer to her question. But in that same instant Flavia's father noticed her absence. Striding over with swelled importance, he barked her name. She blinked as one recovering from a trance and whirled with an audible gasp at his expression of dark disapproval.

Quin still held her hand. She squeezed his and offered a faint, "I'm sorry." Hurrying back to her father, she followed in his powerful wake as he swept off to join their relatives who would return with them to their lands that lay close by to the north.

The youth hoped the lass would look back at him, but she did not. Although he could not hear the words the father was speaking to admonish his daughter, he was aware of the sentiment. It was well known that students at the Ynys Witrin university came from foreign lands or distant tribes. Upon completing their studies, they were likely to return home.

To this particular father's mind, no Silurian parent would allow his only daughter, his most precious child, to be carried off by a druid—no matter how grand an office the graduate in question might attain.

The underlying fact was that, unlike many Silurian leaders who were his superiors in rank and power, Flavia's father was jealous of the druids' hidden knowledge and mysterious abilities, as well as the Decurio's wealth and prestige among his kinfolk.

As Quin would learn later, for years the father had been sowing seeds of mistrust within his own extended family and others of similar opinions which, long after the man's death, resulted in terrible consequences for his daughter.

The ocean passage from Éire to Albion can provide many hours of reflection—or rumination, as the thirty-year-old Quin was now doing. With frustration, he was recalling how several years had passed without him catching more than an occasional glimpse of Flavia. Her father had made certain of her seclusion. However, as she matured and gained a modicum of independence, she and Quin had found ways to meet in secret—though all too infrequently as far as he was concerned.

He felt she did not try hard enough to discover or create opportunities for them to be together. In her mind, she was torn between duty to her father and the love for Quin that flooded her with emotions and memories of their shared past lives which she found almost impossible to contain—especially when she was with him.

In fact, it seemed the father had won. In the past two years, Flavia had all but disappeared from Quin's life. Her father instituted new obstacles to her visiting Ynys Witrin, while the maturing druid's duties increased.

Recalling these many scenes, Quin stood on the bow of the ship as it sailed around a westerly peninsula of Albion before entering the channel that would signal its final approach to the River Brue and his home at Ynys Witrin where he had lived for most of his life.

The sea was turbulent today, though not as rough as his initiations had been. He knew better than the neophyte students he had met on this voyage that becoming a master druid was not for the faint of heart, body or spirit. Advanced trials tested every fiber of an aspirant's constitution and resolve.

Perhaps most challenging were the days of silent meditation in darkened caves where food and water were brought only every other day by equally silent helpers. The purpose of these periods of isolation was to quicken and then heighten powers of clairvoyance and clairaudience, as well as the kinetic abilities that were some of the most secret of a master druid's powers.

Arcane chants handed down from the days of Atlantis and ancient Egypt had to be memorized along with knowledge of occult mysteries of the soul's origin and its destiny. Graduating druids were also expected to have mastered astronomy, arithmetic, geometry, medicine, law, poetry, natural philosophy and oratory.

All in all, as Quin returned to the rigors of his duties as a newly confirmed master druid, he admitted to himself that he would not have been available to wed Flavia, even if her father had relented.

Future Revealed

Quin had been back at Ynys Witrin for only a few weeks when, toward the end of the sixteen years which Racham had predicted, worlds turned. Flavia's father died. *Nobilis Decurio* returned. And Racham was with him.

As soon as the two friends had warmly greeted each other and settled the Decurio in his lodging, they set off to visit the tabernacle they had built together in what seemed ages in the past.

The structure was as fresh as the day it was completed. Interior and exterior wattle weavings had been refreshed and the thatched roof had been recently repaired. Racham's eyes filled as he stood and beheld the service he knew that Quin had done him.

"I had help," his friend explained. "None of us wanted to see it deteriorate. Wattle is highly perishable. We—mostly I—used it as a place to recite some of the prayers you taught us so its vibration would be familiar to you when you returned."

Racham could only nod and place his hand on Quin's shoulder. Reading each other's thoughts, the two robust men—one in his thirties, the other nearly that age—walked silently to the doorway of the tabernacle, entered and sat down on the hand-carved benches to pray.

Racham had always been exceptionally bright. In his previous visits to Ynys Witrin, he had enchanted the local young people with his wisdom and his humor. When discoursing with the elders, he had often asked questions or made statements about cosmic law that prompted even the most learned to pause and consider his unique perspective.

Today he was still himself—only more so.

For one thing, he was no longer a youth. A man of nearly thirty, he was fully grown into his mind and heart, as well as his taller body. People who could see such things observed an aura of radiance surrounding him that would change from waves of gold and white light into vibrant rays of other colors, depending on what he was doing.

He had become a powerful speaker—an obvious leader whose presence drew people of all ages and interests to him like iron to a magnet. Racham said that he planned to remain in Ynys Witrin for a year or longer while his uncle traveled about the country seeing to his mines and trade routes. Or, he had added quietly, until he was called home.

Quin was once again torn. He was elated that he and Flavia might finally be married. He wanted to spend as much time with her as possible. However, his inner guidance, which was very strong, said that he must focus his attention on his conversations with Racham—as if the days of their friendship were numbered and fleeting.

His friend agreed.

"Bring Flavia with you when the public gathers. I will be doing a lot of preaching when I return home. I want to practice here where people hold a favorable opinion of me. Such may not always be the case. You and your beloved will be together for these gatherings. Then you and I will hold our private conversations. I have much to share with you."

And so it was that Flavia and her Silurian cousins and many others from the surrounding areas flocked to hear Racham speak about *An Síoraí,* the Eternal One, and how the sublime wisdom of ages past was meant to be the guiding light in the age to come.

He spoke with deep respect for the druids and their teachings. He elaborated on some points while making even the most arcane concepts accessible to all. It was as if the words he uttered could be understood on many levels, according to the listener's receptivity.

Those who heard Racham hung on his every word. Many wanted to be like him.

Flavia's love for Quin grew with her devotion to her new teacher. Yet, while she blossomed like a flower in springtime, she maintained an odd emotional remove from Quin that he did not understand. Finally, one day he asked Racham about it. Did he understand this apparent reticence of his beloved, even as she declared her undying love for him?

"You and Flavia are soul of each other's soul, heart of each other's heart," replied his friend. "You were born of a single light and one day you will return to that light. But your paths to that destiny are not the same. I believe she may understand this better than you, Old Quin. More than that, I cannot tell you."

Though Quin was puzzled, he let the matter rest. When he did so, he observed Flavia becoming more relaxed. As he released a certain anxiety he had not realized he'd been holding, their togetherness took on a fluidity devoid of expectation and full of devotion. They would look back on these days as the best of their lives.

True to his word, Racham taught Quin, and those who were attracted to the deeper mysteries, about his travels in the Far East. His listeners often felt themselves lifted into realms of wisdom they had never before attained.

Where allowed, he shared with them much of what he had learned while studying with master rishis of India, the lamas of Tibet and mystery school lineage holders of Egypt. Most remarkable of all, he had found his own teacher, whom he referred to as "my Father."

"My Father was not physical," Racham explained. "He could be approached only in spirit and not by externally seeking. Only by becoming.

"Learn this of me," he continued. "Become as I am and we will never be apart. Seeking by human willing to fill an emptiness only pushes the true source of wholeness away. The Way is ever-present and can be as tangible as you see me with you in this moment. Walk the pathless path with me and no darkness will ever prevail against you. That is my Father's promise and my own."

One day, Quin felt compelled to seek out Racham. He found the man in his tabernacle. "I heard you call," he said simply. They had long ago established telepathic communication.

Racham stood. He looked at his companion with unusual gravity. His grey eyes were serious. "Come with me," he said.

Together they walked in silence across the lush green of the holy space around the tabernacle and entered the avenue of massive oak trees which had been planted in centuries past as a processional path that led to the summit of *Cnoc Glas.*

At the top was a *Gorsedd,* an elevated place used for extraordinary rituals and communion with exalted spiritual forces. The commanding three-hundred-sixty-degree view of the countryside was breathtaking.

The two men stood at the top, gazing and chanting a ritual to the Sun, turning around from east to west in imitation of the Sun's track around the Earth. As master astronomers, they knew that Earth was the planetary body which did the circling. Still, an ancient adoration of the spiritual Sun came alive in this ritual of cycles which they reverently performed.

When they had finished, they walked a few paces to the side of the hill to talk. Unfortunately, the wind had picked up from its usual briskness to a ferocity that buffeted them with a severity that felt almost mean.

Quin thought they might have to descend the hill for their conversation, but Racham stood firm. He seemed to grow taller as he faced into the wind that howled around him, whipping his robe and hair as if it meant to fling him from the slope he commanded. He raised his arms, palms facing outward. In a voice of such power and authority that Quin sank to his knees, Racham cried, "Peace! Be still!"

Immediately, the wind not only calmed, it stopped completely— which it never did atop the *Cnoc Glas.*

Racham turned back to where Quin remained immobilized by the miraculous sight he had just witnessed. The newly revealed master of the elements stretched out his hand and raised his friend to his feet.

"Hear me now, Old Quin," said Racham solemnly, "My time has come. You may not know that my human father died some time ago. For that and other reasons, I must return home."

"I am sorry to hear of this loss," said Quin with genuine affection. "Is your mother alone, then?"

"No, she has been living with my brothers. However, the Decurio, as younger brother of her deceased father, is her legal guardian. His trading duties have not allowed him to be with her until now. He is firm that we must hasten. I know that changes are also imminent in my own life."

Quin began to offer further condolences, but Racham stopped him. "Our ship sails tomorrow and I will not return. We will not see each other again in the physical, though I will always know where you are."

He touched Quin in the center of his brow, which sent a flash of light through the druid's third eye, opening his awareness in a manner not even his hours of silent meditation in darkened caves had accomplished.

"Now you will know where I am," Racham said simply. "The days to come will be difficult for you, Quin. This insight is the best answer that can be given to your request to go with me whenever I should leave here."

Indeed, Quin had declared his desire to accompany Racham to his home in the Levant. He hoped that Flavia's growing devotion to the man they and others called "Teacher" would convince her to go with them. He expected that at least his own request would be granted. His friend's saying otherwise caught Quin by surprise. He became uncharacteristically agitated and began to plead.

"Racham, please let me go with you. I can help you. I understand your teachings better than anyone here. You will need a friend, someone to look after your well-being. I can help explain your mission to those who do not understand. Have you not told me that many who will be drawn to you will not comprehend what you are telling them?"

Quin had raised his voice and was pacing, looking back at his friend for any sign of confirmation. Racham's grey eyes met his friend's blue ones, which were ablaze with emotion, but the man did not speak.

"You have said we have much in common. Is that not still true? I have studied my entire life for this moment. Please, Racham, my dearest friend, take me with you!"

The two men were standing now, face to face. In that moment, Quin swore he saw an almost unearthly light in Racham's eyes that pierced his heart. The intensity of the man's expression and the firmness of his words shook him to the core.

"Hear me, Quin, because this is the final teaching I can give you. You are correct. You have studied all your life for this moment, but not to go with me. You are needed in Éire. Urgently so. My ship sails tomorrow. Yours departs the following day."

Racham held up his hand to silence his friend. "No arguments, Quin.

Go home and tend your flock at Tearmann. That is your mission."

"And Flavia?" Quin choked as he said his beloved's name.

"She will remain here in Albion. Her duty lies with her family as they face the trials that will surely come upon them because of their courage. Love her for her obedience and your hearts will be forever joined."

Quin had never felt so wounded, so angry. His body was shaking. He had no thought in his mind except the sensation of being utterly and totally abandoned by those he loved most. Despite Racham's warning, he cried out like a child, "No! You need me!"

Racham took him by the shoulders, his grey eyes burning into Quin's desperate countenance. His voice was calm and firm as iron.

"Obey me in this, or you are not my friend."

Without another word, he turned and strode down the opposite side of *Cnoc Glas,* leaving Quin struggling to stand in the blast of cold wind that suddenly swirled around the *Gorsedd* with a strength unlike any he had ever felt.

Quin slept little that night. Anger, disappointment, shock—a thousand thoughts and emotions rushed through him as if he were still standing atop the *Cnoc Glas.* He could barely recall making his way back through the Avenue of the Oaks. He remembered hiding himself in his hut, knowing he dared not speak to anyone.

Throughout the night, as he thrashed on his sleeping mat, he vowed not to witness the departure of the merchant ship. But in the morning, after he had dozed for perhaps an hour, he realized that the tide would be turning. He ran to the dock only in time to see the great sails catch a stiff breeze and bear the ship and his dear friend away forever. Tears streamed down his face and he did not care who saw them.

Yet, as he stood, wretched in grief, he saw Racham's figure appear on the ship's bow. Even from a distance he felt the man's eyes meet his and in that moment he heard the familiar voice speak firmly into his heart, "Old Quin, my friend, never doubt that I love thee."

Simply No Words

The scene faded from view and the Circle of Close Companions blinked open their eyes, astonished to find themselves seated once more in Tim and Maggie O'Toole's living room where the turf fire had faded to the warm glow that makes peat such a comforting fuel.

No one spoke as Maggie served them a special tea meant to help them anchor back in their bodies. Although only two hours had elapsed in real time, they had traveled centuries. Such an experience tended to give one's soul the need to pause and catch up. While their bodies had been at rest, their souls had been on a rigorous journey.

"Sarah, darlin'," Lucky gently addressed his scribe. "Will you be able to recount all you've witnessed? This review holds much to remember."

"The scenes are emblazoned in my memory," she said gravely and reached out to touch his hand. "If I don't remember part of the story, I know Kevin will."

She turned to her husband and smiled. "We have some experience with remembering life reviews."

"We do," he agreed solemnly, as the Companions carefully returned their chairs to their original placement around the room.

As soon as they were settled, Lucky spoke again.

"I know you'll be wanting to know what happened to Old Quin. To be sure, there is more to the story, though I don't know when or how much I'll be able or allowed to share with you.

"What I can tell you is that Quin did set sail for Éire the following day in the company of several fellow druids from Tearmann. Most were students going home to visit or possibly to complete their studies with Ard-Mháistir Óengus at his school in Cois Abhann."

"Flavia didn't go with Quin, did she?" Debbie asked quietly, though she was sure of the answer.

"No, lass, she didn't. Racham was correct about her being obedient to her own path. She and Quin did say their good-byes before he left and she repeated Racham's words to him, 'Never doubt that I love thee.'

"She had received her own advanced training from Racham and she would receive more in coming years—interestingly, from his mother, who did eventually sail to Ynys Witrin with her uncle, the *Nobilis Decurio.*

"When the group that traveled together under miraculous circumstances arrived at the island, they found the little tabernacle which the two great friends and fellow students had built together. Some years later a magnificent chapel was erected on the spot where a spring still flows.

"This small group of Racham's close disciples became the source of dramatic healings and many conversions to his teachings. They and the druids maintained close ties throughout the ensuing years as the wisdom and ancient precepts shared between them created the foundation for the spread of spiritual truths that changed the world.

"Now, that's getting ahead of the story—except to say that Racham's mother and her uncle the Decurio lived out the remainder of their days there at the place that came to be known as Avalon.

"In the end, they both passed peacefully into the arms of the luminous son and nephew who had risen to etheric realms at the end of his mission."

Once more, the group sat in silence, allowing the profound scenes they had witnessed to settle in their hearts. Many felt tears trickle down their cheeks as they took into their beings the felt sense of Quin's final view of Racham when his ship sailed away from Ynys Witrin, never to return.

After several minutes, they rose to take their leave. Though not before each one had stopped to hug Lucky.

He had shared with them his most heartfelt memories of his twin flame, Flavia, and their beloved friend and teacher, Racham. There were simply no words to express how deeply moved was the entire Circle of Close Companions.

"Be careful driving home," Maggie gently admonished them. "You've plenty of daylight to see your way clear, but don't dawdle. Be good to yourselves in the coming days and contact us if you have any questions or problems during the week."

"I fear 'the game's afoot,' as our Master likes to say," added Tim. "We're not yet sure what that game may be. Still, 'tis an hour for watchfulness and prayer."

Part Four

Inescapable Records of the Past

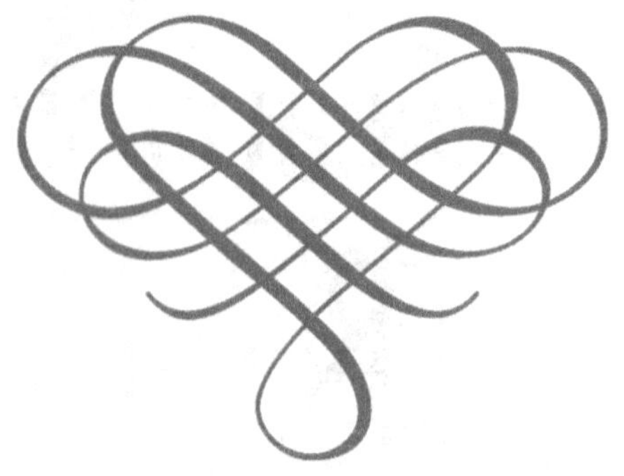

Showdown

Brian and Hank would have been glad for some spiritual advice from Lucky and the O'Tooles. Unfortunately, they had not been present at yesterday's life review, so they did not know to ask. Instead, they followed their own plan and phoned Brian's attorneys first thing Monday morning to request an emergency meeting.

The fact that Brian had not received any money from Stan's associates, nor had he drawn any checks on the promised bank account, made the circumstances less dire than they might have been. The absence of any written agreements about transferring money was also helpful.

However, the attorneys said there was little they could do without tangible proof of illegal activity. So far, everything was hearsay.

In the meantime, Hank and Brian would proceed with meeting Stan for lunch. That part of the drama could be tricky, but they were determined to play it straight. They would simply explain that the financial situation of Callahan & Logan had improved.

If Conway was not able to pay for the computer project, then Brian would exercise his option to terminate their contract. The two business partners and their attorneys agreed that this was the best explanation. They hoped it would work.

In the interest of meeting on neutral ground, the men were convening at a moderately priced restaurant several blocks from Fibonacci's. Hank and Brian arrived early and secured a table in a quiet corner where their conversation would not be heard and where they could watch the door.

"You don't want to miss Stan's entrance," Brian explained grimly. He found himself wishing he could order a glass of wine, but Hank didn't drink and they both needed their wits about them.

Indeed, when Stan arrived at the appointed hour, he swept in with an air of ownership, as if he were a generous benefactor who'd come to spread peace and good will among men.

"Let the games begin," said Hank softly as he and Brian rose to shake hands with the man who apparently intended to embroil them in illegal activities that could ruin them and everything they had worked for since college. It did not occur to them that a larger ruination had always been the ultimate target.

"Let's get down to business." Stan believed in a strong offense and took control of the conversation. Hank and Brian had dealt individually with men who thought of themselves as players. Now that they were facing one together, they felt on firm ground. Let the man talk and see what he had to say. Which was quite a lot.

"Brian, you'll be glad to know that I went back to my associates to discuss our mutual money challenges. They have another suggestion. Part of their reticence was unfamiliarity with the health food business. The good news is that they understand technology.

"They would like to invest in Callahan & Logan Computer Systems as a way to offset the cost of my new system. That solves my cash flow problem and takes care of your invoices. Plus, it gives my associates an investment, which they are confident will pay them significant dividends in the future. Seems like a sweet deal to me. What do you say?"

Conway's a stream roller, thought Hank. *And what was that weird flicker of a smile? Did the man actually lick his lips?*

Brian looked Stan in the eye, businessman to businessman.

"That is very generous of your associates, Stan. But, as it turns out, Callahan & Logan doesn't need a cash infusion after all. You see, we're going to be selling our Boston branch so we can concentrate on the New York market. That was an option unknown to me until yesterday."

He paused for a beat to let that news sink in, then continued.

"As you can imagine, we're going to be very busy with that sale and integrating into the New York office some of our functions that have been handled in Boston. Since Conway's isn't in a position to pay for the system upgrade we had planned, we feel it's best that we exercise our option to terminate the contract now."

Hank jumped in. "And, as a gesture of good will, we're going to forgive the few invoices you haven't paid. Some of that balance due was a down-payment. Brian's team hadn't started on the detailed customization programming yet. So there's no harm done."

Brian picked up the conversation. "Your new system would have been an interesting project, Stan. It just isn't going to work for us right now."

His words hung in the air that was thick with tension, though Conway was playing it cool. Hank thought he looked like a poker player, holding his cards close to the vest, speaking smoothly while sweating out a tough hand.

"I must admit you surprise me, gentlemen. My associates will be disappointed. I sincerely regret that this small matter of a few invoices has become a sticking point between us. Especially since the health food store is located within Fibonacci's property."

"As a tenant," Brian reminded him, countering the veiled threat. "We do still have a lease agreement, which I'm sure you will want to honor."

"Oh, by all means," said Stan hastily. "We are certainly able to pay our rent. It was the system upgrade that was stretching my budget."

"We understand," said Brian and he turned to his partner. "Didn't I tell you that Stan Conway was a real businessman?"

"You did. And I appreciate his honesty." Hank managed to say this without irony, then quickly changed the subject. No need to prolong the conversation. "Let's order. I'm famished." He signaled for the waiter.

Point to Callahan & Logan, Stan said to himself, *but nowhere near game, set, match.* He checked his watch and stood abruptly. "You'll have to excuse me. I just realized that I have another appointment and I need to inform my associates that you have declined their offer."

Not waiting for a reply or parting handshake, he turned, narrowly missed colliding with the waiter and barreled out of the restaurant—leaving the revolving door spinning in his wake.

"What do you think?" Brian asked as soon as Stan was gone.

"Not sure." Hank drew out the words. "That was a guy in a hurry who was not trying to hide his haste. I don't know if Stan is in big trouble with his associates or if we are. I think we'd better have that chat with Kevin and Jeremy now."

"Agreed. Do you still want lunch?"

"No. I'm not very hungry. Let's get back to Fibonacci's."

Kevin, Jeremy, Brian and Hank were seated at a round table in the ball-room upstairs at Fibonacci's. Kevin had suggested they meet there. He was feeling called to be in that forcefield more frequently these days—as if times and circumstances required the support of the spirit beings who gathered there. Today his intuition was more than correct.

He and Jeremy listened without comment while Brian and Hank described the situation with Stan Conway. When the two partners had finished, Jeremy spoke first.

"I knew something suspicious was going on in that store, but Kevin and I agreed we had to let events play out. I had no idea the situation might be illegal."

"Nor did I," Kevin agreed, "although Debbie did come to me with her concerns because of Glenna's reaction to one of Stacey's herbs—which she didn't take, by the way. And then there was that incident with another customer and her daughter."

"I'm glad to know this isn't a total shock to you," said Brian. "The last thing I wanted was to put Fibonacci's in jeopardy, but that's exactly what I've done."

"Don't be too hard on yourself," Kevin reassured his brother-in-law. "Often there are larger reasons than we can see underlying what appears on the surface. I'm sensing this is one of those situations."

"I agree," said Jeremy. "I've always had an uneasy feeling about the Conways—even though, at the time, their buying the store from Cyndi was a perfect solution for her and for Fibonacci's."

"That's what I'd thought," Brian agreed. "'Synchronicity', Cyndi called it. I called it the good luck that can happen sometimes in business."

"Still, the Conways have always reminded me of somebody." Jeremy furrowed his brow, searching for an answer. "No, I still don't know who. Only a vibe, I guess—that they were up to no good."

"I'm grateful we're all on the same page, here," said Hank. "As I see it, the question remains: How do we turn that page and finish this chapter of our mutual story?"

The four men were silent. Consulting inner guidance. Considering options. After several minutes, Kevin spoke.

"I think we're all making a mistake here. We're trying to solve this without Lucky. I know we've been giving him space to mourn the loss of Róisín and to work out his legacy, but we need him."

"You're right," said Jeremy. "We've fallen into the same old 'divide and conquer' trap that made Brian think he had to do a deal with the devil to save his business."

"That's harsh," said Hank, rising to his partner's defense.

"Sorry, Hank. That's just how I see Stan. I'm not blaming Brian. You don't know me. But Kevin can tell you that I've had some experience with people like the Conways who have an ability to cloak their real identity or intentions."

"It's okay, Hank," Brian intervened. "I get the picture."

"In fact..." Jeremy drew out the words.

"What is it?" asked Kevin. "What do you see?"

"Arán Bán and Una."

"But we got rid of them. With a lot of help from the Masters."

"We did, but they aren't the only ne'er-do-wells in the Universe."

"Catch me up, here," said Hank. "Brian, do you know about this?"

"Not really." Brian furrowed his brow. "This is where these guys lose me in their talk about spiritual warfare. Although the situation they're referring to is what led to Callahan & Logan investing in this building. That crook A. B. Ryan—who I guess was this Arán Bán character in a previous life—is the one who managed to burn down the original Fibonacci's."

"Yeah," said Hank. "That was a scary deal. But what does that have to do with the Conways? Are they relatives or something?"

Jeremy nodded his head. "Hank, you've hit the mark. A. B. Ryan and the Conways probably are not related by blood in this life, but there is a family connection. I see it clearly now."

Kevin's eyes were wide as saucers. "We've got talk to Lucky. We can't sideline him here. This is his fight, as much as ours. Maybe more. This situation goes far back in time and it affects the entire community. I know it involves me and Sarah. I'll call the O'Tooles and ask how soon they can bring Lucky over here. Jeremy, we need our wives and the other couples, too. It's time to call in the troops."

Kevin started to rise from his chair when Jeremy put a hand on his arm. His friend didn't usually act in haste. Was that fear he saw in the man's normally calm blue-green eyes?

"You're right, Kevin, but let's hold on a minute. It's almost dinner time. You and Brian have families, and don't forget that Glenna's pregnant."

Jeremy was about to continue when Hank's stomach made its empty condition known with a loud growl. He grimaced. "Brian and I missed lunch."

"Understood," Jeremy chuckled. "Besides, we need to give our store managers time to cover their shifts for tomorrow at the bookstore and the coffee shop. And Lucky may want to consider if he's ready to come back to Fibonacci's."

Kevin rubbed his eyes and brushed a hand over his forehead.

"Sorry, I don't know what came over me. I'll talk to Lucky. If he agrees, will ten o'clock tomorrow morning work for everybody else?"

"Good for me and Hank—and Ivy," added Brian. "Jeremy?"

"Sounds good. As soon as you get the okay from Lucky, I'll ask Debbie to help me call the others."

The four men stood together and shook hands as they prepared to leave for the evening.

"Thanks, guys," said Brian. "I'm realizing how important this community is to me—in a way I never have before."

Patience

Kevin knew exactly what had come over him. When he told Sarah the full story of events at the health food store, she did as well.

"Does an ancient family connection between the Conways and Arán Bán have anything to do with your nightmare?" she asked.

"More than likely. I'm not sure I want to learn the particulars, but I have a feeling that's a big part of this whole situation. If we're going to resolve this attack on the community, we've got to get to the core of where it started."

"You're right. But, Kevin, it's late. Our babies are here. We can't go exploring a perilous past life on our own. Master Saint Germain would never want us to put ourselves in that kind of danger."

"I know. Part of me just wants to get this over with."

"Let's be wise here. Lucky agreed to meet everyone tomorrow at the ballroom. That should give us more insight into what the community wants to do. Then we can ask Lucky, and probably Tim and Maggie, for their read on how we should proceed."

"Good idea. Meanwhile, let's contact our Master for his guidance. I'm sensing tremendous opposition to the community's stability. I think it's time we talked to him directly."

As soon as little Gareth and Naimh were fast asleep, Sarah and Kevin each made attunement with their Higher Self and settled into the state of awareness that reflected the attainment they knew they must engage in this hour. They gave the mantras that raised their consciousness to the level where they could receive the spiritual guidance they were beginning to feel was a matter of life or death.

Master Saint Germain instantly responded to the couple's request for his counsel and was now standing in their living room in his light body.

Sarah and Kevin listened keenly to his instruction as he spoke into their hearts. To receive his discourses was always an experience of being lifted into refined states of consciousness where his words were emblazoned in their total awareness.

You were wise to call me. There are reasons why you have not been allowed to access this past life record until these cycles had turned. Even now, the danger to your souls is significant.

You are no strangers to scenes of warfare and malevolence. But never have you witnessed events in which you were a purely innocent victim (he looked at Sarah) or the perpetrator of regrettable violence.

The Master's violet eyes fell upon Kevin with a mixture of firmness and deep compassion. These revelations were never easy to deliver, even for one who had long ago attained his liberation from the limitations of earthly karma.

When the timing is appropriate, I will sponsor you in this initiation, as I have for more lifetimes than any of us cares to count. Let us observe how tomorrow's meeting evolves and what transpires in the days that follow. This is a complex equation of an entire community, not only the Circle of Close Companions.

Although your roles are primary here, all must be weighed in the balance scales of life. Lucky and his ascended twin flame are both deeply involved. For that alchemy to come to fruition, he requires your support as much as you do his.

Having so said, the Master's image faded from view. Kevin and Sarah were once more alone, now comforted in the knowledge that they had received the blessing of the gracious being who would—as much as divinely possible—ensure their safety and that of their children. How the wider Friends of Ancient Wisdom community would be affected was a matter for watchfulness and deep prayer.

One thing you have to say about the Circle of Close Companions, when you need them, they do not hesitate, Kevin thought to himself the next morning as he prepared for the group meeting. He had felt certain that he could depend upon their attendance, and he was right. Hank, Brian and Ivy had also promised to be present.

Maggie and Tim had arrived early with Lucky so he could meditate alone before the others joined him. At ten o'clock he was standing in front of the altar where the curtain had been opened to reveal the golden disc that shimmered like an actual sun.

As the adults began to assemble, their friend and mentor beamed his greeting to each of them as if he were welcoming them to Fibonacci's for the first time. Here was his deep love that had been hard-won through many trials and triumphs. It wove them together with threads of loyalty and devotion to higher purpose that must be refreshed to be maintained.

Lucky was doing that now.

When everyone was gathered, he motioned for them to stand. Then he turned and lit the tapers on the spiral candelabra on either side of the altar. Moving to the center with his hands upraised, he repeated the prayer that had been handed down to this community from ancient times.

O Spirits of East and West, South and North, give ear, we pray, to our supplications. Angels of our world and the next, bless this assembly with your protection and inspiration.

Beloved An Síoraí, O Eternal One, may the words of our mouths and the deeds of our hands bring health and abundance to all our people and safety to our homes, our leaders and those we love both near and far, here with us and in gracious Tír na n'Óg, Land of the Ever-Living.

Facing them again, he signaled for them to be seated.

"'Tis grand to see you in this blessed space, *a chairde*. Thank you, Kevin and all, for insisting that we meet here today. I didn't realize how much I've missed Fibonacci's. I've missed watching you go about tending to customers and each other as Róisín and I always knew you would. And I've missed working with you like the old days.

"Truth be told, I think I've been hiding out in my sorrow over missing Róisín. We've been together as soulmates for so many lifetimes, I actually haven't known how to get along without her.

"Much as I've needed and appreciated Maggie and Tim's hospitality, I think I've been dragging my feet about coming back. You see, though we've been working on recording my stories—and thanks for giving up your Sunday afternoons to listen to my tales—I've never been sure that storytelling was the whole of the cloth as far as leaving a legacy for others to follow.

"There are more memories to share and some difficult ones that I'm still reluctant to recall. I see now that being here in this place that we've built together and dedicated with our love is an element that I've been overlooking."

For a moment, Lucky's voice caught with emotion. He cleared his throat and gathered himself like the disciplined adept he was.

"Now, then. These lads, Brian and Kevin, have some news that each of you will need to consider carefully. However, before they take the floor, I want to share some musings from my heart that apply to the matter they're going to tell you about."

He smiled at the puzzled expressions on the faces of those who as yet did not know about the Conway situation.

"'Tis the way of the Eternal One, my dears. *An Síoraí* often provides an answer before a question is asked. Our job is to listen and take wise action. In this case, I am responding to the question Róisín and I used to ask of our bookstore customers in Limerick: 'What do you value most?'

"Now each of us can ruminate about the idea. But to elicit a proper response, the question must be asked by another. Sarah, darlin', will you pose the question to me as if you were going to ferret out the perfect book that I, as a new customer, had no idea I was looking for?"

Sarah stood and, sending her own deepest love and gratitude back to him, said in her clear voice, "Lucky, *a chara,* what do you value most in this life? What is important to you above all else?"

"Thank you darlin'. If one of the lads will bring me a chair—and if you'll gather 'round so I can see your faces and you can see mine—I'll sit here like an old *seanchaí* and I'll tell you."

What I value most in this life is you, my dear friends. 'Tis our Circle of Close Companions, our Friends of Ancient Wisdom and Fibonacci's itself. This grand place is the newest home of my heart. Here is where our Master and many others chose to put down roots so that community might grow in this age as it has in other places in other eras.

We did the same in Éire two thousand years ago. We did the same in Egypt and Atlantis and other parts of this beautiful blue planet we call Earth in civilizations that have long since faded into myth and mystery.

In every age we have framed and threaded a loom like we've done at Fibonacci's where the warp and weft of love and light can be woven to fit the times.

Community is a tapestry, you see. 'Tis a tangible place and a vibration. 'Tis a forcefield and a state of consciousness of hope for the hundreds, like you, who are its physical members and for others who belong in their souls.

A community like ours benefits thousands more, perhaps even millions, by the energy we invoke and focus to roll back the darkness that has threatened the light ever since Michael and his angels fought the good fight eons ago.

Our Master Pythagoras always said that consciousness is mathematical. I believe what he meant is that the balance of light and dark can be measured if you happen to possess instruments that are sufficiently sensitive.

You do possess those instruments, *a chairde.* Each of you is a receiving station for vibrations that constantly swirl around the Universe. Ideally, whatever you value most is the vibration you pick up and live in. If you've found yourself burdened by not-so-good signals, you need to adjust the dial on your receiver.

Lucky paused and focused intense love on his Close Companions—as if to infuse them with the depth of his own passion for community and for the mission the Masters of Wisdom had bequeathed to him and Róisín. Soon, responsibility for the continued success of that mission would be upon the shoulders of these souls he cherished with his entire being.

"So now I've given you the answer to the question you'll surely be asking when the lads have told you their story. 'Lucky, what shall we do?' you'll be wanting to know. And you'll see that I've told you in advance.

"We—all of us—must adjust the dial of our consciousness and practice what we preach. We must tune into more light. Invoke more light. Take the wise steps that are ours to take, and empower the Masters to dissolve the inner causes of the problems we're facing.

"When we do that, *a chairde*, miracles can happen. You'll see."

When Lucky went to sleep that night, he was more at peace than he'd been since Róisín's ascension. He felt that he had prepared the Circle of Close Companions as best he could for the challenging days ahead.

To be sure, the information that Brian and Kevin had given them was troubling. It had not been difficult to gain everyone's promise not to visit the health food store and not to discuss the situation with anyone from the larger Friends of Ancient Wisdom community.

No one knew exactly how events would play out. The Conways still owned their business and their rental agreement remained in effect. By no means was "money laundering" to be mentioned in conversation. Any questions or observations were to be directed to Kevin, Brian or Lucky himself. Otherwise, the health food store was to be a non-subject.

In the meantime, what the Companions *could* do was gather more frequently in the ballroom for general chanting. Individuals and groups from the larger community were welcome to commune there at any time. The curtain that shielded the altar would remain open so anyone could light a candle and say a prayer for whatever burdened them.

'*Tis a good plan*, Lucky assured himself. As he drifted off to sleep, he heard the voice of his dear Flavia confirming that he was doing the right thing. She was also reminding him that next Sunday's story would be one he had never wanted to tell.

Courage & Insight

When Lucky awoke on the last Sunday of September, he found himself wondering if it was always a bit of a shock when a long-awaited day finally arrives.

On such a bright morning, does the bride say to herself, "Today I will walk down the aisle to my beloved." And does she pinch herself to know that her wedding day is no longer in the future?

Does the warrior, coming awake on the dawn of a big invasion, say to himself, "Today is the day I will walk through fire and I likely will not live to see the end of it."

These thoughts went through Lucky's mind as he readied himself to receive his Circle of Close Companions. They were all coming today. He had warned Brian, Ivy and Hank that this narrative might be difficult, but they had insisted on being part of the gathering.

Hank had been especially keen—that is if Sarah would give him a synopsis of stories told so far—which she had declared herself more than happy to do. Tim had invited him to stop by on Saturday for a tour of the round tower so he could get a feel for the energy in the place.

By Sunday morning, Hank felt himself well-primed and already an accepted member of the group. He really liked these people and was glad he was going to be living among them instead of alone in Boston.

The atmosphere at the O'Tooles' was alive with conversation and admiration for the brilliantly colored flowers that seemed to have outdone themselves in their early-autumn display in Maggie's garden.

As Lucky looked around the room at his audience, he noticed expressions of concern on the part of Glenna and Cyndi, although their faces immediately brightened when he caught their eye.

Are they afraid of what I am going to tell them? he wondered. Or were they concerned about the Conway situation? Regardless, today's story might not ease their minds, but there was no holding back. He was committed. He had promised Flavia and he would not let her down.

"Because of the need to fit a lot of material into a short period of time, we conducted last week's session as a life review," Lucky began. "Your souls can absorb more than your minds. That process moved us ahead.

"Today, however, I am bound by a promise to my dear Flavia to tell you the story in first person. She says there are things that can only be learned this way."

He paused to gather himself. "I'll try not to burden you with my own emotion, but there's no guarantee. I beg your pardon in advance. This is the hardest thing I have ever done."

"We're with you," said Sarah and all agreed. "The recorder is on. You may start any time."

Lucky breathed in and out, in and out. When he was set, he raised his eyes and, gazing out toward the Infinite, let the story carry him.

We are in the year AD 52—when the murderous edict declared by Roman Emperor Claudius to exterminate the druids of Albion (known to Rome as Britain) was running at full tilt.

Although the island of Ynys Witrin had been spared and would continue to be protected by powerful unseen forces, the druidic culture and religion had been under siege by Rome's ablest generals and their legions for the past ten years.

To the great astonishment of the Romans, the Silurians—Britain's fiercest warriors—could not be defeated. In battle after battle, they bested the world's most powerful fighting machine. It eventually became evident that they would not give up their freedom or their ancient culture in regular warfare. Unfortunately, treachery often finds a way. And that is what happened.

Though Flavia's father was long dead, the poisonous seeds of envy he had sown among his like-minded kinsmen and neigh-boring tribes sprouted in the black heart of the queen of the Celtic Brigantes. Greedy for power, she refused to give sanctuary to the brilliant Silurian military leader Pendragon Caradoc—or Caractacus as the Romans called him.

This betrayal occurred after a disastrous battle that was won by the Romans only because the Emperor himself had brought two additional legions along with elephants to reinforce the two legions that were struggling against Caractacus.

The details are complex, except to say that the Silurian leader was taken in his sleep, bound in chains and hauled off to Rome along with many members of his family. Flavia was among them. With my inner sight I always knew where she was. I witnessed the entire drama.

Even in apparent defeat, Caractacus was magnificent. At his trial, he defended the right of his people to live in peace while addressing the Roman Senate in fluent Latin, accusing Rome of being the aggressor against Britain. He so impressed the Emperor that the family was miraculously released.

The only condition was that Caractacus must stay in Rome for seven years. Other members of his family were free to leave. Some did depart, while others, including Flavia, remained.

In one of history's strangest twists, a wary friendship developed between Caractacus and Emperor Claudius—the very one who, a decade earlier, had declared the destruction of the druidic culture and its next incarnation as Racham's teachings that had been brought to Britain by *Nobilis Decurio,* his nephew's mother and a dozen close disciples.

Along with diplomatic immunity, the Emperor bestowed upon the Silurians the largest house in Rome—a compound where the entire family could live in considerable luxury and protection. The home was known as the "Palace of the Britains." In time, it became an important center for spreading 'The Way,' as Christianity was known in those days. 'Tis a fascinating story, but one whose telling must wait for another time.

There were also personal reasons for some of the Silurian family to remain in Rome. A few years earlier, Flavia's distant cousin, the sister of Caractacus, had married a prominent Roman military leader while he was stationed in Britain. When he was recalled to Rome in AD 47, his wife came with him.

Perhaps even more amazing—Gladys, a teenaged daughter of Caractacus, so impressed the Emperor with her character and beauty that he adopted her as his own daughter. She changed her name to Claudia and a year later married a Roman Senator and former soldier whom she had met in Britain and deeply loved.

So, as long as old Emperor Claudius remained alive and in power, the family's unprecedented protection continued. However, as the only constant in this world is change, the situation abruptly halted when Nero became emperor. Then persecutions resumed with a fury—a hurricane of terror that caught my Flavia in its maelstrom.

Lucky's voice cracked in the emotion that suddenly swamped him. He tried valiantly to choke back the tears that poured unbidden from his eyes, but he failed to stem the tide.

Maggie rushed to bring him a glass of water and Sarah stopped the recording. Kevin hurried to the man's side and helped him stand.

"Let's give him a moment," he said quietly to the others. With his arm around Lucky's shoulder, he led their friend down the hall to his rooms where he could collect himself in private.

Maggie made a fresh pot of tea while Tim encouraged the Companions to adjourn to the terrace and gardens where they could compose themselves. And where they would not hear the cry of grief that erupted from Lucky's being like the howl of a wounded animal.

"Let the tears come," said Kevin as he sat with his mentor of many lifetimes on the small sofa in Lucky's sitting room. "This dam was bound to break after so many years of holding back the flood."

He kept his hand on the man's shoulder until the storm abated. A moment later Maggie knocked on the door with mugs of tea for both men. "The others are wondering if you'd like to adjourn," she asked gently.

Lucky looked up at her with reddened eyes, and gave her a weak but determined smile.

"No, lass, but tell them 'thanks.' I'll be fine in a few more minutes. I'll understand if anybody wants to leave, but could you tell them I'd be grateful if they'd stay. Now that I've had this old breakdown, I should be able to finish the tale without blubbering. It needs to be told today."

Everyone had remained and all were in their seats when he emerged. He looked a bit wrung out. Still, a weight had been lifted. For those who could see such things, there was a brightness in his aura, like one sees after washing windows that had been clouded by an all-but-invisible film.

"Sure, and 'tis the sign of true friendship when you can fall apart and still be accepted, despite your tears," Lucky said warmly. "Remember that, *a chairde*. Uncried tears will make you ill. Sorrow held in can take you out of embodiment before your time. I speak from experience.

"Now, let's get back to our story."

As I was saying, it was the custom in Rome that the Silurian family from Britain was not to be molested. Unfortunately, the rules changed over night and no one was the wiser until it was too late. Until disaster struck my sweet Flavia.

Lucky faltered briefly. Kevin started to rise, but the *seanchaí* raised his hand to signal that he was fine to continue. He took several deep breaths and steadily carried on.

My darling and two of her female cousins, in the company of two strong young men of the household, had been in the habit of walking to an open-air market they particularly favored.

On the day in question, they had only just left the family compound when they were accosted by three Roman soldiers. These men recognized them from past peaceful encounters, but this time the meeting turned violent. With a vicious thrust of their short swords, they killed the two young men and carried the screaming women off to prison.

The family was powerless to free them. In fact, their panicked petitions for the Emperor's clemency served only to worsen the conditions of the women's imprisonment.

I was frantic to sail to Rome myself, though I don't know what I could have done. In my soul body, I sent the whole of my heart and soul to Flavia in prison, to give her courage and strength for the ordeal we both feared was coming.

Two weeks after they had been seized, the three women were loaded onto a cart and driven into the vastnesses of the Coliseum. We prayed their death might be quick. That was not to be.

Nero harbored a virulent hatred of female followers of The Way. He considered their being devoured by ravenous beasts as too swiftly completed. On that wretched day, my beloved and her companions were hung on rough crosses to endure a dying process that dragged on for many hours.

In my finer body I stayed with Flavia. I could only watch and marvel at her courage. She suffered horribly, but never once gave the jeering Roman crowds the satisfaction of crying out. At last, when her soul took flight from her mangled body, she looked at me and smiled. I see now that Racham was with her, but I did not then.

In that moment of shock and astonishment, I collapsed back into my physical body that lay in my dwelling at Tearmann in Éire. Soon after, I fell ill with a fever that even the ministrations of Dearbhla could not cure.

Lucky looked over at Debbie, who had been embodied in Tearmann as that gifted healer. She nodded to him through shimmering tears.

"Yes, darlin', you did your best. Yet I think you knew I could not live in such soul agony. Despite Flavia's efforts to console me, I could not accept that her death was meant to be. Others urged me to resume my duties as *ceann-druí*, but I could not will myself to rally. At last, on a cold day in March of AD 61, I died.

"My soul was never the same—until today, my dears. Until today." He gazed at his audience, his eyes bright with a stunning new awareness.

"Can you explain what you mean?" Sarah asked gently.

"I can, darlin'. You see, Flavia was correct in her insistence that I tell you this story in the first person. For in the recitation and the moments you have granted me for reflection, I've gained an insight that had escaped me until this moment.

"Before relating the dramatic details of these events to you today, I've never understood why my mission and Flavia's seemed not to coincide in that lifetime. For centuries I've asked myself why Racham instructed her to remain in Albion, which resulted in her going to Rome. And why he insisted that I return to Éire. The reason is clear to me now."

Lucky smiled at the puzzled expressions on the faces of his listeners.

"The reason is community, *a chairde*. Flavia had soul obligations to several groups in Albion and Rome. My duty was with Tearmann in Éire, which I'll tell you about next week. For that's a tale involving many of you.

"The point is that, although Flavia and I were physically separated, our souls were engaged in the same work. She completed hers in Rome by laying down her life as a martyr to truth in what was a judgment of Nero and the entire force of darkness that opposed the light in those days.

"For me, in demonstrating to you—and to those who will read my book—how twin souls may be tasked differently on the outer but similarly on the inner, I see now that staying to tell our story is part of my mission that I did not understand and could not accept. With your help, I have an opportunity to complete that mission in this life.

"Your willingness to witness this saga is a blessing to me and Flavia." Lucky gestured toward the terrace. "Some of you may observe her standing in the garden, sending you her thanks."

The company turned and there was Flavia in her light body, clearly visible for all to see. She was dressed in a linen robe belted at the waist with a simple blue cord. Her flaxen hair was arranged in a long braid that she wore over her left shoulder.

Her soft blue eyes were glistening and her radiant smile emanated a vibration of profound love that arced from her heart to Lucky and to these souls whom they had cherished for many, many years.

Constant Vigilance

Debbie often worked the opening shift at Róisín's Coffee Shop. She and Jeremy were both early risers who enjoyed their morning ritual of prayers and meditations.

Since they lived on the third floor of Fibonacci's in the tower room apartment, it was easy for them to have their second cup of coffee and a muffin warm from the oven at the coffee shop. They often sat in the back booth where miraculous conversations had been taking place ever since Lucky and Róisín had opened their first business on Long Island.

Debbie liked to set the shop's sail for the day—to catch the breeze of whatever events would unfold in the next few hours. She smiled to think of that phrase which her father had used. He'd been a sailor in his youth and loved to take his children out on the sailboat which he had insisted was vital to his family's well-being.

The siblings had kept the boat for a few months after their parents were killed in a car accident. In reality, none of them could manage the craft with their father's skill. They sold it after one feebly attempted voyage that nearly ended before they'd maneuvered out of the marina.

Would Cyndi remember more about our family outings? Debbie wondered. She would ask her sister today when they took a break. *And where was Cyndi? She was uncharacteristically late coming in this morning.*

No sooner had that thought crossed Debbie's mind than her sister entered through the back door. She looked a bit "peek-ed," as one of the ladies from the South called the pale color in her usually rosy cheeks. Even her freckles looked washed out.

"Rough night?" Debbie asked as she filled a large urn with the day's special blend of Costa Rican coffee.

"Not really," said Cyndi. "I'm just tired." She hesitated then added, "Glenna will be here in an hour. Could we talk to you?"

"Of course. Is anything the matter?"

"No. Well, sort of. I'd tell you now but Glenna has more of the story. Do you mind waiting until she gets here?"

"Of course not. Why don't you sit down and have a cup of tea. You really do look tired. We're staffed for now. Is Phelan coming in?"

"He's at the bookstore having a chat with Rory. You know, Irishman to Irishman. If he doesn't get his regular dose of Gaelic, he gets—I don't know—lonesome, I guess."

Cyndi paused and lowered her voice. "Actually, I think they're talking about the situation with the health food store. I know Phelan is really bothered by the fact that we had to sell it to pay for Lucky's house. There wasn't another option at the time, but I can tell he regrets it now."

"I think we all do," said Debbie quietly, "though it was a good decision when you made it. Now go have your tea. You can help later if we get busy."

Cyndi hesitated, then said apologetically, "Sarah's coming over, too. I hope you don't mind. Glenna figured we should talk to both of you about our concerns."

"That's fine. Do you want Ivy to be here?"

"No, not yet. We don't know her as well and this is kind of private."

As it happened, Ivy was busy anyway. It had been a difficult morning. Even though she had fixed a delicious breakfast, Brian had snapped at her.

He and Hank had argued about how they should handle liquidating the Boston office. Brian knew how much debt they were carrying and Hank knew the Boston operations better. Each thought he knew more than the other and they'd come to an impasse.

Brian slammed the back door as he left for his office and Hank slammed the front door as he strode out to his car to go for a very long drive. Neither of them thought his partner was showing any common sense about how they should proceed.

Ivy was glad to have them both out of the house. She could have used

Brian's help with the twins, though not if he was in such a foul mood.

Kerry and Kaitlyn were also in a mood. Today was a school day, but they had whined that they had sore throats and should be allowed to stay home. Ivy knew they used that excuse when they didn't want to go to school. This morning they really did have a fever, so she made them their favorite breakfast of oatmeal with raisins and sent them back to bed.

Although they each had their own room now, she could hear them in Kaitlyn's room, arguing that Kerry had entered without her permission. He was refusing to leave, so his sister had run to his room and locked the door so he couldn't get in.

Ivy sat down at the kitchen table and put her head in her hands. What was going on with this family? Everybody was bristling, and she felt like knocking all of their heads together.

Why were they so angry all of a sudden? Were they under some kind of spell or something? While Ivy's imagination was searching for answers, she was more right than she could have known.

By the time Glenna and Sarah arrived at the coffee shop, Debbie, Cyndi and Phelan were ready to tear their hair out. The baker, who also prepared the breakfast and lunch wraps they offered, had gone home sick before all of the items had been completed.

A couple of tourists had complained about the service being slow and said their lattés weren't hot enough. One of the baristas had burned herself on the steam as she made them new, very hot drinks. Two of their regular customers were having a snit over sharing *The New York Times*.

Debbie motioned for Glenna and Sarah to help themselves to tea at the counter and take a seat in the back booth. She and Cyndi would be with them as soon as they calmed down the children's sandbox that seemed to have erupted in the middle of their business.

She was on the verge of closing for the day, when Lucky walked in like a breath of fresh air and a calming presence. He looked around and grinned. It was grand to be back and he radiated joy.

"Lucky! Thank God you're here," said Debbie. "I don't know what hit us this morning. I'm ready to throw cold water on every customer in the place."

"So that's why I got such a strong prompting to have Tim drive me over here," he said knowingly. "Lass, we've got some energy to deal with. Tell you what, I'm going upstairs to do some chants. Why don't you come with me? Looks like Phelan has things under control for now."

"Actually, I was about to have a conversation with my sisters." Debbie pointed to her friends. "Something's up with them too."

Lucky was silent for a minute in the way that told her he was reading the energy in the room as well as the auras of everyone in it.

"Come with me," he said and guided her to where the other three women were seated.

"Good morning, lasses," he said cheerfully. "I understand you were about to have a conversation. Instead, I'd like to suggest that you come upstairs with me for a visit with *An Síoraí*, the Eternal One."

When they started to resist, he became very firm. "I can see that you're worried or upset or afraid of something. Am I right?"

They nodded.

"Then before you start stirring up more of the negative energy that's already having a field day around here, I want you upstairs in that ballroom. What you need is light and we're going to invoke it."

Sarah chuckled to herself as she and the other women dutifully followed Lucky to the elevator that carried them to the second floor. This must have been how Ah-Lahn felt when Old Quin disciplined him. The man meant business and there was no point in disagreeing with him.

There was nothing like chanting with Lucky. His voice resonated with the depth of a pipe organ. Being in his presence as he invoked light energy with the OM and the prayers he sometimes spoke in Gaelic was to be lifted into another plane of consciousness.

Who needs a round tower when you can pray with Lucky? Sarah thought. Then, oh, how her heart skipped a beat when she remembered that he would not be with them forever. They must learn to cut through negative energy like this morning's tidal wave by themselves.

After thirty minutes Lucky brought their session to a close. "That's better. Now, let's go downstairs and have a cup of tea while you tell me what's bothering you."

Glenna spoke up. "Actually, Debbie, could we go to your apartment? What we have to say shouldn't be discussed in the coffee shop where we might be overheard."

"Of course, go ahead. I'll tell Phelan where we are in case he needs us. Cyndi, will you put the kettle on while I let your husband know you haven't been kidnapped?"

When Debbie joined the others in her dining room, she was laughing. "Phelan said the coffee shop is as calm as a chapel after mass. I guess the chants worked, Lucky."

"They were meant to."

"I'm glad," said Debbie. "Phelan was as jumpy this morning as Cyndi was pale. I was concerned the two of you had had a fight. Everybody else seemed to be on tenterhooks this morning."

"No, nothing like that." Cyndi suddenly brightened. "I'm pregnant."

"How wonderful!" exclaimed Sarah. "Glenna, did you know?"

"Cyndi told me the other day when I talked to her about prenatal supplements."

"Had you guessed?" Cyndi asked her sister.

"Debbie has baby radar," laughed Glenna. "I think she knew I was pregnant before I did. Well, almost."

Their friend smiled. "I could see the souls of your babies hovering in your auras. Then Glenna was glowing and now Cyndi is pale. Very clear signs. Lucky, I hope we're not embarrassing you with pregnancy talk."

"On the contrary. 'Tis pleased I am to hear such news. And I believe this has something to do with why Glenna and Cyndi were keen to talk to Debbie and Sarah. Am I right?"

"You are, of course, so I'll come right to the point," said Glenna. "We're afraid—for our babies, our husbands, ourselves. For the community. Lucky, what's going to happen? We don't want to go to war on the outer or the inner."

"That goes for all of us," Debbie agreed. She could see how earnestly

Glenna was trying to state her concerns calmly.

"I was scared witless during the battle with Una, even though we had legions of angels and lady masters on our side. I know that Rory has been a soldier in the past. I can't bear the thought of him fighting ever again. I've lost him in too many wars in too many embodiments. You know what that's like, Lucky."

"We all do," Sarah added soberly. "Perhaps it's possible this situation with the Conways can be fought through the legal system. At least that's my hope."

"Mine, too," said Lucky, "but we don't know yet. I can promise you that everything possible is being done to protect you and your families. We all have too much to lose. I still believe our prayers are the strongest weapon we have."

He stood, his aura shimmering with the *ceann-druí's* authority.

"My admonition to you is this: The minute you feel the slightest discord trying to take hold of you, stop what you're doing and say a prayer. If you're here at Fibonacci's, get someone to cover for you. Go to the ballroom and chant away.

"The darkness cannot bear the light. Take every opportunity to invoke that light for those who know about the situation we're dealing with and especially for those who don't. 'Divide and conquer' is the same old tune the malignant ones have played for eons. Don't fall for it, in even the slightest manner."

He looked purposefully at each of the women to gain their assent. "We will, Lucky," they said as one voice.

"Good. I want you to feel my resolve and that of our Master. He is still the sponsor of Fibonacci's. We need to remember that and give him the ability to act on our behalf. Our free will to ask for spiritual assistance remains the number one rule of the Universe. 'Tis the simplest solution and the hardest to remember when you're being bombarded by forces that want you to forget."

Lucky's paused, letting his words sink into the hearts of these stalwart females. When he felt their unanimous acceptance, his expression changed to a smile.

"Back to work with you now, my darlin' lasses, while I have a chat with

Sarah about our book project."

Wanting to know more about Cyndi's pregnancy, the women gathered around her with hugs and the loving concern for her well-being that they cherished in each other. They were full of questions. When was she due? How had Phelan taken the news? Did they have any names in mind?

The joy of new life in their midst buoyed their spirits.

On their way back to the tasks that called them, each one stopped to kiss Lucky's cheek, which sobered them a bit. What in the world were they going to do without him? They knew they shouldn't think about a future that would arrive in its own time, but they couldn't seem to stop themselves from being concerned.

After this chanting session, the need for constant vigilance was the topic of conversation in all homes of the Circle of Close Companions. The problem was that nobody thought to tell Brian, Ivy or Hank.

Fortunately, Lucky had included them in his prayers, as he would continue to do. Unfortunately, he couldn't watch them every minute—although he was aware that everybody had returned to their best behavior that evening at the Callahan residence. The men had reconciled. Brian had apologized to Ivy. The twins were all smiles and were getting along as was their normal behavior.

However, there were situations in their past lives that Lucky was not allowed to reveal to them. The fact that they remained on the periphery of the Circle of Close Companions concerned him. He would like to set the three adults down and tell them they had serious need of coming in closer to the fold. But he was aware that his options in this situation were limited by their individual karma. Still, he would do what he could.

Hank seemed very interested in being part of the community. Perhaps Tim would encourage the lad to attend the next story session on Sunday and bring his two friends. Now that they weren't busy with the Conway computer project, they had no reason not to be present.

"Is it enough?" Lucky whispered to Flavia, but she did not respond. Or perhaps she was not allowed to answer. That was likely the case.

Home Life

Complicated. If anyone had asked Sarah to describe her life in a single word, that is the one she would have used without hesitation. Nothing in her daily routine was as easy to manage as she had expected.

Certainly not keeping track of thirteen-month-old twins who had transformed into perpetual-motion machines. Sarah had been eager for them to walk. But now that they were gaining more stability and confidence every day, she had to watch them constantly.

Gareth was a runner. His balance was amazing for such a tiny body and he worked hard at staying upright. He was in a hurry to go everywhere and play with every toy he could get his hands on. Of course, all objects in the house were potential toys. Toddler-proofing had become an urgent and comprehensive task at the MacCauleys'.

Naimh was a climber. She has mastered crib escape very early and was up and over chairs, sofas—any obstacle her parents might erect in her path. She loved going upstairs and had figured out how to turn around and scoot backwards on her tummy when she wanted to go downstairs.

She was also the more cautious walker. Where Gareth would fearlessly cross a room, Naimh would walk around the edges, holding on to furniture until she came to the other side of a doorway that her brother would have toddled across.

Hero remained their favorite entertainment. The fascination had been mutual almost as soon as the babies could recognize his presence. Now that they could walk, Hero woofed and scampered and urged them to interact with him. As Sarah had mentioned to Charlotte, inside or outside, the big dog viewed the twins as his personal responsibility.

Gareth followed Hero around until they both were tired. Then he would join Naimh as she nestled against the wolfhound, all three of them taking a shared nap on the parents' bed or one of the dog beds that were placed around the house so Hero and Sprite could snooze comfortably in the same room as their humans.

The cat still kept her distance, except for meal time when the twins were safely contained in their high chairs. Then she would venture over to help Hero clean up any food tidbits the kiddos dropped. Otherwise, tiny hands and kitty paws did not mix well.

Sarah was fascinated by her children's development. She was grateful to work at home where she was privy to the changes that emerged in them almost daily. She was also grateful that when she needed to spend a couple of hours working on Lucky's book, one or both of her parents would come over to watch the children at her house or take them on outings.

One day, when the grandparents were securing the toddlers in their car seats for a trip to the park, Eileen Callahan laughed at her daughter's amazement at how much time and attention were required in the raising of twins.

"You and Brian were close enough in age, you might as well have been twins," she replied to Sarah's complaint about double everything.

"Be grateful for the small moments," she advised. "These two will be telling you how to run your life soon enough. Think of Ivy. It's a wonder that girl survived her twins' first years. Brian wasn't nearly the help to her that Kevin is to you."

"He is wonderful with the babies," Sarah agreed. "For years I was so obsessed with getting pregnant, I never stopped to imagine what kind of father Kevin would be. I think the children's bath time is one of his favorite activities."

"Your father was the same, especially with you. Brian was a stubborn little tyke who required my firmer hand. You were more—I won't say compliant. You were never compliant. You were just more interested in social interactions. Brian liked things. He started stacking blocks and never looked back. He and your father did have a grand time building contraptions from their own designs."

Eileen's bright blue eyes misted as she looked over at her daughter. "I'm glad you were able to birth these babies, Sarah. So you could experience the joy and the frustration. And so you'd share them with me and your father. I never wanted to pressure you about giving us grandchildren. You were stressed enough for all of us. These two are more than I ever dared hope for. Double everything," she quipped with a watery smile.

Yes, Sarah had to admit that her mother was right. Although life as the mother of twins was definitely complicated, she did have a lot of help. Writing Lucky's book was a challenge, though. Compiling his stories was taking more time than she had anticipated. Transcribing from the recordings was a laborious task.

The audios were high quality, so she wasn't straining to hear what the *seanchaí* said. Still, the task was slow going. Being true to his voice and not inserting her own thoughts or opinions or style was a discipline she was working to perfect.

I am very opinionated, she laughed at herself. Plus, she and Lucky had not decided on the overall approach they would take to editing the stories for print. A few of his narratives were in first person. He had told some tales in third person. Still others were the record of an actual life review— which she and Kevin were re-creating from memory.

Perhaps she should be the narrator who tells the stories as they were told to her. That way she could fill in her own commentary and answers to the questions she occasionally posed to Lucky when they reviewed the transcripts from the previous week.

For instance, after last Sunday's story, Sarah had wanted to know, "Did Flavia greet Old Quin on the inner when he died—when his soul left his body?"

"She did," Lucky had replied thoughtfully. "Our souls spent many blissful hours together—however you count time in the realm beyond time. Initiations and soul growth don't end with the death of the body. We each had our own lessons to learn."

Sarah agreed. She was thinking back to her own experiences between embodiments. "I remember that about Alana and Ah-Lahn after he was killed by Arán Bán."

Lucky nodded. "Our situation was similar, yet different. In Ah-Lahn's case, his soul required several embodiments before this lifetime as Kevin.

Flavia had no such requirement to be reborn in another time or place. Though she did not ascend to the Great Silence, like Róisín's twin flame did, she had balanced enough of her karma so she could make progress from inner planes."

"Did your remaining in embodiment help or hinder that process?"

"I like to think I helped both of us by pursuing a spiritual path—though I could not seem to conquer my grief over losing her and Racham, and over the destruction of the druid communities.

"Between embodiments I was shown many aspects of our lives spent together and apart. Still, though inner lessons resonate in the soul, what we attain in outer consciousness is proof of the pudding, so to speak."

"Is this one of the reasons for sharing your stories with us?" Sarah asked. "That seems to be what you were saying last Sunday."

"It is, lass. The treasure is in the telling. A lesson you and Kevin have learned and have more to uncover."

They were both silent, an unspoken question hanging between them which Sarah knew she had to ask.

"Is this Sunday the last story?"

Lucky reached over and gently laid a hand on her shoulder.

"'Tis possible, lass. Though I don't feel the actual end approaching. We've yet to resolve the situation with the Conways, and I won't leave our community till I know that Fibonacci's is safely transferred to Kevin as my successor. And to each of you in the portion that is yours to hold."

Sarah kissed him on the cheek. "I'm glad to hear that."

"'Tis glad I am to say it," Lucky affirmed with a thoughtful nod. Then a cloud furrowed his brow. "Be prepared, my girl. There are dark days ahead and not even this old druid knows exactly what storms they may portend."

A Tale of the Heart

October swept onto Long Island with ominous clouds and a chill off the sea that reminded Lucky of his childhood home in Connemara. There were no cliffs at Tim and Maggie O'Toole's house on the bay, but the salty air was enough to tug at any Irishman's heart strings. Lucky's were playing a melancholy tune today.

Was this the last day for his Circle of Close Companions to gather 'round him while he told them of his past that had much to do with their future? He was not willing to say it was. As his mind drifted back to scenes of the rural life he'd lived as a child, he could almost hear that final story calling from the high mountains shrouded in mists and clouds.

Similar mists and clouds were hanging over the home of the O'Tooles where he'd landed some months ago to heal, to listen and to speak of sights and insights he'd not spoken of for many a year. The turf fire was especially welcome in today's blustery weather, and the couples hugged each other a little closer than on former Sundays.

'Tis a good setting for a tale of the heart, thought Lucky. First, he had a question for Jeremy. The lad was a seer of considerable gifts. The others needed to hear what he had to say.

His inquiry surprised them all, especially the tall young man with the deep brown eyes that didn't miss a thing. And who, like many in the group, often forgot how much Lucky himself could see.

"Jeremy, will you tell the group what you observed about the inner connection between A. B. Ryan and the Conways?"

Jeremy paused, then nodded with an amused smile. He enjoyed Lucky's sporting with him about being a seer.

"I can't say much specifically about an inner connection, except that

I believe there is one. I didn't pick up any significant details. Only that the Conways and A. B. Ryan had that look about them like they were family. You know how you can tell when people are kin, even if they've not been introduced as such? Kevin, you know what I mean."

"In theory, yes. Though when it comes to the Conways, I honestly can't offer an opinion. I met them at our Grand Re-Opening in May, but I've never had any dealings with them."

"I thought you had," said Jeremy.

"No, I haven't. Cyndi sold them the health food business and they rent space from Brian. Come to think of it, I haven't been in the store since we moved Fibonacci's over here to our new location."

"Were you avoiding them?" Lucky wanted to know.

"Maybe. Not consciously. I've never been prompted to interact with them, that's all. Sarah, what about you?"

"Same here. If I've needed any products for us or the babies, the herbalist sisters have supplied me. Family discount." She winked at Debbie, who had been embodied in the druidic community of Tearmann as her aunt Dearbhla, the seer and healer.

"Interesting," said Lucky, drawing out the words. "Your lack of interaction does have a bearing on today's story, as you will see later.

"Kevin, I'm going to answer your question from our first meeting about why Old Quin was so tough on all the druids, the younger ones in particular. You may yet be required to discover why he singled you out for the most rigorous disciplines. Today's story will likely give you some of the clues you need to unlock that mystery."

When Old Quin arrived back in Tearmann, the weather was harsh, as if he and the land of his birth were at odds. He felt lost, abandoned, without purpose. He compared himself to those he'd loved best and felt even worse about his current circumstance.

Racham was off in the Levant, pursuing his mission as a powerful teacher, healer and spiritual leader. He was loved by the thousands who flocked to hear him. The crowds followed him so closely that he often escaped to a ship or a distant shore to be at peace with his disciples—to whom he gave advanced teachings.

Old Quin was often frustrated when he observed how little of Racham's wisdom many of those twelve comprehended. *If I'd been there, I could have helped them understand,* he thought to himself.

Instead, he was stuck in a *túath* on the coast of Éire where his father was *ceann-druí,* while he was little more than a newly minted master druid without position or office.

Then there was Flavia. She had remained with her family and was sharing with them what she had learned from Racham. She also had taken it upon herself to see that the wattle tabernacle was kept in good repair. She prayed there often and was happy with her life. Quin could feel her deep love for him, but she was far more content than he.

One day Quin's father came to him, a serious expression on his ruddy face. 'My son, what do you observe in the Levant? Our seers are concerned and we are getting reports from travelers that things are not going well for your friend Racham.'

'Truth be told, Father, I've not been watching. Now that his mission is proceeding apace, he does not need my attention or poor prayers.'

'Did you learn nothing at Ynys Witrin!' boomed his father. He was a giant of a man in physical stature and in the authority he wore like a suit of armor.

'Your friend needs every prayer you can send him. Those loving throngs are loyal only when he is teaching them. As soon as they leave his presence, the whisperings of Racham's enemies sway them to doubt their own eyes and ears.'

Quin was stunned by his father's intensity.

'Racham is accused of being a devil or worse. Watch and learn, my son. The world is turning and your friend is the very hub of the wheel—the axis on which the future of every soul in this universe depends.'

From that day forward, Quin did watch. He learned first-hand the strategies of dark forces who plotted and planned and lied and manipulated the very laws they themselves had created in order to trap Racham and destroy him.

If Quin had not witnessed with his own eyes the tragedy that unfolded in the Levant, he would not have believed it. How could it be that his brilliant friend was tried and condemned in the dark of night, tortured and scourged and hung on a cross like the vilest of criminals? It was unthinkable. Yet it happened.

In his finer body, Quin stood on that wretched hill and wept with the holy women. Even when he learned that Racham's uncle, the *Nobilis Decurio,* had courageously secured the precious body and given it a proper entombment, grief overwhelmed him.

Quin was devastated—disillusioned that such cruelty could have been perpetrated against the man who had shone like the brightest star in the firmament.

When he'd learned of the astonishing miracles that followed, he had wanted to believe. But witnessing Racham's death seemed to have erected a wall between himself and the man's spirit. For many months he could not feel his friend's presence.

In those desperate hours, his telepathic communion with Flavia helped him build a bridge back to his friend. She knew Racham would live on. The Way of his teachings would spread throughout the world, and she intended to do her part. When Racham's uncle, his mother and other disciples arrived at Ynys Witrin in AD 36, Flavia was there, ready to help.

In the years that followed, Old Quin did succeed his father as *ceann-druí.* And he was fortunate to find a friend in the woman named Róisín—an elder seer, healer and his soulmate of many past lives. She listened with a heart of compassion and offered the wisdom of her vast experience.

Their conversations were solace to both of them. Yet, even in that relationship, loss was inevitable. Róisín's own lifespan came to a close when Old Quin was only in his late forties.

While Old Quin proved himself a wise adviser to Toíseach Cróga the elder and later to the younger, his real skill was as a mentor. He did not create his own school. Instead, students from his *túath* went to Ynys Môn or Ynys Witrin or to the school of Ard-Mháistir Óengus at Cois Abhann.

What Old Quin provided was the practical application of the *ceann-druí's* obligation to the law, the land and the oral heritage that had been handed down from generation to generation for thousands of years.

Above all, he championed the druid motto: 'Truth Against the World!' He was determined that a true path of ancient wisdom be the guiding light for all of his students.

He was tough because he had seen what the dark forces were capable of. He harbored no naïveté when it came to dealing with their lies and those who told them.

Now in his sixties, he had in his tutelage a group of aspiring druids who were remarkably intelligent. He saw them as the hope of his community. He also observed in them a danger that carried the potential to destroy that community from within.

They were Riordan, Ah-Lahn and a difficult young man named Arán Bán. The first two were dedicated and enthusiastic with a welcome touch of humility. The third was ambitious with a cruel streak that Old Quin was determined to curb.

He sought to understand why the man was sly, rigid and competitive beyond necessity, especially toward Ah-Lahn. One day, when Arán Bán's behavior had been notably unacceptable, he challenged the man to explain his motivation.

'Ask my mother,' was the reply delivered with a malice that seethed under his cryptic answer. That woman had been dead for several years, so her history remained a mystery until Old Quin probed the akashic records for an answer.

What his inner sight revealed to him was so troubling that he vowed to *An Síoraí,* the Eternal One, that he would do everything in his power to shore up the higher consciousness of these three men whose destinies were so tightly interwoven that, in all likelihood, none of them would escape the consequences.

He could not disclose these insights to the young druids, so he gave them the individual direction that might possibly bring them to their own inner awareness of the truth.

Riordan's heart was his own best guide, which Old Quin encouraged with opportunities for the young man to prove himself and boost the self-confidence he would need in years to come.

He treated Arán Bán with kindness—attempting to show him that being merciful to others was strength, not weakness. In fact, before he died, he named Arán Bán as his temporary successor to serve in that position until Ard-Mháistir Óengus could choose a permanent *ceann-druí*. He hoped that filling the office would convince the young man that community required care of more than the mind.

Finally, Old Quin focused his most rigorous disciplines on Ah-Lahn. Here was a man of character and intelligence who would prove to be a skilled leader—if he could wake up to the realities which the *ceann-druí* was not allowed to reveal.

Unfortunately, Old Quin had his own problems. His heart had been severely wounded by the death of Racham. When the Romans decimated the druid university and community at Ynys Môn in AD 60, the shock sent him reeling.

Had either of those horrific events not taken place, he might have withstood the cruelty of Flavia's martyrdom that same year. But compounding all these losses was more than he could bear.

And so, he died. Sadly, before he could turn the inevitable tide away from the malice that had blackened the soul of Arán Bán and that would be carried on in two of the children he sired who have reembodied in our time as the store owners we know.

Good God!" Phelan exclaimed when he had recovered himself enough to speak. "Are you suggesting that the Conways are the reembodied children of Arán Bán?"

"It makes sense," said Jeremy. "These family connections can go back in history for eons. The loves, the hates, the rivalries. The karma made among themselves and with other people."

"I remember those children—the spawn of Arán Bán and his consort, Una," said Rory in a low voice. "After Ah-Lahn died and Riordan became *ceann-druí,* they began a vicious campaign against Toíseach Cróga and the Druid Counsel. They split the *túath* of Tearmann into warring factions that resulted in many lives lost."

"Including Riordan's," said Glenna grimly.

"Including Riordan's," Rory nodded.

"I guess they're still at it," commented Hank. He was grateful that Tim had filled him in on the back story of the Friends of Ancient Wisdom during his tour of the tower. Apparently, the congenial adept had known that Hank would need an accelerated course in the mysteries surrounding Fibonacci's.

"If I'm hearing you all correctly," Hank continued, "the Conways are likely those people in this life. And the origin of their hatred could go back to before Atlantis."

"You have the right of it," said Lucky.

"But you haven't told us what caused the hatred Arán Bán harbored so vehemently against Ah-Lahn. And we don't know if there is an actual blood-kinship in this life between the Conways and A. B. Ryan."

Debbie suddenly gasped. "Oh, my God."

"What is it?" Jeremy put his arm around her shoulder and looked at her searchingly.

"I don't think there is a blood connection, but I'm pretty sure there is a business one. Sarah, you won't remember this because I was already working for A. B. Ryan before you joined his marketing team. In the early days when I was first employed in his office, he used to talk about a pal— he called him a pal—in one of his operations.

"I always had a hunch that operation was illegal and I'm thinking now it may have been one source of the cash he used to bribe judges and the police. That relationship seems to have soured, because I didn't hear the name mentioned more than once or twice."

"What was the name?" asked Sarah. "I'm afraid I already know."

Debbie nodded. "Stan. I once heard A. B. refer to 'My pal, Stan, the conman.'"

Stunned silence blanketed the room until Brian spoke. His tone was hopeful. "Maybe there's a way to tie whatever illegal deals the conman's got going now to his past with A. B. Ryan."

"It's a long shot," said Kevin. "Most of A. B.'s crimes were mafia-related. Actual references to Conway in official files are probably obscure or have been deleted."

"You're right," agreed Brian. "Still, if there were indictments that could be traced, Stan's name might show up. I'll call my attorneys in the morning. Maybe they can find something in court records. It's worth a try."

"I can't believe these are the people I sold my wonderful business to," said Cyndi tearfully. Pregnancy hormones were making her emotional. "Lucky, did this all have to play out?"

"It did, lass, and the play isn't over."

The afternoon sun had broken through the clouds and was dipping low, creating deep shadows across the lawn and terrace. Sarah shivered and not only from the waning warmth of the turf fire going to ashes.

"It's getting late, and it's time that Kevin and I picked up our little ones." She glanced over at Ivy and Brian. "I imagine your twins are ready to go home, too." They nodded wearily.

"Lucky, will you offer a prayer before we leave? I have to say that contacting these records is making me nervous. It wasn't very long ago that several of us had some horrific encounters with Arán Bán. Thankfully, he's been eliminated. But if his relations are still plotting and planning against Fibonacci's, we need to be extremely careful."

"Sarah is right," said Lucky. "Let's join hands and give our OM. Then I'll send you on your way with a blessing."

The Lifetime of Greatest Import

Monday, October 4 - at the MacCauleys'

Sarah had good reason to be concerned, as did Kevin. She could see it in the deep lines that furrowed his brow. They had awakened at the same time and looked straight into each other's eyes.

"Today's the day for our life review, isn't it?" she said before he could tell her the news he was reluctant to share.

"It is. Did our Master appear to you?"

"He did."

She was about to elaborate when two little voices began calling "Mama! Dada!" from the nursery. "Oh, they're awake. Guess we'll talk at breakfast. Will you call my mom and ask if we can drop off the twins in a couple of hours?"

Kevin picked up his phone. "I have a feeling the O'Tooles and Lucky already know we'll be arriving soon. I'll call them anyway, just in case."

Two hours later Maggie was serving the MacCauleys a much-needed cup of tea and a second breakfast. Lucky joined them briefly, then retired to his rooms. His consciousness was already highly attuned to the life review. He would be giving powerful chants throughout the entire experience.

Sarah had pulled her long auburn hair back in a clip and she wore no make-up. She had given up trying not to look frazzled this morning.

"I still underestimate how long it takes to get two wiggly toddlers ready to go out for the day," she apologized. "Fortunately, my mother understands. Better than I do."

"You are forgiven for being human, *a chara*," chuckled Maggie. "Now, drink your tea and tell us how our Master wants you to proceed."

"On the way over here we compared our dreams from last night," said

Kevin. "Saint Germain's instruction to each of us was identical."

Sarah elaborated. "He will meet us in the tower after we've completed the chants and prayers we always use to invoke his presence. He asks that both of you sit with us to guard our physical forms."

"We expected as much," said Tim. "We'll make sure you return to your bodies safely."

Maggie turned to Kevin. He was gazing off into the distance and shivering as a cool breeze blew in through the French doors that were open to a sunny October morning.

"Don't fret, lad, you're secure with us beside you."

Kevin ran his hands through his dark brown hair and came back to himself. "Thanks, Maggie. I trust you both. It's our safety while we're in the scenes of the life review I'm concerned about. This initiation—for it feels like a major test—is requiring every ounce of my willpower to enter."

Sarah was unnerved to see her husband so troubled. "I'm here with you, Kevin. We're doing this together." She put her hand on his arm.

"I know," he said. "That's what worries me."

As soon as the four had completed the necessary spiritual preparation in Tim's Tower, the Master Saint Germain appeared to them in his light body which was visible only to those with advanced second sight.

You are well met, my son and daughter and faithful guardians. I greet you to provide a prologue for today's experience.

You will be entering a drama with a cast of many characters, all of whom you know in this life, though names and roles differ from lifetime to lifetime. I believe the only one of your company who has retained her soul name through the centuries is our dear Róisín.

You will not be surprised to observe your adversaries in these scenes as the very ones you are now facing. What you may find most troubling is the relationships in which you were involved in the past.

The lifetime, which begins in 28 B.C. when the souls of Kevin and the Conways were born, was not the first instance of conflict between you. However, it is the lifetime of greatest import for your understanding and resolution of the present difficulties confronting you.

Now visualize the necessary orbs of light as they will appear here in the tower. When the scenes materialize before you, Sarah and Kevin will step onto the stage of life when your entrance is required. That step may not occur as soon as you expect and your exit may be abrupt.

The Master addressed that final sentence to Sarah. He immediately disappeared as spheres of violet light beckoned her and her twin flame into the life review which neither of them had wanted to experience.

In the year 28 B.C., three souls were born in the *túath* of Tearmann on the eastern coast of Éire. They were reared in a community of the powerful Brigantes tribe and grew up expecting to become druids, as were their respective parents.

The druidic oral tradition taught the importance of maintaining personal and interpersonal harmony. Only a person whose mind and soul were in alignment with inner universal laws was capable of fulfilling the complex teachings that set these adepts apart from even the most erudite Greek philosophers of the time.

Therefore, it was surprising to all who were aware of such things that there should be severe enmity between the families of these young people. No one could account for it, except to suppose that its origin lay centuries in the past—perhaps before the sinking of Atlantis or even earlier.

Nevertheless, the three waxed strong and gained in mastery. The two who were twin flames wed at an early age and produced two children—a boy and a girl, whose roles as teenagers in this drama give them import. At a later date, the daughter would give birth to Arán Bán and his older sister, Casidhe.

The unmarried lad had a younger sister. She adored her brother throughout childhood and into adulthood, when she married a warrior who was in service to the local *toíseach*.

Unfortunately, the sister was not the only one enthralled by the many gifts of her handsome brother. The druidess, who ironically insisted on being addressed as Bantiarna (though she was no lady) was also obsessed with the man.

She and her husband—whom many in the *túath* thought of as the Sly Druid—had become highly skilled in certain ancient practices, though they tended to live on the fringe of the druidic community. For neither of them cared much about marital fidelity.

In fact, the further their eyes roamed, the better they liked it. They frequently told each other about their sexual conquests—as if they were competing to see who could bag the biggest prize. Who among the mighty druids could they bring low in order to raise themselves up?

One day it happened that Bantiarna won the competition.

While her husband focused on power politics within the *túath*, she had a way with herbs and potions and spells that were difficult to detect and powerful in their effects on her unwitting prey. Many men and a few women had fallen victim to her schemes.

Plotting and planning, she had saved her most potent concoctions for the sister's older brother. For a few months Bantiarna watched and waited for an opportunity to use them. Then, like a viper, she struck.

She had hoped to find the man in the grove he favored, since he had recently been named *ceann-druí*. However, realizing that perfect timing was essential to her long-term plans, she went to his hut where he lived alone—as was often the custom of master druids until they were firmly settled in their offices.

Bantiarna was a voluptuous woman who was very aware of her physical attributes. On this day she had adorned herself in her finest garments and scented herself with aromatics that only heightened her appeal.

As she entered the *ceann-druí's* dwelling, her demeanor was demure, her eyes reflecting the soul of innocence she wished him to perceive.

Gliding into his private space, she could not help but congratulate herself on the deception. The man was so trusting. He was making this far too easy. She was about to land the biggest fish of her life.

Her unsuspecting prey stood and addressed her cordially. "Greetings, Bantiarna. How may I be of service?"

"I am sorry to disturb you, *Ceann-Druí*." She used his title as a way of demonstrating the respect that, in fact, she did not feel. "I have been creating some excellent new herbal compounds that I believe will benefit our people. The best one is taken orally as a tincture. Will you try it for me and give your approval?"

The *ceann-druí* faced his visitor.

"I will be pleased to assist you, though I wonder why you are not presenting your work to our healers."

"They have already pronounced this one superlative," Bantiarna lied. "However, they know how skilled you are in these matters and have asked for your additional comment."

"Very well. How shall I take it?"

"You may sample this dose." She held out a small flask. The instant the *ceann-druí* touched the container, a sensation that he could not quite identify ran up his arm.

"Oh, I see you are already feeling its power," cooed the woman. "Drink it all and you will discover an even more potent effect." She took hold of his hand that held the flask, pulled out the stopper and poured the contents into his mouth.

The *ceann-druí's* body shuddered as the tincture slid down his throat. A fire flashed into his brain, then dove straight to his loins. His eyes went wide as he looked upon Bantiarna. She was the most alluring creature he had ever beheld. He instantly desired her with an overwhelming passion.

Delighted that her potion was working so quickly, she led him to his sleeping platform and began to undress. Aflame with lust, he shed his own garments and had his way with her—exactly as she had planned.

A Wicked Fate

When the *ceann-druí* awoke hours later, his head ached and he lay naked as the day he was born. A strong, nauseating scent lingered on his body and an empty flask lay on the floor where the seductress had made certain he would find it.

He hurriedly dressed in his clothes which he also found on the floor and began to reconstruct the afternoon's events. Though his mind was severely muddled, he did not require much thought to realize what had taken place. And why.

The druids were not by nature licentious and they expected the most scrupulous behavior from their leaders. What should he do?

He ruminated for over an hour and eventually convinced himself that, considering Bantiarna's unsavory reputation (which he had failed to take into account when she approached him), perhaps no real harm had been done. He certainly would be wary of any interaction with her in the future.

Fortunately, nothing came of this event. Neither the Sly Druid nor his wife said a word about the *ceann-druí's* moment of weakness. In fact, he need not have worried about escaping Bantiarna's attention. She scrupulously avoided him and made herself known to him only many months later. On that day, he was shocked when she appeared at his hut and entered as brazenly as she had done nearly a year earlier.

"I am not available," the *ceann-druí* stated flatly.

"I will take but a moment of your time," said the woman with a smirk. "I have come to introduce you to your daughter."

She held out a tiny bundle. The infant opened her clear blue eyes and looked directly into the astonished face of her twin soul.

The *ceann-druí* recognized her instantly.

"We call her Little Sarah." Bantiarna oozed the self-satisfaction she saw no reason to hide. "We will take good care of her. My children are delighted to have an infant to play with."

"You cannot...," the *ceann-druí* stammered. "You...you do not deserve her. Give her to me and I will raise her. She is my blood, my soul."

He tried to wrest the baby from her mother, but the woman was too quick. She was out the door and on her way back to the dwelling she shared with her husband and their two teenaged children who were cut from the same dark cloth as their parents.

Disgusted and horrified beyond belief, the *ceann-druí* sank onto the edge of his sleeping platform, his head in his hands. He could hear Bantiarna's taunting laughter echoing across the *túath*. The sound shook him to the core of his being.

As time passed, the *ceann-druí* was surprised that the woman did not prevent him from interacting with Little Sarah. In fact, she clearly drew pleasure from allowing him to hold the child. Naturally, she claimed the baby was the product of the loving relationship between her and her husband.

"The *ceann-druí* has no children of his own," she explained to her neighbors. "It gives me such joy to share our daughter with him."

As soon as Little Sarah could walk, her mother often let her wander. Unsupervised, the child would toddle her way around hut and grove until she found the *ceann-druí*. She would sit with him as he prayed and often fell asleep in his arms until he, duty-bound, carried the wailing child back to her mother.

Bantiarna never failed to bestow upon the *ceann-druí* her most supercilious smile. She often patted him on the shoulder like a pet dog as he laid the child in the undeserving mother's arms. She knew each separation was a knife in the man's back and she relished his pain.

The Sly Druid welcomed his wife's reports on the effect her treachery was having on their victim—and for which they mocked him at every opportunity. They knew the cause of his suffering and worked hard to increase his turmoil.

The *ceann-druí* was beginning to falter in the execution of his duties. When required to accompany the *toíseach* on occasional skirmishes in which the leader engaged with neighboring tribes, he became so ineffective that the Druid Counsel began to express concern.

However, the *ceann-druí* was well-loved and respected, so they agreed to let him carry on until some event or action should take place that would necessitate his removal from office.

That event did transpire, in the most unforeseen manner.

One day, when Little Sarah was five years of age, Bantiarna once more made her way to the *ceann-druí's* hut. He was eating the simple midday meal that was his custom when she barged in like a gale-force wind.

The man had long since ceased to be civil when confronted with her intrusions. He rose from his seat, prepared to usher her out the way she'd entered. Then he saw that she carried Little Sarah. The child appeared to be asleep, though she hung limply in the woman's arms, her head lolling back, her mouth open.

"I've brought you the child," said Bantiarna in a voice filled with malice. "You've always wanted her. Now she's yours."

Without another word, she dumped Little Sarah's lifeless body at the *ceann-druí's* feet.

"I'm sorry she's somewhat the worse for wear. My children were teaching her to fly. Sadly, when she jumped off that big boulder and hit her head—well, as you see, the child did not have wings after all."

Years of pent-up anger overcame the *ceann-druí* with a rage unlike any emotion he would have imagined himself capable. The strength of a giant rippled through his veins.

Without the benefit of spells or potions to weaken her foil, Bantiarna was at a disadvantage. Full-figured as she was, the man was taller and stronger. When he fastened his hands around her neck, he did not let go until she fell as lifeless as the child she had destroyed.

The *ceann-druí* knew he was a dead man. With nothing to lose, he seized a sword from the ceremonial weaponry he rarely used and raced to the Sly Druid's hut. He found the man alone, his back to the door. Afraid to hesitate lest he lose his nerve, the *ceann-druí* raised the sword and struck. The weapon was sharp, the blow clean, the death instantaneous.

For a moment he stood stunned. Numb as rage left him, he dropped the sword on the floor and turned to leave. When he crossed the threshold, dazed and spattered with blood, he literally ran into the couple's teenaged daughter.

She had come to deliver a new cloak to her father. He prized her garments for the magic she wove into them and often wore them during the dark rituals he conducted.

"What have you done?" The daughter shrieked and rushed to the side of her father who lay in a crimson pool. Rising with astonishing fury, she screamed at the *ceann-druí,* "You will pay with your life! My family will haunt you and yours till the end of time! You will never be forgiven! That is my promise and my curse!"

Devastated beyond reason, the *ceann-druí* whirled and ran back to his hut. Tenderly gathering the broken body of Little Sarah in his arms, he carried her into the deepest part of forest. There he buried her and soon vanished from Tearmann.

His sister searched for him for several weeks—until her own life's tragedy overtook her. Eventually, she abandoned all hope for her brother as she did for herself.

For years, rumors circulated about a lone druid wandering the forests of eastern Éire. However, his peers knew that, soon after burying the child whose soul was the twin of his own, the *ceann-druí* had died of grief.

The shock of Little Sarah's death and the murders he had committed had shattered his heart. He died lying next to the child's grave he had dug with his bare hands. Only days later, wolves devoured his body.

Those who could see such things were aware that, once out of embodiment, he had begged the Great Masters of Wisdom for an opportunity to repay the terrible debt to life he had incurred. He vowed to serve his community selflessly until the karma was balanced. He would willingly lay down his own life many times so the kin of the slain couple might live.

His petition was granted and in a dozen years he was born to a family of fishermen in the *túath* of Tearmann. They named him Ah-Lahn and in time he became a great master druid. As he had agreed, while still in his prime and married to Alana, the reembodied soul of his beloved Little Sarah, he was murdered by Arán Bán—the grandson of Bantiarna and her husband, the Sly Druid.

The grandson's mind had been poisoned by his mother—the teenaged daughter who had cursed her father's killer. The infection had not been difficult, for these same individuals had been wreaking havoc on Ah-Lahn and his loved ones for eons.

The reasons were long lost in the mists of antiquity. And as Old Quin had foreseen, the deadly fruits sown from those poisonous seeds were ripening now in modern times in a way that none of the players in this drama were likely to escape.

The O'Tooles remained huddled with the MacCauleys in the tower. Tim and Maggie were sitting with their arms around Kevin and Sarah. The two were clutching each other, sobbing as their guardians had never witnessed in their long years of service to the Masters.

"Release it all," Maggie softly encouraged the couple. "We will stay here with you for as long as you need us. The floodgates must open for the record to be cleared. The storm will pass in its own time."

Eventually their sobbing ceased. Kevin and Sarah tentatively released each other from the fierce embrace that had seemed to them the only way they could possibly survive. They were utterly and completely spent and so weak they wondered if they had the strength to descend the tower's ladder and stairs back to ground level.

"Take your time, *a chairde*," said Tim as they gingerly made their way out of the round tower and across the lawn to the O'Tooles' house.

Still gripping each other's hands, Kevin and Sarah headed straight for a sofa in front of the fireplace where Tim set a huge pile of turf bricks ablaze. They were cold to the bone and welcomed the tea and hot soup Maggie brought them on a tray so they could eat by the fire.

As promised, Lucky had been holding vigil in his rooms. He soon joined them and sat quietly with Tim and Maggie at the dining table until their friends were able to speak. The pair finished their meal in silence and then turned to their faithful guardians.

"Will you sit with us?" Sarah said softly. "We have some questions."

When they were all gathered around the fire, Kevin spoke gravely. "I have only one question: Is this karma balanced or must others suffer?"

"Or must Kevin die?" Sarah asked wearily.

This was an hour for absolute honesty and Lucky knew he must tell them the truth.

"Until this afternoon, there was no guarantee that Kevin would live out this life as an old man. Our Master has given me permission to tell you that unless you do something foolish, you will live to witness the birth of your grandchildren."

Sarah put her arms around her husband and held him with a fierce strength that rose up from the depths of her soul. Grateful beyond words, they looked to Lucky.

"What else can you tell us?" Kevin asked. "Or are you allowed to say more?"

"I am," Lucky nodded. "For you must understand how the Great Law has worked in your favor.

"Several lifetimes are usually required to pay the debt for murder. Fortunately, you balanced some of that karma by your sincere remorse after that lifetime and in losing your next life at the hands of your ancient nemesis, Arán Bán.

"During intervening centuries, you have been given many opportunities to serve Stan and Stacey, which greatly reduced your debt to them. Unfortunately, that family's desire for revenge has never abated. Two years ago in Ireland, Arán Bán tried again to kill you with a poisoned knife. When he instigated the fire at Fibonacci's, you were severely injured. Those situations all served to tip the karmic scales in your favor.

"*A chairde,* the strength you both have displayed in going through this very painful life review has achieved a balance sufficient to spare Kevin's life. Many souls are neither willing nor able to summon the courage necessary to witness the record of their worst misdeeds and accept the karma they have incurred. That determination opens the door to mercy.

"Our Master is grateful to you. The entire Friends of Ancient Wisdom community is safer now because of your courage. Debts may remain which others must pay, and you will likely face additional challenges in the future. Nevertheless, as of this moment, your soul is clear of this record."

Revelations

When Kevin emerged from the long, hot shower that felt like a welcome cleansing, he discovered that Sarah wasn't in bed. Although he was exhausted from the day's ordeal, he padded down the hallway where he found her in the nursery.

She was curled up in her favorite overstuffed chair, watching Naimh and Gareth as they slept. At first Kevin thought she was quietly musing on their children, but then he noticed that her body was tense.

"Are you coming to bed?" he whispered.

Without answering, Sarah rose and walked to their bedroom. Instead of retiring as Kevin had hoped, she sat on the loveseat that flanked the window where morning sun was often the first greeting of the day.

She motioned for Kevin to join her. "Will you sit with me?"

"Is something wrong?" he asked. Sarah clearly wanted to talk.

"Yes," she said. There was desperation in her voice and she seemed on the verge of tears. "I was watching the babies resting so peacefully in their cribs. They were smiling those little toddler smiles. They have no idea of the malice that lives in the hearts of some people. They are so trusting and vulnerable. Until today's life review, I don't think I ever realized how completely dependent they are on us for their safety."

"I know what you mean," said Kevin softly. "Is that what you want to talk about?"

"Not the safety of our children. The safety of one child at the center of the events we witnessed today."

"Little Sarah." Kevin shuddered and his chest tightened with the pain that still resonated in him over the death of his twin flame in that lifetime. Then a thought crossed his mind.

"I know Lucky said my soul is clear of the life record we witnessed. Now I'm wondering if he meant only the record of the murders, not of my failure to protect you." He turned to Sarah. "Can you forgive me for not saving you from that wicked woman?"

Without warning, Sarah burst into white hot tears that made her want to shout, except she didn't want wake the children.

Kevin reached over to take her hand, but she pulled it away.

"Why *didn't* you save me?" She spoke in a stage whisper yet with an intensity that surprised them both. She squeezed her eyes shut and made herself get a grip on her emotions. Kevin didn't deserve this.

"I'm sorry. While we were still at the O'Tooles', I didn't realize how deeply the life review affected me. Since we've been home, I keep hearing Little Sarah crying, 'Why won't you save me?' That's what I was thinking every time you gave me back to that horrible woman."

Kevin was dumbfounded. "I honestly don't know," he said bleakly. "Cowardice?"

"You've never shied from danger." Sarah looked him in the eye. "I've watched you run toward mortal threats in too many lifetimes to ever call you a coward. What else could have been going through your mind?"

They were both silent while Kevin forced his awareness to return to the scenes he had hoped never to witness again. At last, a veil lifted.

"I *did* want to keep you with me, but I knew I couldn't care for a very small child. As *ceann-druí* I was bound to serve the *toíseach*. I was often away from the *túath* for days or weeks at a time. I do remember thinking, 'A child needs her mother.' I convinced myself that even such a mother was better than none. She appeared to be fond of you."

Sarah stood abruptly and began pacing. "Surely you could have found a way. If you'd really loved me, you would have found a way." She stopped and planted herself in front of Kevin—desperately willing him to understand what she had experienced. "I was terrified of that woman and her children—the way they tormented me."

"That was your dream about being smothered, wasn't it?" Puzzling events were coming together in Kevin's mind. "Sarah, I swear I didn't know they were mistreating you. If I'd been aware, I would have..."

He stopped mid-sentence.

"You would have what?" Sarah's eyes flashed at him.

He returned the intensity of her expression.

"I'd like to think I would have kidnapped you and we'd have escaped to the farthest island of the known world."

"But you didn't."

"No, I didn't. And I will be sorry for that failure for the rest of my life. But, Sarah, I didn't know what you were going through."

"You were unaware of the lies she told me about you?"

"What lies? Come, sit and tell me. I want to understand."

Sarah sighed from the depths of her soul and moved back to the loveseat. A light was beginning to dawn in her own understanding.

"I see now that Bantiarna recognized the love between us. She went after our soul connection with a vengeance. I remember her telling me, 'You think he loves you. Well, he doesn't. He was angry that I got pregnant when he ruthlessly attacked and raped me. He's disgusted with you. A mewling infant he called you.' Imagine anyone saying that to a tiny child."

"That is so vile."

"It was. Even when I was little more than a baby, she hounded me, saying over and over, 'He wishes you'd never been born.' I was so confused. When I was with you, I could feel your love. Then you would give me back to her, which only confirmed in my mind that you really didn't care if I was alive or dead."

When Kevin reached for Sarah's hand this time, she did not pull away.

"I was so desperate that when those teenagers told me I could fly, I believed them. By that time, I was accustomed to accepting their lies as truth. When they said all I had to do was leap off that big rock, I spread my arms and jumped as far and as high as I could. We know how that turned out."

Kevin enfolded Sarah in his arms. "I am so sorry," he said, stroking her hair. "Please, forgive me. I promise I will never let you down again."

She sat up and looked into his eyes, now as red as hers, seeking the assurance neither of them could give the other. "Do you think life will let you keep that promise?"

"God, I hope so."

Once more, Sarah leaned into her husband's embrace and sent her mind back through the past two thousand years. There she discovered the consequences of her own unknowing.

She sat up abruptly. "Oh my God, Kevin. I am so terribly sorry. I have to apologize to you."

"Why?"

"For all of these centuries—until this very moment—I have harbored unconscious anger against you." She took both his hands in hers.

"I never knew that *you* did not know how that terrible woman was manipulating both of us. I may have been told the truth between embodiments, but Little Sarah's anger was buried in my psyche and couldn't be resolved until the record was revealed."

"How do you feel now?"

"Completely spent and empty—as if *An Síorai*, the Eternal One, has rolled up the entire record of my anger and our mutual misunderstanding in that lifetime and tossed it into a giant bonfire. Thank God we could face this together."

"And yet, we are still responsible for our personal karma," Kevin said quietly. He was thinking of his own obligations to life. "Even as twin flames, we must achieve our individual wholeness. Though we walk the path together, our mastery remains a do-it-yourself project."

Sarah rested her head on his chest as he renewed his embrace. "That's sobering, isn't it?" she said. "In the end, I think love is all we can actually give each other."

"And forgiveness, *a ghrá*."

"And forgiveness."

Turning the Tide

Starting the very next day, Lucky could be found at Róisín's Coffee Shop every day of the week. He usually worked all morning, then returned in the evening to conduct devotional services for the entire Friends of Ancient Wisdom community

People loved it and turned out in large numbers. A side benefit was that they talked to him and told him what they'd been hearing—mostly rumors being whispered about the Fibonacci's businesses and those who ran them.

Some rumors were silly. Others mean. A few truly dangerous. The worst accused Kevin and Jeremy of embezzlement or claimed that Brian had reneged on a contract, costing Stan and Stacey thousands of dollars.

Lucky was able to dispel most of them. Old timers who had known him for years carried the truth back to the ears of newer members who had been most susceptible to the untruths. Longtime customers gave their assurance to anyone who would listen that Fibonacci's bookstore and coffee shop were supremely honest establishments. Managers all breathed a sigh of relief. Lucky's presence had made all the difference.

Then the dam broke.

Early Monday morning of the following week, investigators from multiple federal agencies descended on Conway's health food store. As if they had been tipped off, reporters were waiting outside to capture images of Stan and Stacey being led away in handcuffs.

Because the store was located in the Fibonacci's block, the authorities also raided Brian's office—as well as Kevin's and Jeremy's—carrying off computers and boxes of files. All of the businesses were shuttered until further notice. It was a complete disaster.

To make matters worse, all three of Fibonacci's administrators plus Lucky were taken into custody for questioning. They barely had time to call their attorneys before the interrogation began.

Questioning went on for hours. Anyone else probably would have been thrown in jail or indicted on multiple charges. But the agents were not accustomed to dealing with two master druids, a seer, a very smart businessman and his even smarter attorneys.

Brian and his lawyers had out-negotiated A. B. Ryan when he tried to ruin Lucky financially. They were not about to lose this assault on the integrity of their client.

Fortunately, when Brian and Hank first told Kevin and Jeremy about the situation with the Conways, they had conducted a quick audit of their own financials. They had always maintained impeccable records, as had Hank for the Boston branch of Callahan & Logan.

The agents were able to review all of these files as well as the rental agreement between Fibonacci's and Conway's health food store. Brian had also taken the step of legally terminating the contract for Stan's computer upgrade. All of those documents were available for review. Tax returns were in order, having been subject to an outside audit, which Kevin and Jeremy had requested last spring.

At one point the agents left the room to confer with each other. Who were these people? They were obviously highly professional and appeared to be honest beyond all doubt. Incredibly, the four men had remained completely calm, even under the most intense interrogation. In fact, they appeared to be anticipating the authorities' demands for information.

Shaking their heads, the agents returned to the room. "No more questions," they said flatly. "You're free to go and take your materials with you."

Such was not the case with the health food store. The business was padlocked, and not even Brian's attorneys could find out what was going on with his real estate or with the Conways.

Major news stories appeared in the media—all with a negative spin on what had happened to this fine family business. Were the rumors true after all? What were they hiding that not even trained agents could find?

Why were the Conways still in custody when the others were not? Had they bribed the officials?

The damage was mounting by the hour.

Finally, the four men decided to announce a news conference for Tuesday afternoon in front of Fibonacci's bright blue doors. Dozens of reporters showed up and the barrage of insinuating questions began. However, salacious journalists had never tried to trap individuals with such poise and skill. Every leading question was rolled back upon the one who attempted to use it as an attack. The jackals eventually slunk away.

Incredibly, late-night news reported that the Fibonacci's businesses and Callahan & Logan Computer Systems were not being accused of any wrong doing. In fact, Fibonacci's would be open in the morning as usual.

The public was invited to experience for themselves the congenial atmosphere and wholesome products that had made the bookstore and coffee shop community favorites in their former location and now here in their new one. The only comment about the health food store was that it was still under investigation. No additional information was available at this time.

Wednesday morning brought a tidal wave of customers. The immediate world appeared to have assembled on the sidewalk and rushed in the minute Debbie opened the front door. She, Cyndi and Phelan had prepared for an onslaught, but this was extreme. Well-wishers, regular patrons and new ones poured in from as far away as the Hamptons, Yonkers, Newark, even Connecticut.

Phone calls had gone out to longtime Friends of Ancient Wisdom for help, and they were there in force. Bakers were baking. Baristas were filling regular orders. Cyndi and Phelan were creating specialty drinks. Debbie was supervising inside. Hank was managing the crowd outside.

Tim and Maggie appeared to be having the time of their lives, bussing tables, filling coffee urns and chatting away. They were also watching for anybody with a sour expression who still might be harboring doubts about the integrity of the coffee shop and bookstore. They cheerfully answered questions, continued to dispel rumors and filled empty coffee cups.

Lucky was everywhere. When they didn't see him, they knew he was upstairs in the ballroom, chanting and praying with devoted community members who decided that invoking light was the best contribution they could make to the day's success.

Next door, Kevin, Rory and Jeremy were selling books like there was no tomorrow. Under Rory's management, the staff had adopted Lucky's technique of asking patrons what they valued most. Today they were concentrating on ringing up sales and answering questions about the press conference.

At five o'clock, Sarah and Ivy decided it was long past time when they should relieve Eileen and Patrick of the two sets of twins they had been entertaining for most of the day—with some much-appreciated assistance from Charlotte, who had stopped by to help.

When Kevin, Brian and Hank returned home an hour later, everyone was confident that the tide of negative publicity had been turned.

Tomorrow was likely to be another busy day, though hopefully without such a crush of people. The only question on their minds was: What was happening with the Conways? There was still no word from Brian's attorneys. Perhaps no news was good news.

At 7:00 p.m. Kevin's cell phone rang.

"Hey, Kevin, it's Brian. I just got a call from one of the new attorneys who's working on the health food store case. He said they received additional information on the Conways and they need Vee and me to come to the office right away."

"This late on a Wednesday night? That's odd."

"Yeah, I know and he apologized. He said it was urgent that we verify what we know, especially Vee's experience working for those two. All the attorneys are working late to get information ready for the hearing on Friday morning. They're expecting indictments and want to have the documents in order so there are no slip-ups in court."

"This still sounds odd," said Kevin, "but then the whole situation with the Conways has been odd from the beginning. What about your kiddos? Do you need to bring then over here?"

"No, Hank's staying with them. He'd already made popcorn and they were watching a movie. He can put them to bed when it's over. We should be home in a couple of hours. The attorney said our interview would be as short as they could make it."

"Sounds like you've got things covered. Call me when you get back, okay? I'm curious to hear what new information the attorneys have that's so urgent. And I want to make sure you're both still in one piece."

"Will do." Brian paused. "Thanks for everything, Kevin. You've been a rock. Vee and I really appreciate it."

When the Bough Breaks

When Brian and Ivy arrived at the attorney's office the building was dark. No lights were on and the front door was locked.

"The attorney who called said not to worry if the front lights were off," explained Brian. "They're working in the back. We should just ring the bell and somebody will let us in."

Ivy tried peering through the glass door. "I don't like this."

"Nor should you, little lady," a familiar voice growled behind them. They both turned to see Stan pointing a gun at Ivy.

"Stan? What are you...?" started Brian.

"Shut up and get in the car." He motioned to a black sedan. Stacey was in the driver's seat. "Ivy, in the back with me. Brian, in the front where I can see you. Don't try anything or the wife gets it."

"I don't know what you're up to," said Brian firmly, "but Ivy has nothing to do with the problems you and I have. Let her go."

"Now, why would I give up my bargaining chip? Ivy's my leverage to help you see your way clear to assisting me and my associates with our financial arrangements."

Stan sat behind his wife and snarled at her. "What are you waiting for? Get going. And watch your speed. We don't want any cops pulling us over."

"I know what I'm doing. Stop bullying me," she snapped.

After she had driven about ten miles along a dark, tree-lined, two-lane road, Stan barked, "Turn left up here." He still had the gun pointed at Ivy and menacingly waved it at her every few minutes to make sure she behaved herself.

"That's not the turn," Stacey argued. "It's another mile yet."

"All right, all right. But watch your speed."

After another minute, Stacey slowed the car.

"What are you doing?" Stan demanded.

"I think I missed the turn."

"You stupid dame. Keep going. There's another road up ahead that circles around. And do what I tell you."

Stacey stomped on the gas. She hated it when Stan was right.

"Where's the stupid road?" she peered through the windshield.

"Straight over this bridge."

"I don't see it." Stacey took her eyes off the road and glowered at Stan in the rear view mirror. Before she realized what was happening, the car started drifting into the left lane, into the path of an oncoming truck that was halfway across the bridge that spanned the deep end of a large pond.

"Look out!" shouted Brian as he reached over to help Stacey.

"Sit down!" Stan yelled and turned his gun on Brian, aiming at his head, his hand poised on the trigger.

Stacey wrenched the steering wheel right and left and then back to the right. She was driving too fast and couldn't stop. The car was out of control, fishtailing wildly. It smashed the guardrail and flew into the water. The right front tire hit a rock, causing the car to roll onto the driver's side.

The passengers were bounced around and the gun went off. So did the air bags, which ruined Stan's aim. That saved Brian from immediate death, but a bullet struck him obliquely in the back of his neck. He began to bleed profusely.

The car was sinking fast, filling with water. The two men who were in the approaching truck had witnessed the whole thing. They pulled over and dialed 911. The larger of the two grabbed a flashlight and hurried down the embankment to the right side of the car.

"Bring the crowbar and get down here!" he yelled to the second man. "The driver's side is blocked, but we can get the other passengers out."

By that time more cars had stopped and several men rushed to help while the car was still sinking. Working together, two groups were able to pry open both right side doors in time to pull Ivy and Brian out and carry them to safety. Emergency vehicles and paramedics arrived within minutes.

When Kevin's cell phone rang, he and Sarah were drinking a cup of tea after putting the twins to bed. "At last!" he said. "This should be Brian."

But, of course, it wasn't.

"Kevin, it's Hank." The voice on the other end of the line was frantic. "There's been an accident. Brian and Ivy were in a car with the Conways. They went off a bridge. Car's all smashed. The O'Tooles just showed up to take care of the twins. That's all I know. I gotta get to the hospital."

"Hank! Hank!" Kevin shouted, but the call had dropped. Then the phone rang again. "Hank?"

"No, it's Maggie. Tim's on the other line with the highway patrol. The officer didn't know much except that Ivy's conscious and Brian's badly hurt. Somehow he was shot. The ambulance took them to Glen Cove Hospital. Eileen and Patrick are on their way there now. Debbie and Jeremy will be at your house in a few minutes to watch your twins so you can leave. Lucky's at Fibonacci's praying. Glenna, Rory, Cyndi and Phelan are joining him, and others will be taking turns around the clock."

"What about the Conways?"

"They're dead, Kevin," said Maggie simply. "Hang on, Tim wants to talk to you." She handed the phone to her husband.

"Here's what I found out. Seems that when the car went into the water, pieces of the guardrail smashed into the driver's side, blocking the doors. Stan was in the backseat, trapped under a piece of metal that had shattered the window next to him. Stacey had been driving. They were both dead at the scene. Maybe drowned. Maybe other injuries. The officer didn't know.

"He said it was a bizarre accident. It was like the left side of the car was totally demolished and the right side was nearly intact so the people who responded were able to save the other passengers. I'll call you if we hear anything else. You may learn more once you get to the hospital."

"The whole thing was a set-up," said Jeremy when he and Debbie arrived at the MacCauleys'. "I called Brian's attorney at home. He said there were no new people on the case. Nobody's working late and, as far as he was aware, indictments were not imminent. There was no additional information, except that the Conways had been let out on bail, which he hadn't expected."

"Stay at the hospital as long as you're needed," said Debbie, helping Sarah put on a jacket. She knew her friend was remembering how Brian's family had survived an accident two years ago. Hopefully, they would again. At least the twins hadn't been with them this time.

Kevin and Sarah found her parents in the emergency room waiting area. The elder Callahans stood as they came in. Mother and daughter embraced—speechless. Kevin put his arm around his father-in-law's shoulder. He'd never seen the man so shaken.

"Ivy's on the other side of those doors," said Patrick. He pointed to the entry marked No ADMITTANCE. Always the rock of the family, he was doing his best to keep it together for his wife, but he was having a hard time.

"Our girl has whiplash and a mild concussion. The docs don't want her falling asleep right now, so Hank's with her. Brian's in surgery. He was shot at the back of the neck and lost a lot of blood. They're really worried about his brain stem and they don't know if he's going to..."

Patrick's voice cracked and he buried his face in Kevin's shoulder. The two men managed to move to the sofa beside Sarah and Eileen when Hank walked out from the emergency room.

"The docs are with Ivy now. She's doing better."

"Thank God," said Kevin. "When we drove up we spoke to a couple of police detectives who want to talk to her about what caused the accident and why Brian was shot."

"Well, they can't see her yet," said Hank firmly. He pulled up a chair facing the family. "I don't think she knows about Brian. The docs told me not to ask her about the accident. She's worried enough."

"We'll just pray for the best," said Sarah. Reversing the roles she and her mother had played in each other's lives, she brushed a soothing hand over Eileen's brow and softly cradled the distraught woman in her arms.

About an hour later, Hank and Kevin were inserting coins into vending machines that were located around a corner some distance away from the waiting area where Sarah was sitting with her parents. They were selecting hot beverages and snacks from the paltry offering that seemed to be common fare for waiting rooms.

"You know, this whole thing is really strange," said Hank. "Last week, when Brian and I were reviewing financial statements, analyzing how to start liquidating the Boston branch of our business, he looked over at me with the oddest expression I've ever seen on that rugged face of his.

"He said, 'Hank, if anything ever happens to me, I want you to take care of Ivy and the twins.' I figured he still might be expecting to spend some time in prison.

"'You know I will,' I told him. Then he totally shocked me. 'You've always loved her. That's been plain since the beginning. If she's with you, I won't worry.'

"And that was it. He went back to inputting figures on a spreadsheet while I could only sit there dumbfounded. I mean, what do you say to your best friend and business partner when he articulates what's always been in your heart?"

"I can't imagine," said Kevin quietly.

They walked back to the family with the snacks they hoped would sustain them for several hours longer. When they rounded the hallway corner, they knew the waiting was over. Three stricken faces greeted them as they turned from the doctor who had obviously just delivered the news they had dreaded.

Brian was gone.

"Will you let me tell her?" Hank asked the others after they learned more from the doctors. "She's my responsibility now. I'd like her to know that."

"Go on, Hank," said Sarah. She caught the look in Kevin's eyes that reminded her of Ivy's life review. *Yes, this is right,* she thought.

"What did he mean?" Eileen turned to Kevin as Hank went back to the emergency room.

"Not long ago, Brian asked Hank to take care of his family, should anything happen to him."

"I wonder if my boy knew he wasn't going to live," Eileen said, her voice barely audible.

"Perhaps his soul did. I have to pray that's true." Sarah spoke through the unspeakable pain of losing her brother. "Dear God, please take care of Brian's soul." She felt an instant response that told her he was in safe hands.

"Let's get you home," said Kevin to the Callahans. "Sarah and I will stay with you until Millie and Frank arrive from New Bedford." He checked his watch. "I called them earlier. They should be here in a couple of hours."

Even before the terrible news of Brian's death, Kevin had known that Patrick's older sister and her husband would want to be notified about the accident. They had not hesitated. They would drive down to New York immediately.

"How will we tell the children?" Eileen said softly—more to herself than to the others. Her mind began to whirl as she imagined the many things that would have to be taken care of. A funeral. Childcare and school for the twins while Ivy recuperated. There was the computer business to run. And the Boston branch to sell. Hank had said he would take care of Brian's family, but what did that mean?

Patrick knew when his wife's mental wheels started spinning.

"*A ghra,*" he said softly, "let it be until tomorrow. There's nothing more we can do tonight. Our boy is gone. That's enough to deal with right now. Kevin will drive us home and Sarah will put us to bed."

He blinked back the tears he felt he might cry for the rest of his life and allowed himself and the devastated mother of his son to be escorted to the car.

Transitions

Eileen need not have worried about how to tell her grandchildren their father was dead. They already knew.

When the twins' friends Maggie and Tim appeared at their house and Uncle Hank rushed away, the adults they loved almost as much as their parents told them that Mommy and Daddy had been in a car accident and were in the hospital.

"Can we pray for them?" Kaitlyn asked.

"Absolutely," Maggie agreed. The four of them stayed up saying all of the children's favorite prayers until two little redheads were nodding. It was very late when the O'Tooles finally tucked them into the twin beds in Kaitlyn's room where they insisted they wanted to sleep that night.

The adults had just tiptoed to the doorway and switched off the light when they heard Kerry whisper to his sister, "Katy, I think Daddy has gone to heaven."

"I know," she whispered back and both little voices were silent.

In the morning, they were full of news for Maggie and Tim—and Hank, who had stayed at the hospital until the nurses assured him that Ivy would rest better if he would do the same. The doctors said she would likely be released the following afternoon.

The O'Tooles had waited up for him so they could tell him what they'd heard the youngsters whisper. He was as eager as they to learn what else the children would have to say at breakfast. The twins needed no prompting to share their experiences.

"The Rose Lady came to see us last night," Kerry began. "She told us that Daddy was going to heaven and she was going to take him."

"Then we saw Daddy," said Kaitlyn.

"Did you, now, lass?" asked Tim. "And where was this?"

"He was standing with the Rose Lady."

"He told us he loves us, and Uncle Hank is going to stay with us," said Kerry, casting an affectionate eye at the man.

"Daddy said it was his idea for Uncle Hank to take care of us and Mommy. And we're to be really good because he has a lot on his mind," Kaitlyn explained with firm conviction.

"You're right," said Hank, matching her tone. "We're going to be a team now and your mommy needs all of us to help her."

"We will," said Kerry. "But we haven't finished our story."

"Go ahead, darlin'," said Maggie. "We're listening."

"Then the Rose Lady said it was time for Daddy to go to heaven. So we said, 'Good-bye, Daddy. We love you.' And he said, 'I love you, too. Remember me always.' Then we waved and he waved back. And the Rose Lady put her arm around him and they walked away into a big white cloud."

"We cried a little," said Kaitlyn, "but not too much. The Rose Lady said it's fine to cry when we feel like it and not to feel bad about missing Daddy even though Uncle Hank is going to stay with us. She said Daddy gets to go to school in heaven, so that made us happy for him."

Kerry abruptly changed the subject. "Can we go see Gareth and Naimh, now?"

"We need to tell them about Daddy going to heaven with the Rose Lady so they're not too sad," Kaitlyn explained.

"And we don't want Hero and Sprite to feel left out," added Kerry.

"You bet," said Hank. "Let's finish breakfast and we'll go for a walk." He turned to the O'Tooles. "I've got this. Thanks for everything."

"We'll take them any time," said Tim. "Don't try to do it all, lad. There's lots of help for you here. You've only to ask."

After leaving the hospital with Hank at her side, Ivy had described for the police the events that led up to the car accident. By the next day, she was able to resume caring for her children. They were her first priority.

The next few days were a whirlwind of activity which, at least temporarily, helped alleviate some of the pain of losing Brian. There was to be a private cremation service and then a small reception with the Circle of Close Companions at Debbie and Jeremy's apartment. The family would hold a larger memorial service later.

Ivy was relieved to let Brian's family do the planning. They welcomed her input, but gave her no responsibility unless she wanted to say a few words. Lucky would conduct the service.

These were rough times for Ivy and Hank. In losing Brian they had lost their anchor, their rock. Although they were strong, independent people, they had looked to Brian to lead them. The big ideas, the bold business moves, the major innovations had come mostly from him.

Of course, the three of them were excellent collaborators who made the decisions together that had created the success of their company's two branches. But now Ivy and Hank felt themselves adrift.

The trauma of Brian's sudden death had shocked them into depths of grief they wondered how their souls could survive. They did lean on each other, but that relationship was a bit awkward. For Hank because of his love for Ivy, which Brian had recognized. And for her because, while she was in and out of sleep in the hospital, she had gained a clear image of Hank as the stranger from her life review.

They were grateful that Kerry and Kaitlyn seemed so balanced about losing their father. In fact, the twins were doing their best to comfort their mother and Uncle Hank by reminding them of what they had seen when the Rose Lady took their daddy to heaven.

The adults agreed that having the children's perspective eased their minds. Still, they missed the man they both had dearly loved for all of his amazing gifts and for his strength which they now would have to find within themselves.

Fortunately, the Circle of Close Companions and an unexpected gift came to their rescue.

Gifts from Above

The cremation service had taken place on Saturday following Brian's passing. Over the next few days, the Companions did whatever they could to help Ivy and Hank cope with their loss. Maggie, Tim and Lucky were especially helpful to Brian's parents.

Sarah and Kevin found their meditations going deep into the mystery of life after death. And on Wednesday they received a surprising offer that seemed to come straight from heaven. They contacted Lucky and the other Companions. Everyone was on board. They all felt the need to be together.

Two days later, Ivy and the twins were finishing a quiet, Friday-morning breakfast with Hank when the doorbell rang. He opened the front door to find Sarah and Kevin standing there with huge grins on their faces. They were accompanied by Millie and Frank who were holding Gareth and Naimh by the hand.

"Come in." Hank laughed as Kerry and Kaitlyn joined him and immediately took charge of their little cousins. "What's the occasion?"

"An excursion," said Kevin, his eyes bright with anticipation. "And the Circle of Close Companions will be your fellow voyagers."

"What kind of excursion?" asked Ivy. She had come in from the breakfast room when she heard familiar voices.

"Two days ago, Brian's lead attorney called me to say that he is gifting us with a yacht cruise around the New York Harbor as a way of expressing his condolences and also his own sorrow over losing Brian. He said they had become good friends."

"Here's the plan," said Sarah eagerly. "Millie and Frank have said they would love to join us on the cruise to help take care of the twins. Then later we'll all rendezvous at Fibonacci's. The coffee shop will be closed by then. We can have pizzas delivered and stay as long as we like."

"We'll wait now while you get ready, but don't dawdle," Kevin laughed. He realized he was having way too much fun executing this plan.

"Just grab whatever gear you need for a few hours on the water. We have no obligations today except to enjoy this beautiful weather and feel the love that is the gift I know Brian would want us to share."

'Twas a grand day, as Lucky would say. The weather was unusually sunny and pleasantly warm. The breeze was perfect for sailing and New York Harbor was not particularly crowded.

"Wow!" exclaimed the group when they discovered that their yacht was an 80-foot schooner with four sails and spacious seating that allowed room for conversation as well as sightseeing. They learned later that the cruise company actually offered memorial events. They hadn't planned a service, but what emerged was a spontaneous celebration of Brian's life.

The Circle of Close Companions enfolded Hank and the Callahan family in the profound affection that comes from lifetimes of soul friendship. Uplifted by stunning views of Manhattan, they all grieved together. Losing Brian had affected each of them in myriad and significant ways.

Everybody had a story to share about him. They cried. They laughed. And laughed and cried some more until hearts were opened wide and sorrow was eased—at least as much as could be released in three hours of compassionate fellowship aboard a beautiful yacht.

When they gathered at Fibonacci's later that day, the stories, tears and laughter continued. And some conversations became more private as individuals were drawn together to talk quietly while they ate. The experience of being transformed in the spirit of community touched them all deeply.

"Today's celebration has been better than any send-off for Brian I could have imagined!" exclaimed Ivy as daytime faded into evening. "Thank you so much for knowing what we needed."

"I'm sure it was also what Brian's soul needed," said Sarah, placing a gentle hand on her sister-in-law's shoulder.

"Godspeed, Brian!" declared Hank. He raised his coffee cup in salute.

"Godspeed, Brian!" repeated the Companions. "We love you!"

Following this healing experience, Hank and Ivy finally had the emotional and mental energy they needed to begin implementing the plans that he and Brian had drawn up for liquidating the Boston branch of Callahan & Logan and consolidating operations in New York.

After they had spent Saturday morning working up initial task lists, Ivy decided to take the plunge she could feel her soul urging her to take.

Yes, it's time, she thought. Over a simple lunch, she told Hank the full story of her life review—and who she had identified as her lover in that lifetime. To her considerable relief, Hank was not surprised. The night before, he'd had a dream about the same events.

"I'm sure it was the Rose Lady who told me to expect a story that would change my life," he said. "The woman I saw in my dream looked like a goddess. She definitely fit the twins' description. I don't often recall my dreams, but I'll never forget this one."

"Tell me," said Ivy softly.

"I'm glad I *can* tell you," Hank began. "You know I've always cared for you and I told you what Brian said—which is still a shock to me."

Ivy nodded. "Go on."

"The first thing I remember about the dream is the setting. It was like a Greek temple with a rose quartz fountain where music seemed to be coming from the flowers that were everywhere. I might have just stopped to listen, except I saw the Rose Lady. She was beckoning for me to join her. We sat on a bench by the fountain and she spoke in a voice like an angel's.

"'Henry Wadsworth,' she said and her eyes twinkled. Only special people call me that. 'You have obligations in this life—duties you will cherish because you have long desired to fulfill the role of family man.'"

"I never knew you wanted that." Ivy reached over to touch his hand.

He took hers. "Well, I only wanted it with you, so I didn't give the idea any room in my mind. You and Brian and I had a business to run. And that became enough for me. I think I could have continued that way..."

"...if we hadn't lost Brian," said Ivy.

"If we hadn't lost Brian. But we did—and now things are different. Which is what the Rose Lady told me. She said, 'Ivy is going to share with you a weight that has been on her heart. I want you to accept her story as true. Your acceptance is the open door for both of you to make amends for misdeeds of the past and to build the future that your souls need, as do Kaitlyn's and Kerry's. The opportunity to help Brian's children grow to maturity is a blessing that surrendering your love for Ivy has earned you. Continue as the honorable man you are and all will be well.'"

Tears were rolling down Ivy's cheeks. She was happy and sad and more than a little overwhelmed by how quickly things seemed to be moving—thanks to the Rose Lady, of all people.

"How do you feel about all of this?" She searched Hank's face.

"I'm grateful and at peace. I hope you are, too, because I do want to make a life with you and the twins. If I ask you to marry me, will you?"

Ivy did not hesitate. "I will."

"Then I'm asking." Hank held out his arms to the woman he had loved forever and welcomed her into the embrace he had longed to give her.

"Yes," she smiled. "Henry Wadsworth Logan, I will marry you."

As they talked about their future, Ivy and Hank agreed there was more to learn about their souls and Brian's. And for now, they weren't going to say anything about the amazing shift in their relationship—even if some people tuned in to the change, which they knew could happen.

They phoned Lucky to ask if he would fill in the pieces of their past lives that they felt were missing. Despite the short notice, they wondered if he, the O'Tooles and the other couples might be willing to hold a gathering tomorrow to complete the story. Of course, everyone accepted.

The next day, surrounded by the Companions in the tranquil atmosphere of *Teach an tSolais,* Ivy showed real courage as she related the story of the past-life situation between her and Brian and Hank—and why she had been determined to support her husband because of her previous betrayal.

When she'd finished, she turned to Lucky. "I'm hoping you can explain why Brian was entangled with the Conways. Kevin told us that he himself was involved with them during the same lifetime when he was my brother, the chief druid. However, that debt has been paid. So what about Brian?"

"There is a story to tell," said Lucky, "and 'tis a complex tale."

A Complex Tale

First a bit of prologue," explained Lucky. "As you can imagine from Ivy's description, the warrior and his wife did not have an easy time after her lover was killed. They both felt remorse, for there had been genuine love between them.

"They vowed to stay together to rear their children, which would have balanced some of their karma. Unfortunately, the warrior was killed in battle soon after. We don't see him again until the time of Arán Bán—who, it turns out, is the linchpin of the past and present of Brian's involvement with the Conways.

"Most of you know quite a bit about Arán Bán because you've been defending yourselves against him for centuries. Yet there are things you don't know that are pertinent to Ivy's question: What about Brian and the Conways?

"So we all understand the complexity of the family connections, I'm going to begin at the beginning of Arán Bán's life in first-century Ireland."

In the year AD 21, Arán Bán was born in the *túath* of Tearmann. In that same year, Kevin was born as Ah-Lahn, the future *ceann-druí* who would succeed Old Quin. This was the embodiment that Kevin's soul had requested as recompense for having killed the druids who were Arán Bán's grandparents.

Ah-Lahn was outwardly unaware of these lives, but Old Quin had read the akashic record, so he knew. The other person who might have become aware of the connection was Arán Bán's mother—the daughter of the Sly Druid and Bantiarna.

'Tis not entirely clear if the daughter recognized Ah-Lahn as the *ceann-druí* who killed her parents, though she seems to have suspected his identity. From the time her son could understand, she filled the lad with hatred for Ah-Lahn and those he held dear—his twin flame Alana and their closest friends: Dearbhla, Madwyn, Gormlaith and Riordan—now the Twin Flames of Éire: Debbie, Jeremy, Glenna and Rory, along with Kevin and Sarah.

So the seeds of enmity that had existed for centuries were sown again at Tearmann in the soul of Arán Bán.

Now we know that planting was not difficult, for the man had been a treacherous High Priest on Atlantis and a self-styled enemy in countless other lifetimes when he plotted to eliminate Kevin. He tried again only two years ago. He failed this time as well, and that brings up a point I've only recently learned about.

You see, the souls of Arán Bán's grandparents were watching from the astral plane where the wickedness they had chosen had landed them after their death.

Because they had possessed advanced spiritual attainment before the Luciferian rebellion, the Great Law allowed them multiple opportunities to forsake the dark arts and turn to the light. That was an option they had not chosen. However, they did seize upon the opportunity to take embodiment again—as the son and daughter of Arán Bán.

"Wait a minute," said Hank. "Are you telling us that Arán Bán was also the father of his own grandparents? Can people die and be reborn as their own relatives with hardly any time in between?"

"They can and they did," explained Lucky. "Sometimes when there is serious karma between individuals or groups of souls, the Masters who govern such things will bring them together again quickly—always with the hope that they will resolve their differences and stop repeating the cycles of vengeance."

"I guess that didn't happen, did it?" said Hank. "Sorry to interrupt."

"You're fine, lad. 'Tis a lot to take in. And there's more to tell."

One thing I didn't know until our Master showed me following Brian's death is that the grandparents had always harbored a low opinion of Arán Bán. Though he fashioned himself as a mighty druid with extraordinary powers, he was not nearly as clever or calculating as his ancestors.

In fact, they considered him a failure because he had never been able to destroy Kevin's soul. Their grandson may have taken his target out of embodiment more than once, but Kevin actually gained in mastery with every successive lifetime.

The one aspect of Arán Bán's nature that strongly resembled his grandparents was his lechery. In addition to his legitimate son and daughter, he fathered at least two younger illegitimate sons—one of whom was Brian.

Ivy had been listening intently without comment, but with this revelation about her late husband, she gasped and clutched Hank's hand. He put his arm around her. Maggie brought her a glass of water. The other twin flames couples drew closer together. They had not expected Brian to be so intricately woven into the family of Arán Bán.

"Go on, Lucky, I'm fine," said Ivy after another minute, though she remained pale for the rest of the afternoon.

Our story skips ahead now to the year AD 62 when Arán Bán killed Ah-Lahn, and he himself died while attempting to escape from Tearmann.

As we've said, their deaths meant that Riordan became *ceann-druí* to Toíseach Cróga. All of you living in the community were faced with betrayal by Arán Bán's adult children, who turned many of the less-enlightened druids against their leaders.

We know that Riordan was the great hero of that war. His laying down his own life saved Tearmann. However, the son and daughter had come close to destroying that *túath* and others within the Brigantes tribe because they manipulated their half-brother, Brian, into helping them.

The lad was not involved as a combatant in the war against

the community, but he did inadvertently aid his half-siblings in ways he would later regret. When he discovered that he had been duped, he fled Tearmann and lived out his life trying to be of service to others.

"So Brian was not a bad soul, then," said Hank. "I'm relieved to hear that. But how did he end up with such a family in the first place? I am astounded at how the same players keep reembodying."

"'Tis an important point to understand," explained Lucky. "Sometimes a soul of light volunteers to be born into a family that has chosen dark ways. The Masters hope that such a one can lend a positive influence. Unfortunately, that single soul may suffer terribly when the family instinctively opposes the individual who could have turned them from their bad choices—and whose presence among them actually reveals their darkness."

Hank picked up the thread. "So those people—the son and daughter of Arán Bán—tried to use Brian, just like the Conways did this time."

"That's right," said Lucky. He paused and looked straight at Hank, as if to draw out of him the answer that was hanging in the air.

Jeremy got there first. "I knew there was a family connection. Stan and Stacey were the grandparents of Arán Bán as well as his children. And in this life they were the same souls, the heirs of his treachery. Am I right?"

Lucky nodded. "Truth be told, they were instigators from the beginning—being higher up in the hierarchy of archdeceivers. They became convinced that Arán Bán was going to botch the job of eliminating the soul of Ah-Lahn—which he did again in this life when he failed to kill Kevin in Ireland.

"In his final attempt as A. B. Ryan, he caused the fire at the original Fibonacci's and then attacked me from the astral plane. None of those acts succeeded in getting rid of us. But his many lifetimes of choices made on behalf of the fallen ones eventually compounded into an irredeemable weight of karma that extinguished his soul in the Second Death."

"And Stan and Stacey were waiting in the wings to finish me off," said Kevin—as amazed as anyone. "They couldn't get to me directly, so they went after Brian as a way to savage my soul and destroy all of us who are connected with Fibonacci's."

"You have the truth of it," said Lucky. "The battle isn't over until those we call lightbearers make the ultimate choice for the light and the fallen ones either turn to the light or make their final choice for darkness."

He looked over at Ivy, who was still clutching Hank's hand. "Don't worry lass, I won't let you down. We'll finish Brian's story now."

Over the following centuries, the lad's soul made significant progress. Sadly, he was wary of involvement with the spiritual communities we and others formed on behalf of the Masters. And though Brian tended to remain on the periphery of our gatherings, he did his best to live exemplary lives, which eventually earned him an extraordinary mercy that included being born into the Callahan family.

Before this present lifetime, he was offered an opportunity by the Masters of Wisdom to balance a large portion of his karma by helping to bring the Conways and others to justice. He was made aware of how, for centuries, they had practiced their treachery against our communities of light and especially against Kevin, who was always their main target.

The danger this opportunity presented to Brian was that his actions could mean forfeiting his life. Nevertheless, because of his soul's profound remorse for his past deeds and his deep love for all of you, he agreed.

"Did he really understand what he was promising?" Hank interrupted again. "Agreeing to forfeit your life so a couple of bad apples can get what they deserve is a tall order."

"'Tis, indeed," said Lucky. "These are matters our souls likely know but that do not become conscious to our outer minds, except during life reviews or insights that emerge in meditation or prayer."

"Then Brian didn't actually know, did he?" Ivy said quietly.

"I believe he did," said Patrick. "At least, I believe he was warned, though, as Lucky says, his outer mind did not comprehend the message."

"What do you mean?" asked Eileen. "I don't understand."

"A few weeks ago, our son told me about a vision he'd had during a group meditation with many of you in Tim's Tower. He said a beautiful goddess, who was surrounded in white light, was warning him about something that he didn't understand. The vision faded before he could ask her what she meant."

"That makes sense," said Lucky thoughtfully. "'Tis how initiations work sometimes. We may be given warnings, but we're not told the details. Passing a certain test depends on our free will. In this case, I can see how Brian was required to make the decision on his own not to help Stan and Stacey with their devilish plans.

"Against his better judgment and out of fear of what they might do to him or his family, he nearly fell into their trap. Fortunately, you, Hank, arrived with your proposal to sell part of your company. That saved Brian from Stan's aggressive energy and his own karma that had blinded him and was your soul's way of forgiving him for your murder centuries earlier.

"You see how exacting is the law of cause and effect over time."

"What about our family's karma?" asked Ivy. "The four of us were in a car accident a couple of years ago. Brian's injury was to his head then, too, and my injuries were minor in comparison. The children were not hurt at all."

"Your twins were under the protection of the Wisdom Masters," said Lucky, "which is why that accident was not fatal to any of you. Ivy, in past embodiments you've made positive karma by being faithful to your spouse, including lifetimes when you were married to Brian. In this most recent accident, your stronger connection with our community through Kevin and Sarah, your twins and your loyalty to Brian kept you safe from serious harm."

Lucky paused briefly, listening. "That's all this old druid is allowed to reveal to you. I hope 'tis enough to help you move forward in your lives."

When it came to moving forward, one more vital question involving the Fibonacci's community remained to be answered: What was to be done with the health food store property?

The government had seized all of the inventory, display cabinets and shelving to be auctioned for back taxes. Investigators had discovered enough evidence on Stan's computer, in his desk and other hiding places to put a number of criminals behind bars. Even a local bank used by his associates had been seized.

As landlords of the health food store's portion of the Fibonacci's block, Ivy and Hank gave the Circle of Close Companions permission to conduct an energy clearance on the property, which they did the following day. The astral creatures that had frightened Kerry and Kaitlyn and all residual pockets of darkness were consigned to the spiritual fire. The store front was now clear of negative vibrations and stood empty.

When everyone had gathered in the coffee shop after their clearance session, the O'Tooles had an idea.

"What would you say about Maggie and me opening a rock shop in this space?" Tim proposed. "We've been collecting hundreds of crystals, geodes and fossils from all over the world. Seems like a good time to put them to use."

Maggie chimed in. "Stacey was generating some interest in crystals in what she called her 'Ritual Section.' Of course hers were permeated with dark energy. Ours contain wonderful healing light that can help the people who buy them. Having a crystal shop as part of the Fibonacci's block could boost the general vibration of all the other businesses and the entire neighborhood."

Hank gave Ivy a hopeful look. She nodded serenely to him and said to the group, "We think it's a super idea."

Phelan joined in with another proposal. "Cyndi and I also have an idea. With her being pregnant, we're not in a position to start a new health food store business—even if we could afford the inventory."

"Still, we'd like to keep our hand in," added Cyndi. "Do you think we could create a small herbal corner in the coffee shop? You know, to offer a few special blends as supplements. We're already serving the healthy teas that Stacey wanted no part of."

"I'm all for it," said Debbie with a smile that lit up the room. "I know Róisín would love the idea of an herbal corner. We can call it: 'Phelan's Organic Pharmacy.'"

The Call of Home

The day was soft. That's how the Irish call the drizzly damp that hugs you like mittens on cold hands. This soft makes you cold, but in a cozy sort of way. Or maybe the cold damp makes a body long for the soft warmth of a turf fire that can seep into your bones and ease out the cold.

Warm and dry, cold and damp. In Ireland both sensations can be soft, and that makes the fluctuations tolerable. One gives way to the other like lovers in a dance.

Tim O'Toole noticed how today's low clouds and the promise of rain made him think of home—though he was a sunshine man, himself. Sunny disposition with a ready laugh and a glint in his crystalline blue eyes. Still, he was enough of an Irishman—one hundred percent he'd have you know—that the melancholy air could tug at his heart and make him long for the home that hadn't been all that difficult to leave.

The Emerald Isle could be as hard as she was soft. And there had been plenty of hardships to leave behind for the bright promise of American shores.

Give me the sunshine, Tim declared to himself. He blessed the ray that broke through the gloom to sparkle on the bay where his good friend Lucky O'Connor was standing, staring and leaning out toward the water as if willing himself across the Atlantic to the land of his birth.

Tim decided to take a stroll across the lawn from the terrace where he'd been watching his friend. Just then, the big Irishman turned toward the gardens. The mists of deep contemplation glistened in his eyes.

Lucky did not linger in the gardens that were still bursting with the last roses of summer and the gold and rust-colored chrysanthemums of autumn. Instead, he continued walking toward the round tower. Which is where Tim met him, standing very still, looking up at the conical roof.

Tim joined his friend of many ages. Remembering how they had helped build a similar structure twice as large in height and girth, he asked, "Do you miss it, lad?"

Lucky turned and laughed the rich chortle that had been missing from him except for when he was at Fibonacci's.

"Tower building? Can't say as I do."

"The land, then. Éire. Your soul's home."

Lucky faced his friend. "Have you ever felt like your heart wants to pluck itself out of your chest and sail off across the Wild Atlantic?"

"I have, yes. Not of late, though. I've been back more times than you. You've not made that journey in thirty years."

"'Tis true."

"Why not?"

"Too busy. Too many memories. They've come up anyway in the telling of my stories. Róisín always said the more painful memories are the ones we most need to let in. And Flavia told me I'd discover things about myself that could only come out in the telling."

"Have they come out?"

"They have. And along with them a tenderness toward home and the seeking lad I was in Connemara—gazing out over my pondering spot by the lake, searching for answers to questions I didn't know to ask. Or was afraid to ask."

"Do you know the definition of a seeker?" The twinkle in Tim's eye made Lucky laugh again.

"I believe you're going to tell me."

"A seeker is a person who looks in all the wrong places. Because if he looked in the right places, he would find what he's only been pretending to look for. Then everything would have to change."

"I don't think finding Róisín, meeting F. M. Bellamarre, taking over Fibonacci's from Joshua and expanding the Friends of Ancient Wisdom community is looking in all the wrong places." Lucky pushed back against the idea that he'd misspent his life. He knew he hadn't.

"Not at all," Tim reassured his friend. "Those were all worthy accomplishments. Still, even with all the mastery you've gained in his life—which is considerable—where is the one place you've not explored sufficiently? Or maybe, who is the one person you've neglected in all the years you've been serving and teaching and encouraging others?"

"Can't think of anybody."

"Put your mind to it, lad. You never much liked his name."

Lucky paused. Then a light dawned and he rolled his eyes in recognition. Hadn't he been thinking of his childhood self only minutes earlier?

"Lúcháir," he said simply. "I think I left pieces of him in Ireland when I came to the States."

"Then 'tis time to retrieve those bits of your soul. Seems to me that's what's missing from the legacy you're meant to bequeath to your Circle of Close Companions."

"You've the right of it," Lucky agreed. "And there are sights I want to see. I want to breathe the air, feel my feet on that land, put my hands in that earth. I want to walk along the cliffs and feel my whole body shake in the wind and the spray and the millennial crashing of water against rock. I've become too tame, lad. There's a wildness gone out of me."

"I don't remember you being all that wild," remarked Tim, raising an eyebrow and cocking his head. "Well, maybe a time or two. You were usually the serious one of O'Connor and O'Toole," he grinned.

"Till I married Róisín," said Lucky wistfully. "She's the one who sparked the joy in me. Flavia would have done, but there's only so much you can generate from the spirit realms. Most of the time, when I'd think of her, the pain would be all I'd feel. I avoided those thoughts."

Tim studied the man who had braved storms of unthinkable loss.

"If you don't mind my saying, you seem becalmed. Like a boat stuck in the marina waiting for somebody to take you out to unfurl your sails in a grand old breeze."

"Exactly."

"Then what are you waiting for? You can't sit around here wondering if today's the day that *An Síoraí,* the Eternal One, is going to send the bus marked *Tír na n'Óg.* I don't see you dying any time soon."

"Nor do I. I've never felt fitter in my life. Ever since Kevin's life review, I've had the sense that we'll both keep going for many a year. I may even outlive him."

Tim rolled his eyes and Lucky hooted with laughter at the image of him and Kevin doddering around Fibonacci's in extreme old age. Then he turned serious.

"I think the lad and I need to go to Ireland together. There's something I'm meant to reclaim that can be found only in Connemara. That's the missing piece of my legacy and the last bit to gather up and hand off to our new *ceann-druí*."

"That's the spirit!" exclaimed Tim. "What a grand adventure you'll be having. I almost wish I could go with you."

"Could you?"

"No, 'tis for you and Kevin. If I suggested taking off for Ireland right now, Maggie would accuse me of having rocks in my head as well as in the new shop."

"More than likely," said Lucky and turned toward the house. He put his arm around Tim's shoulder. "Let's ask Kevin and Sarah to come over. I can't wait to tell them the news."

"Sorry it took us so long to get here," Sarah apologized. "I know you said you have something important to tell us. We have fantastic news that I'm bursting to share. You won't believe what's happened."

"What is it, lass? Nothing bad, I hope," said Maggie warily. "We've had enough heartbreaks to last several lifetimes." She put out two hands to take a wiggly Gareth from his mother.

"Oh, no, this is a wonderful surprise," Sarah assured her, "though I had to sit down when Ivy told me. I still can't believe it. I never thought my mother would do a thing like this."

"Like what?" asked Tim. "Out with it, lass."

"Ivy phoned to say that my mother had informed her and Hank that they should secure a marriage license, gather up their friends and get married this afternoon. The ceremony is today at 4:00 p.m. at the Justice of the Peace. You're all invited."

Kevin chimed in. "Eileen told them there was no point in waiting.

The twins need a father. They adore Hank. He and Ivy have known each other for years. It's clear that they share a deep affection and they need to be together."

Sarah picked up the story. "I think this is my mother's way of handling her grief over losing Brian. She told Ivy they could plan a proper wedding and reception for next spring at *Bealtaine*. But right now, life needs to move on."

Kevin took over. "Then Hank called me with the news that his Boston manager, Dev, has a wealthy cousin from India who wants to buy their branch of the computer business. That's the other reason for Hank and Ivy to marry today. As soon as they take a brief honeymoon, he's heading north to work out details of the sale."

"That *is* a lot of news," agreed Lucky, "and I'm truly glad to hear it. Makes me think that Brian may be negotiating some heavenly assistance from the Other Side."

"We couldn't wait to tell you." Sarah was radiant with joy. "Now what did you want to tell us?"

"'Tis more of a question." Lucky's bright blue eyes had regained their old sparkle. "Kevin, lad, how soon can you leave for Ireland?"

Of course, Kevin declared that he was too busy to take off for Ireland for several weeks, but his resistance was uniformly overruled.

Sarah encouraged him to accompany Lucky on this voyage that was taking on the quality of a pilgrimage. Jeremy, Rory and Debbie assured him that the Fibonacci's businesses would hum along fine in his absence. The clincher came when Lucky focused his full attention on Kevin with an intensity worthy of Old Quin.

"Initiations are not scheduled for your convenience, lad. This trip is as much for you as it is for me. That's become clear as I've searched my heart for reasons. *An Síoraí*, the Eternal One, is very firm that we're neither of us finished with our work here on planet Earth."

"Then you're on!" declared Kevin. "When do we leave?"

Part Five

The Invisible Weaving Continues

Samhain

This year's Celtic New Year celebration was less complex than previous ones, though it was certainly no less enthusiastically attended.

In light of Brian's recent passing and the burdens on his family and the Fibonacci's businesses, other members of the Friends of Ancient Wisdom community had organized themselves to furnish refreshments and issue invitations so everyone would know that Lucky and Kevin were leaving tomorrow for a grand adventure in Ireland.

The ballroom was full to capacity with well-wishers and stirring Irish music provided by musicians who seemed to come out of the woodwork for such occasions. The mood was festive with the touch of melancholy the Irish have of blending together a keen sense that threads of tragedy as well as triumph are perpetually interwoven in life's tapestry.

Which is what Sarah and Kevin saw when they entered, a bit later than they had planned, with their twins happily babbling in their stroller.

"Hon, look!" she exclaimed, grabbing his arm. "It's the scene from the tapestry in the nursery!"

"Amazing." Kevin drew out the word. "Who knew a piece of woven art could hold a prophecy."

Sure enough, there was Lucky, standing and talking with dozens of friends who surrounded him like moths to a flame. Smaller groups were clustered in little tableaux of conversation and gaiety. The other twin flames couples were mixing with community friends they had not seen since the post-press-conference rush at the coffee shop.

A person whom Sarah had thought might be visible in the nursery weaving came forward to greet her and Kevin.

"Charlotte," she enthused, "thank you for all your hard work. I understand you had a lot to do with this wonderful gathering."

"You know I love to help," said the young woman as she extended her hand to Sarah's husband. "You must be Kevin. I've waited a long time for this moment."

"I'm sorry, I thought you two had already met," Sarah apologized.

"No, I haven't had the pleasure of meeting the father of these gorgeous children. How proud you must be, *Ceann-Druí.*" Her tone was matter-of-face, as if she used Kevin's title every day.

Charlotte reached out to take both of his hands, but he gave her a strange look and pulled his hand away.

"Was I not supposed to use your title?" She looked him in the eye.

"It's not usual," said Kevin, returning her directness. *What is it about this person?* he wondered and offered no other comment.

Sarah stepped in to cover a surprisingly awkward moment.

"Lucky is still our *ceann-druí,*" she hastily explained. "We know that many of us were part of a druidic community many centuries ago. You probably were there, too, Charlotte. We're not trying to recreate Tearmann. As modern-day mystics, we're only bringing forward the values and esoteric understanding of eternal truths from all ages."

"That's what I find so fascinating about all of you," said Charlotte. She apparently was unaware of Sarah's discomfort. "And of course, the Celtic connection. I've never been to Ireland, but I hope to go one day. Just like Lucky and you, Kevin. I hope you have a lovely vacation."

"It's more like a pilgrimage, really," said Sarah. *Why isn't Kevin saying anything? He's got that faraway look about him again.*

"Kevin? Charlotte just wished you well for your trip to Ireland."

"What? Oh, sorry." Kevin came back to himself. "Lots on my mind getting ready to leave tomorrow. Thanks for the babysitting help, by the way. I know Sarah and her mom appreciate the assistance."

"I love children," said Charlotte. "I don't have any of my own yet in this life, but I do remember the joys and challenges of motherhood from past embodiments. Every day is a new adventure."

"That's for sure," agreed Sarah.

"I am glad to meet you, at last, Kevin. I've heard so much about you and how skillfully you managed all that mess with the health food store.

And Brian's loss, of course. Such a tragedy for your family. You have my deepest sympathy."

"Thank you," said Kevin. "It's been a rough couple of weeks, but we're getting through it. As you can see, our community has rallied."

"They obviously have deep feelings for all of you. I do have one question. Did the Conways have family? I heard that someone showed up to claim their bodies, but the police didn't say who."

"I'm sorry, Charlotte," said Kevin rather flatly. "I'm not at liberty to discuss any details of that situation."

"Oh, I understand. I just feel bad for people who die suddenly without family. You all are so fortunate to be surrounded with such loving support." She heard someone call her name and looked away. "Excuse me, I see I'm needed at the refreshments table."

As Charlotte turned to leave, she focused her attention on Sarah with an air of familiarity. "Let me know if you need me while Kevin is away. Last minute is no problem. I can pop over any time."

"What was that with Charlotte?" Sarah confronted Kevin in a stage whisper as soon as they were alone. "You were barely civil to her. She's been a lot of help to me and my mom. I thought you would be more gracious."

"Don't you think it was odd that she called me *Ceann-Druí*?"

"Maybe a bit presumptuous. She's still learning how we do things. Most people in the Friends of Ancient Wisdom have known you by that title. It is fairly common knowledge that our Master sent us to Ireland to merge with our past attainment as druids. Stories like that do travel."

"I suppose you're right. I'm just not used to someone using the title in everyday conversation. And...," Kevin paused. "I felt like there was an edge to how she said *Ceann-Druí*. Did you pick that up?"

"I think you're making too much of her directness. I like her and I'm grateful there's somebody I can call in a pinch."

"Okay. I didn't mean to be rude. I really do have a lot on my mind."

"I know. You're forgiven." Sarah kissed him on the cheek. When she started to push the twins' stroller, Kevin put his hand on her arm.

"Be careful is all I'm saying. We don't really know much about her. How is it that she's always available to babysit? Doesn't she work?"

"She told me she has a trust fund. Rich relatives or something like that. She can follow her interests where they lead her. It's kind of sweet, really. She said she was feeling at loose ends until she found Fibonacci's. Now that she's getting to know the Friends of Ancient Wisdom, she feels more grounded—like she's discovered purpose in meeting all of us."

"That makes sense," agreed Kevin.

"Good." Sarah gave him another kiss on the cheek. "Let's mingle. We haven't seen some of these folks in weeks."

The atmosphere at Fibonacci's was jubilant until leave-taking time when Lucky grew melancholy and eloquent.

"My dear friends, a new year is turning for us Celts and a new cycle of life and love is dawning. I ask you all to care for one another, to love each other as Róisín and I have loved you. Let no divisions come between you. Be kind, be brave and let nothing deter you from the path of light the Friends of Ancient Wisdom represents. You are our hope and our joy. I give you all my love and assurance that this parting is not good-bye but only a fare-thee-well. *Beannachtaí daoibh, a chairde.*"

No one tried to hide the tears that misted their eyes as they gathered around Lucky for the personal hug he gave each one. To close the evening, they sounded the OM together and he sent them home with his blessing.

"Did he say he would be back?" Glenna asked Rory as they drove home to their apartment.

"Not specifically, but he didn't say he wouldn't."

"I don't want to think about it. We've known him for such a short time. I'm only beginning to understand that we've had an incredible adept in our midst."

"I know. 'Tis funny. When I was Riordan, I felt the same about Old Quin. It wasn't till he was gone that I really appreciated him."

"We humans are kind of dense, aren't we?" said Glenna.

"We are, yes," agreed Rory. "Still, I do think we're making progress."

"I hope so."

Travelers

I am still amazed that Maggie got us *Aer Lingus* tickets from JFK to Shannon on such notice," said Kevin as he settled into his business-class seat for the red-eye flight that signaled the beginning of the Celtic adventure he and Lucky were embarking upon.

"She always has reservations on hold with her travel agent," explained his fellow traveler. "When our Master calls, she and Tim can hop on a plane and be where he needs them in a flash. They've been doing that for more years than I can count."

"Probably more embodiments, too," Kevin grinned. "Only without the benefit of air travel. Why do I have a feeling they actually bilocate and the flight arrangements are just for show?"

Saying nothing, Lucky hummed a little tune and watched as the lights of New York disappeared from view. He and Kevin had agreed he would take the window seat so he could catch a first glimpse of Ireland's lights when they appeared the next morning.

Departing after sundown and arriving before sunrise. From dark to dark in search of illumination's light. Truly a pilgrimage into the Unknown. he thought to himself and turned to Kevin.

"Are you convinced you don't want to include Sarah in real time as we travel? Until we get into the wilds of Connemara, we can connect with her in the towns. Tim told me that most cafés and hotels have wifi."

"No. We agreed that with the time difference and her managing the twins' without me around, it would be too complicated. She did say if I could change diapers over the Internet, she would consider the option."

Both men chuckled at that idea.

"Otherwise, unless some event or bit of information is really timely,

I'm supposed to send her updates by email and take lots of photos so we can relive the whole trip when we get back. Besides, she wants to have your book completely drafted by then."

Lucky nodded. "'Tis true. She's promised to email me some pages to review. We both thought 'twould be interesting for me to read how she's integrating my childhood recollections while I'm visiting the very places."

A cloud passed over his face—so quickly that only a fellow adept would have noticed.

"Are you okay?" asked Kevin.

"Guess I've got a bit of the jitters, that's all. 'Tis thirty years since I've been on an airplane."

"I understand. This is quite an adventure for both of us."

Kevin decided to change the subject. "Tell me about Connemara. What do you remember loving the most about your homeland?"

Lucky understood what his friend was doing and gratefully began to wax poetical about the land of his birth.

"'Tis precious country to me. There was no national park when I was a lad. I've walked many a mile on faint paths and across untrammeled hills and valleys that took me deep into myself.

"To be sure, I loved the vistas that often included herds of Connemara ponies. I never tired of the constant changes in color between the brown bogs, the green fields dotted with white sheep, the golden furze and purple moor grass. And the blues—aye, the blues of the lakes. 'Twas a work of Nature's mighty art.

"Then you've got the sounds. Even in winter, songbirds would call out to me as I passed. And the music of water. The gentle splashing along lake shores, the noisy flow of streams, the rush of waterfalls, the crash of the sea. They all lifted my spirits in their different ways.

"And when you venture out to the edge of Cleggan Cliffs or climb up Diamond Hill to view the sheer expanse of the world that lies before you, the wind howls and whistles like a chorus of the gods tuning up for a mighty concert.

"Still, the stone of Connemara is my favorite. Maybe because the land is formed of stone in grand conflagrations. The boulders and ridges scattered across the landscape as far as you can see always looked to me like warriors formed in ranks or waging their private battles for the soul free-dom this land offers to those who'll be still long enough to feel it."

Kevin shared his friend's exultation as he was transported by the vivid images Lucky's memories painted. He felt his entire being expanding to embrace the immensity his soul was eager to explore in the physical.

"Ah, there 'tis." Lucky was jubilant as he breathed in huge lungs full of Irish air when they exited the Shannon Airport terminal. "No aroma touches the heart quite like the fragrance of this land."

"And no food satisfies the stomach like a full Irish breakfast," Kevin said eagerly. "Let's check into our hotel. We've got three meals paid for, thanks to Maggie's planning. Glenna says the hotel's breakfast will warm us body and soul. We can pick up our rental car when we're ready to drive to Limerick."

As they crossed the parking lot, Kevin paused to look over at Lucky.

"Are you still up for exploring this part of your past today?"

"I'm wide awake if you are, since you'll be doing the driving. And won't people be impressed with my American chauffeur." Lucky grinned.

"Well, I've done more driving on the left in recent years than you have," said Kevin.

"Truth be told, I never actually drove on the left or the right when I lived here," said Lucky somewhat sheepishly.

"You didn't?"

"I didn't drive as a lad. Tim had an old rattler of a car when we were in seminary, but he was the only one brave enough to get behind the wheel. Once I moved to Limerick, I walked everywhere or took a bus. Cars were still very dear in those days. And remember, Róisín and I were saving our money to emigrate. Limerick is a walkable town, so that's what we did."

"Okay then," Kevin agreed. "I'll drive and you navigate. Rory has marked all the roads for us on the detailed map he gave me. I think the lad missed his calling as a tour guide. Maggie and Glenna made our hotel reservations, so we're set all the way to Connemara."

"At that point I think we'd best let *An Síoraí,* the Eternal One, be our guide," said Lucky. "I've no idea what we'll find when we get there."

"Agreed," said Kevin. "Now, let's have breakfast!"

"Are you going to eat your way across Ireland, lad?" Lucky chuckled. They'd been exploring Limerick for only two hours when Kevin declared himself ready for lunch. They left the walking tour Lucky had decided they should take first (to get the feel of the city) and stopped at one of many historic pubs in the busy city center.

"I can see that you'll be talking your way across the country," Kevin joked, drinking the tea he said tasted this good only in Ireland. "You don't know any of these people we've met in the shops or on the walking tour, yet you're talking with them like old friends."

"In a way they are," said Lucky. "People are like archetypes. You see a man or a woman or a child who reminds you of someone you know. You may as well treat them as if you do and find out how life is treating them these days. Who knows? You could have been great friends in the past. We're all part of the same old tapestry of life, lad. It lifts my spirits to greet my fellow weavers. I believe my interest in them lifts theirs as well."

"I know it does," Kevin agreed. "You're a ray of sunshine, Lucky. I remember that from the first day I met you and Róisín. You gladdened my heart when I was very low. Thanks for reminding me."

"I've come to believe that easing another's burden is a main job of the *ceann-druí*," said Lucky. "At least in these days that are so mixed up with sorrow and joy. Speaking of mixed up days, I'm ready to show you the sights of my former life in Limerick. Finish your tea, and let's walk."

And walk they did. It took some searching to discover where Róisín had lived with her little boy and abusive husband. Their tenement building had been razed and rebuilt in the 1990s. Finding Lucky's old bookstore was easier, as it had been located in a shopping area that was still thriving in Limerick's active tourist trade.

The park where he used to eat his lunch and where he'd first glimpsed Róisín was smaller than he remembered. The trees were bigger and offered significantly more shade.

St. John's Hospital was where it had always been—across the street from the cathedral named for St. John the Baptist. Lucky and Kevin spent over an hour in the cathedral, but decided against entering the hospital.

After that, they simply wandered the streets to see what sights might catch their attention. Some hours later, they spontaneously sensed their visit was complete and walked back to their rental car.

That evening over another hearty meal at their hotel, Lucky answered Kevin's unspoken query.

"Sure, the city has changed. I knew it would, as have I. Still, much was familiar. Every so often I would catch myself remembering how Róisín and I loved a certain park or church or stroll by our grand River Shannon."

"The question is: Do you feel fulfilled with only this much time spent in Limerick?" Kevin asked. "We could go back tomorrow."

"Today was enough," said Lucky thoughtfully. "We have many more sights to see. These hours of walking the old streets tugged at my heart, and my heart says it's satisfied. Tomorrow we go up-country like a couple of tourists. No obligations for either of us for a couple of days."

"What a relief," said Kevin with a lilt in his voice. "Onward to the Cliffs of Moher, the Burren, Galway and beautiful Irish landscapes. God, how I love this country! I hadn't realized how much I needed to return."

"Aye," was all Lucky said for the rest of the evening.

The Visitor

While the two travelers were exploring Limerick and plotting their sightseeing excursions for the next few days, Sarah was busy at work on Lucky's memoirs.

She had wondered what to do about childcare because her parents were taking care of Ivy's twins while she and Hank were on their short honeymoon. Fortunately, Maggie and Tim had invited Sarah to work at their house so they could watch Gareth and Naimh. The O'Tooles' new crystal shop was still being redecorated. They were at home and happy for the company.

Sarah was grateful for this quiet time in the extraordinary forcefield of *Teach an tSolais*. Being surrounded with so much light was definitely enhancing her attunement with Lucky's stories—especially since she was working in his sitting room where an antique oak desk with beautifully carved legs provided ample space for her laptop and notes.

She and Lucky had agreed on a narrative strategy which she was eager to implement while he was away. She knew he trusted her to maintain his voice and unique expressions. That trust was like wind in her sails as she set about entering into the flow of some of the most important chapters.

Today she was reviewing her notes from the life review of Lúcháir, Flavia and Racham that the Circle of Close Companions had witnessed in September. Between her and Kevin, they had reconstructed the events that she was now ready to insert into the narrative of Lucky's memoirs.

As Sarah typed, she felt herself sliding once more into the inspiring scenes. The events were coming alive through her fingertips, yet she was not submerged in them. Instead, she was aware of her own thoughts and feelings as separate from the events. Which is what caused her to say out loud, "I wish I could talk to Flavia—to get her perspective on Quin, on her decision to go to Rome with her family. Why did she remain when she was free to leave?"

Those words had barely escaped Sarah's lips when the atmosphere in Lucky's sitting room went all "shimmery" and a figure began to materialize before her in the shape of a young woman. She was dressed in a linen robe. She wore her flaxen hair in a long braid draped over one shoulder. Her soft blue eyes were the last feature of her form to come into focus.

Fixing those beautiful orbs on Sarah, she spoke with a voice that was calm and kind and full of the graciousness that befitted Flavia. For it was she who said, "I loved my family, especially my cousins from whom I did not wish to be separated. Did I know of the dangers that awaited us? Not until it was too late. Then I saw Racham in my mind's eye.

"He opened his heart to me with such holy love, I knew I could face any fate. He transferred to me the profound joy he experienced in living his life as the Son. His passion was to be that One. His time on the cross was a brief but necessary event to demonstrate the power of life over death.

"In reality, he had prepared me for the same test. My agony was great, but my ecstasy was greater. Is that what you wanted to know, dear Sarah?"

Other individuals might have been stunned at the appearance of this radiant spirit being whose form emanated white light that filled the room. Other individuals were not a reembodied female druid—a *bandruí*.

"I know you." Sarah felt a glimmer of recognition stir in her heart.

"Yes, my dear, and that is why I have permission to greet you in this manner. We share a purpose, you and I, which you have not realized. My coming today is to spark your recollection. I am not allowed to reveal what you cannot intuit."

"I never expected you to answer me," said Sarah.

"Cannot old friends have a chat when one calls to the other? What are you beginning to remember?"

"As I've been transcribing Lucky's stories, you have seemed familiar. Until now, I thought I was just seeing you through his eyes."

"You were. And now you can see me through your own."

"I do sense that we've had more than a few friendly chats like this, though I don't know when or where. Am I allowed to ask you questions?"

"No, but I will ask you some—beginning with this one: Why do you think my dear Lúcháir asked you to be his scribe?"

Sarah thought a minute. "Because I am a writer?"

"Others could have fulfilled the task. Maggie O'Toole herself has the skills. But she is not you. Imagine our connection, Sarah. Think back. You are adept enough to recall. I am here merely as a catalyst, as you yourself have been in many ages. I can give you one clue: Nhada-lihn."

"The Rose Lady's name on Atlantis."

At the mention of this beloved lady master, Sarah felt an instant spark of ancient memory. "Of course, you and I were sister priestesses in the Temple of Light. Such golden days those were—until it all went wrong."

"And we both earned good karma in the mission we shared. Now go deeper, Sarah. What next relationship did we cherish?"

Aware that Flavia was not allowed to articulate the vital message that her appearance was meant to convey, Sarah closed her eyes and willed herself back into the eras that followed Atlantis. Then she saw the scenes— the majestic temples, the enormous statues, the blue river that nurtured the desert kingdom where she was queen.

"I see now. You were my mother—the wise woman who taught me the skills I would need to be the wife and partner of Per-aa, the pharaoh. Oh, you were wonderful. How I grieved when you died. Our kingdom had such potential. What a tragedy that the degenerate priest class with their jealousy and black arts would not have it."

In Sarah's excitement to know more, she asked, "What about Sparta? Did we know each other then?"

"What does your inner sight tell you?"

By now, Sarah's intuition was flowing like water. "I see you again as my mother when my father was the king. (*Was Lucky my father then?* she wondered to herself.) I was born a princess and when I grew up I married the next king. I'm surprised that I didn't remember you until now."

"These revelations come in their own time," Flavia reminded her.

Sarah had witnessed the record of her Sparta embodiment in a life review she experienced during her first trip to Ireland. Now a deeper meaning came to mind as she mused on this fresh recollection.

"I have a lot of royal obligations, don't I?"

"What does that tell you?" Flavia asked. "Do you see a pattern? When you contact the record of yourself in those roles, what do you sense as the lesson? What were you missing?"

A theme came to Sarah's mind with a clarity she had never seen until this moment. "I was an accomplished leader, but I was not humble. All too often I mistook myself for the doer. I know my expertise was needed in those embodiments. But my service was not as effective as it could have been because I did not acknowledge *An Síoraí,* the Eternal One, as the one who was truly meant to be acting."

"Racham taught me that same lesson," said Flavia. "We are meant to be the vessel, the conduit for divine mysteries to act in this world. Go deeper now. What or who is the thread that links the embodiments you remember?"

"That is an easy question to answer. Kevin has been the constant in all of my lifetimes. Even if we weren't married, he was close to me. When we weren't sharing an embodiment, our souls were still eternally one. Sometimes I can see or feel a golden thread connecting us heart to heart."

"What is important about that thread now?"

"I've been thinking about how we need to live more from the spiritual attainment we achieved as Alana and Ah-Lahn. Kevin needs to express that level of his adeptship so he can take over for Lucky. I mean Lúcháir."

"What about you? What about Alana's attainment?"

Sarah paused, reflecting. "As a mother and as a writer, I try hard to use the attunement that comes from my attainment. I guess that partially answers my question about what it means to live as a modern-day mystic. And I can tell by the way you're looking at me that I'm missing something."

Flavia said nothing. With the intensity of timeless love, she focused her soft blue eyes on this dear friend and daughter of ages past.

"Okay, I'm thinking, said Sarah. "Whenever you and I have known each other, you have urged me to be my authentic self, to be real."

"What about being real has been most opposed in all your lifetimes?"

"My relationship with Kevin. Our work together has rarely gone as we had hoped. Arán Bán and his wretched family have done their worst to keep us apart. They aborted our mission in Tearmann."

"Now do you understand why I am here?" asked Flavia. "Lúcháir needs Kevin to succeed him. And I..." She paused again and looked meaningfully at the young woman in whom she had placed enormous faith.

A light dawned in Sarah's awareness. "You need me to succeed you," she said softly. "You need me like Lúcháir needs Kevin. Our twin flames in resonance with your twin flames. Equal dedication and determination. But how do I succeed you, Flavia?"

"That is a question I may answer. Pass your tests, Sarah. Be watchful and keep your wits about you. Mind your children. More than that I cannot say. I will help you where I can. And remember what Kevin said about the spiritual path we each walk."

"The path is a do-it-yourself-project."

Flavia nodded. "Be mindful of what you are doing and who is the doer," she said as her light body began fading from view. "You have my love and a promise that I long to keep—if you will earn it."

A short while later, Lúcháir and Flavia were in a conversation of their own.

"Is Sarah ready?" he asked.

"As ready as I can help her be. You know I am not allowed to tell her anything she cannot intuit."

"She understands that she is your successor?"

"She does. Offering her that much insight is all I can do."

Lúcháir gazed into Flavia's clear blue eyes as he poured out his love to her. "I'll be with you soon, *a ghra*," he said.

"Finish well." Flavia's own longing for their reunion was palpable. "I will be waiting."

"This is the life, isn't it?" Lúcháir asked, though he was well-aware of the answer to the question that had percolated in his soul since childhood.

"There are many threads remaining to be woven before this tapestry is complete, my love. And yes, this is the life when you can fulfill all."

In the Heart of the Goddess

Hungry. If anyone had asked Kevin, that is how he would have characterized himself. Not only was he ready for another serving of the Irish food he considered true home cooking. He was also hungry for the textures and sensorial experiences he was sure lay ahead.

Today he and Lucky were beginning their trek through County Clare for a day or two of sightseeing before heading into Galway and their final destination—Connemara.

Of course, they were more than casual tourists. They were both adepts whose intuitive gaze could penetrate the surface of places and the masks that people wore to protect themselves from the unrealities, and sometimes the realities, of what frightened them.

The desire to find spiritual truths that lie beneath mundane appearances has always been the mystic's way. Knowing themselves to be of that lineage, the two men from America followed the leadings of their Celtic blood and druidic past into the mysteries of Éire.

After a good night's sleep, they were preparing to enjoy a leisurely breakfast when they began to feel an urgency—a pull on the heart that told them to not delay their arrival in Connemara. Each man read the other's mind—'twas the Goddess Éire herself urging them onward.

The distance from Shannon through Ennis and into Galway can be driven in less than ninety minutes. Despite their shared sense of urgency, Lucky and Kevin agreed that such rapid travel would be too fast and too urban. As soon as they reached Ennis, they took off across County Clare to the Cliffs of Moher.

With few other visitors abroad that day in early November, they were nearly alone with the ferocious winds that chilled them to the bone and thrilled them with the primal power of land and sea and sky collaborating to create a scene of unmitigated immensity.

"If you've ever wondered where the wild Celtic spirit of the Irish still thrives, 'tis here!" Lucky shouted above the crash of pounding waves 700 feet below. He could sense Kevin's entire being opening to the power that was also moving him body and soul.

"Freedom, lad!" Lucky boomed again. "And the refusal to give in to greedy principalities and false dominions. 'Tis the power of the goddess to stand against all invaders!"

"This is what I came for!" Kevin shouted in response. He promised himself he would not forget the ecstasy he was feeling in this moment at the cliff-edge of the world.

"Let's walk on before Goddess Éire blows us off her island," Lucky grinned. "We've only begun to experience her presence."

"Did you feel that?" Lucky asked the next morning as they escaped the traffic of Galway. Though they had enjoyed rambling around the City of the Tribes throughout the previous afternoon and evening, today they were eager to drive along the coast of Galway Bay and then turn inland.

"We've entered Connemara, haven't we?" Kevin had felt the change.

"We're still in County Galway, yet in a different world entirely."

"Are you ready for this?" Kevin asked, keeping his eyes on the road.

"I am, though I've no idea what 'this' may be. 'Twill be good to stay in Clifden. I remember it as a special place—a sort of magical treat for a child. Our family rarely went there. 'Tis only an hour or so from here and there are a couple of stops I want to make on the way. The first is the Patrick Pearse cottage site. They've built a visitor center in the last few years. I'd like to see what they've done for Connemara's hero."

"Wasn't he a key figure in the Easter Uprising of 1916?"

"The very man. Educator, writer, revolutionary. He was a big deal to me when I was a lad. People say we wouldn't have an Irish Republic had it not been for Pearse. An odd fellow to be our first president. He was too poetical to lead a government. But he surely had the heart and the gift of words to inspire a movement. They say he fancied himself a sort of Christ figure who willingly sacrificed himself for his country. He died a martyr for the cause of Irish freedom."

Kevin was pensive as he negotiated the roadway's turn to the north.

"What are you thinking, lad?" asked Lucky.

"I'm remembering how many times we've done the same—sacrificed for the freedom of our people, I mean."

"Over the centuries? Too many to count."

"Is it worth it, do you think?"

"It depends." Lucky drew out the words, considering the hundreds of wars he had personally experienced.

"On what?"

"Who the players are and what's at stake. The circumstance is always an equation of light and dark which no adept or even a powerful spiritual master can predict. The Great Law acts impartially. All we can do is play our parts, as you've done yourself."

"On Atlantis, for sure. I bought time for many to escape before the continent sank."

"You did. And Riordan's death after Ah-Lahn was killed turned the tide of battle and saved Tearmann."

"Brian's soul made the decision to safeguard the future of his family and friends." Kevin felt his throat clutch. The loss was so recent.

"Think of Róisín." Lucky's voice was equally wistful. "She laid down her life to bring about the final judgment of the fallen one that was Una. Of course, Racham's sacrifice remains the greatest. He saved a universe of souls until they could gain the mastery to save themselves. These passings were all prompted by *An Síoraí*, the Eternal One."

"Then the source of the prompting makes the difference between a sacrifice that flows from the heart, not from the ego," said Kevin.

Lucky nodded firmly. "Remember that, lad. There are people who would trick us into making sacrifices that are not the will of the Masters who guide our destiny. We're meant to choose life. Not put ourselves in mortal danger if another solution can be found. If we can fight and win our battles on inner planes, physical war may not be necessary."

They remained silent for several minutes, watching the warming morning sun as it played on sea and land, while the sky above Connemara opened to ever-widening vistas.

"Where's the other stop you want to make?" Kevin eased them back into conversation as he pulled into the car park at the Pearse memorial visitors center.

"There's a famous pub at Maam Cross where we can have lunch. It's on the main road to Clifden. And..." Lucky paused.

"And what?"

"And the future that is hidden until *An Síoraí,* the Eternal One, lifts the veil," he said with a tone of resignation in his voice that Kevin had not heard before.

Remembering how A. B. Ryan had tried to kill Lucky from the astral plane after their adversary had died, he asked, "Are you worried about the Conways mounting an attack, even though they're out of embodiment?"

"No. Tim checked with our Master before we left New York. He said not to worry. Archangel Michael is taking care of them."

"Good to know. At least that's one problem we don't have to be concerned about. I suppose there will be others at some point."

"You know the answer to that, my friend. 'Tis always a matter of when, not if." Lucky rested a reassuring hand on Kevin's shoulder as they walked toward the entrance.

"Now, let's go soak up some Connemara courage from the poet who declared our independence. Pearse situated his cottage with grand views of the land he loved more than life itself. I want to see what he was looking at when he wrote his most inspiring words."

Initiation

Wednesday, November 3 - at Fibonacci's ballroom

Sarah was restless. After Flavia's appearance and their enlightening conversation, she felt an overwhelming need to work on Lucky's book in the ballroom at Fibonacci's where angels gathered and where her beloved mentor had conducted many soul-stirring services.

Her animals were also restless at home, so she decided to bring them with her. Hero was accustomed to hanging out in the bookstore. He was a popular addition to the children's corner where he listened patiently in the Paws to Read program. He loved the affection he received from the young readers, and the children adored the big dog's non-judgmental attention.

Sprite enjoyed her own niche as occasional bookstore cat. She had a special fondness for napping in the front window display, which attracted curious passers-by to inquire about the cat who loved books.

In fact, one young customer had written a children's book called *Sprite, the Antiquarian Cat.* The cover featured a picture another youngster had painted of Sprite curled around a stack of the oldest books in the Esoterica section upstairs in the bookstore loft.

Sarah was feeling a bit guilty about leaving the twins at home all morning, but the prompting to work in the ballroom was overwhelming. The intensity of that sensation convinced her that the children would be fine in Charlotte's care. They were familiar with her now and she knew their routines.

Normally, Sarah's parents would have been glad to babysit, but they were visiting Millie and Frank in New Bedford, Massachusetts. Ivy and Hank were back from their honeymoon, but they were very busy working out details of the New York consolidation of Callahan & Logan Computer Systems while Kerry and Kaitlyn were in school.

Maggie and Tim had whisked off last night on an impromptu mission for the Master. So Charlotte was in charge of daycare for Gareth and Naimh. As always, she seemed thrilled with the opportunity.

Sarah took a cue from the angel presences she detected in the ballroom. Sounding the OM, she continued the chant until she felt surrounded in light. After that, the work flowed smoothly. Any questions that arose in her mind about wording and formatting seemed to answer themselves.

She was pleased with how the different stories, conversations and reminiscences of Lucky's narrative were falling into place. They had finished reviewing the final transcripts before he and Kevin left for Ireland. Sarah's current task was one of assembling the many complex pieces—a challenge she thoroughly enjoyed.

At around 10:30 a.m. she looked at her watch. Another hour until lunchtime when she planned to pack up her laptop, dog and cat, and go home to feed her children. And make sure they took a good, long nap.

Sarah's only complaint about Charlotte's caring for them was that she seemed to get them overly excited. That made it hard to settle them for a couple of hours. She'd put off saying anything to this young woman who was so helpful, but she did have in the back of her mind that a correction needed to be made—diplomatically, of course.

Realizing that her thoughts had wandered, Sarah brought her attention back to Lucky's deeply moving story about his love for Flavia. She was studying the printed correction copy she was working from when a glint of light caught her eye. She looked up and there was Flavia, even more tangible than she had been the day before.

Her eyes were blazing with uncharacteristic intensity as she spoke three words and vanished: "Go home! Now!"

Sarah threw her laptop and papers in her briefcase and rushed downstairs to the bookstore. "Rory!" she shouted breathlessly. "I have to go home this instant. Will you keep the fur kids until I can come back for them?"

"What's wrong?" He had never seen her so frantic. "Do you need me to come with you?" Then he realized he was the only staff on duty. "Sorry, *a chara*, I can't leave the store. Shall I call Debbie?"

"I don't know!" exclaimed Sarah. "I've got to go!"

"Be careful, lass," Rory called after her as she sprinted out of the store.

Sarah knew to be careful. As soon as she was behind the wheel of her car, she took a deep breath and sounded an OM that she visualized piercing through the ethers.

"An Síoraí! Archangel Michael! Help me!" she cried aloud. Instantly she felt the mantle and mastery of her spiritual identity, Bandruí Alana, descend around her like a sheath of light.

She started driving with focused intensity. The traffic seemed to part before her, allowing her to pull into her driveway in record time. Steady as a rock now, she moved swiftly from her car, locked it and strode in the full power of her inner reality, up the steps to her front door—which she opened just in time to see little Naimh standing on the back of an armchair in the living room, ready to leap off.

The child was beaming with joy. Her little arms were extended like the wings she seemed unaware that she didn't have. Charlotte was standing on the far side of the room, holding Gareth back from protecting his sister. She was urging the little girl to fly—where she surely would have hit her head on the coffee table's sharp metal edge.

"Naimh! No!" Sarah yelled as she rushed to scoop her daughter into her arms. She turned to confront Charlotte. The woman had released little Gareth, who nearly fell onto the coffee table trying to get to his mother and sister.

Sarah gasped at the scene that suddenly materialized before her. For the raven-haired woman now standing menacingly in her living room was none other than the teenaged daughter of Bantiarna and the Sly Druid from Sarah and Kevin's horrific life review.

Their eyes locked and Charlotte declared with an accusatory smirk, "Sarah! Look what you've done. You've spoiled our game, just when we were having so much fun. Naimh was learning to fly, but now she won't get a chance to try her wings."

She turned to leave, but Sarah called out with the full power of a mother's ferocity that halted the woman in her tracks. "Stop! Whoever you are. You're not going anywhere until you explain yourself."

"You know exactly who I am," Charlotte sneered with oily condescension. "Surely you know why I'm here. Your precious *ceann-druí* killed my parents. I promised him over my father's dead body that my family would haunt him and his own till the end of time.

"My Aunt Stacey and Uncle Stan couldn't get close to the coward, so we've been chipping away at his family. They managed to take out your weak-willed brother before they died. And I nearly had your sniveling brat Naimh, who is even more gullible than you were, Little Sarah."

Charlotte opened her mouth as if to utter a curse, but Sarah's hand went up with a loud, "No! You have no power here. Now get out and do not dare show your face in our community again!"

"Don't worry, I'm leaving," said Charlotte with a wicked smile. "But you haven't heard the last of me! I will strike when you least expect it and there is nothing you can do to stop me!"

She whirled and dashed out the front door, nearly knocking Debbie off the porch. As soon as Rory had alerted her that something was terribly wrong with Sarah, she had rushed to her friend's house.

She hurried into the living room where Sarah was sitting on the sofa with her twins huddled against her. They were crying and she was trying unsuccessfully to calm them. The energy of the confrontation between their mother and Charlotte had frightened them beyond comprehension.

Debbie moved swiftly to gather Sarah and the children into her arms. "Are you all okay? What happened? Why was Charlotte blazing out of here like a banshee?"

Sarah couldn't speak. What she could do was send her seer friend a mental image of the situation she had confronted. Debbie already knew the heart-wrenching story. She instantly understood that a deadly record of past events had been revived.

"My God," she gasped. "Charlotte was the teenager who killed you when Kevin was your father, the *ceann-druí*."

"She was." Sarah found her voice as the twins began to settle now that their mother's devoted friend had arrived.

"I did it, Debbie. I saved my baby. I don't entirely understand what happened, except that the minute I stopped Naimh from jumping and hitting her head on the coffee table, somehow I was not only saving her, I was saving Little Sarah. Those terrible people killed Brian, but I saved my child. Do you know Charlotte called Stacey and Stan her aunt and uncle."

Debbie was aghast.

"I knew I would fight her to the death," Sarah continued. "I'm glad it didn't come to that."

"So am I," said Debbie, hugging her friend and her precious children even closer.

"Is everybody safe?" called Jeremy as he rushed through the open front door with Sprite in his arms. "Rory called me right after he called you, Debbie. He said Sarah's fur kids were practically knocking down the door to the bookstore, trying to get home."

Hero bounded past him and rushed over to the twins. Wagging his whole body, he was whimpering and licking their hands and faces—the perfect remedy to calm frightened children.

"Meow!" cried Sprite as she jumped out of Jeremy's arms. The sleek feline made a beeline for her mistress. In a single leap she was on the sofa and wrapping herself around Sarah's shoulders where she began purring vigorously to physically comfort the woman she had tended in spirit for centuries.

"What can we do?" Debbie asked. "Looks like your kids have got you covered." They all laughed. Sarah was completely surrounded with pets and children.

"It's lunchtime. If you don't mind foraging, I know there are sandwich makings in the fridge and canned soup in the cupboard. Jeremy, you're welcome to stay."

Then she gasped. "Oh my God, Jeremy. Could you call Kevin? I can feel him trying to reach me. My cell phone's in the car and I haven't been calm enough to answer his telepath. He probably got a flash of Charlotte's menacing image at the same time I saw her for who she really is."

"I'm sure he did. The energy whipping around this room easily sent sparks across the cosmos, not to mention the ocean. What shall I tell him?"

"Let him know that the image he no doubt saw was true and that you and Debbie have made sure we're all safe. I'll call him after lunch, as soon as the twins are settled."

"Don't worry," Jeremy said reassuringly. "You relax. I'll encourage your husband to do the same."

"Are you sure you're okay?" asked a very worried Kevin when Sarah reached him by phone an hour later. He was trying to sound calm, but he couldn't remember ever being this desperate about the safety of his family.

"Do I need to come home? We're in Clifden, but I could catch a flight from Shannon tomorrow."

"No, Hon, we're fine now. Debbie fed us and the twins went right to sleep for their afternoon nap. Poor little things. They were bewildered to feel so much negative energy—not to mention their mother shouting like a *Valkyrie* in battle."

"I definitely felt it from here," said Kevin. "When you didn't answer my telepath or your phone, I feared the worst."

"It was so weird," Sarah explained. "You know how the atmosphere goes all 'shimmery' when you contact a record that's right on the surface?"

"Yeah. It's always a surprise."

"This was like that. At first Charlotte was standing in front of me, appearing like her present-day self. Then the mask she's been wearing fell off and I saw her as the teenaged daughter of those two vile druids—the grandparents of Arán Bán who are now Stan and Stacey."

"Thank God you got home in time."

"It's as if the whole thing was being orchestrated to reveal Charlotte's hidden identity and for me to save Naimh—and, curiously, myself. She was full of revenge. She started to curse us again, but I rolled it back on her as she was about to speak."

"Good for you, Hon. And you're positive that you're safe? Not frightened? The twins are at peace?"

"Yes. Debbie and I are doing extra prayers for them. She's spending the night and the fur kids are on duty. Hero is in the nursery and Sprite hasn't left my side. I'm not going to tell my folks anything about this until they return from Massachusetts. Maggie texted me that she and Tim will be home tomorrow. And besides, you have work to do with Lucky."

Sarah paused, remembering to ask about Kevin's travels. "How are you two doing, by the way? Are you having a good time so far?"

"'Grand,' as Lucky would say."

"Give him my love. And tell him it was Flavia who sent me home at the precise time I needed to arrive to save Naimh and reveal Charlotte."

Kevin could feel that his inner guidance was on high alert. "Sarah, I think this was a big deal."

"So do I. I'm grateful we got through it. Your family is safe for now, but I can't help being concerned. Even if Charlotte never shows her face around Fibonacci's again, she's is still on the loose. She said we haven't heard the last of her.

"She was absolutely furious that I thwarted her plan to kill Naimh. And who knows what she would have done to Gareth. She had him a vice grip so he couldn't move. I wouldn't put anything past her. She's the last hand that wicked family has left to play."

"I'll let Lucky know. We may be able to tune in to where she is or what she's up to, although she's proved her ability to cloak her identity and probably her location. We'll just have to be watchful."

"And prayerful," said Sarah, "as will all of us here. Oh, Kevin, please be careful. I want you and Lucky to come home in one piece when your mission in Connemara is complete."

"'Don't worry, lass,' to quote Lucky again. Charlotte is dealing with two master druids who've got her number now. We'll be fine, I promise."

"I expect you to keep that promise," said Sarah gently. She closed her eyes and concentrated on sending a powerful ray of love from her heart, across the ethers to her soul's beloved twin.

Kevin's own heart caught the ray, and it moved him to tears. He felt the golden thread of their eternal soul connection grow stronger and more precious. Come what may, he knew they would hold fast.

At last he was able to relax. He breathed a deep sigh and said softly in Irish, *"Oíche mhaith, a ghrá."*

"Good night to you, too, my love," Sarah answered. "I'll see you in my dreams."

Connemara

Anyone viewing Connemara from the air could easily imagine that the last ice age had only recently melted, leaving every valley, gully or crack in the earth filled with water.

Here was the land of the Goddess Éire in her most plentiful manifestation of lakes and ponds and streams. Her rugged presence was equally visible in wild landscapes of rocky hills and vales carved thousands of years ago by the retreating ice.

Here also was the land of Lucky's birth where he was deeply feeling the meaning of his birth name—Lúcháir, the soul of welcoming joy.

As Kevin had predicted, the man was talking his way across Connemara. Starting at the Pearse memorial, through lunch at the Maam Cross pub and into the afternoon with the staff of the Clifden Station House Hotel where Maggie had booked their accommodations, Lucky happily introduced himself as Lúcháir—a returning son of County Galway.

"Now that you're calling yourself Lúcháir, it seems appropriate that I should use your birth name," Kevin smiled at his friend as they unpacked in their hotel room.

"Aye, lad. I'm ready to claim that identity. I can feel there are reasons I don't understand yet—except to say that the name carries the vibration I'm meant to embody for whatever comes next."

Despite the brisk breeze and drizzle that prompted the need for hats and rain gear, after settling into their accommodations, they walked through the market square, inspecting the few streets and charming shops that comprise the small town of Clifden. Excellent food and friendly conversation with locals kept their spirits light that evening. They retired for the night feeling themselves generously enfolded in Connemara hospitality.

Early the next morning—a Friday—after the full Irish breakfast they had agreed was in order, they walked the short distance to St. Joseph's Catholic Church. They knew that Father Kenneally had transferred there from Letterfrack before he retired.

He would have been well over one hundred years old, had he still been living. But they were hopeful of meeting someone who might have known the wise old prelate. *An Síoraí,* the Eternal One, smiled on their wishes.

"Sure, I knew him," said Father Turley—a handsome priest about fifty years of age, with a Celt's dark hair, blue eyes and instant openness that marked him as a kindred soul. "I feel like I know you, too. Though when Father first mentioned the lad he'd rescued from idleness, he called you by your surname: O'Connor."

Lúcháir smiled at the recollection. "He must have been long in the tooth when you knew him. When was that? The first time I met him, I thought he already looked ancient."

"He took me under his wing here in Clifden shortly after you went to seminary," Father Turley answered. "I was one of the last to have the privilege of his care. The older he got, the more ancient his wisdom seemed to grow. Like he was seeing far back in time. I often imagined I was being tutored by a senior druid and not a Catholic priest. He was that deep. Did you pick up on that, at all?"

Caught up in Father Turley's memories, Lúcháir let his own mind slip back to his adolescence.

"I did have the odd past-life flash now and again. Though truth be told, when I was a lad I was most keen to read all I could find about King Arthur, his knights and ladies of the Round Table. When Father Kenneally urged me back to school, the nuns made sure that class lessons were my focus. Later in life, I became mightily aware of druid times."

The priest nodded. "I think that's what happened to the Father. Later in life, I mean. That's when he started mentioning you with a faraway look in his eyes. 'My best student. Aye, he was a special one,' he'd say. But in those recollections he didn't call you 'O'Connor.' He called you 'Quin.' Then I knew you'd been a druid."

Lúchair was not entirely surprised.

"'Tis a funny thing," Father Turley went on. "When Father Kenneally called you Quin, I seemed to recall us being his students in those long-ago days when he wanted me to follow in your footsteps. Like I did in this lifetime."

Spontaneously, the two men reached out and clasped hands and forearms in the double handshake the druids had used for centuries. Anyone observing them—as Kevin did—would have seen the atmosphere in the priest's office where they'd been talking shimmer with a radiance that instilled in the hearts of the three men a deep knowing and gratitude for past connections, now renewed.

Coming back to himself, Lúchair realized that Kevin had been standing by during this spontaneous reunion of two acquaintances from ages past. "Excuse my poor manners," he said. "This is my fellow druid and successor, Kevin MacCauley."

"'Tis grand to meet you, Kevin," Father Turley said with a knowing smile. "Or should I say 'Ah-Lahn'?"

After this conversation, Lúchair and Kevin fairly floated back to their hotel room—no doubt aided by the wind they were beginning to realize would be with them throughout their sojourn in the country of Lúchair's birth.

Without a word, they seated themselves in armchairs that flanked a window which offered a clear view of the bay. However, viewing the outer landscape was not their intention in this moment. Instead, they went into a deep meditation that lasted into the early afternoon.

Hunger finally caught Lúchair's attention as well as Kevin's. Father Turley had recommended their hotel's restaurant. 'Twas an easy choice.

When they returned from their meal, Lúchair discovered an email from Sarah with the promised pages of his childhood stories.

"I'll leave you to read," said Kevin. "I feel a prompting to walk down by the bay while there's still some daylight."

"Come back in an hour," said Lúchair, "and mind your surroundings, lad. Something's afoot, though I can't say what."

As soon as Kevin left the hotel, he felt it, too. He could not identify the source of the disturbance he detected—only that he did detect it. He walked a short distance, then changed his mind and returned to the hotel lobby where he sat and watched the comings and goings of other patrons for the remainder of an hour.

Lúcháir was waiting for him when he entered their room. Kevin could see his friend's eyes were moist, but he was wearing a bright smile.

"Our Sarah is doing a grand job with the writing. She's capturing the tone and flow I was hoping for. I know you've been helping her with remembering the life review. Thanks for that."

"You're more than welcome, Lúcháir. You're giving us a priceless gift—threads of our lineage we never knew before."

"Then let's celebrate the progress of our legacy book with some good fun tonight. Father Turley just texted an invitation for us to join him at a local pub that's known as Clifden's home of traditional Irish music.

"Turns out a talented musician family is holding a *seisiún* tonight. He said they're not to be missed. He'll meet us at the crossroads by the church and we'll walk the rest of the way together. 'Tisn't far, though we'd best plan for some weather. He said a storm is brewing—a typical forecast for this time of year.

"Tomorrow we'll see if we can find where I grew up—though I suspect the old house is gone by now and my sisters and parents all passed away with it."

Lúcháir paused, knowing that was true. Then he brightened again.

"However, if *An Síoraí,* the Eternal One, agrees, I'm sure we can locate my childhood pondering spot. I've another story to tell you, and it needs a lake and a boulder to set the stage. We'll get to where we're going soon enough, but we've got to be sure we know where we're standing."

As circumstances are wont to take an unexpected turn for mystics who have embarked upon a pilgrimage, a vital event awaited the two reembodied druids before they could enter into the recollections that were so necessary to their seeking souls.

Indeed, a storm was brewing, though one not strictly weather-related.

Justice

The two travelers were preparing to join Father Turley when Lúcháir paused, listening to his inner guidance. He turned to Kevin. Looking him in the eye, he asked, "Do you trust me?"

Though surprised, Kevin did not hesitate. "With my life."

"As I trust you with mine. God willing, we'll neither of us come to that. Still, promise me that whatever happens tonight, you'll follow my lead."

"That's a bit mysterious, even for you, Lúcháir. But I promise."

"Connemara folks don't let a little thing like rain and sleet stop them from enjoying some good music, do they?" Kevin observed as he, Lúcháir and Father Turley made their way down Main Street, through The Square and halfway up Market Street to the popular pub that was hosting Clifden's main attraction that evening.

The wind was blowing fiercely with a promise of snow before the night was over. Nevertheless, several dozen patrons were hurrying through the brightly painted entrance to the popular establishment.

The musicians could be heard tuning up, playing a few licks on their instruments amidst a growing volume of conversation. Excitement was building for an entertaining *seisiún*.

As the three men prepared to join the crowd, a raven-haired young woman stepped in front of them, her cobalt-blue eyes flashing. When she aggressively blocked their way, they needed only a fraction of a second to recognize Charlotte. Not even Father Turley expressed surprise at her arrival.

"I'll bet you didn't expect to see me here in Connemara," she boasted.

Kevin noticed that Charlotte seemed extremely anxious. Her voice was pitched higher than he remembered. Her faced was flushed as if she had rushed to intercept the men before they could join the other people entering the pub.

"Actually, we've been expecting you," said Lúcháir calmly.

"Don't talk to me, old man!" Charlotte snapped. She jerked a revolver from her jacket pocket and pointed it at Kevin. "He's the one I'm after."

"Now, there's no need for that," said Father Turley gently. "Why don't we find a place to sit and talk about what's troubling you." He took a step toward Charlotte as if to lead her away from the door to the pub, but she waved the gun at him.

"Stay where you are, Father. You have no part here. This is between me and the *ceann-druí*. The time for talking is over." She turned back to her prey and, ironically, began to talk. Her speech was coming out rapidly, breathlessly. She was rambling, not entirely making sense.

"Though after all these centuries, I'll find little satisfaction," she said. "My family is dead—again. But killing you will help. It's what you deserve."

She was pointing the gun at Kevin, but her hand was shaking as if the weight of the weapon was too much for her to hold steady. Though the gun was not large, she was using both hands to keep it level.

Kevin made a conscious effort to still his heart and not be drawn into Charlotte's chaotic aura. He could sense that Father Turley and Lúcháir were doing the same. In his mind's eye he saw three master druids being confronted by an overwrought woman who had the potential of doing one or all of them great harm.

"Charlotte," he said, matching Father Turley's gentle tone, "your aunt and uncle died in a car accident. No one else is to blame for that."

"That's not what I'm talking about, you fool! You killed my parents! You know you did!"

"Lass, that was centuries ago," said Lúcháir. He spoke to her with a kindness that caught her off guard. "Kevin has atoned for his errors. Surely you don't want to burden your own soul with more bloodshed. You said that Kevin deserves to die. But what do you deserve?"

She looked at him with disbelief and swung around to face him, waving the gun. Now it was pointing at Lúcháir.

"Justice! And I'm here to get it!"

"I believe Kevin wants justice as much as you do," said Father Turley, "but this isn't the way."

"I told you to stay out of this!" Charlotte was becoming more and more agitated. Things weren't going the way she'd planned. She'd wanted to get Kevin alone and make him beg for his life. Instead, she was outnumbered by three men who kept talking to her. Worse yet, the angrier she got, the calmer they became.

She had her finger on the trigger now.

"Stop trying to trick me!" She was practically yelling and was moving the weapon back and forth, as if she suddenly was not sure where to aim. She was becoming seriously unhinged. The energy whipping through her was making her extremely dangerous.

Then something unexpected happened.

Lúcháir took a small step toward Charlotte. At the same time, he made a subtle motion with his right hand—a gesture that Kevin remembered. He had seen Old Quin alter the shape and function of objects without touching them. That is exactly what Lúcháir did.

Charlotte was so shocked by his movements that she squeezed the trigger. But nothing happened. Not even a click.

As if a slow motion film scene were unfolding before them, Kevin, Lúcháir and Father Turley watched as the would-be executioner fiddled with her weapon. She was rambling again—cursing the man who'd sold her an old gun with old ammunition, cursing the damp weather that made everything wet. And cursing her prey who stood before her like a statue, expressionless. Or was that pity in his eyes?

Charlotte was wise enough not to look down the barrel of the gun, but when she spun the chamber, it went off in her hand. Violently tossing the weapon aside, she lost her balance, caught her foot on the uneven pavement and pitched backward where she fell, hitting her head on a jagged piece of concrete that had broken loose.

"Charlotte, lie still!" cried Kevin. "We'll find a doctor!"

He bent down to help the woman who had meant to kill him. But she lived only long enough to answer him with a fury.

"I spit on your mercy. You'll get none from me," she sneered. "I swear my wrath will visit you yet," she croaked as she died in the pool of hatred she had carried for more than two thousand years.

For a moment, silence fell like a shroud. Then chaos broke out as patrons who had witnessed the gun go off in Charlotte's hand gathered around. At the sound of gunfire and shouts from the crowd, two off-duty *garda* who happened to be in the pub rushed out into the cold night air that had gone strangely calm.

They immediately took control of the situation, moving by-standers back and calling an ambulance. They asked many questions of the three men as well as other witnesses and soon appeared satisfied that Charlotte's fatal head wound was accidental—the result of unprovoked malice on the part of the dead woman.

"There'll be an inquiry, sir," the lead officer spoke to Lúcháir. "But since Father, here, vouches for you, and your story rings true according to these folks who saw what happened, the magistrate'll surely move things along so's we don't keep you from your travels."

Eventually, the *garda* finished taking photos and the ambulance left with Charlotte's body. Kevin wondered what they would do with her. Neither he nor Lúcháir had any idea of her next of kin who might be living. The authorities would have to deal with that problem.

Father Turley found a relatively quiet corner in the pub where they could warm up and discuss this strange event.

Kevin shook his head in amazement "Like son, like mother," he murmured, briefly explaining to Father Turley how Arán Bán had mocked Ah-Lahn's compassion. Which, strangely, was what he was feeling for the soul of this woman who, at least once, had given birth to the man who had for eons intended to kill him.

"Justice is what she asked for," said Father Turley thoughtfully.

"And what she will receive," agreed Lúcháir, "though not in the way she imagined. The meting out of karmic retribution belongs to *An Síoraí*, the Eternal One, not to us. All we can do is play our parts."

"As we've seen in the past and surely will again," agreed Kevin.

"Aye, though not any time soon, I hope."

Interlude

After last night's unnerving confrontation with Charlotte, both Lúcháir and Kevin felt they needed a day to imbibe the healing atmosphere of Nature. Diving into the drama of past lives could wait. They made the most of a hearty breakfast before beginning their journey eastward from Clifden toward Lúcháir's former home.

They drove slowly, stopped often and walked purposefully, feeling the land under their feet and breathing deeply of the air that smelled alternately of sea and earth and distant turf fires.

Kevin eagerly joined Lúcháir when his friend would suddenly halt and bend down to inspect a native plant or inhale the sweet coconut scent of golden furze that managed to bloom even in November.

They filled their beings with the sensations each acre shared with them—body, heart, mind and soul. With calmer weather today they were able to climb some hills, negotiating rough-hewn stone steps and rugged pathways. They soon noticed a different kind of strength in their limbs that life in the city never engaged quite like this.

As November's afternoon sun began to wane, Kevin once again declared that food was the need of the hour. Lúcháir agreed.

"I've no need to track down the old house after all," he admitted. "'Tis probably gone derelict by now and contacting that desolation doesn't feel right. Not after this grand walkabout."

"Then how about a meal at Kylemore Abbey and a wander through their gardens?" Kevin suggested. "Even this late in the season, I'm thinking their well-ordered beauty offers an interesting balance to Connemara's wildness. Nature and man in collaboration."

Lúcháir nodded. "Today we wander; tomorrow we ponder. All in the perfect timing of *An Síoraí,* the Eternal One."

Sunday morning dawned full of promise. Both men could feel it. They knew they had passed a major test in surviving the threat from Charlotte. The local magistrate had confirmed that they bore no responsibility for her actions.

Father Turley and other witnesses had all agreed that the woman's death was the fault of her own aggression. With apologies for any inconvenience caused by necessary questions, the visitors from America were free to continue their vacation in Connemara.

"We're very close to my pondering spot now," Lúcháir said after they had walked a couple of miles away from the national park's visitors center. "In fact, my feet know the way exactly, like they did when I was a lad."

He was right, of course. Within ten more minutes, the two men were standing by the shore of a tiny lake with a few scattered boulders on one side and a breathtaking view of the Maumturks Mountains on the other.

They found a flat rock which Lúcháir declared was the very one upon which he had sat during his childhood musings. Settling into the scene before him, he prepared to relate the tale he had said was an important recollection.

"You'd best turn on the little recorder Sarah sent with you," he said to Kevin. "I promised her this story for the book. 'Tis a vital thread we're meant to weave into my legacy."

Lúcháir looked intently around the lake shore. Spying a large boulder that was half in, half out of the water, he pointed. "See that big rock over there? That boulder is where this part of the story begins."

A Lake & A Boulder

Kevin was relieved that Lúcháir was slipping once again into *seanchaí* mode. They both relaxed and settled into the receptivity that welcomes a story to speak its truth. For that is the storyteller's gift—to allow even the grandest fiction to reveal the reality that lies at its source.

As I've told you, I spent many an hour here at my pondering spot, dreaming about King Arthur, his knights and ladies. Now, this was more than boyhood wishing or fantasy. I knew in my soul I'd lived among them.

One day I decided to climb up there on that boulder so I could look into the lake from a different perspective. There was no wind blowing, not even the ripple of a breeze to disturb the water's surface. Lack of wind is unheard of in Connemara, so I knew 'twas an auspicious day.

I'd read how the druids, as well as seers and mystics from many ages, had used large bowls of water as what they called a scrying device—a tool for seeing into realms of the unseen. So I perched there above the face of the lake that was smooth as glass and focused my entire being on its surface.

At first, nothing happened. Then suddenly images began to appear. Though I didn't remember doing such a thing before, I felt my soul step out of my body and into the scenes as naturally as if I was walking out of my father's house to visit a neighbor.

At the time, I didn't know what to call the experience. You

and I would call it a life review, because that's what it was. But it wasn't a review in the way we usually experience. Instead, 'twas a series of life reviews that continued over a period of a month.

If you'd have asked me what I expected to see in such scenes, I would have told you the twelve battles Arthur fought against the Angles, Saxons and Jutes who threatened sixth-century Britain. That was after the Roman legions had departed, leaving the Celtic Britons to fend for themselves.

That's not all I experienced, and the real facts were more amazing than the poetical romances from the High Middle Ages I had read. For the life reviews revealed Arthur as an initiate of spiritual mysteries. He was knowledgeable in the ways of ancient wisdom, as were many of the men and women he gathered around him—including me.

As a youth, he had been trained by Merlin the magician—the wizard and high initiate who was skilled in hidden abilities some call occult that had been handed down from the days of Atlantis. He taught the lad how to take the perspective of other beings and how to use his wise heart and gifts of insight to pass the many difficult tests he would confront as a leader in both war and the fragile peace that he won for a time.

As I sat enthralled on my scrying boulder, I learned more about the person I served with—and that is what I've come to see was most important. Arthur was a man of his era in history, yet one who transcended the age in which he lived.

He was fierce when necessary, yet kind and unfailingly fair. Demanding though always just, he required of his knights only the rigors he required of himself. And we loved him for it. We dedicated our lives to his service because he gave the totality of his being for us, for our homeland and for the freedom he understood at deeper levels than did most of his people.

What Arthur knew—and what my life reviews revealed— was that the twelve battles he fought to save Britain from invasion were more than physical confrontations. Each one was a spiritual initiation against a specific source of anti-freedom that was being fed by dark forces on inner as well as outer planes.

I was with him for the twelfth battle, the mighty victory on the Hill of Badon. And I was with him for the next twenty years when he ruled from the real Camelot—a fortress that lay within sight of Ynys Witrin.

Arthur often went alone to the sacred isle which retained the light and power of the Grail cup that Racham's uncle had brought from the Holy Land. 'Twas a place of retreat and inspiration for him. There was always a radiance in his aura when he returned. As long as he was able, he shared his wisdom with us, though we knew there were mysteries he could not share.

Some have called the years when the real Arthur lived the Dark Ages. But with such a noble soul in the world, there was light indeed. In the end, 'tis not the accuracy of the dates that really matters. 'Tis the legacy of the soul and his determination to fight for freedom wherever it is threatened.

For a few minutes, no sound disturbed Connemara's vast expanse except for a lone peregrine falcon soaring high overhead, calling to its mate who answered from across the valley.

Kevin gently broke the silence.

"Is there more to your story?" He had a feeling that a major point remained to be made.

"There is, yes. For this is a tale in two parts. The first we'll finish here, as 'tis key to your personal inheritance. The second part we'll finish in New York."

Lúcháir gazed off into the distance, then turned back to the man who would be his successor and laughed.

"Lad, your question is as loud in your head as it has been in mine. These life reviews are all well and good, and I could talk for days about what I saw and experienced. But what's the purpose? What lesson was I meant to glean from watching Arthur leading his people in the battles and political intrigues that have fascinated storytellers and poets for centuries?

"That question remained a puzzle to me until the weeks I passed in prayer and contemplation at Tim and Maggie's home of light while preparing to share my legacy.

"One day our Master appeared to me at *Teach an tSolais* looking like Merlin himself. Except for how his violet eyes sparkled, I might not have recognized him in his long robe, white beard and purple velvet cap.

"With a touch of humor in his voice, yet in all seriousness, he said to me, 'Lúcháir, I will answer your question with a question of my own: What would I, as magician and master of the deepest mysteries, have been teaching Arthur? What insights did I impart that made him so vital to his people and to you personally?'

"With that clue, it did not take long for a single word to flash into my mind—almost like bold letters were written across my forehead."

Lúcháir paused and looked intently at his fellow adept.

"Leadership!" declared Kevin.

"Aye, lad, you've the right of it. Leadership from the heart of a great soul whose concern was always the spiritual welfare of his people as well as their physical survival. He was like a protective father. He was also like a mother in the way he saw to the human needs that made life more than merely tolerable for his followers.

"Arthur was always a soldier first and considered myriad issues with military precision. Yet, there was a caring about him that made him unique. That's what I've tried to emulate and what I admonish you to carry on when you're *ceann-druí* to our Friends of Ancient Wisdom."

The Rest of the Story

"Twas like one of Connemara's old stone warriors rose up out of the pavement and dealt her a fatal blow to the head." Lúcháir was explaining to the Circle of Close Companions how Charlotte's life had come to an abrupt end.

All of the twin flames couples, including Sarah's parents and two sets of twins, had gathered at Tim and Maggie's house to listen to the recording of Lúcháir's story about his boyhood life reviews and to hear the details of the harrowing confrontation with the Conways' niece in Clifden.

Now they had questions.

Rory began, "In the recording you mentioned that there were two lessons involved in your fascination with King Arthur."

Surprisingly, Lúcháir looked to Kevin to explain.

"Yes," he obliged. "As the story showed, the first lesson is to follow Arthur's example as a wise and compassionate leader. Which I believe we all can affirm that our *ceann-druí* has done and which I pledge to you that I will do my best to continue whenever that time comes."

The group applauded this statement as Kevin gestured to his mentor.

"Lúcháir, the floor is yours. We're ready for what's next."

"I'm recording," said Sarah, prompting their *seanchaí* to tell them the rest of the story.

A chairde, through insights this old druid has gained in telling his stories, there is a vital thought I want to convey to you: We must, all of us, identify and understand our divine inheritance. From

our many experiences, and also from their source.

That is the story I have told you about Racham and Old Quin. What I have not told you is the reminder my soul required because I had forgotten the lesson of my friend's unending love.

After Flavia died, my grief and confusion about the larger purposes of *An Síoraí*, the Eternal One, had blinded me. For nearly half a century I was like a lost soul. Even during lifetimes when I was a monk in the early Celtic Church, I did not actually connect with Racham's spirit in the way he'd meant for me to do.

My heart never seemed able to open all the way to accept the blessing he offered when he said, 'Never doubt that I love thee.'

Arthur became for me an open door to that love through his recollection of his own significant past life. His visits to Ynys Witrin surely helped him on his spiritual path. One such visit made all the difference to mine, for he let me go with him.

This is the occasion I've remembered only recently in a life review that happened right before Kevin and I went to Ireland. I've not revealed it until now—not even to Tim and Maggie.

Lúcháir paused to let his Circle of Close Companions take in this new revelation. Here was the final and most important aspect of the legacy Saint Germain had wanted him to convey to them.

On that amazing journey, 'twas only Arthur and me and a burly rower who navigated our small currach boat through the marshes and wetlands surrounding Ynys Witrin. Even before we reached the small dock, I began to weep.

Being a knight, I tried to hide my emotion, but Arthur knew. As soon as we landed, he placed his hands on my shoulders. He turned me to face him and looked me in the eye with an expression of unspeakable kindness and understanding.

Did he know I'd lived and studied on the island as a young druid in centuries past? Perhaps. I don't know if he had second sight, but he felt the light in people, places and situations. And he had his own memory of Racham from an earlier embodiment.

Without prefacing his story, he said to me, 'I know the myths are true about him and his mother. Long ago, I was one of the first to meet them. I remember the babe's eyes. He looked at me as if to say, "We are on Earth for the same cause." I've seen his mother in my dreams. 'Tis why I wore her image on my shield at the battle for Badon. She and her son surely won us our victory that day.'

Saying no more, he turned and went about his own business.

'Twas the only time I went with him to Ynys Witrin. But that one experience was enough to quicken my recollection of the lifetime when Flavia and Racham and I had been together. Most important, I finally contacted the love we shared.

Of course, I have had to remember that love again in each lifetime. That is what my soul was trying to do in my relentless reading about King Arthur.

And to answer the question I can hear some of you asking, I never left Camelot to go on a Grail quest like many of Arthur's knights. I had no need. In remembering my days in Racham's company, I knew I had been in the presence of the very source of the living Grail.

Like the cauldron of Celtic spirituality that gives to the ones who find it everything they need for their life, Racham's presence did that for me and for Flavia. She realized it before I did, but I got there in the end. And that's what I want you to know.

Lúcháir paused again. Would he be able to convey to these precious souls the real gift he was leaving them? All he could do was try.

"*A chairde,* please understand me as I explain. Here is the theme that has run through all of my embodiments and is the key to the legacy that I learned from Racham: 'Tis the thread of contact with our divine source, with love, with the reality of freedom that is the nature of our souls.

"In the days before Racham was called to leave Ynys Witrin for the last time—when he was teaching Flavia and me, her cousins and our other friends—he would say to us with the deepest passion of his heart, 'Become as I am. Hold fast to the thread of contact with my Father and your Father, and we will never lose each other.'

"Such a simple statement and so difficult to achieve. Yet that one idea is my legacy to you, *a chairde:* Hold fast to the mystical thread that connects us heart to heart, soul to soul, and we will forever be linked in a circle of a oneness that endures beyond time and space.

"Hold fast to the thread of contact with your own inner divinity, and you will never be lost in this world."

When Lúcháir finished speaking, his Companions gathered silently around him. Each one in turn hugged their beloved mentor. Then quietly taking their leave of *Teach an tSolais,* they made their way home.

For many weeks thereafter, they pondered in their heart of hearts the memories and profound meaning of their *ceann-druí's* legacy of love.

And so it was that winter passed with Lúcháir and Sarah spending many hours together readying his book for publication in the spring. There were no more story sessions at the O'Tooles', although there was a big Thanksgiving Day feast at Fibonacci's for all of the Friends of Ancient Wisdom to celebrate the safe return of the two Connemara travelers.

That event was also a perfect occasion for the full community to learn that Lucky was now officially called Lúcháir and to hear some well-chosen tales from the adventures he and Kevin had shared.

The two told stories about the rugged landscape they'd walked and the gracious people they'd met. Their listeners enjoyed hearing about Father Turley. And those who hadn't been to the Emerald Isle declared it was time they booked their own visit.

Little was mentioned about Charlotte's conspicuous absence—except to say that she had made a dramatic decision about her future and would not be rejoining the Friends of Ancient Wisdom.

Lúcháir also let the community know that he was retiring, though he would be glad to see them occasionally for a fine cup of coffee brewed by Phelan, the new Caffeine Alchemist.

After this event, Kevin became more visible at Fibonacci's. He made a point of being available to answer questions or simply chat with community members who stopped in for the food, beverages and conversation they preferred to enjoy at Róisín's over any other gathering place.

Sometimes he sat alone in the back booth where he discovered that his poetical muse had awakened—a renewal of his old bardic talents. Mostly, he was reviewing everything he had learned about being *ceann-druí* from his own past-life reviews and recollections, and from Lúcháir's stories.

Together, he and Sarah were deepening their meditation practice as well as refining their ability to communicate telepathically. Lúcháir had also begun inviting the two of them to join him regularly at the O'Tooles' home for advanced teachings which he said Flavia was very intent on his sharing with them.

On an unusually sunny Sunday in January, Sarah noticed that their dear friend appeared to be growing thinner, even as his eyes sparkled with remarkable brightness.

"Lúcháir, are you going to dematerialize before our very eyes?"

He gave her a wistful smile. "Wouldn't that be grand."

Finally, the book was ready for release on February 1—St. Brigid's Day and the Celtic early spring festival called *Imbolc*. A jubilant celebration was held at Fibonacci's ballroom with Lúcháir himself acting as master of ceremonies. He had asked that the curtain be opened to reveal the great sun disk which radiated sublime luminosity over the assembled company.

Once he was certain that everyone had arrived, he went to the altar and lit the candles on the spiral candelabra. A hush fell over the crowd as he turned and faced them. His entire being emanated such profound love that many hearts swelled and eyes misted.

Enfolding this community he cherished in the warmth of his heart, he offered the invocation he had been giving since time immemorial.

O Spirits of East and West, South and North, give ear, we pray, to our supplications. Angels of our world and the next, bless this assembly with your protection and inspiration.

Beloved An Síoraí, O Eternal One, may the words of our

*mouths and the deeds of our hands bring health and abundance
to all our people and safety to our homes, our leaders and those we
love both near and far, here with us and in gracious Tír na n'Óg,
Land of the Ever-Living.*

"*A chairde,* my dear friends," he began, "please join me in chanting the
OM and then Sarah will give you our grand announcement."

For weeks following, those who were in attendance would remark to
each other that never had the chant been so powerfully heartfelt in all the
years they had been gathering to share the experience.

Too emotional for a long speech, Sarah found she could only hold up
a copy of the new book and declare, "Beloved Friends of Ancient Wisdom,
I am honored to present to you *A Heart of Welcoming Joy*—the legacy our
dear Lúcháir has bequeathed to us for all time."

The Fibonacci's building shook to its foundation with the applause
and cheers that followed.

For the remainder of the week, Lúcháir did not appear at Fibonacci's.
No one was really surprised. The book release party had proved highly
emotional for everyone, especially for him. Those in casual conversation
avoided mentioning that the book's publication probably meant their
friend and *ceann-druí* had earned his release from this world. However,
the thought did weigh on many hearts.

The thought weighed with particular heaviness on Kevin and Sarah.
Lúcháir had hinted that the timing of his leave-taking had at least as much
to do with their preparation as his own. His comment to them after the
book party had left them pondering.

"Watch and listen, *a chairde,*" he'd said, placing an affectionate hand
on each one's shoulder. "Listen carefully. Your keen hearing is essential.
'Tis all I can say."

Indeed, those were his last words to them in the physical plane. He
had gone into seclusion at the O'Tooles' where, Maggie told them, he was
spending many hours a day in Tim's Tower.

Kevin and Sarah continued to focus on their own spiritual practice as
much as work and active toddlers allowed—and they waited.

Love's Victory

Less than a week later, Kevin went to work as usual, though he was reluctant to leave Sarah and the children. Something had changed during the night. However, neither Maggie nor Tim had called, which they had promised to do if Lúcháir's demeanor altered dramatically.

Still, when Kevin opened the bright blue door to Fibonacci's, he was not surprised to see the other Twin Flames of Éire couples waiting for him. Even a very pregnant Glenna was there with Rory.

Debbie acted as spokesperson for the group. "We each received a strong prompting to meet you here this morning. Something has changed."

"Sarah and I sensed it, too," agreed Kevin. "I expected to hear from the O'Tooles, but nothing yet."

"You know we all support you and Sarah in whatever happens with Lúcháir," said Jeremy and the others concurred. "Let us know when, where or how you need us, and we'll be there."

Kevin was about to express his deepest thanks when his cell phone rang. It was Sarah. "Maggie just called. We're needed at the O'Tooles' right away. The twins and I will be ready as soon as you can get home, and please tell the others. The 'something' we were feeling is happening now."

Maggie and Tim were waiting for the couples when they arrived at *Teach an tSolais*. So were Sarah's parents along with Ivy, Hank and their twins.

Maggie ushered everyone into the living room and calmly offered the explanation the group awaited with some trepidation.

"All is well, my dears," she assured them. "Our Master is with Lúcháir in the crystal room, preparing him to take his seat in the accelerator chair. To receive our own acceleration, our Master has asked that we give you some instruction for the ritual we're about to undertake."

"Do we get to help?" Kerry asked eagerly. His eyes were bright with anticipation.

"You do, darlin'," said Maggie. "Your Uncle Lúcháir wants you and Kaitlyn to participate. Our lessons together have proved your readiness. You and your cousins will join the adults in your ageless soul bodies. You will appear as grown-up as you often see yourselves."

Kerry's turned to his sister. "I told you!" he silently mouthed. Kaitlyn's own blue eyes glowed in acknowledgement. Both twins were already feeling the acceleration of what was to come.

Tim knew how they felt. "Though we've never tried an experiment like this, we have faith that your hearts and voices united in mighty chants and prayers will give our brother the boost he needs to take off for higher realms."

Maggie continued. "Although the crystal room is located here at *Teach an tSolais,* the physical space is merely a replica of an etheric chamber where our ritual will take place. As we have done in the past, we will pray and visualize ourselves being enfolded in light to prepare our consciousness for the extraordinary radiance we will experience. Then, as we are guided from within, we will step into an orb of light that appears in the flames in the fireplace. The orbs will transport us to the actual chamber where we will join our dear friend, Lúcháir."

"We were going to gather in the tower," offered Tim.

"That is true," said Maggie with a smile, "but our Master suggested that we gather here by the fire instead. With Glenna's baby due any day now and Cyndi's coming in a few months, we wanted our pregnant ladies to be comfortable. Ivy, I believe this is better for you, too."

Ivy blushed six shades of red and nodded. She squeezed Hank's hand and grinned at him. His face was as ruby-tinged as hers.

"How wonderful! Congratulations!" the others exclaimed and then laughed when Kaitlyn announced with obvious delight, "We're going to have a brother."

Amidst the excitement, Sarah caught the joy in her mother's eyes that meant one of her plans had succeeded. *So that's why Ma wanted Ivy and Hank to marry right away. She knew another soul was eager to be born.*

Sarah winked at Eileen, then returned her attention to Maggie, who brought the group back to the matter at hand.

"*A chairde*, whatever you perceive during the ritual, continue sending your deepest love to Lúcháir. Focus on the presence of your inner divinity, invoke the light and follow the light as it flows in and around you. And be at peace. Our Master would not be sponsoring this event unless he was sure of Lúcháir's loyal Circle of Close Companions."

"Please sit where you can see the flames," said Tim. "I will lead us as we chant. When we've done sufficient inner work, the orbs will appear and we will step in. I am told that angels will tend our physical bodies, so be assured of your physical safety."

With tremendous fervor, everyone—including Gareth and Naimh in their sweet little voices—sounded the OM, sang and chanted until their auras were glowing. Sarah gazed lovingly at her children as they prayed with their cousins and the adults. Had she ever doubted in their spiritual gifts (which she had not), here was proof of their souls' intention to be active participants in the Circle of Close Companions.

Time disappeared as a forcefield of scintillating light enveloped the group and each one felt mightily prepared for whatever was going to transpire. Guided from within, together they opened their eyes. The turf fire was alive with brilliant orbs that beckoned them to enter. In a single, united motion—they did.

Now in their soul bodies, the Companions found themselves in a chamber that was shaped like the inside of an enormous egg. There were no windows or apparent sources of light. Still, the space was illumined with a soft glow that emanated from the clear quartz crystals that lined the walls and vaulted ceiling. Even the floor was covered with the same crystalline substance they recognized from Tim's Tower.

On a slightly raised dais at the far end of the chamber was the accelerator chair. It had been fashioned from an enormous quartz crystal that glistened with ribboned veins and threads of purest gold. The Master was standing behind the chair where Lúcháir was now seated in meditation.

As they had done in previous rituals, the women arranged themselves on the right side just below and facing the dais. The men did the same on the left. They formed a circle with Maggie and Tim on either side of Lúcháir while Sarah and Kevin stood directly across from him.

All were now highly attuned to the ritual that was unfolding before them. At a nod from the Master, who remained standing behind the chair, they began sounding the OM in deep devotion. Gradually they increased the volume of their chants until the chamber was filled with many voices, as if a heavenly choir were joining them to replicate the sound of Creation.

The Companions continued chanting for several minutes until the celestial choir began to sing the most exquisite song of Love's Victory they had ever heard. Their hearts were filled to overflowing with gratitude for this experience that flooded the chamber with the scent of roses.

As they stood in rapture, the song completed and a sound like wind rustling through trees or perhaps the beat of angel wings caused them to look up. Chords from a mighty organ began to play and the chamber's ceiling opened to reveal a luminous firmament.

A shaft of light the width of the accelerator chair flashed down through the opening like a ray of pure sunshine. Softly at first, it grew and grew in intensity and brilliance, enveloping Lúcháir's form, causing it to glow more and more vibrantly.

With majestic organ music resounding in the chamber, the Companions watched—riveted in amazement. The Master lifted his arms to the heavens and Lúcháir's body began to rise so that he was standing in front of and slightly above the chair. As he did, the radiant figure of Flavia became visible. She was descending from the ethers to join her beloved twin flame. And she was not alone.

Gently escorting her—like a father presenting his daughter the bride to her waiting bridegroom—was Racham. The two resplendent beings met Lúcháir in midair where Flavia embraced him as she had longed to do for two thousand years. Racham placed his hands on their heads in blessing, then gestured for them to step forward toward their successors.

As Lúcháir and Flavia approached Kevin and Sarah, the figures of the two ascending ones were barely visible, although their voices were clearly audible to these souls who would carry on their legacy. Other Companions saw their lips moving, but only the two initiates heard the long-awaited instruction.

Their auras had expanded and their souls rejoiced in the realization that they were hearing the words for which they had prayed they might be worthy. In that same moment, capes of royal blue with ruby lining and Celtic patterns woven in golden threads descended upon their shoulders.

Then—as Sarah had imagined might happen—Lúcháir's form along with Flavia's grew intensely bright. In a burst of blazing luminescence accompanied by the music of a triumphant fanfare, they vanished.

In profound gratitude for the extraordinary love that was bathing the chamber and the entire company in crystalline light, Lúcháir and Flavia's Close Companions clasped hands around the circle and stood connected in deep reverence.

Saint Germain and Racham had remained in the chamber. They were now hovering above the accelerator chair with their hands raised in blessing. Immediately, the soul-stirring strains of a choral benediction enveloped the Companions in tangible waves of comfort and peace which they perceived the two Masters transmitting to them.

This was the vibration in which they found themselves—returned to their physical forms and seated once more before the turf fire at *Teach an tSolais*—changed forever in heart, mind, body, soul and spirit.

Weaving New Threads

Sarah and Kevin instinctively checked to make sure that Naimh and Gareth were safely back in their toddler bodies. There was no need for their concern. The twins' violet eyes sparkled with joyful exuberance and they smiled at their parents with an inner knowing far beyond their eighteen months of age.

Kaitlyn and Kerry were more than usually bright-eyed. Upon returning to their bodies, they had discovered an enhanced telepathic ability. They were doing their best not to giggle in delight as they sent each other thoughts about what they had seen as their Uncle Lúcháir rose up in the air to meet the luminous woman they knew was his twin flame.

Thanks to Maggie's restorative teas and the comforting food that she and Eileen had prepared in advance, the Companions began easing into a more grounded state of awareness, although conversation remained minimal. Even this group's familiarity with life reviews and their witnessing Róisín's translation to higher realms had not completely prepared them for this experience. Being present at a physical ascension had been profoundly moving for all of them.

After a few minutes, Tim posed the question he was eager to ask of Lúcháir's successor. He had witnessed Kevin and Sarah receiving their mantles. Still, he wanted to be certain that the transfer of light, love and authority from Lúcháir and Flavia to these two reembodied druids had fully taken place.

In this moment, more than either of them understood depended on the continuation of the Master's sponsorship of the Friends of Ancient Wisdom community.

"How does it feel to be *ceann-druí* again?" Tim ventured.

Kevin paused, thoughtful. "I can't really say yet. Familiar, I suppose, and also unique. We're living in an age that is very different from first-century Ireland, with new opportunities and responsibilities. That much I know. Ask me again in a month. I may have a better answer by then."

"And may you wear your mantles well," said Rory affectionately. "You did in ages past. I know you will this time. You, too, Sarah. 'Tis strange, I find myself wanting to call you Ah-Lahn and Alana."

"I have the same impression," said Glenna softly. She was still floating from her experience in the crystal chamber and had begun to notice other more physical sensations moving through her body. "In fact, I'm seeing you both as if you were the druids we have known so well."

Sarah could feel her heart bursting with love for the Companions. "We will always be ourselves—as Sarah and Kevin who are blessed to have integrated their identities as Alana and Ah-Lahn. Whatever of our attainment is needed will always be given in service to our community."

Now as *ceann-druí*, Kevin was prompted to address his friends.

"*A chairde*, I believe everyone has accelerated today. The blessing to us from Lúchair's ascension was the final thread in the tapestry of his legacy. I believe that completion is an increase in our personal spiritual awareness and a heightened collective ability to enhance light and combat darkness wherever we find ourselves engaged in that confrontation. May we all remember this day as a turning point toward greater and greater light."

The Companions were still full of the powerful rays of ascension's light that had lifted them into a feeling of unspeakable joy. They met this outpouring of their *ceann-druí's* love and wisdom with their own exclamations of acceptance.

"Absolutely! Well said! Thank you! We agree!"

Kevin's heart was overflowing with such immense joy, he could have said more. He even heard the beginning of a poem he would like to share with these dear soul friends. However, any further comments he might have had in mind would wait for another day.

For just then, Glenna cried out and grabbed her husband's arm.

"Rory, it's time! We need to get to the hospital!"

He leapt into action—a broad smile on his face and eyes shining as he hurried out. "Sorry to leave so suddenly. But seems we have an urgent calling."

"We'll be right behind you," said Debbie as she helped Glenna put on her coat while Rory fetched their car. She and Jeremy had promised to be with the O'Donnells for the birth.

Ever the efficient organizer when quick thinking was required, Eileen jumped in with suggestions for the others—this time more gently than she had done in the past. She was still floating a bit herself.

"Phelan and Hank, you may want to take your families home." She smiled at the two men. "Rest up while you can, lads. Your time will come soon enough. Sarah, you and Kevin are free go to the hospital with your friends. Your father and I are very happy to take Gareth and Naimh home with us."

Patrick reached over and took his wife's hand. He could feel the shift in her being and loved her all the more for it.

After helping the Callahan grandparents bundle children and adults into the appropriate cars, Maggie and Tim stood at their front door, arms around each other, waving the Circle of Close Companions off to their next adventures.

"They still need us," said Maggie wistfully.

"Aye, lass, they surely do," Tim agreed. "Our voyage to *Tír na n'Óg* can wait a while longer. I don't see us taking off for the Land of Ever-Living any time soon."

"Nor do I," Maggie agreed as she took his hand.

They turned, crossed the threshold into *Teach an tSolais* and prepared to welcome whatever new summits *An Síoraí*, the Eternal One, had in mind for them to climb.

"What did Lúcháir say to you at the end?" Sarah asked while Kevin kept their car close behind the O'Donnells and the Maddens for the short drive to the hospital. "We haven't had a chance to compare our experiences. I only heard Flavia speak to me."

"Lúcháir's message was nearly what I expected. Though to receive it from his lips was truly a life-changing transfer of light to my heart. I heard him say: 'Accept this mantle of leadership and wear it with my love. Hold fast the thread of contact and become as I am.'

"What was Flavia's message to you?"

"Her words were exactly the same. And there was something more. Maybe you saw it, too. She extended to me what, at first, looked like a large bunch of flowers. Then I realized there were hundreds of threads in all colors, cascading down from her hand like an elegant wedding bouquet.

"As she passed the bouquet to me, I saw that each thread represents a soul whose gifts are vital to our community—past, present and future."

Kevin could feel his aura glowing. Here was more insight into the future than he had hoped for.

"I did see the colors," he said, "but not the threads or what they represented. This seems like Flavia's special gift to you. And I can see that we've got a lot of weaving to do."

His heart was near to bursting as he sensed Sarah's complete attunement with the vision he was seeing of the future they would share.

"I agree. It's as if our acceptance of the entire message—the loving transfer of our leadership mantles from Lúcháir and Flavia and the thread of contact we're meant to maintain are interwoven with these gorgeous threads like the warp and weft of a new tapestry of being—becoming as I am."

"Are you ready for this next adventure, Bandruí Alana?"

"I am, if you are, Ceann-Druí Ah-Lahn."

"Then let's go help the Twin Flames of Éire welcome a colorful new soul-thread into the next rich tapestry of our Friends of Ancient Wisdom."

"I already see the master weavers setting up their loom," smiled Sarah.

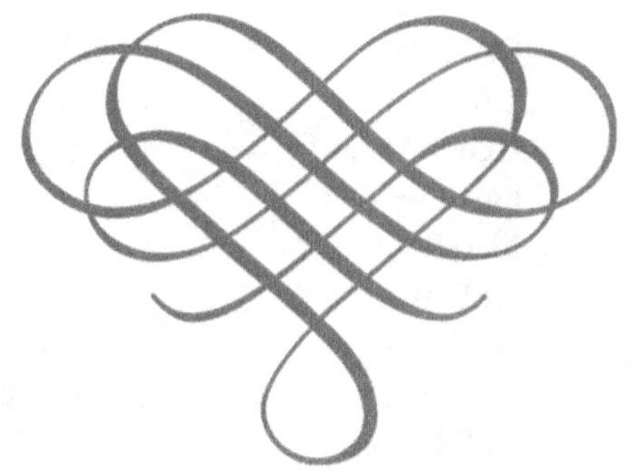

Glossary & Pronunciation Guide

Letters ch (written phonetically as chk or hk) are pronounced as in loch

<u>Names</u>	<u>Pronunciation</u>	<u>Meaning</u>
Ah-Lahn	ah-LAHN	Var. Alan, noble, rock
Alana	ah-LAN-ah	Dear child
Arán Bán	rahn BAHN	White bread
Bantiarna	ban-TEER-na	Lady
Cois Abhann	cush OW-enn	Riverside
Cróga	KRO-guh	Brave, hardy
Dearbhla	DAR-vla	Daughter of the poet
Gareth	GEHR-eth	Gentle, watchful (Welsh)
Gormlaith	GOORM-luh	Blue princess
Lúcháir	loo-HAH(ih)	Welcoming joy
Madwyn	MAHD-oo-en	Forthright (Welsh)
Naimh	NEE-av	Luster, sheen
Óengus	O-en-gus	Singular strength
Racham	RAH-hkam	Friend (Aramaic)
Riordan	REER-duhn	Royal poet
Róisín	roh-SHEEN	Little Rose
Una	OO-nuh	Variation *uan*, Lamb

<u>Place Names</u>	<u>Pronunciation</u>	<u>Meaning</u>
Éire	AY-(rhe)	Ireland
Muir Éireann	moyr AY-(r)enn	Irish Sea
Teach an tSolais	Chahk an Tullish	House of Light
Tearmann	TAR-a-mun	Place of refuge
Ynys Môn	in-ish MOHN	Anglesey Island, Wales
Ynys Witrin	in-ish WIT-rin	Avalon Island, Britain

<u>Endearments</u>	<u>Pronunciation</u>	<u>Meaning</u>
A chairde	a-CHKAR-dyeh	My friends
A chara	a-CHKAR-uh	O friend, my friend
A chara dhílis	a-CHKAR-uh YEE-lish	My faithful friend
A ghrá	a-GHRAH	My love
A pháistí	a-FAHSH-tee	My children
Mo chroí	mu-CHKREE	My heart
Mo mhuirnín	mu-WOOR-neen	My darling

Terms	**Pronunciation**	**Meaning**
An Síoraí	un SHEE-uh-ree	The Eternal One
Ard mháistir	ard WOHSH-ti(d)	Grandmaster
Bealtaine (festival)	bee-YOWL-tin-uh	May Day, bright fire
Ceann-druí	KYAHN-dree	Chief Druid
Currach	KER-uchk	Traditional boat
Druí, bandruí	dree, ban-DREE	Druid, druidess
Garda	GAHR-deh	Police
Imbolc (festival)	IM-bolk	Feb. 1, St. Brigid's Day
Lughnasa (festival)	LOO-nuh-suh	Aug. 1, first harvest
Ollamh	AH-luv	Master poet/bard
Samhain (festival)	SOW-en	Nov. 1, Celtic New Year
Seanchaí	SHAN-a-chkee	Storyteller
Seisiún	SEH-shoon	Session of trad. Irish music
Toísech	TEE-shuck	Chieftain
Túath	TOO-uh	Territory, village

Phrases with Pronunciation and Translation

Beannachtaí daoibh	BAN-ach-tee deev	Blessings to you (plural)
Bí fós, a ghrá.	bee fohsh, ah-grah	Be still, my love
Céad míle fáilte	cayd MEE-luh FAL-tyuh	A hundred thousand welcomes
Go raibh maith agat	GUH-ruh MAH haht	Thank you
Go raibh míle maith agat	GUH-ruh-MEE-luh MAH hah-gut	Thank you very much
Is mise le meas	is mish leh mess	Sincerely yours
Le de thoil	led deh HOL	Please
Oíche mhaith	EE-uh wah	Good night
Slán abhaile	SLAWN a-WILE-eh	May you go safely home
Tá fáilte romhat	tah FAHL-tyuh ROOT	You're welcome
Táim anseo agus tá tú slán	tah(i)m AN-shah ah-gus tah too SLAWN	I'm here and you're safe
Teacht ar ais	tachkt ahr ASH	Come back

Read the story that sparked the
Twin Flames of Éire Trilogy,
and learn where the path of reunion began
for Sarah and Kevin and their Friends of Ancient Wisdom.

Sometimes to move forward
you have to go back...

Sarah and Kevin recognized their connection as twin flames within minutes of meeting at a party that neither had wanted to attend.

They soon vowed to stay together forever. Yet, seven years later they are on the verge of losing each other—and not for the first time. For as they discover through dreams and visions, their shared embodiments were often scarred by painful separations.

Will Sarah and Kevin find a way to reconcile past and present to escape a future neither of them wants?

Only going back in time will tell.

Don't miss these exciting sequels to *The Weaving*
in the Twin Flames of Éire Trilogy

The Ancients and The Call - Sarah and Kevin believe they resolved all of their differences last summer in the luminous atmosphere of Éire. But that experience was only the beginning of their mission on behalf of twin flames. Now they know that love can be lost unless they return to Ireland and merge with their ancient attainment as druids Alana and Ah-Lahn.

The Water and The Flame - Broadway actress Glenna and Irish monk Rory are worlds apart. The chances of their meeting and realizing they are twin flames are slim. Until the magic of Éire and the support of their Friends of Ancient Wisdom sends them on a voyage of self-discovery and overcoming malevolent forces they never could have imagined.

The Mystics and The Mystery - The path of reunion for twin flames has never been more perilous than for seers Debbie and Jeremy. Must she surrender her visions of the love they shared in the past for the sake of his soul? Or will he summon his inner strength to join her and other mystics to combat the ancient forces that have opposed them?

Acknowledgements

Every life is a journey through many planes of existence, both seen and unseen. Every person, place or event we encounter on that journey is a teacher. Their lessons may bring us exquisite joy. Or they may challenge us to the very core of our beliefs about ourselves and others.

All are equally valuable because they form the warp and weft of the tapestry we weave that becomes the fabric of the life we create.

Gratitude for life's ups and downs allows us to observe the threads that belong to our partnership with the spirit of *An Síoraí,* the Eternal One, who lives in the deepest part of us. And, if we are wise, we will also acknowledge the many threads that others have woven into this miraculous creation we could not have fashioned alone.

I am blessed with colleagues Theresa McNicholas and James Bennett, Janice Haugen and Paula Kehoe who share my passion for publishing.

Special thanks to my dear friends Mary Wallace, Dónall Ó Héalaí and his father, Dr. Pádraig Ó Héalaí, for their priceless assistance with the Gaelic terms that speak to the beauty of the ancient Irish culture that has inspired each of my twin flames novels. I have done my best to make faithful use of their suggestions. Any errors in spelling, usage, or pronunciation are mine alone.

These stories reach far back in time and point to a future that is still unfolding, which gives me the opportunity to gather several millennia of thanks and send them out to countless teachers and mentors for all the lessons, including more than a few dark nights.

The story of twin flames belongs to all of us. Thank you, Mother, for letting me tell one small part of it. And to my beloved Stephen, whether together or apart, I live in you as you live in me. Thanks to you and to our great Masters of Wisdom for helping me finally understand what that means.

Cheryl Lafferty Eckl has played many roles since she began her career as a singer/actress in musical theatre. Among those roles are award-winning author, mystical poet, professional development trainer, life coach, inspirational speaker and retreat facilitator.

These days, her favorite role is *seanchaí*—that's Irish for storyteller.

If you ask, she'll tell you it's her love of Ireland—its people, language, land and culture—that continues to inspire characters and stories in thrilling novels that follow the trials and triumphs of twin flames who sometimes struggle and very often succeed in unlocking Love's mystery.

Learn more about Cheryl's books, and enjoy her videos, audios and articles at www.CherylEckl.com.